The GIRL WHO ESCAPED

BOOKS BY ANGELA PETCH

The Tuscan Secret

The Tuscan Girl

A Tuscan Memory

The Tuscan House

The Postcard from Italy

The GIRL WHO ESCAPED

ANGELA PETCH

bookouture

Published by Bookouture in 2023

An imprint of Storyfire Ltd.
Carmelite House
50 Victoria Embankment
London EC4Y 0DZ

www.bookouture.com

ISBN: 978-1-83790-129-6
eBook ISBN: 978-1-83790-128-9

To Luigi Micheli (1903–1990)
Partigiano combattente, awarded La Croce al merito di guerra
and other unsung heroes and heroines of the Italian Campaign.

'Rescue those who are being taken away to death;
hold back those who are stumbling to the
slaughter.
If you say, "Behold, we did not know this,"
does not he who weighs the heart perceive it?
Does not he who keeps watch over your soul
know it,
and will he not repay man according to his
work?'

— PROVERBS XXIV, 11–12 ENGLISH STANDARD VERSION

PROLOGUE

20 AUGUST 1988

The black and white photograph, five centimetres square, was creased and faded. It showed four young people, one with a dog at his feet, grouped by the side of a stony path, bare-legged, kerchiefs round the two young men's necks and straw hats on the girls' heads. In the background, peaks of over two thousand metres soared into a clear sky like spines of ancient monsters. The youngsters were squinting, one of the girls shading her eyes with her hand against the sun. The location was the Gran Sasso in the region of Abruzzo, southern Italy. On the back was scribbled, *August 1938. See you in fifty years.*

Each of these young people had long grown up now, but all had memories of that hiking trip. For Devora Lassa, it was the pearly grey of the mountains and the yellow-mossy-green of the scrub where edelweiss and tiny alpine flowers nodded their heads. She'd visualised the pathway they had trodden that day like a pathway stretching to eternity. At eighteen, everything had seemed possible.

Nineteen-year-old Luigi Michelozzi had seen it as an amazing place to escape with Tuffo, his young, bouncy Pointer. There were endless paths to explore and freedom from dull accountancy studies. Every now and again he'd stopped to use his binoculars.

Sabrina Merli remembered the day as tiring and tedious. Her feet had ached in heavy walking boots she hadn't broken in before coming on the week away. It was too hot, she'd complained, and she'd constantly asked how much further they had to trek. Everybody had known why she was there: not for the scenery, but because of Enrico.

Conte Enrico di Villanova had received a brand-new Kodak pocket camera for his nineteenth birthday and this trip was an opportunity to practise on it. Back home in Urbino after the break, he had arranged to have three copies of the photograph made to give to his friends as a memento. Throughout the trip he'd constantly asked them to pose, but mostly Devora, observing the way the sun highlighted the dark gold of her shoulder-length hair, wondering how it would show up on black and white film.

And now here he was, his life much changed, standing in Piazza della Repubblica in the centre of Urbino, at nine thirty in the morning, fifty years to the day.

As he directed his Canon professional at sections of the portico, Enrico wondered if anybody would bother to turn up. He clicked away, forgetting time as he crouched to direct his lens upwards to catch the contrast of a cloudless sky. His composition would look best in black and white as opposed to colour. The way the light fell, the angles of the shadows, reminded him of an Escher drawing.

'Enrico?'

He swivelled to see her. Devora was still stunning, strands of silver threading hair cut in a bob, puppy fat replaced with angles, her cheekbones sharper. As he straightened up, he stepped towards her to give the customary kiss on each cheek but she moved back, her expression frosty.

'It's been a lifetime since we saw you last,' she said in a snappy tone as she glanced behind her.

'Now you're going to say I haven't changed a bit,' Enrico replied, his gravelly smoker's voice trailing away as he followed her towards the café.

'Well, I'm not going to flatter you with that type of comment.'

'Are you angry with me, Biondina?'

She stopped and he almost collided into her.

'Hah! Your conscience finally catching up with you? And – while we're at it – I'm Devora to you. Maybe this wasn't such a good idea, Enrico.'

'What did I do?'

'Perhaps you should think about what you *didn't* do.'

'Now, I'm *completely* baffled.' He replaced the lens on his camera and packed it away. 'Come on, Devora. I'll buy us a drink and you can tell me what's bugging you.'

CHAPTER 1

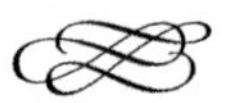

9 JUNE 1940, URBINO, ITALY

DEVORA

Sabrina was wearing another new dress for the contessa's monthly Friday tea party: a soft-cotton voile frock in peach satin, tiny buttons down the front, a lacy collar and soft pleats to cleverly disguise her stout body. The shoes were new too, Devora observed, feeling dowdy in her one and only best outfit. It was a muddy beige and had once belonged to her mother, who was at least a head shorter. Anna Maria, their maid servant, had added a hem in a contrasting olive-green frill to lengthen it, adding bone buttons resurrected from another garment and flap pockets at the hips to bring it up to date. She was clever at making do and mending but Devora was still envious of her friend's new clothes.

Enrico's mother, Contessa Giulietta di Villanova, air-kissed Devora when she walked into the *salone,* as she liked to call the living room of her apartment in the cathedral square of Urbino. Its long windows were draped in heavy velvet and overlooked the elaborate renaissance façade of the Ducal Palace. The furniture was painted gold and upholstered with brocades and silks.

Portraits of sombre, bewigged ladies and gentlemen hung against silk-wallpapered walls, and whatnots were cluttered with antique porcelain. It was not a room where Devora could imagine herself curling up to read a book.

In one corner, partly hidden by a potted palm, a large gilded cage housed a parrot called Amadeo. Devora felt sorry for the creature and went over to talk to him. If encouraged, he occasionally came out with some of the contessa's expressions: 'Don't flick your duster, girl,' or 'If I've told you once, I've told you twice: your cigars stink of old socks.' Some of Amadeo's quotes had obviously been picked up from careless servants: 'Have you seen the old cow?' and 'Tell the contessa to get stuffed.' Listening to Amadeo made a pleasant diversion from having to engage in vacuous tea-party talk.

'*Lovely* to see you, *cara*,' the contessa said, approaching Devora. Taking a puff from the cigarette in her holder, she exhaled smoke in Devora's face. Devora never believed these endearments, certain she was invited from a sense of duty, like most of the guests. She'd noticed the butcher's wife as well as the manager of the Raffaello Sanzio Theatre. *Cutlets and tickets*, Devora assessed, guessing why they'd been invited. Devora knew she was here because Enrico insisted his friends be included to cushion him from what he dubbed Monthly Friday Ordeals.

This afternoon the contessa wore cream leather gloves pulled above her elbow. Devora could not see the point. Why on earth bother in this summer heat? The apartment windows were shut fast and Devora longed to fling them wide to let in air from the piazza. Maybe the contessa's gloves were meant to protect her from contamination by the hoi polloi? It was common knowledge her side of the family was not from aristocracy, that she had married her elderly husband for his title and she put on airs to keep up with the wealthy set. Bent on finding a suitable match for Enrico, her only son, she was forever casting her net over the daughters of the wealthy, which did not include Devora, daughter of a factory owner turned tailor's assistant, and Jewish to boot. Far from suitable for the contessa's precious son. Occasionally Devora noticed a slight slip of the tongue, the wrong interpretation or mispronunciation of a word in the contessa's speech as she tried to emulate her aristocratic husband. Language was important to Devora, her nose stuck in a book unless she was enjoying her time fencing or running for the *Circolo Atletico*, banned to her now because of racial laws.

She made her way over to the refreshments table where Enrico was chatting to Sabrina and some girls Devora recognised from the university crowd. He caught her glance and beckoned her over.

'*Ciao*, Devora,' he said, bending to kiss her on both cheeks.

He'd never openly done this before. Devora's heart stopped a beat and she felt herself blush. To cover her confusion, she grabbed a cake from the tiered stand on a side table. The *diplomatico* was larger than she'd estimated and now her mouth bulged with cream and flaky pastry, and she was sure she looked like her twin brothers' pet hamster, recently eaten by the neighbours' cat. One of the girls sniggered and Sabrina came to Devora's rescue, taking her arm and suggesting they go and fetch a cup of lemon tea together.

Out of earshot and glancing round to where Enrico stood, the girls fluttering around him like giddy butterflies, Sabrina rolled her eyes. 'I'd like to take them a cup after lacing it with arsenic. Pestilential creatures. But doesn't Enrico look so handsome this afternoon? I can't believe he actually kissed you on *both* cheeks. What did you do to deserve that, Biondina?' She used Devora's pet name, given to her on account of her dark blonde hair – unusual amongst the predominant black of most Italians.

'I don't actually know. It surprised me too,' Devora said,

swallowing the last of the fancy cake and licking her sticky fingers.

'I wish he would surprise *me*. Honestly, he's so gorgeous. And I wish I could study medicine like you and see him every day at university. Instead, I have to work in the shop for Papà and help old men choose suits.'

'I don't see him each day. I'm not allowed to study at university anymore. Or had you forgotten?'

'Whoops, sorry, Devora. I just don't think of you as being different from us. But, anyway, you still fence with him.'

'Once a week, if that. And with all the racial laws about what we can and cannot do, I'm not going to stop my fencing in the park. I've been banned from the *Circolo* but nobody has told me I can't meet a friend to practise with.'

Devora chose to ignore Sabrina's comment about her being different. From anybody else it would have been an insult, but poor Sabrina was not the brightest. She was sweet, but oh so dizzy. And Devora was not going to open up and tell Sabrina how much she enjoyed Enrico's company either. Those stolen hours spent fencing and chatting with him up at the Fortezza were the highlight of her week.

Her friend had a long-standing crush on Enrico. Back in her early teens, Sabrina had stolen his scarf from his peg at school and taken it home to breathe in his masculine scent – as she'd put it – keeping it under her pillow at night, 'So I can dream of him', she'd said. If she wanted to bitch, Devora had plenty of ammunition with which to tease Sabrina, but she wasn't like that. Her friend had enough to contend with, being slow, and prone to acne.

Their on-off friendship had endured thirteen years, since Devora had helped Sabrina on their first day in infants' class. Sabrina had wet herself and hidden behind a piano, crying and refusing to come out. Devora had managed to coax her from her hiding place and from that day onwards, Sabrina had relied on their friendship. She had failed her end of school examinations, but it didn't matter, as she'd always been destined to work in the family business, the tailor's shop in the main square.

Devora's father worked there too, cutting cloth in the back room and bringing alterations home for his wife to finish. It was a comedown from when he'd owned his own textile business in Frankfurt am Main, but needs must, and he'd had to hone up on tailoring skills. His new occupation put food in his family's bellies and provided a roof over their heads. Owning his own business was a thing of the past for the time being.

Devora gazed with longing through the window at the view over the rooftops and mountains in the distance, blue in the summer haze. Her parents made her come to these parties. Mamma wanted her to learn social graces, while Papà said it was important to become part of the community, especially since the introduction of the racial laws two years earlier.

'Any chance you have of merging with people, the better. Sometimes in life, it's not what you know, but who you know that counts,' he had said, polishing his glasses and picking up his treasured copy of Kafka's *Das Schloss*. He had read it from cover to cover so often that he could quote whole passages.

'But the parties are so... so stuffy and boring. I only ever end up talking to my friends and I could do that in the piazza or the park. *Uffa!*' was Devora's response as she puffed out air and pulled a face.

'You need to integrate to make your way in society. In Germany we attended soirées and concerts. We mixed with the right people,' her mother had said.

'But we're not in Germany now, Mütti, and what good did it do you anyway? And I already mix with the right people. My *friends*. The contessa is such a snob and barely hides her dislike of me. I *hate* her tea parties.'

'Be honoured that you are invited.'

'So, I have to be honoured because I'm a Jewess?'

Her mother tutted at that. 'We came to Italy for a better life,' she snapped. 'Don't ruin your chances, *Mädchen*.'

'Chances? What chances... Look what Mussolini has done for us,' Devora retorted. 'His stupid laws kicked in with a vengeance meaning no more university for me. How am I going to catch up on my medical studies? No school for the boys either. And we're not supposed to employ Anna Maria because she's Aryan. Don't talk about chances to me.'

'Hush, Devora. Life is difficult enough. Leave your mother alone,' her father admonished, snapping shut his book and slamming it down on the table to bring the discussion to an end.

On and on and back and forth went the arguments, but it made no difference. The tea parties were the deadliest thing on earth, even if her friends were there, but her parents insisted and, to keep the peace, she obeyed.

'I need the cloakroom,' she told Sabrina. She didn't, but the toilet reserved for guests was near the front door and she planned to slip away unnoticed. As she was about to exit, Enrico approached.

'Don't blame you, Biondina. How about we meet for fencing practice in an hour? Usual place?'

'It's a deal,' she said, her mood instantly lifting. 'Make sure you eat plenty of those cakes and then you'll be too full to move.'

She stuck out her tongue at him as she opened the door to escape, freedom and Enrico beckoning. One hour to go. She willed the minutes to whizz by.

It was less suffocating outside and as she dawdled along the portico to the side of the main piazza; the cooler air filtering through was welcome. She descended to the shade of the warren of alleyways leading to her home in the ghetto area of Via delle Stallacce. For a minute she leant against the mossy wall, enjoying a light breeze on her face, to gaze at the inviting Apennines. If she was a falcon, she thought, she could spread her wings and soar above the twin towers of the Ducal Palace and the marketplace at its foot, to land in the forests on the mountain slopes. There, in the family's favourite picnic spot, it would be cool. She could sit against a tree, read more chapters of her novel and then dip in the stream to refresh herself. *Mamma mia!* Verga's story about Eva was so passionate. As she descended the steps leading to the door of her home, it was wrenched open and her father hurried out.

'Good timing, Devora. Come fetch the boys with me,' he said. 'They're flying their kites up at the fortress. It's time for them to come home.'

From inside the little house, her mother called out, 'Make sure you hurry, Friedrich. There's much to do. No dawdling.'

Vati's face was drawn and he mopped sweat with his handkerchief as they hurried down the narrow alleys towards Corso Garibaldi. Devora nearly tripped over a box overflowing with clothes and bags of food outside one of the ghetto houses and for the first time, she took note of agitated voices coming from neighbours' homes. Something was up. Her disappointment at not being able to meet up with Enrico was overtaken by concern.

'Slow down, Papà,' she said. 'It's too hot. What's going on?'

He lowered his voice and urged her on. 'Mussolini has published further racial laws today. We have to pack up and leave.'

She stopped still. 'What are you talking about? Why? Where are we going?'

'You and the boys will not be going, Devora. Just Mütti and I.'

Devora tugged at his sleeve. They were now climbing the other side of town, up the almost perpendicular rise past carpenters' workshops and the house where Raffaello had been born. Although she was fit, she was finding it hard to keep up with her father. She increased her pace, perspiration trickling down her face and back. Her father, normally placid and calm, was a fury of anger. When they arrived at the grassy area round the Fortezza Albornoz, he slumped onto a tree trunk, his head in his hands.

She noticed for the first time how bald he'd become. He looked old and lost and she wondered how she could help. 'I don't understand, Vati. Explain to me what's going on.'

He looked up at her and she sat beside him.

'Devora, before we collect the boys, you must listen. You have to be brave and do exactly what I tell you. This morning, my friend in the police department – one of the customers I look after in the shop – he warned me that tomorrow they'll come to fetch your mother and me because an important announcement is about to be made. He's a good man. He warned us to make preparations.'

'What announcement? What are you talking about?'

'Italy is entering the war alongside Germany. Foreign Jews are to be arrested and sent to internment camps.'

Fear gripped her. The world about her stopped still as she stammered, 'But, the boys... and I... we're *all* Jewish. Why should they take only you?'

A breeze stirred, causing a pine cone to thud from the branches above father and daughter. Devora waited for her father to respond, giving him time, noting how he bit his lip as he stared into the distance. He was Vati again: weighing up the right way to express himself, considerate, measured. At last he drew a deep breath and took hold of her hands.

'Listen to me, Devora. You and the boys were born in Italy so this new rule doesn't apply to you. You're not considered foreign Jews, as we are.'

'I hate the way you're making us sound different from you. We are *one* family,' Devora exclaimed, pulling her hands from him as she stood up to face him. 'We should stay together.'

He shook his head. 'Devora, Devora, my beautiful *Tochter*. Things could be far worse for us. At least we're not being deported. The poor wretches who live next door, the Levingers, who only came to Urbino last year, they will be dispatched from Italy entirely.'

'I don't understand. Why them and not you? This is all so ridiculous. Why are we being sorted like this – it's as if we're a herd of cattle, branded with different colours because of our worth.'

'I know, I know. But these are the laws at the moment. This country has been good to us and we mustn't make more trouble for ourselves. The thing is, Mütti and I arrived here back in 1918 and have Italian citizenship so, according to the laws, we're allowed to stay. Any Jew who acquired nationality after 1 January 1919 now loses citizenship.'

'*Allowed* to stay! Pah!' Devora crushed the pine cone beneath her foot as she stamped her frustration. 'You say Italy has been good to you but look what the *fascisti* are putting us through. I'm not allowed to pursue my medical studies any longer or attend the athletic club. The boys can't attend school with the friends they've grown up with. I was always top of my class. I *know* I'll make a fantastic doctor if they'd only let me. You've been forced to do work beneath your station. It's all so outrageous, Papà. I can't stand it. We *have* to stick together. I'm not going to let you leave us here without you.'

Her tears fell as life as she'd known it cracked into tiny shards. How could they live apart?

'I know, I know and I have always feared this would happen again,' Friedrich said, his voice shaking. 'There have been rumblings and pogroms in Germany from way back. And Hitler was already blaming the Jews for losing the Great War. I could see even back then that life was to become more difficult for us. That is why Mütti and I left. And I was right.'

In the distance a dog howled and Devora heard the claxon of the daily *corriera* hooting as it trundled its way round the bends towards the market square. Life for everybody else continued unabated but life for the Lassa family had been dealt another bitter blow. Her father began to talk again, his voice resigned.

'Devora, you know all this already, I don't need to repeat it. I've told you often enough why we left Germany in the first place, but I always hoped this hatred wouldn't spread to Italy. I know the goodness of the people here. We must trust in them and hope it all blows over soon. But in the meantime, we shall follow the rules.'

'But it's so unfair. What have we done to deserve it?' She picked up a stone and hurled it against the walls of the fortress. 'I won't let it happen.' She came back to sit beside him, her fingers gripping the cloth of her skirt.

'Listen to me, *Kind*.' In his distress, he was using more German than Italian. 'There is nothing you can do. Mütti and I are adamant you will not come with us.'

'Where will they take you? I can't bear it. This cannot be happening.' She crept into his arms, sobbing, and he stroked her hair, patting her back like when she was a tiny child.

'To a place near Arezzo. A former orphanage, according to my policeman friend. He came in today for a final measurement. He thinks you'll be able to come and visit. But, Devora, until we know what it will be like for sure, you and the boys have to stay. Now, dry your eyes and put on a brave face for your little brothers. You have to be strong and look after them. God willing, it won't be for long. Anna Maria will help look after you all. She's a good woman.'

So far, their servant, Anna Maria, from Lucania, a desolate, arid corner of southern Italy, had worked for her Jewish family without any interference from the authorities. An orphan, without a bean to her name, she knew how to make and mend and cook anything. She had been a lifesaver for Mütti, frail since the difficult birth of Devora's ten-year-old twin brothers, Arturo and Alfredo. Anna Maria's language was as ripe as seasoned Gorgonzola but, fortunately, most of it was lost on Devora's parents, their grasp of Italian not as fluent as their children's.

Father and daughter trailed over the grass towards a group of children flying kites, their gleeful shouts and free spirits at variance with Devora's misery. Against the clean blue sky, paper birds, planes, butterflies and kites of all shapes, colours and sizes swooped and soared as the children tugged on their strings.

'Are you *sure* you have to go, Papà? Can't we find somewhere in the forest to hide together?'

'*Shh!* Devora. No more talk about this in front of the boys. Running away will only make it worse. If the *fascisti* were to find us, they might shoot us all on the spot. That is what happened in Frankfurt.'

'But we're not in Germany now. That surely wouldn't happen here. Never in a million years.'

'*Halt die Klappe*. Be quiet. You're very naïve, Devora. You must learn to accept.'

Papà was not himself. This nightmare would end soon. He'd got it all wrong. And if he thought she was going to accept this ridiculous situation, he was mistaken. She would ask Enrico if his family could help. They knew people in high places who might pull strings.

Ten-year-old Alfredo and Arturo chattered all the way home. The knowledge that their carefree worlds were about to change broke her heart.

'My kite flew the highest,' Arturo said. 'My aeroplane climbed almost as high as the towers.'

'My lines tangled in a tree,' Alfredo, taller and sturdier than his twin, butted in. 'And I had to climb to the top branch to untangle them. Look, Papà, it has a rip. I'll ask Mamma to sew it up for me tonight.'

'Tonight she's busy, Alfred. She has too much to do.'

'I'll do it for you,' Devora said, noticing that her father had used Alfred, the German version of Alfredo. He was resorting more and more to his native language with the stress.

'But you don't know how to sew,' Alfredo said.

'Of course I do. I had to sew up a wound on a corpse in anatomy class. I'm an expert.'

'Yuck. That's disgusting. Was there blood everywhere?'

She bent to tickle him, forcing herself to be jolly. 'Loads of blood. And guts. And a squishy eyeball as well. Be careful I don't sew *you* up right now.'

The twins squealed and ran off and she gave chase. If it was falling to her to look after her two brothers, then she would do her best. But first she had to try all avenues to find a better solution. Her heart brimmed with anger at this latest downturn for her family, her hopes now pinned on securing Enrico's help. She had to see him later, no matter what.

CHAPTER 2

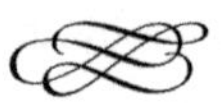

The house was upside down, clothes and possessions piled on every surface. Anna Maria was busy at the stove stirring soup while Mamma was fussing by her side, showing her how to make *latkes*, the crispy potato pancakes so loved by the family.

'It will be your task to make them now for the children, Anna Maria,' she wailed and Anna Maria tried to calm her, telling her they would be back soon.

'Don't worry, signora. These new rules won't last for long. We're not good at sticking to regulations in Italy. You'll see. Look at me, for example. Am I, an Aryan woman, supposed to be working for you?' Anna Maria stood solid in the middle of the small kitchen, squaring up to the situation, hands on her broad hips.

'And don't forget the chicken soup and always keep a stock of candles in the house,' Devora's mother said as she dropped egg mixture into the hot oil and it hissed and splashed. 'Devora, go now and buy more candles for the cupboard. And if you find potatoes at a good price, buy plenty.'

She lifted the tin from the shelf above the fireplace and pushed a handful of lire into Devora's hands. 'And be quick.

Your father wants to light the candles tonight. And fetch more flour for me. I will make *matzahs* too.'

'But...' Devora began but her mother snapped at her.

'No buts. You are always full of buts. But will be the end of you, my girl. Do as you're told and hurry straight back.' She pushed her daughter out of the door with unexpected strength. Devora had been about to ask why they were eating *matzah* when it wasn't even Passover. They were not a particularly religious family. Everything was topsy-turvy at the moment. But if it made Mamma happy, then so be it.

Her first destination was not the store in the piazza. Glancing at the clock outside the chemist, she noted it was almost six o'clock. If she was lucky, Enrico would still be waiting for her in the park. There would be no time for fencing but she hoped he could come up with a solution to this nightmare.

Enrico was in their usual place in the far corner of the park where only lovers, and youngsters smoking illicit cigarettes, ventured. He was practising footwork, perfecting advanced lunges in his trademark style of jumping before propelling his whole body forward. In centuries past, swordsmen would have fought by the fortress for their lives, she thought. Fencing for her was a pastime she'd picked up while she was able to belong to Mussolini's *giovani italiane*, before racial laws had changed everything and ruined her time at university. Her brothers had left their primary school and now joined in with the small group of Jewish children in the synagogue round the corner from their home. Devora couldn't bear to think that life was going to become even worse. Enrico would help, she was sure of it.

From a distance, she watched him move, his body lean and lithe. It was like watching a dancer. She would never tire of it.

'Hey, Biondina. Where are your sabre and mask?' he called.

As she drew nearer, he said, 'Never mind. We can practise footwork instead. I've learned new drills to pass on to you.'

There were no kisses on each cheek as at the tea party. That had probably been bravado, she thought, to show off in front of the girls.

'I've no time today for fencing,' she said. 'I need your help, Rico.'

'What's up? You look awful. Have you been crying?'

He stepped forward and tilted up her face. 'Yes, you have. Are you in trouble again?' He winked.

She pushed away his hand. 'My parents have to leave Urbino tomorrow. Because of yet another new regulation devised by your wonderful hero Mussolini.' She all but spat out the name.

He gave a low whistle. 'So, the wheels are already turning.'

'You knew about this?'

'At the GUF meeting of the university fascists last week, there was talk. *Sì*.'

'What talk? Why didn't you say anything to me?'

He turned away to execute a lunge, his sabre slicing the air. 'Because I thought it wouldn't happen. Not here in Urbino where there are so few of you.'

She pulled him by his sword-bearing arm. 'What wouldn't happen? What?'

He sighed and placed his sabre on the grass, flinging his glove on top.

'There was talk of war. Of foreign Jews being arrested before the announcement, because they would be potential enemies.'

She looked at him in horror. 'Your Mussolini is *pazzo*, a mad man. Weak, fawning to that monster Hitler. What more is going to happen to us? In fact, what have *any* Jews ever done to hurt their fellow Italians? Enrico, I can't believe what you're telling me.'

'But I never think of you as being a Jew. You're—'

'I'm what?' she yelled. 'I'm not a monkey playing jazz on a saxophone like on those posters Papà was told about by his friends in letters from Germany.' She started to pace backwards and forwards, waving her arms in anger. 'I'm not one of those Jews who will weaken the blood of the pure Italian race. I'm not tainted and evil and growing devil horns, I'm ...'

She beat her fists against him as she shouted and he clamped his hand over her mouth. '*Zitta*. Be quiet. People will hear you. Calm down and let me speak.'

Her breathing steadied and eventually he removed his hand.

She shook her head. 'What am I going to do? Mamma and Papà are leaving tomorrow. They insist I stay behind and look after the boys. But what about their schooling? The synagogue will shut down and I shall worry every minute about my parents if we're apart. And... my studies... You've got to help. You must know somebody who can put in a good word for us.' Her words trailed away in anguish, replaced by hot tears. She was angry with herself for showing weakness in front of Enrico.

He pulled her close and the strong, steady beat of his heart was a comfort as her tears soaked into his fencing jacket. 'Rico, tell me you don't believe in all this rubbish,' she sobbed.

He dropped a kiss on top of her head. 'I'm convinced it will blow over. You'll have to bear it for a while and then Il Duce will relent, just as he has done in the past. And as for your medical studies, I'll continue to help you. I'll cadge notes from medical student friends and I'll keep you up to date just as I've done during these past months. I promise. And I shall find out if you can sit the exams in some way. So then, when this is all over, you'll be ahead of the game and pass with honours. Don't worry, Biondina, there are ways to get through this.'

She hoped with all her heart that was true, her troubles momentarily forgotten. He was so handsome. So strong. The white of his jacket accentuated the tan of his skin; his eyes were pools of flecked brown that she wanted to drown in. Before she could ask him anything else, he bent to kiss her on her mouth and she didn't stop him, delicious feelings stirring in the pit of her stomach. Sabrina was not the only girl who had dreamt about doing this with the handsomest boy in Urbino and she pulled him closer as their kisses grew deeper. With him on her side, maybe she could get through this next turn of events.

The clock on the palace struck the half hour and she pulled away.

'*Dio mio.* Mamma's shopping! I have to go, Rico. *Grazie.* Please pull all the strings you can. I beg of you.'

The last evening together in Via delle Stallacce was strange. Papà had retrieved his cap from the pile of clothes Mamma had stuffed into the leather suitcase they had last used over twenty years earlier to flee Germany. At that time, Italy allowed entry to immigrants without an official visa and they had felt safe since then, despite the recent mounting anti-Semitic laws. Most Italians ignored the rules, with mutters of, '*Siete Cristiani come noi.* You are the same as us.' The word *Cristiani* was the common way of saying 'human beings'.

Mütti lit the seven candles to place on the table, the dim lights both eerie and a comfort in the tiny room that served as kitchen and living room, as well as bedroom for Anna Maria.

'Listen to what the candles say to you,' she murmured to her family.

Vati, his kippah on his head, moved his hands over the unleavened bread in a blessing. Anna Maria was invited to share and after chanting a Hebrew prayer that Devora barely remembered – she'd heard her father so seldom use it – Vati spoke in a mixture of German and Italian, passing pieces of flat-bread to each person.

'As you receive the matzah, share with us how you will use your resourcefulness in these difficult times. We eat this bread as our ancestors have done since flights immemorial from persecution. Remember *their* resourcefulness and take courage, my dearest ones.'

They responded with 'Amen' and he spoke again after a moment of silence. 'Mütti and I will not be far away and we shall carry you in our hearts, knowing that the Lord will keep you safe.'

As he put the bread in his mouth, their mother stifled a sob. 'Stay together, look after each other, say your prayers,' she said, her voice trembling with emotion. 'Be kind to one another. Be safe. Do what Anna Maria tells you.' She blew her nose. 'And, Devora, my only daughter, be good and watch your impulsive nature.' That was all she could manage before disintegrating into silent sobs.

Alfredo was next. 'I don't know these prayers you ask us to say, Mütti, but I shall light a candle in the cathedral and recite the *Pater Noster* we learned at school. And I will help Arturo with his maths.' He nudged Arturo, who stuttered his own contribution.

'I don't want you to leave. I want to go with you. Who will sit by me when I have nightmares?'

Mütti's sobs were loud now.

Alfredo glared at his brother. '*I* will. Don't upset Mütti. Think of something courageous you can do, Arturo.'

After a moment, Arturo turned to Anna Maria. 'I will eat your pasta with turnip tops, even though I hate it.'

This brought a moment of light relief. With a smile, Anna Maria spoke up. 'I'm used to managing in difficult times, signori. I promise to look after your family. Alfredo and Arturo can come with me to the cathedral and we will light candles together and pray for your safe return to Urbino. God listens to everybody. We don't need priests to pray to Him on our behalf. We are all the same, no matter how we pray.'

Devora tried to swallow a huge lump in her throat but it wouldn't budge. Willing her tears to keep away, she chewed on a morsel of the simple bread.

'Mütti, Vater, rest assured I shall do everything to take care of our family. Everything in my power.' The pieces of crisp bread felt like thorns in her mouth but she chewed on, swallowing with difficulty.

They retired to bed soon afterwards. The muffled conversations of her parents through the flimsy walls of their bedroom, Anna Maria below in the kitchen sweeping the floor, snores of her brothers in the bed next to hers, cats yowling in the alleyway were all normal sounds. And then, the mournful notes of their neighbour's clarinet, the sounds of the klezmer, playing a tune that echoed round the simple houses of the ghetto like wailing and moaning, invaded her senses. It was music that represented the dreams and prayers of persecuted Jews. Devora turned her face into her pillow and sobbed.

CHAPTER 3

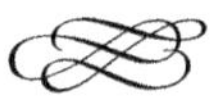

SEPTEMBER 1940

With their parents away in the internment camp near Arezzo, the children settled into a kind of routine. Vati had sent a couple of postcards, one showing Villa Oliveto, an arrow pointing to their bedroom. If anything, the turn-of-the-century building looked more like a guesthouse than a prison and she took some comfort in her father's words: *alles gut*. Everything is fine. She hoped he was telling the truth.

Little things pulled Devora up sharp, a red cloth of anger filling her head at the injustice of their situation. She came across one of Papà's slippers in the corner of the kitchen and stored it in a box of items to take to her parents if they were ever allowed to visit. He must have dropped it in the rush to pack for departure. There was a hole in the toe and she held the slipper to her chest, biting back furious words about Mussolini and his unreasonable racial laws.

Her mother's tuneless singing as she carried out household tasks was absent. Devora regretted all those occasions when she had blocked her ears and complained about the caterwaul. Alfredo's brave attempts at comforting his twin brother at bedtimes, when he was so obviously upset himself, encouraged

Devora to snap out of her mood and up her game. In the mornings the three siblings took to sitting at the kitchen table, while Anna Maria peeled potatoes or rolled out thin sheets of pasta and Devora tried to find ways to home school her brothers.

'If you finish this page of fractions by ten o'clock, we'll go and fly your kites up at the fortress.'

'But it's pouring with rain,' Arturo moaned.

'Well... if it's still raining, we'll play cards,' she attempted, trying to cajole them into completing their work.

She found she was better at helping them with maths and science and resorted to reading from Papá's bulging bookshelf in her parents' bedroom for history and language lessons. The sight of their bed, the counterpane not hiding the dents of their bodies, upset her the first time, until she told herself off for being miserable.

One morning she started a pillow fight with the boys in the main bedroom, letting them bounce and roll on the bed. One of the pillows burst and feathers fell around them like snow. The boys had stopped still, expecting a reprimand, Arturo's eyes round like saucers, and then all three of them had burst out laughing. It was laughter bordering on tears, but their parents' bed no longer looked like a marble tomb from the cathedral.

Anna Maria had made them clean the room up. The innards of the pillows had scattered everywhere and every now and again in the next months when a window was open or somebody walked past, a tiny goose feather would flutter in the air, a memory of their high jinx and instead of feeling sad, they smiled conspiratorially at each other. Their parents might be one hundred kilometres away, but the feathers were a reminder and they were never far from their thoughts. Devora tried not to worry but it was impossible. What was Villa Oliveto really like and how were they coping?

Devora decided that Italian lessons, in the form of reading from her father's precious classics, such as Dante's *Divine*

Comedy or Verga's *Sicilian Stories*, should take place on the bed, the three of them snuggled together. Devora loved reading but she didn't dwell on the whys and wherefores of the stories or dissect passages with explanations and comprehension exercises as in a proper classroom. It was enough for the boys to enjoy the sounds of the words and follow the stories.

It was hard to fit in her own studies. Devora had already had two years of being barred from studying at university. She missed attending lectures, carrying out procedures on the mannequins in the practice lab. She had no equipment at Via delle Stallacce, no stethoscope or blood pressure monitor to practise on the boys or Anna Maria. Enrico's promise of bringing notes for her to study became more and more sporadic and when he had eventually given her a bundle of untidy notes, she had trouble deciphering the scrawl and patchy sketches.

It had been a privilege to be amongst the very few women studying medicine and she strongly resented that privilege having been snatched from her purely because she was a Jew. She was falling behind and there was always so much to do to help Anna Maria. It was boring dusting and scrubbing floors, but she felt bad that Anna Maria was doing so much for them and tried to do her bit.

'Can't we leave the cobwebs hanging where they are?' she'd asked one day. 'They're so beautiful. And think how long it must have taken the poor spiders to weave them.'

Anna Maria had smiled and removed a strand of web from Devora's unruly curls. 'Any excuse to get out of housework, *ragazza mia*! Listen, if you prefer to hoe between our seedlings, then I'll finish off in here and come and join you later.'

Anna Maria had requisitioned a patch of earth behind the houses where stray cats lay on sunny days and fought at night. As summer had faded into autumn, she'd dug it over. She'd encouraged the boys to help, telling them they would grow strong muscles on their arms and legs and be able to run faster and fly their kites higher. It was too late to plant salads or tomatoes but as the September days passed, she acquired seeds for fennel, turnips, cabbage and spinach. And the boys helped her build cloches with the springs of a discarded bed frame. Anna Maria made covers to place over them from an old net curtain from the trunk at the end of the marital bed.

'In October we can sow garlic, peas and onions and in November and December we'll sow rocket and then put our little *orto* to bed for the winter,' Anna Maria had said, straightening up, leaning on her hoe to rest her weary back.

Devora hoped her parents would be back in Via delle Stallacce long before then – that Mussolini's rules would prove to be a mistake, like other foolish things he had agreed to.

The garden became a place of sanctuary. Protected by the walls of the surrounding buildings, it was a suntrap and Devora joked it was their own miniature cloister. It might not be as ornate as the *cortile* in the Ducal Palace, but it served its purpose perfectly. One morning, when the boys had been huffing and puffing about a science lesson on fulcrums and levers and they weren't paying attention, she suggested a ten-minute break in their little cloister.

Anna Maria brought out a tray with glasses of her homemade *limonata* and a handful of dry *cantuccini* biscuits and they'd stood together in a rare break, watching the boys wrestle on the ground, Anna Maria threatening to skin them like rabbits if they crushed her seedlings.

'Give them a project, signorina Devora. They need something to get rid of that energy. They're bored.'

'It's so much harder being a teacher than I ever imagined. And please drop the "signorina", Anna Maria. You're family. Don't you realise that by now?'

Anna Maria rarely smiled but her lips twitched and Devora recognised a smile in her eyes.

'You were not meant to be a teacher... Devora,' she said.

'One day you'll be a fine doctor, and you'll need to deal with difficult situations and patients. So, there's no harm in practising patience and resourcefulness now. Remember what your papà said before he went away?'

'I miss him so much.'

'I know. But I feel in my bones you'll see him again soon.'

Now, as she worked fast to catch the last light of day, hoeing carefully between rows of fennel plants, she clung to Anna Maria's optimism and wished her parents could see how hard she was trying to keep their little family together.

'Need any help?' a male voice called. She turned to see one of her close school friends approach, carrying a large sack. Luigi Michelozzi had dropped by once a week in the months since her parents had left and always arrived bearing gifts and news.

He raised his free hand in greeting.

Devora stood up, leaning on the hoe and he smiled. 'You look the part,' he said. 'A typical *contadina* working on the land.'

She laughed and turned her hand to show him the blisters on her palm. 'It's probably a good thing I'm not working on a patient today. This term was supposed to be the start of practical sessions on real patients, but with my filthy fingernails and these callouses I'm developing, I'm sure I'd be failed.'

He placed a sack carefully at her feet. 'We had spare potatoes at home and there are some eggs too. My uncle from the countryside brought them to us and we can't eat them all.'

'*Grazie*, Luigi. You're always so thoughtful.'

'How are you managing?'

She paused. 'If I'm honest, it's not easy. It's hard running everything here. And although Papà writes that they're fine, I can't stop worrying about them. Anna Maria is wonderful, but it's not the same.'

'Come and escape. Have a coffee with me in the piazza.'

Her eyes lit up at the thought of a momentary escape and then she shook her head. 'Look at me.' She lifted one foot after the other, encased in her father's old shoes caked in mud. 'Do you really want to accompany a *contadina* to the piazza?'

'I think you look rather fetching with your hair tied up in that scarf. Like a present-day version of Raffaello's veiled lady. *La velata*.'

She laughed. 'The things you come out with, Luigi.'

When he looked crestfallen at her remark, she leant her hoe against the stone building and pulled the scarf from her head, her tangle of dark blonde curls spilling to her shoulders. 'Let me check with Anna Maria that she can watch the boys and if you give me a moment, I'll try and make myself respectable.'

He smiled and his smile was even wider when she reappeared ten minutes later in her one and only best outfit, hair brushed and hands passably clean, her fingernails still lined with soil. She'd slung one of her mother's shawls around her shoulders to keep off the chill.

'*Andiamo*,' she said, linking her arm through his.

CHAPTER 4

The tables under the portico were full, so Luigi and Devora found a place to sit on the steps and waited to be served.

'Are you sure you don't want to try a cocktail, Devora? *Un martini*? Gin?'

She looked around at the sophisticated customers drinking from tall glasses, cocktail sticks spiked through a cherry or an olive adorning the drinks. A couple of the girls had fox stoles draped over their shoulders and she felt dowdy. Sabrina was sitting with a large group near the fountain, two tables pushed together, and Devora waved, hoping to catch a chance to chat, but Sabrina didn't seem to notice her. It wasn't the first time her friend had looked the other way.

'I'm fine with coffee, Luigi.'

A couple vacated their table and a group of four turned up, pushing past Luigi and Devora, who had stood up to make their move. The waiter jumped to welcome the newcomers and take their orders. Luigi frowned and beckoned him over.

'We were here first,' he said.

The waiter looked embarrassed, taking in Devora, and explained the group were regular customers who had booked.

'How long are we expected to wait?' Luigi asked and the waiter shrugged.

'That's absolutely fine,' Devora said, pulling herself up as tall as she could. 'I know of somewhere more welcoming. Let's go.'

The table where Sabrina and her friends had been sitting was now empty and she thought to herself that she and Luigi could quite easily have sat themselves down and clicked their fingers to order drinks. But she didn't want to spoil her evening with a scene so she walked away, her back straight, head held high and lips pursed, for she knew her words would have been sharp.

As they climbed Via Vittorio Veneto, she stopped at a shop window to read a notice pinned next to a display.

THIS SHOP IS ARYAN. JEWS NOT PERMITTED.

Luigi stood beside her. 'If that was on the outside, I'd tear it down immediately,' he said. 'The world has gone mad.'

'They would only put up a fresh one in the morning. It would serve no purpose.'

'It would show that not everybody is in agreement with that sentiment,' he said. 'And I don't believe I'm the only one who knows what is right and what is wrong.'

Devora's defiance at the bar had now deflated. She stood, shoulders slumped, fighting back tears.

'Come to the bar I go to,' Luigi said, seeing her face. 'Who wants to sit in the piazza anyway with people who only go there to be seen? *Su*, Devora! Come on. I think we need more than coffee.'

This time he linked his arm through hers as they crossed the wide square, passing the ornate façade of the cathedral and the Ducal Palace before making their way towards the district that housed most of the university offices. The street narrowed into a web of alleyways, thin light showing through some of the shutters of simple dwellings, and they walked on towards the westernmost tip of the little city.

She had often walked through this district in the past, hurrying to be on time for a lecture, but she had never noticed the tiny bar where Luigi stopped. There was no sign outside. Light and voices spilled from a small barred window set to the right of three steps leading down to an old door. He pushed it open and Devora was met by a fug of smoke and friendly voices calling a welcome to Luigi.

'*Ciao*, Luigi. Long time, no see! Is it because it's been your round for some time? Now you've a cushy job in the Town Hall, you have no excuse.'

Laughter rang out as well as the stamping of feet and cheers.

'*Porca miseria, amici*. Bloody hell, my friends. I thought I'd got away with leaving my wallet firmly in my pocket,' Luigi responded, a huge grin on his face.

He ordered a couple of jugs of red wine, plonking down one in the middle of his friends' table. There were wolf whistles as he led Devora to an empty table for two in the far corner next to the fire. Luigi muttered not to take any notice of his uncouth friends.

'I'm so sorry that I never asked you how your new job is going. Are you enjoying working for the *comune*, Luigi?' she asked as she settled herself at the table. A candle stuck in a round Chianti bottle lit up Luigi's face. His eyes were like the eyes of the robin who came to peck for worms in their little *orto*, she thought to herself. Warm and brown.

He pulled a face. 'Most of the work is boring.' He poured wine into their glasses: stubby vessels, unlike the long-stemmed glasses used in the busy piazza bar. 'I have to register births, deaths, marriages. It's by no means exciting. But it's a job and I suppose I should be happy to have one. You've no idea how many little boys have been christened Benito and Adolfo in the last years.'

She took a mouthful of the wine. It was strong and she imagined it fuelling her insides, warming up the cold she felt each day, not only within her body. Two small logs in the grate gave off more heat than she would have imagined possible and she removed the shawl from her shoulders. She liked this cosy place and began to relax for the first time since Mamma and Papà had left. When Luigi topped up her glass, she didn't stop him.

'I'm disgusted about that shop sign and what is happening to our country,' Luigi said, lowering his voice, his fingers tracing the rim of his glass. 'I'm ashamed our so-called leader is letting his pursuit of military valour cloud his judgement. And as for this discrimination against your people, it's another terrible mistake in a long litany of blunders.'

Devora felt the cold return and she pulled on her shawl as she listened to her friend's words.

'First it was Abyssinia,' Luigi continued. 'Then Spain. And now Mussolini is throwing himself into the arms of Hitler. He thinks that Germany has already won the war. That's why he signed the Pact of Steel last year.'

'Do you think things are going to get worse, Luigi? Enrico said things would blow over.'

'Pah! Enrico. He's one-sided. Following the mantra that we were all taught when we were little kids in the Balilla: *Credere, obbedire, combattere... morire per Il Duce...* Believe, obey, fight and die for Mussolini. Do you remember, Devora, how we all blindly did what we were told? Those Saturday mornings we spent marching about the piazza with our toy guns? But we're not children anymore. We should make up our own minds now. He's been indoctrinated, hook, line and sinker. I'm fed up with him, to be honest.'

'Pour me more wine, Gigi, and let's talk about something

else,' Devora said, using his pet-name used by friends and family.

But a couple of his friends had overheard Luigi's diatribe and there followed a lively discussion about the good and the bad of the political situation.

'Never forget Mussolini has also changed things for the better, Luigi,' said a burly young man, his hair razor-short, a scar above his nose. He dragged his chair over and turned it round to sit astride. 'You have to admit Il Duce helped many of us have a decent education. My father had to leave school because my grandparents were unable to pay the fees. Babbo was one of the many who marched to Rome with Mussolini. He's been a staunch follower ever since he was elected prime minister.'

'I grant you he provided education to the people, Franco,' Luigi replied, 'but have you ever thought it might have been purely in order to win votes? Get the masses on his side?'

'Like the church,' another voice piped up, 'stuffing people's heads with hellfire and brimstone, so they follow out of fear.'

'Absolutely, Gianni,' Luigi continued. 'Don't forget how Il Duce shut down opposition newspapers, how Matteotti mysteriously disappeared after speaking out against him, and then how he banned all other parties straight after his election. That was twenty years ago and look how his power has crept up. Where is democracy in all this?'

The middle-aged owner wiping glasses at the bar spoke up. 'And if you lot don't keep your voices down,' he said, coming from behind the counter to turn the key in the door and bang closed the shutters on the window, 'they'll be banning me too. And then how do I put food in my children's bellies?'

Franco lowered his voice, turning to the owner of the bar. 'You've got food for your family because he created work for us so that we could drink in establishments like yours. And he improved wages.'

'And then banned trade unions,' Luigi interrupted. 'The

man is obsessed with building up the might of our country through force. Look what he did in Libya and Abyssinia, spending the people's money and wasting Italian lives on building up his empire. You mark my words: this war he has entered us into, against the *inglesi*, it will be our nation's downfall.'

'Our King won't let that happen,' Franco said and Luigi shrugged.

'If you believe that, you'll believe anything.'

'Time, *ragazzi*! Off to your homes. It's late,' the owner of the bar shouted, pushing past Luigi's table to fling open the door. 'Careful how you go. Get home safely.'

One by one they filed out. After the fug of the little bar, the air felt cooler and Devora wrapped her mother's shawl around her shoulders.

Just before Piazza Rinascimento, Franco tugged on Luigi's sleeve and Devora heard him say, 'Come round to my place tomorrow evening, Michelozzi. Nine o'clock. It would be good to talk.'

'I'm not sure if I'm free. I'll see,' Luigi said, walking on with Devora. Franco disappeared down Via del Poggio and Luigi muttered to Devora, 'I have nothing in common with him. Why should he want to talk with me?'

'To convert you?' she said. 'To make you *obbedire*?' She smiled to herself in the dark. Franco would no sooner be able to get Luigi to obey the fascist rule book than she could fly to the moon.

She gazed upwards, hunting for the little people Vati used to invent in his bedtime stories when she was tiny. The moon was full tonight, the stars bright. Devora could hear a prayer in her head, the one Mütti recited in her terrible Italian, adapting it as she went along from Hebrew, which the children barely knew. She was more devout than Vati, taking the family outside to bless a new moon, come frost or summer heat. 'Praise Him, sun and moon, praise Him, all stars of the night,' she would say and they would have to answer, 'Amen.'

Vati was more open-minded, advising his children that one should respect others' beliefs. Devora and the boys had followed instruction in the Roman Catholic faith at school, although they hadn't been baptised. But Devora wondered what God the Father was doing at this moment to prevent turmoil in people's lives. Why should a people be punished for what they believed? What was wrong with individual faith if it harmed nobody?

She missed her parents more than she knew how to express. She couldn't imagine what Mütti would be doing with herself without the boys to fuss over. Devora even missed her mother's chastising. Her tongue could be harsh, but she knew her mother's heart was tender. On lighter moments, her father called Mütti Sabra instead of addressing her as her usual Miriam. Sabra was the word for the fruit of the prickly pear: tough and spiky on the outside, but soft inside. *Sabra, Sabra*, she could hear Vati now in her head. *What on earth did you say that for, Sabra? What nonsense you come out with sometimes!*

Music abruptly interrupted the night's silence and echoed round the piazza. A dance tune started up by an accordion player and a group of youngsters erupted from the central bar, skirts swirling, feet tapping. One of the men started to sing along to an old folk tune, the words sentimental, something about his girl's blue eyes shining like stars. 'Speak to me of love,' he crooned in his trained voice.

'*Posso*? May I?' Enrico asked as he appeared from the throng and swept Devora round before she could refuse, dancing her to the middle of the group of revellers. She looked over to Luigi, who lifted his hands as if to say, *what can I do?*

Enrico was as good at dancing as he was at fencing. Not surprising with all the footwork practice he'd put in over the years. He pulled her closer, spinning her faster as the music changed and a trumpeter joined in with the accordion player, sounding the notes of a modern swing piece popular with young Italians and hated by their parents. To be in his arms after so long was heavenly. He hadn't visited her once since her parents had been sent away but all that was forgotten as he swept her round the cobbled piazza. Her shawl fell to the ground and Enrico picked it up and flung it over the back of a chair, returning quickly to reach for her again, his arm extended to pull her towards him. Her hand fast in his, he swung her away and then reeled her in again and again until she was breathless and giddy. The music slowed to a romantic folk tune and when her head stopped spinning, she looked for Luigi but he was gone.

'Don't worry, I'll walk you home, Biondina. Stay with me and enjoy the music.'

While she danced under the moon and stars, she switched off from politics and stupid Mussolini. She was carefree again, lost in the moment, moving with Enrico to the tunes, enjoying his closeness, his eyes and smiles encouraging her to dance with abandon. As the bells struck twelve chimes of midnight, the youngsters disbanded. Enrico fetched her shawl, holding it up with disgust. 'What in God's name is this rag you're wearing? Did you clean the floor with it before coming out?'

She snatched it from him and he laughed.

'It belongs to my mother.'

With that, the spell of the last hour and a half was broken and she stormed away, hurrying down Corso Garibaldi. He caught up with her and hugged her. 'Forgive me, Biondina.'

'You didn't lift a finger to stop my parents being sent away. Why should I forgive you?'

'Because tomorrow I leave Urbino. I've enlisted. I've been waiting to be called up. Let's not say goodbye on bad terms.'

She brought her hand to her mouth. What was going to be the next thing to stamp joy from her world?

CHAPTER 5

He pulled her into a doorway, opened his arms and she crept into them, forgetting her anger.

'Why, Enrico?' she said. 'Why?'

'Because I have to do my duty. It's three months now since Italy allied itself with Germany. I can't stay in Urbino forever.'

She buried her face in his chest, his scent of expensive cologne and male sweat strong after their lively dances. 'First my parents leave, then you, Rico. What next? I can't bear it.' She looked up at him. 'If you know so much about what is going on, why didn't you do something about Mamma and Papà? It's not right that the boys be separated from them. They're too young. It's cruel.'

'I am doing what I can,' he said enigmatically. 'But it isn't easy. *Su*, Biondina, it's late. I'll walk you home. Let's forget about everything else except what's happening this evening.'

He held her hand as they continued downwards towards the marketplace beneath the Ducal Palace. Any other time, she would have felt the luckiest girl in the world to be walking out with him as his *fidanzata*, the girlfriend of the most eligible and good-looking young man in Urbino. The twin towers of the palace were outlined against a soft black sky, stars shining like the setting for a romantic scene in a movie. But her heart was heavy instead of light.

At the door to her house, he pulled her close again and tilted her face to kiss her. He was gentle, his lips soft and warm. She was missing her parents, their affection and the happy, loving atmosphere gone from Via delle Stallacce and she pressed her body against his, enjoying the comfort. Desire mounted as their kisses increased, her stomach flipping over as he nibbled at her ears and neck. And then his tongue parted her lips. He murmured her name as he pressed his hand against her breast and moved to undo the top button of her blouse.

Light spilled over them as Anna Maria wrenched open the door.

'Devora, I think it's time your young man went to his home,' she said. '*Buonanotte*, signor conte.' Anna Maria stood, legs planted akimbo on the threshold. 'It's late.'

He gave a slight bow. 'I have delivered Devora safely to her door.'

'I can see that, Conte. Well, she's back now. So, you can go,' she said, pulling Devora in and closing the door in Enrico's face.

'How dare you, Anna Maria. I didn't say goodbye properly to him. He's leaving tomorrow to enlist.'

'From what I can tell, you were doing a whole lot more than saying goodbye, signorina.'

Devora blushed. 'You're not my mother.'

'No, I'm not. But your parents entrusted me to look after you.'

'I don't need looking after.'

'Keep your voice down. You'll wake the boys. Come, I'll make us hot drinks. It will help calm you before you sleep.'

'I don't want to sleep and I don't need to calm down.'

'Then share a glass of *liquore* with me. It will help *me* calm down.' Anna Maria took hold of Devora's hands. 'Don't be angry with me. Please. I promised your parents I would look after you. Not let you fall pregnant within the first weeks.'

Devora was shocked at this comment but she shrugged her shoulders as if to say, *what nonsense.* She was far from ready for her bed, Enrico having woken up all her senses, and she sat at the kitchen table in a sulk, watching as the stout countrywoman poured generous measures of potent home-made walnut *liquore.*

'I was saving this for Christmas,' Anna Maria said. 'But we can test it now.'

Devora sipped the sweet spirit and leant back in her chair.

'Have you ever been in love, Anna Maria?' she asked, the fiery *liquore* helping to open her heart. There was no one else to confide in, although Anna Maria would not have been the first person in whom she usually confided. Sabrina was proving herself elusive and, anyway, her erstwhile best friend was in love with Enrico. A straightforward conversation was what she needed at the moment.

'Me? In love? What do you think?' the older woman said, topping up their glasses.

'I don't know.'

'Do you think it's impossible for a woman like me to be in love? A woman past her prime, not beautiful, uneducated, with no dowry to her name?'

'I don't think any of those are necessary for a woman to... have feelings,' Devora finished lamely.

'I was in love with a man, yes. And that is why I had to leave Lucania.'

'Why? Was he married?'

'Yes. But not in the way you think. Not to a woman.' She drained her glass and then slammed it down on the table. 'He was married to the church.'

Devora stared at her, open-mouthed. 'You were in love with a priest?'

'*Sì.*'

'*Really?*' Devora gasped.

'Really. And I thought he loved me back.'

'*Dio mio.* What was he like?'

'Handsome. Tall. He knew how to give a good sermon.' She pulled a wry face. 'Yes, he knew how to talk and I liked to listen to what he said to me when we were in his bed in the presbytery. You see, I have no family. No family I know about. I was a foundling, left on the convent doorsteps. And when I was fourteen, the nuns gave me back to the church as his housekeeper. It was all very convenient... for our parish priest.'

'That's dreadful.'

'I didn't think it was dreadful. I loved him. I was his *perpetua,* his permanent, live-in servant, and he cared for me, kept me warm at night, praised me for the food I prepared, the vestments I mended. I swept the church, polished the candlesticks, worked all day and at night we kept each other warm.'

'So, what happened?'

'The thing that happens when a man and a woman make love night after night. Because love is what I believed it was. I fell pregnant.'

A sharp intake of breath from Devora was followed by, 'And...?'

'And, nothing. *Niente,*' Anna Maria said, pouring herself another glass of *liquore.*

Devora put her hand over her glass, refusing more of the strong spirit. Her head was spinning enough with this revelation as well as the wine and dancing of earlier.

'But... the baby... You're a mother. Where is your child?'

'In the village cemetery. There's no tombstone, only a simple wooden cross. Amato was stillborn.'

'And your priest?'

'The bishop decided he should be sent to a mission school in Abyssinia. If that was not bad enough, my priest, as you call him, he blamed the child on me.' Anna Maria wiped her hand over her mouth as if he was a bad taste. 'It was all my fault, he said: I had lured him into my bed and seduced him, he said. Me, an innocent fourteen-year-old who knew nothing about men or love before he seduced me. *Figlio di un cane*. Son of a bitch.'

'I'm so sorry, Anna Maria.'

'No need for *you* to be sorry. But there's no need for you to make the same mistake as I did either and fall for the first man who pays you attention. That young man, Enrico. He's not good enough for a girl like you.'

'He kissed me, that's all.'

'Yes. He kissed you. I saw, through the window. But, *cara mia*, that is only the start. He will be kissing more than your lips soon if you let him. And you will be the one who suffers. And he's going away. You'll be the one left behind, sorting out the gift he presents to your belly.'

Devora felt sorry for Anna Maria. Not only losing her baby but being banished from her home town because of it. Punished for accepting what she thought was love from a man of the cloth who should have known better. But what was happening between her and Enrico was entirely different from what the scoundrel parish priest had done. Anna Maria did not understand. She might be a wonder at keeping house, cooking up meals and growing vegetables, but she really knew nothing about her and Enrico.

'I'm sorry, Anna Maria. I appreciate your concern but you don't really know Enrico. I've known him since I was at nursery school.'

'You *think* you know him. Remember, a little boy in short trousers is not the same as a grown man.'

Anna Maria had been traumatised by a man, Devora thought. Her attitude was scarred. Their two worlds were entirely different.

'I'll think about what you've told me, Anna Maria,' she said, not wishing to say anything further to offend the poor woman. 'Let's not quarrel. I'm tired. See you in the morning.'

Devora took ages to fall asleep. She wasn't tired. She lay under the covers, imagining what might have happened if Anna Maria hadn't disturbed Enrico at the door. She would count the days until she saw him again. To whatever God was listening, she prayed to keep him safe for her in the meantime.

CHAPTER 6

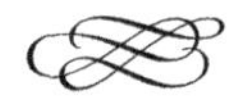

Devora's head ached next morning and Anna Maria brewed her a *tisana*, made with dried slices of prickly pear she had brought from her native Lucania. She added a sprinkle of black pepper to the mixture and told Devora to drink every last drop.

It was bitter but it helped.

'Fresh air for you now. See if the weeds have grown and hoe them for me. I'll look after the boys for an hour. They can help me by sweeping the bedroom. There are still feathers under the bed.'

Mornings were fresher now and Devora tied her mother's shawl close, hoping Enrico was already gone and would not find her dressed like a peasant girl. Luigi had admired the look but she was sure that Enrico didn't.

She picked the last of the cherry tomatoes and started to pull up the yellowing plants to add to the compost heap.

'Signorina Devora?'

She looked up to see the chaplain of the elementary school the boys used to attend, dressed in his black soutane. He raised his wide-brimmed hat and approached the little space Anna Maria had appropriated.

'*Buongiorno, padre,*' she said, wondering why he had called. Perhaps he had been sent to tell them the land wasn't theirs to work.

'We needed to plant here,' she said. 'Since our parents left, it's been hard and...'

He lifted his hands and shook his head. 'It's not why I have come, signorina. Can we sit?'

She indicated a simple bench. 'My little brothers made that. It's not that comfortable, *padre*. Won't you come inside? Anna Maria can make you coffee.'

'No. It is you I want to talk to. Without the boys hearing.'

She frowned. 'What's the matter?'

He sighed and folded his arms, his hands disappearing into the wide sleeves of his cassock.

'Your brothers... I caught them yesterday stealing money in the cathedral.'

'Arturo? Alfredo? Are you sure? They know stealing is wrong.'

'I am sure they do. In your religion, "thou shalt not steal" is the eighth commandment, while in our Catholic faith it's the seventh. I remember teaching them scripture at school. Delightful boys. And I am sure your parents will have instilled these rules too.'

'Of course. We've never been strict followers of our faith, but of course the boys know it's wrong to steal. I'm so sorry. What did they take? I'll have to punish them. But... it's so hard without Mamma and Papà...'

'I am sure it is, my dear. When I tell you that they broke open the offerings box beneath the candles to take coins so they themselves could buy a candle each to light – to ask God to bring their mother and father back soon – you will understand that punishment is not in order. No... my idea is to let them join in with the football team again. To give them some joy in their young lives. Football is surely not against the rules. And I have spoken to one of the *maestre* at school and she is prepared to come to your house for one hour each afternoon to coach them in their lessons. What do you think? I have done some investigations and you are the only Jewish children left in Urbino. The numbers in your community were never very high anyway.'

'I don't know what to say, *padre*. I know they'll love the football.' She smiled. 'Maybe they won't be so enthusiastic about the lessons, but I have to admit I'm struggling to keep them interested. I take my hat off to all teachers.'

'It's different when the children are not yours,' he said. 'Teachers can go home in the afternoons and switch off.'

The old priest stood up. 'And I shall pray for you all. The situation in our land at the moment is appalling. We have to do the right thing and help each other. Love they neighbour as thyself. That commandment is as central to the Torah as it is to our own religion. But it has vanished from some politicians' minds. May the Lord bless and keep you.'

He made the sign of the cross in the air and tears came into Devora's eyes. Her tears never seemed far away these days. His blessing was identical to the words her mother sometimes used. Why were Jewish people considered so very different? The question seemed too huge to express at this moment. For now, she was grateful for the old man's kindly response.

'*Grazie infinite, padre,*' she said. '*Grazie.*'

That afternoon she had a quiet word with the boys as they lay together on their parents' bed before she started to read, explaining she didn't approve of what they had done, that Mamma and Papà would be mortified if they knew.

'But I'm not going to tell them, *ragazzi*. Promise me you won't do anything like that again. If you need money, then I shall see what I can do. And...' She wagged her finger at them. 'There will be no football if I hear you misbehave with the teacher. *Padre* Valentini has been very good to us.'

Later that evening, there was a knock on the door and the old priest presented Devora with a brown parcel. 'I found old boots for the boys and there's a bag of flour for your maid to make bread.'

Devora slept well that night, feeling some of the burden had lifted from her young shoulders.

Seven months later, a letter finally arrived, with some proper news.

Villa Oliveto, 5 April 1941
Val di Chiana, Tuscany

Liebe Kinder,

At last I am able to send good news. There is an organisation called DELASEM helping us and others. They provide assistance to Jewish immigrants, including correspondence. Normally we are only permitted to send a short, censored postcard.

Now that we have been here for almost one year, Mütti and I feel it is safe for you to come to Villa Oliveto. We should be together. It has been far too long. Not only is it safe, but it is absolutely permitted. I have permissions from the capitano of the camp. Bracciaforte is a good family man. He was shocked when he understood our three children were living apart from us. He insists it is in order for you all to come. There is a school here for the boys to attend and a spare room next to ours for you all to sleep. There are a few other children of the twins' age with their parents, so they will have company.

Devora, make arrangements to travel and we shall pay back the driver. It is a long way – more than one hundred kilometres. We receive an allowance of 6.50 lire a day for food and clothing. We have to keep to a curfew and are only allowed to walk in the local hamlet, so our freedom is limited.

Make sure to bring your study notes. There is a retired doctor from Berlin in the camp and I've asked if you can follow him on his visits to the sick. Doktor Kempe may have time to help you with your studies as well. Please bring me my books from the shelf in our bedroom. We have started up a lending library and I would like to contribute something. What good are they languishing there, collecting damp and dust?

Send our regards to Anna Maria and tell her there is money for her concealed in the usual place. She knows where. Let her have two hundred lire and thank her from the bottom of our hearts. Take one hundred for your journey. The rest can stay safe in its hiding place for when we come back. Because that is what we must cling to. Hope. For a better future.

Your ever-loving Vati and Mütti

The letter sent Devora into a spin and she rushed to find Anna Maria.

'Look! A letter from Mamma and Papà. They say we must join them.' She read the letter aloud, translating from the German.

'What does Vati mean by the "hiding place"?' she asked Anna Maria.

Anna Maria wiped her hands on her pinafore and asked Devora to help her move the kitchen table to one side. Then with her back to the sink, she counted six floor tiles towards the fireplace, and then pivoting to the right, she counted three tiles to beneath where the table usually stood. Kneeling down, she felt with her hands.

'Bring me a kitchen knife, Devora.'

Devora handed her one from the drawer and watched as the servant prised up a tile, gently placing it to one side. A small hole had been dug out underneath, slightly smaller than the dimensions of the floor tile, and Anna Maria retrieved a small hessian pouch and handed it to her charge.

'Your papà made sure I memorised the numbers. Six by three. Not three by six. Best not to tell anyone else. Not even your brothers.'

Devora smiled to herself. *Six times three makes eighteen. The lucky Jewish number. Multiples of eighteen are given at special occasions: Mitzvahs and weddings. Eighteen is the gift of life. Clever Papà.*

Inside the pouch was a tight roll of banknotes and Devora counted out two hundred for Anna Maria and one hundred for the journey, proud of her father's generosity and sacrifice. It must have taken him ages to save on his meagre new income at the back of the tailor's shop.

'Will you be all right if we leave, Anna Maria? Where will you go?'

The woman shrugged. 'I'll be fine. I can look after myself.'

'Why don't you stay here?'

'I think if your parents had wanted me to, they would have said so. Now, we must start with packing for you and the boys. You can wear as many clothes as possible to save you from carrying too much.'

'If Enrico was here...'

She stopped. Anna Maria was staring at her, shaking her head in disapproval.

'I was simply going to say that if he had been in Urbino,' Devora continued, her voice raised slightly, 'I'd have asked him for a lift to this place.'

She hadn't heard from him once since he'd left. Luigi dropped by occasionally with food or books but Sabrina kept her distance. Enrico had disappeared from her life.

'Well, he's not. And he can't. Let us see about a *corriera* or the train. But first, we must pack.'

To her dismay, another sign forbidding entrance to Jews had appeared in the centre of town. This time on the door to Sabrina's family shop. Later that afternoon, Devora peered through the window, pressing her nose against the glass. A woman wearing a mink coat had her back to her and was chatting at length to Sabrina, who was busy wrapping a garment in tissue paper. At last the transaction was finished and Devora waited at the door to slip inside.

'Oh, it's you, Devora. I believe you're not supposed to enter these premises.' The woman in the fur coat was Enrico's mother and she looked Devora up and down at the doorway, her eyebrows raised. 'Why are you still here in Urbino?'

Devora drew herself up tall. 'And why shouldn't I be, Contessa? Mussolini's new laws are intended for *foreign* Jews. *I* am Italian.'

There was no point in telling her she was leaving and she had wanted to ask about Enrico. The timing was wrong. Instead, she stepped into the shop and shut the door smartly behind her.

'Sabbi,' she hissed. 'Can we talk?'

Sabrina looked up from the lengths of material she was folding and waved her hands at Devora, as if shooing away a wasp.

'Devora, don't let Papà see you. Go outside and I'll meet you at the back door as soon as I can slip away.'

To reach the rear entrance, Devora stepped along a dingy alleyway, pigeon droppings littering the ground and windowsills. A cold breeze funnelled through the narrow space and she stamped her feet to keep warm while waiting for her friend.

'I can only spare a couple of minutes,' Sabrina said when, ten minutes later, she opened the door a crack. 'If Papà sees you here, he'll be mad with me.'

This explained Sabrina's distancing herself but Devora was disappointed in her friend.

Sabrina remained on the other side of the barely opened door, as if barricading herself. She gave Sabrina the benefit of the doubt. Maybe she was cold in her thin silk frock, cleverly cut to disguise her plump thighs, but Devora's instincts told her it was really nothing to do with the climate. Sabrina's coldness was tantamount to dislike and she looked different too. Her hair was dressed in the latest fashion: two bouffant curls rolled up at one side of her crown. With her bright red lipstick and brushed and tinted eyebrows, she looked sophisticated, almost elegant. Gone was the retiring, gawky friend of before.

'I'm leaving Urbino very soon, Sabbi. I wanted to say goodbye.'

Sabrina shook her head and sighed. 'First of all Enrico and now you. It will be Luigi next. Enrico sent me a postcard from Libya. Just imagine! I've stuck it to my dressing table mirror where I can see it morning and night.' She sighed and grimaced. 'I worry so much for his safety. Have you received a card too?'

'No. Is he all right?'

'*Tutto bene.* All good. Those two words only. Everything else on the card was blocked out. Censored.' She lowered her voice. 'In case of spies, I suppose. What a hero he is.'

Devora felt a pang of disappointment she hadn't received a card too. That was Anna Maria's fault. For sending him away with such hostility.

'Anyway, Devora. You mustn't come here It's against the

law. We're not supposed to frequent with Jews anymore. And... I don't know if we can see each other again.'

'What are you talking about, Sabrina? So much for friendship. Surely you don't believe in all this rubbish about Jews? Can't we snatch time together later on when you've finished work?'

'Papà says the reason why Italy is going through such difficulties with business is because of the Jews. And it's not about the religion, it's about weakening the Aryan race.'

Devora spluttered. 'You're not serious, surely? What twaddle are you spouting? Papà says this, Papà says that. What does *Sabrina* say? If you could only hear yourself. I cannot believe my ears.'

'And by rights, you shouldn't even have Anna Maria working for you. She's Aryan and that's against the law too.'

'What? That too? What dreadful things do you think will happen to her by living with us? Will she turn into a werewolf? Catch Jewish germs... You're being absolutely ludicrous, Sabrina. Tell me you're joking.'

'Papà says... you should have left with your parents too and he can't understand why you and your brothers are still in Urbino.'

Devora placed both hands over her ears. 'Shut up. *Stai zitta, idiota*. I can't bear it. If you can't work it out for yourself, have your own thoughts and come to a sensible opinion, then I don't want to listen to another word you say.'

She wheeled about and ran down the steps, ignoring Sabrina's calls to come back and talk. She hadn't meant it, she said. 'But if Papà came to know...'

But Devora didn't hear the rest of her sentence; she was beyond hearing range now, her feet flying, taking her up to the Fortezza along the cobbled streets, where she and Enrico had enjoyed their fencing sessions. Up there, away from stupid Sabrina and interfering Anna Maria, she might find solace.

. . .

She was alone up at the Fortezza, the wind keener than in the city centre, cold air nipping at her cheeks. The clouds over the mountains were heavy with more snow, not unusual in the spring, and she swung her arms back and forth across her chest to warm her body. And then she threw her head back and screamed, howling at the sky like a wild animal, no longer able to contain her anger and frustration. On the rise opposite, the twin towers that had always seemed to her like an illustration from a book of fairy tales now looked menacing: portals to Hell, holding bands of evil, fascist warriors bent on destroying the hopes and dreams of her family: first her father's livelihood, next her brothers' schooling, her own medical studies and social life all snatched away simply because they were considered different and undesirable.

'*Idioti*, all of you,' she screamed over and over, her words snatched by the cold breeze.

'Devora?'

She didn't hear him at first. So, when Luigi tapped on her shoulder, she jumped and screamed again.

'Devora?' he repeated. 'What on earth is up?' Tuffo bounded over and jumped up at her.

'*Giù*, Tuffo. Down.' Luigi yanked him away, holding on to his collar.

'Leave him be. Let him enjoy himself while he can, Gigi. Soon there'll be laws to curtail the freedom of dogs too.'

'What's up, Biondina?'

The affectionate use of her name made her well up and for a few moments she couldn't answer, a huge lump wedged in her throat.

'Let's sit down in the lee of the walls,' he suggested. 'Take your time. I'm not in a hurry.'

She was shivering and he removed his green Loden cape and put it round her.

'You'll freeze,' she said.

'I'm warm, don't worry. Me and Tuffo have walked back from Castel Cavallino.' He showed her the basket of *prugnoli* mushrooms he'd collected. 'Talk to me. What's up?'

'I despair,' she said eventually. 'These racial laws have become intolerable. And now, with war well underway, we shall start losing all our friends. Enrico has enlisted. Life is *merda*, basically. Absolute shit.'

'I don't believe the majority of Italians take any notice of these racial laws, Biondina. To me, you're simply Devora. I don't go round looking at people and categorising them into race and creed.'

'No. Because *you* are intelligent. Unlike those who have put notices up in their shop windows.'

He sat down beside her and she patted his knee. 'Thank you, Gigi. Thank God – whatever God,' she added ruefully. 'Thank God there are sane people who think the way you do. There are plenty who don't, who follow blindly, afraid of stepping out of line. Can you believe I've just come away from Sabrina. I wanted to say goodbye to her, despite her ignoring me for months. But she didn't want to know.' She mimicked Sabrina's voice: 'Papà says you can't come in, Papà says this, Papà says that. *Porca boia*, Luigi. I'm so angry.' She pulled the cloak tighter round her shoulders, shivering with rage and then apologised, dragging half of it from herself to cover her friend.

'Say goodbye to her? Where are you going?'

'Papà sent a letter. We can go and stay with them in their camp. I have to arrange how to travel. I'm supposed to be finding that out now.' She handed the cloak back to him and stood up.

'But where are you going?'

'Somewhere near Arezzo. Apparently, there's room for us and proper schooling for the boys. It will be easier. *Maestra* Butteri has been kind to come each day to help them, but the little scamps are going wild. One hour a day is not enough.'

'What sort of place is it? Are you sure it's a good idea to leave, Biondina? You might be safer here.'

'If Papà thinks it's all right, then it will be. Honestly, I'm finding everything so difficult here on my own. Anna Maria is good to us, but... controlling two eleven-year-olds is a job and a half. I don't want to leave Urbino but hopefully we'll be back soon. This war can't go on forever... and I do long to see my parents again.'

'But where exactly is this camp? Let me check for you.'

'What do you mean?'

'I mean...' Luigi paused, as if to find the correct words, deep furrows between his eyes. 'Some of these internment camps... the conditions are not the best. You have to be sure before you leave. In my opinion you'd be better off staying here.'

'You're worrying me, Luigi.'

'Listen, Biondina. Let *me* take you there. I'll borrow Father's car. But it will have to be in a couple of days' time. Easter Sunday. Then I can see for myself the lie of the land.'

'You're sounding like another father, rather than a friend,' she said, squeezing his hand. 'Are you sure? That would be so wonderful. I can pay you for the fuel. Papà set money aside...'

'Don't offend me. I don't want money. We're friends, remember.'

She flung her arms round him. 'You're so kind, Luigi. You make me want to cry.'

'Please don't cry,' he said, extricating himself from her arms. 'Come on, I'll walk you back to your place.' He whistled to Tuffo, who was now at the other end of the fortress grounds. The dog raced over to them, his long brown ears streaming behind him.

'*Grazie, amico,*' she said, bending to caress Tuffo. 'Anna Maria will be wondering where I am. There's lots of packing to finish.' She buried her face in Tuffo's furry neck to hide her tears. 'Oh, Luigi, I don't want to leave Urbino. But I know we must.'

CHAPTER 7

LUIGI

Luigi arranged to drive Devora and her brothers to reunite them with their parents. He'd told his father he was invited to have Easter lunch with a university friend who was about to be called up and he'd chosen a good moment to ask for the loan of the Fiat Topolino.

'There's no *corriera* on Easter Sunday, Papà, and I really want to see him. Do you mind?'

His father had been in a good mood, having lunched well with his friends after a successful morning's hare coursing.

'Fine, *ragazzo mio*. But your mother will be very upset you're not spending the *festa in famiglia*. Tread carefully.' He'd puffed on his cigar and chuckled as he'd asked, 'And does this friend of yours have a sister, perhaps? Is that the real reason to go all that way? It's high time you got yourself sorted with a nice girl. Your mother's always going on at me to encourage you.' He relit the cigar and while he sucked air, he winked at his son. 'Take the car with my blessings, *figlio*.'

Yes, the real reason is because of a girl, Luigi thought. But he wasn't sure if his father would approve of her being Devora 'the little Jewish girl', as they always described her. His parents were decent people but they were parochial and mixed with the *borghesia* of Urbino, their political views mainstream, although Papà had been heard once or twice to mutter under his breath about Mussolini and his antics, as he put it. His father was not the sort of man to participate in clandestine meetings or go out on a limb, however. 'Swim with the tide and keep your nose out of trouble,' were the kind of sayings he used.

Luigi wanted to check with don Cecchetti, the priest at Castel Cavallino, and coordinator of the fledgling group of local *partigiani*, if it was wise to transport Devora and her young brothers all the way to this Villa Oliveto on the outskirts of Arezzo. He wondered about some of the decisions taken by the authorities over where Jews were sent. Why had Devora's parents been sent to a camp so far from Urbino? Was it perhaps to make it harder for friends and family to keep in touch?

Stories were already filtering through to the group about poor treatment and conditions in some of the internment camps. At Urbisaglia, for example, a camp within the Marche region, they had received word of overcrowding and an outbreak of typhus. He was anxious to see for himself the living conditions in Villa Oliveto, if the girl he admired most in the world was to stay there. They had also heard that all documents had been removed from the internees at Urbisaglia. If this was also the case at Villa Oliveto, then false papers needed to be provided. Who knew if the day might come when Devora's family needed to escape? Without identity documents they would not get far. The world was going mad. The probability of them being moved on was likely. There was much to do.

Vestments hung from the priest's bedroom windowsill in the presbytery next to the Abbey of San Casciano in Castel

Cavallino: don Cecchetti's way of conveying the coast was clear. Luigi was relieved it meant the meeting would go ahead. Every now and again the militia could arrive unexpectedly at any premises where they suspected the existence of clandestine get-togethers. Churches were supposed to be exempt from raids, but dissidents knew this rule was not adhered to. So, vigilance was paramount. Punishment for anti-fascist meetings could lead to imprisonment or exile.

He knocked four times on the church door with his knuckles. It opened a chink and he whispered the password, 'It's three months since my last confession. I need a priest.'

He heard the correct coded answer, 'The Lord is my Shepherd,' and stepped forward.

It was Franco who drew him inside the musty church and shook his hand, his grip firm. He was a good actor too... Luigi had been convinced of his fascist loyalties on their first meeting months ago when he'd been with Devora, but that had been a charade, to put snoopers off the scent. Franco had told him he'd liked his attitude in the bar; he was on the lookout for fellows like him to help in the cause.

Since 1937 it had been a crime to oppose political decisions made by the Italian state and several political dissidents, deemed a danger to Italy, had been exiled to remote corners of Italy, especially to the south. In reality, Franco was an active member of don Cecchetti's local anti-fascist group and was carefully recruiting more members, fed up with the way Mussolini was ruining the country, exploring ways to undermine his government and to strengthen their ranks, without drawing attention to themselves. The group was growing all the time.

Luigi followed Franco into the sacristy where a dozen men of various ages and a couple of women were already seated. Luigi recognised two men, but the women were new to him. One of them was particularly striking, her hair cropped short like a boy's, her eyes blue as forget-me-nots. She turned her face away at Luigi's appreciative stare.

Don Cecchetti welcomed Luigi with a smile. '*Benvenuto*, Michelozzi.' He turned to the others. 'Now our new *compagno* is here, we can begin. I have to be at the castle in one hour to carry out last rites for the *barone*, so I'll be brief. Who has news?'

Luigi was the first to speak. 'Tomorrow, I drive to Arezzo to take Jewish siblings to their parents already interned in Villa Oliveto, on the outskirts of Arezzo. I have two questions. Does anybody have information about the place and, secondly, is there anything of use I can do while in that part of Tuscany?'

'My classmate from my seminary days is parish priest in nearby Civitella in Val di Chiana, a few kilometres from the villa. Apparently, the villa is not such a bad place to be confined. But are you sure these children have to leave Urbino? Several exceptions have been made. What sort of employment were their parents in? If their father fought in Libya or Spain, they could be exempt.'

'The parents came to Italy back in 1918 and have stayed in Urbino since. The three children were born here and the father worked in the back room of the tailor's in the piazza. I don't see how any of this helps.'

The priest sighed. 'Even so. Do the children really have to leave? We could find somewhere for them to stay. We're doing it for others.' He turned to the two women. 'Is there any room at the farm?'

The girl with the short hair shook her head. 'Full to bursting,' she replied. 'I could scout about, if you need.'

Luigi couldn't quite place her accent. It wasn't from Urbino.

Luigi shook his head. 'It's complicated. At the moment, they're allowed to stay in Urbino: they're Italian-born but their parents wish the family to be together.'

'Well, let's see how it goes, Michelozzi,' the priest said. 'If matters deteriorate, then we can step in. Not everybody is tolerant of these poor people. Life is only going to get worse in this war for our friends.'

'You're right, unfortunately, *padre*. I do hear comments amongst some Urbino citizens. They like to read that dreadful rag, *L'Ora*, and take heed of comments such as Jews being a poisonous virus.'

'Well, that's why we're all here, is it not? To do what we can to counteract. Stay on after the meeting and I'll scribble a note for my colleague in Civitella. You can pay him a visit and see if he has any new information for us.'

Luigi nodded, his worries not entirely settled.

'And, Michelozzi. You work in the Town Hall; I need a dozen blank forms for new identity documents. Can you arrange to get some more *carte in bianco*? I've found a skilled forger. A man I used to visit in Pesaro Prison before the war. He owes me a few favours and I need papers for some new arrivals from Yugoslavia.'

'Of course, *padre*. I can get hold of those forms, no problem. When nobody is around.'

Luigi listened to the rest of the meeting, Tuffo lying patiently at his feet as the group discussed what they had been up to.

The priest explained he had applied to DELASEM for more funds to provide food and clothing to cloistered nuns at the convent who were hiding two families of Slav immigrants in their cellars.

A fresh-faced youth of about fourteen, new to Luigi, was the final speaker. 'Two nights ago, my brother and I painted over anti-semitic slogans that appeared on the city walls: *Nemici d'Italia*, enemies of Italy and, on the door of the synagogue: *Ebreo nemico naturale della patria*. Jews are the natural enemy of the homeland.'

Luigi admired the boy's spirit, but things had come to a pretty pass if schoolchildren were being recruited. Where were all the men with experience?

'Good lad,' don Cecchetti said. 'It's important to show the world we are not all sheep who follow these obscene rules without question. But be careful not to be seen. Your mother needs you, Paolino, now that your father has passed.'

The boy nodded and the priest continued. 'Now, comrades, listen carefully. I have been in close touch with the Fifth Garibaldi Brigade in Pesaro and they are keen for us to join them. However, we all need to be extra vigilant. I entreat you to vary your routines. There are plenty of ardent *fascisti* spies looking out for anything remotely clandestine. If they see you in a huddle, or regularly meeting with the same companions, then they'll suspect something is up. I suggest you avoid the bar in Stretto del Tasso for a while. Go to different places. Keep your ears open too – not just for informers. Be on your guard all the time.'

There were nods of approval between the group as the priest continued.

'In the meantime, let us continue collecting funds and weapons. I'll bless you before you make your way home. Travel separately. We'll meet in a fortnight, unless you hear otherwise, in the usual way. Look for my message on the notices of the dead in the piazza. Always the bottom left announcement. As regards potential new members, don't enrol anyone until you've spoken to me and I've vetted them.'

He raised his right hand and made the sign of the cross in the air: '*In nomine patris, et figlii et spiritus sancti*,' intoning Latin words familiar to Luigi since he'd been a toddler.

The group dispersed after mumbling their goodnights, going their separate ways. The girl with the cropped hair shook his hand, her fingers small in his.

'I'll keep my ears open in case your friends need to hide,' she said. 'I'm Lisa, by the way. At least that's the name I use right now.'

He wanted to talk more but she disappeared into the shadows after the others and he wondered if he would have another chance at a future meeting.

It was dark but Luigi and Tuffo knew their way across the fields. Occasionally Luigi flicked on his torch to check when his pet strayed from his side to sniff out some night creature, the dog's eyes two balls of flame in the torch's glare. Luigi was frustrated that nothing much was happening in terms of an anti-fascist uprising but don Cecchetti was continually urging them to keep things low-key so as not to raise suspicions. The time would come, the priest said, when they might have much to do. It was important to have a consolidated base from which to act.

At least Luigi had found out Villa Oliveto was safe enough. He would seek out the local parish priest after he had delivered Devora and the twins to their parents. He wondered when he would see her again and if out of sight signified out of mind. Maybe absence would ease his lovesick heart, rather than make it grow fonder. He tried to tell himself that she wasn't the only girl in the world. But his heart told him otherwise.

CHAPTER 8

The following morning, Easter Sunday, Luigi's mother was incandescent.

'I never see anything of you nowadays,' she said, pacing the Aubusson rug in the living room. 'You treat this house like an *albergo*. And today of all days. Normal families spend it together.'

'I'm sorry, Mamma. I'm free tomorrow. Will that do? You can have the pleasure of my company from morning to night. What's in a day, after all?'

'What's in a day? Easter Sunday is perhaps the most important day in our calendar and well you know it, Luigi. Domenica has been slaving away in the kitchen to make your favourite stuffed rabbit and *cappelletti*. I'm really disappointed in you. Your father doesn't help matters either. He told me he's hunting until noon. *Again*. I am fed up with both of you, I really am. Why didn't I have a daughter?'

She hadn't let her son near her when he approached to say goodbye. Usually, a kiss and a hug calmed her down. Luigi felt a twinge of guilt but he had deliberately chosen Easter Sunday to accompany Devora and the twins as he knew there would be fewer police around to check comings and goings. But he couldn't explain all that to his mother. Being an only child made it difficult to live an independent life but it would be far more sensible to find his own place as he became more involved with the resistance. He left his mother fuming. He couldn't even promise to get back in time for supper. Arezzo was a good morning's drive in Papà's little Fiat and he was hardly going to drop Devora off and turn round immediately for the long drive back to Urbino over the mountains.

They had to make a couple of journeys back and forth to load the car, Via delle Stallacce being far too narrow for a vehicle to park outside the Lassas' humble house. Luigi left the Topolino in the large market square and the boys, chattering with excitement about the adventure ahead, helped him carry bundles and bags up and down the narrow alley steps. At the last minute, Anna Maria hurried down with a basket of produce and a picnic for the journey, hugging the children to her, asking if they had remembered everything. 'The books for your father, Devora?'

'You've already asked me that twice, *carissima* Anna Maria,' Luigi heard Devora say. 'And, yes, the sheets and candlestick that Mamma asked for too. And her stout shoes. And her favourite hat for Shabbat. And Papà's odd slipper.'

'Your schoolbooks, *ragazzi*?' Anna Maria asked the boys, who looked at each other sheepishly and were immediately sent back by Devora to fetch them, warning that otherwise their football boots would certainly not be coming with them in the car.

And then, Anna Maria began to cry. '*Ahi!* I have an insect in my eye,' she said, wiping her eyes on the apron tied round her middle. 'Hurry up and leave,' she said, instructions coming one after the other as if to hide her upset. 'Go! You'll be late. Keep safe. I'll make sure to tidy up and lock the house. Tell your mother and father it will be clean for their return and the key will be in its usual place. Be good for them and give them my best wishes. See you soon. *A presto!*'

They waved to her from the car as Luigi started the ignition. She presented a lonely figure as they drew away along the road towards Urbania, the boys turning to kneel on the backseat to peer through the window. Everyone was quiet for a few minutes.

'Poor Anna Maria,' Devora said, from the front passenger seat. 'I suppose we've become family for her. She has nobody else.'

'She's a strong woman,' Luigi said. 'And I'll try to keep an eye on her.'

'I'm not sure she'll stay in Urbino.'

The road wound up and down the Apennines in tortuous bends out of Le Marche and into Tuscany. Arturo felt queasy, so before they reached the Tuscan city of Sansepolcro they stopped to stretch their legs and eat Anna Maria's picnic. She'd baked pizza as well as the boys' favourite fried onion rings. And she'd included slices of chocolate cake.

'You're very quiet, Biondina,' Luigi said. It was warmer in the valley and he was lying full-stretched on the verge, his sleeves rolled up, chewing on a blade of grass. The boys were kicking their beloved football in a field sprouting clover and daisies.

'I'm apprehensive. The very word "internment" fills me with dread... I'm nervous,' she said, eventually. 'Of course I can't wait to see Mamma and Papà but who knows how long it will be before we're free again? I mean, in Urbino most people are against these ridiculous laws, don't you think? Sabrina's family aren't, but I think they're the exception, Gigi, am I right? I'm so confused.'

'That's understandable. Unfortunately, they're not the only

bigoted citizens but if you don't want to go, then I can turn the car round right now and...'

'I couldn't do that to my parents. They want us together as a family.' She sat down near him, holding her knees. 'And apparently there's a doctor in the camp, willing to take me under his wing. I haven't had time to study much. And with Enrico being away, and no longer sending me notes, I've rather fallen behind.'

He got up, brushing grass and dust from his trousers. 'This might be the moment to give you my gift. You need cheering up.' He moved to the back of the car and opened the tiny boot, rummaging beneath bags the boys had piled in haphazardly.

'*Eccolo!* Here you are,' he said, handing her what looked like a book wrapped in brown paper.

'It's not my birthday.'

'I know.'

He'd given her a miniature volume of poems on her birthday back in February: *La Vita Nuova*, bound in leather. It was an early work by Dante, describing his love for Beatrice. A girl he'd first seen when she was nine years old. Luigi had written a message inside: *To Devora. Known since you were younger than Beatrice. Best wishes, Gigi.*

She unwrapped the paper to discover a medical text: *Human Anatomy and Physiology*.

'Bedside reading, rather than bedtime,' he quipped.

Already she was leafing through, the pages opening at a detailed coloured illustration of the brain. She looked up at him, a beam on her face. 'It's wonderful, Gigi. But... it must have cost a fortune.'

'No,' he said, shaking his head. 'I bought it from the university second-hand shop.' He leant over her shoulder, one of her curls brushing against his face, distracting him for a moment. 'See.' He pointed at a page where somebody had scribbled comments in the margin and another where a whole passage was underlined in dark pencil. 'It's not new. Sorry!'

'It's perfect. Absolutely perfect and will be such a help. *Grazie*.' She leant to peck him on the cheek.

He couldn't tear his eyes away from her and he watched as she turned to the index, her finger running down the lines, searching, her lips mouthing the headings to herself.

'Skeletal muscles,' she announced, her eyes shining as she punched the air. 'Yes! I find them so hard to memorise. This is *so* useful. When's your birthday, Gigi? I've forgotten.'

'It's July. The thirtieth of July,' he said, envy like a stab in the guts, disappointed she didn't remember.

'Ah yes, you're a Leo. Intelligent and courageous.'

He raised his eyes. 'Don't tell me you believe in all that stuff.'

'No. Not really. But it's fun and I like to read daily horoscopes to see if anything comes true. I'm an Aquarian. Supposed to be imaginative and logical. But I can't conjure up a way out of this intolerable mess we're in. Can you?'

He extended his hand to reluctantly pull her from the ground, wanting this interlude with her to last longer than their picnic on the grass, the view of the cathedral spire and the city walls of Sansepolcro in the distance shimmering in the spring sun. For half an hour today, life had seemed almost normal. The spectre of war distant.

'We should leave, otherwise it will be midnight by the time I drive back,' he said, calling for the boys to climb into the car.

A couple of hours later, Luigi took a road south of Arezzo, turning to tell Devora that one day when there was more time, he would love to bring her to see the beautiful square and cathedral. The boys were fast asleep in the back, tired of asking if they were nearly there.

'I'd love that. But, goodness, Gigi, I didn't realise the villa was so far from Urbino. I'm so sorry.'

'Just be grateful your parents haven't been sent to the far south, like two of my dissident friends. I haven't seen them for two years. And I'm not likely to see them again anytime soon the way things are going.'

It wasn't difficult to find the camp, the signpost for Oliveto pointing up a hill, a quarter of a kilometre off the provincial road. A farmer was guiding two large white oxen ahead of them and Luigi slowed the car down, the engine labouring as they climbed. A handful of flies from the beasts flew into the car and Devora wound up her window.

She stared out at the dense olive groves, separated from the track by stone walls. The road surface was rutted and the boys woke up from the bouncing.

'Are we nearly there?' Alfredo asked, rubbing his eyes.

Luigi and Devora laughed and then, as the track curved to the left, there was Papà, standing with a couple of other men outside a pair of tall, metal gates bearing the sign *Villa Oliveto*. His face lit up when he saw them and he rushed forwards, shouting, 'It's them. They're here. Fetch my wife. Tell her our *Kinder* are here.'

Luigi stood back to let Friedrich enjoy this special moment with his three children.

Their father clasped them in a higgledy-piggledy embrace, the boys jumping up and down, Devora wiping her eyes. He extricated himself, pulling the boys' arms from around his neck, half-crying, half-speaking: 'Let me look at you, my wonderful *Kinder*.' He put his hand to his mouth, gasping as he said, 'Devora, you are more beautiful than ever. Boys, calm down. You're still very noisy. I'd quite forgotten.'

But Luigi sensed he did not really mind their joyful enthusiasm; the boisterousness he had been starved of must be really welcome. The four of them were laughing, trying to speak at the same time. More people had come through the gates now, clapping their hands, joining in with the wonderful moment of reunion. And then the whole thing was repeated all over again as their mother came running from the big house in floods of tears and then the five of them were clinched in another tangled embrace of arms and legs and heads and words.

Luigi felt deep anger and shame at the sight: that a family should be split up like this. All because of racial laws formulated by an Italian government cosying up to Hitler. An Italy that to Luigi had become a laughing stock. He knew the details by heart, his job as registrar requiring him to know facts and figures: regulation 1415 of 8 July 1938, reinforced on 10 June 1940, stating that: *all male Jews between the ages of eighteen and seventy and all foreign Jews be considered enemies of the state in so far as they are capable of bearing arms, and should be sent to internment camps*. It was all wrong. Wrong through and through. His fists clenched by his side, he strode to the car and climbed in, leaving the Lassa family to catch up with each other.

Before he could start the engine, Devora's father wrenched open the car door. 'Luigi. *Caro* Luigi. Thank you, thank you for bringing our children to us today. Stay and eat. There's a feast prepared.' He was joined by the rest of the family and Luigi looked at Devora, who nodded her head and encouraged him out. 'You can't leave just like that,' she said.

He climbed from the car. 'Thank you, signor Lassa. Most kind. I can stay for a while but I have another visit to make.'

Devora's mother reached up to plant two fat kisses on his cheeks and pulled him over to one of the tables positioned in front of the imposing building.

'We have prepared a celebration meal,' she said. 'Please share in our joy.'

She laid a large white cloth on the table. It billowed like a sail and then a couple of women emerged from the house bearing plates of boiled eggs, potato fritters, fresh fruit, olives, a loaf of flat bread and a small chicken to weigh down the cloth. The twins reached out to take a fritter each and they were rewarded by a slap on the back of their hands by their mother.

'Manners, boys. And first, you wash your hands, party or not. I can see you have gone wild in these past months.' She scowled at Devora, who shrugged her shoulders.

'Now, now, Mütti, now, now. Don't start!' Friedrich Lassa said. He turned to Luigi. 'Today is your Easter. We celebrate Pesach in a couple of days. But please accept what we can offer you today.'

'Did you make sure there was nothing leavened in your meal today, Devora?' his wife asked.

'Mütti, I'm sorry. We've found it hard to keep to all the rules while you've been away,' Devora answered, twiddling a curl round her finger.

'Well, never mind, my child. You're here now. We'll soon have you sorted and back to rights.'

'Devora can't cook for toffee,' Arturo said. 'Anna Maria is loads better. She's not strict about what we eat...'

A dig in his ribs from Alfredo stopped him from giving more away. 'But we've missed your gefilte fish and dumplings,' Alfredo said. 'And have you made apple pancakes with cream, Mamma?'

'Here you call me Mütti, boys. I am definitely Mütti now,' was his mother's stern reply.

Luigi glanced at Devora. She looked tense but remained silent. He remembered what she had said at the picnic on the way, how anxious she was about coming to Villa Oliveto. What was it she had said? She was anxious about being confined. Yes, that was it. He felt sorry for her. This place might be a kind of double internment for her, both physically and morally.

As if to blunt the sharpness of his wife's comments, Devora's father said, 'This is not such a bad place, Devora, as you'll discover when we show you round. You'll see there is a library, as well as a living room where we listen to music and occasionally there is a concert. We even have a room set aside for a synagogue. There is plenty to do. And later, you will meet Doktor Kempe.' He lifted a knife and tapped it against his glass for silence. '*Salute,* my friends. *Prost.* And welcome, my beloved family. Together again.' He lifted his glass, a quarter full of beer, like all the other glasses.

'*Zei Gazunt!*' said his wife. '*L'Chayim.* To life!'

Luigi left soon after the meal was finished.

'Come back and see us as soon as you can,' Devora's father said as they shook hands. 'Visits are allowed after written permission. Thank you again for delivering my children safely, Luigi. Take good care of yourself.'

The sparkle had drained from Devora's eyes, telling Luigi all he needed to know.

'Give it a chance,' he whispered as she hugged him goodbye. 'And write to me. Send me a list of everything you need.'

It was obvious to Luigi that she was biting back her emotions, her lips pursed as she nodded and squeezed his hand before following her parents and the twins into the austere building shaded by Mediterranean pines. The wind gusted, tugging at the tablecloth again like a handkerchief waving farewell, and a couple of women set to, clearing away dishes.

Luigi drove his father's car down the track away from the villa, choked at leaving Devora behind. She had looked so lost. His distracted mind caused him to swerve to avoid a group of boys playing in the dust. As he continued to the walled town of Civitella in Val di Chiana, he wondered about the hastily scribbled note in his pocket that don Cecchetti had pushed into his hands. Should he know about the contents? Were there too many disparate groups working towards the same end? It was all a mess: families banished because of their religion, neighbour pitted against neighbour in this crazy civil war. He feared things were only going to get worse, unless more of his fellowmen united to stand up against the *nazifascisti*. As night began to fall, darkness seeped into his heart as he approached the hilltop town.

CHAPTER 9

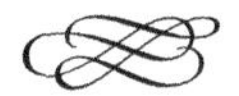

JANUARY 1941, LIBYA

ENRICO

In a dive in the centre of Tripoli's souk district, I met the most beguiling girl. The club was run by the same Italian who had organised Italy's last Grand Prix in the city. The girl was exquisite. Her belly half exposed, a sheer strip of material revealing glimpses of bare thighs as she shook herself, her buttocks twitching as she moved to the music. Towards the end of the dance, she was down on her knees, bending to scrape the floor with her long hair: an act of sensual submission. This girl was no virgin; she knew how to excite. But there was something in the way she moved her feet lightly across the stage that reminded me of Devora and our fencing dances. And yet, not. I felt sure Devora would not writhe in the same way that this girl did later in the back room she had taken me to. I remember hoping at the time she would not give me the pox and yet not caring. If I was going to die on the following day, what did it matter?

. . .

I woke the morning after the night before to a headache and reality: a bugle call to action in a cold desert dawn. A frantic pulling on of uniform, pushing of feet into boots and grabbing of weapons had started the too-early day. I jumped into the semi-circular trench we'd dug under the blistering sun. While we waited, hunkered in the sandy ditches like terrified rabbits, the forward patrol had set out to lure in the enemy. The shouts of men were drowned by the ping of bullets hitting the sides of *inglesi* tanks as they advanced. I lobbed a grenade and watched the crew as they scrambled to the safety of nearby rocks and I yelled at the men assigned to me to set up the Breda and continue firing. Smoke and sand swirling in the scirocco storm blurred our vision. I felt sick, dust clung to my skin, my mind was blank as I wondered what the hell I was doing here: hungover, the scent of the dancer still on my skin, in the middle of a godforsaken desert, shooting with other low-grade soldiers who had little idea of what they were doing. Parading in pristine uniform on a military base back home had been no preparation for this hellhole.

By some miracle, the tank we had attacked suddenly burst into flame, the air filled with the screams of dying men. A British soldier half hung from the cupola, flames streaking up his back like orange wings, his arms in the air as he shrieked for surrender. And then somebody from our dugout shot him. I went berserk as I clambered from the trench, barbed wire tearing at my limbs, to go to his aid and then I heard the whistle of a bullet and felt a sharp pain in my leg. I fell face first, my mouth open in agony, sand filling my mouth, my own screams filling my ears.

When I came to, I was being tended by a dark-skinned nurse. He spoke good Italian, like most Libyans, and he told me the surgeon had removed a bullet from my calf and I should rest.

The surgeon came to see me. He knew my father well.

They'd studied together at Bologna University, apparently. He sat by my bed and talked softly. He told me he was sending me home. My wound needed better care than he could give me here. He said that what I had done to try to save the enemy was foolish but admirable. 'I lost my only son when he was three,' he told me. 'He drowned at Forte dei Marmi when his mother and I were drinking cocktails. I won't let your father lose you. I'm writing a report about your situation and...' he lowered his voice further, 'if what I write is exaggerated, then who will know? We shall keep it between ourselves. It's crazy out here. Our army is badly equipped. We even shoot down our own planes. You need to leave, young man. You're more use back home.'

That is the way it works, you see. *Raccomandazioni.* How wheels are oiled in our country, how jobs are procured. It is who you know not what you know that helps our world grind round. A little push, *la spintarella*, a key to unlock favours, *la chiave*.

I do not complain, neither am I surprised at this turn of events. Often my blue blood has helped me out of sticky situations. I told my father's friend that before I left, there was something I needed to do. My life depended on it, I told him. And when he smiled and asked if it was an affair of the heart and I'd nodded, he'd shrugged his weary shoulders. 'The young will always learn the hardest way,' he said. 'Make sure you're back here in forty-eight hours. There is a plane leaving late Tuesday night.' He rose to leave my bedside. 'And remember! All this stays between us. Give my best wishes to your father...'

How could I have kept away from her? She has cast a spell over me with her bewitching almond eyes, her beautiful face, her hair that I undo to fall beneath her waist in a thick curtain of shining black.

Concerned, she removed the bandage from my leg and told

me it was clean and not too deep. 'You must keep it dry, but it will heal.'

She rubbed oil into my body: myrrh that she told me was used for embalming as well as to bring vigour and good health. Tears of myrrh, she said it was called, as she leant over me, her breasts brushing against my back as she massaged my weary skin, her hands firm as she worked her fingers down my spine. I felt myself harden and wanted to turn round to take her, but she slapped my buttocks playfully and told me to wait. I could not bear it as she moved down to my feet, telling me she was using jasmine oil to relax me even further, carefully avoiding my bandaged leg. But I was anything but relaxed, so that when she turned me round, I was more than ready when she took me in her mouth.

Afterwards, she bathed me, dipping a cloth into scented water to remove the dust of battle, her hair tangled round my limbs like weed, as water steamed like a desert mirage from the bowl. I kissed her on her eyelids, then on her nose, aquiline and classic. I kissed her behind her ears, as delicate as two seashells, and I called her my mermaid. She laughed and told me I was clean now, that I should get dressed, that I would be late otherwise. And that she had another client in half an hour.

I clutched her wrists then, told her she could not, would not, do to others what we had done together and she shook her head.

'You do not tell me what to do,' she said, pulling her hands from my grasp. 'It's my job.'

'I'll rent us an apartment,' I said, consumed with fury that I was not the only man she had known or would know.

She laughed at me. 'Promises, promises. Men always promise, but they never deliver.'

'I shall return in a couple of hours. I promise I shall have found you somewhere.' Even as I said those words, I wondered how I would manage. But I knew I wanted her to myself. I pulled a handful of notes from my wallet and thrust them at her. 'Take this. Tell your customers you can't see them anymore.'

She looked down at the notes in her hands, picking one up from the floor where it had fallen. 'But... this is too much...'

'Good! Then you will no longer have to work.'

It was a kind of craziness I was experiencing. But I always know what I want. And, most often, I get it.

My orderly was waiting for me and he helped me with arrangements.

I returned to her later. She had prepared a meal and lit dozens of candles around the room. 'You gave me enough money so that now I shall never again be frightened of the dark,' she said.

'Are you afraid of the dark? There is much I don't know about you.'

'Sit,' she ordered, pushing me gently down to the cushions heaped against the whitewashed wall in the corner. 'I will serve you.'

She had prepared dishes of *kusku.* A dish I'd never eaten before – a kind of soft grain served with stewed beef, tender and succulent, and *tajin mahshi.* She repeated the names for me and laughed when I clumsily imitated. This was followed by stuffed peppers and aubergines. And *shakshouka:* eggs poached in a rich tomato sauce. We ate a bread, round with a hole in the middle, and she told me her mother baked this bread in the desert in the hot sand that served as an oven. And then she cut me slices of *basbousa* – cake made from semolina, oozing with syrups and almonds, which we washed down with sweet black tea.

She danced for me as I reclined against the cushions, her body sinuous, sensual in the soft candlelight, and then she knelt to kiss me on the mouth for the first time.

'Did you mean what you said earlier? That promise of

finding somewhere for me to live?' she asked as we stretched out together on the cushions, lazy after our lovemaking. 'Even if you don't find anywhere, I am happy about what you said. I like that you want me for yourself. Nobody ever cared enough to feel that way.'

And then she told me of what she had endured. How her father had been killed whilst working for the Italians: building a road between Benghazi and Tripoli. Her mother, unable to look after her, had sold her to a man in the bazaar to work in his club. 'She doesn't know what I really do,' she said, her eyes downcast. 'I can never tell her. She thinks I'm a waitress.'

I pulled the paper from my pocket: the rental agreement for the rooms my Libyan orderly had found near the southern gate to the bazaar. 'You can move there tomorrow.'

She took the paper from me and squealed with joy. 'You will not regret this. But I still have to find a job. To send money to my mother.'

'I will give you the money. I'm not sure when I shall see you again, but I'll be in touch.'

I had my parents' allowance to dip into. All that mattered to me was to keep her safe. And now I had started this madness, I would make damn sure to avoid action as much as possible. There would be plenty of tomorrows, I'd make certain of that. Before I left, I took photographs. At first, she struck poses, almost pornographic, asking me if that was what I wanted.

I shook my head. 'I'm not buying you. Nobody will buy you any longer. I want photographs of you, as you are.'

Her smile as she thanked me brought tears to my eyes and I wondered if perhaps the last time she had smiled that way had been when she was a child. Innocent, untouched. In that moment, I vowed to make sure she smiled this way again.

. . .

On the following morning, I was stretcher-borne to a Caproni transport plane, the letter from my father's friend safely stowed in the top pocket of my jacket. I said a prayer for safe delivery and I feigned sleep during the flight across the sea. It was far easier than explaining why I was being transported away from conflict. We landed at Catania Airport soon after dawn. A light mist hovered over the tarmac like a stage effect and I thought ruefully how I was indeed an actor playing a part. An ambulance was waiting. I was handed a pair of crutches to help me climb into the back. I didn't really need this support but I had to behave as if I were badly injured. The surgeon had written this in his letter and recommended I return to my family home for rest.

Back in Italy, I had plans to set in motion.

CHAPTER 10

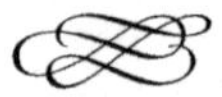

EARLY SUMMER 1941

DEVORA

As the weeks passed, Devora found crowded Villa Oliveto hard to cope with. The building was capacious: a fancy country house built in the last century for a wealthy landowner. Frescoes of bucolic country scenes: plump shepherdesses tending to animals, bunches of grapes, figs, meadow flowers and cherubs gazed down from the ceilings at the motley groups of families below. There were many professional Jews confined in this place: architects, teachers, a doctor, lawyers, faded people like the once smart furnishings of the house, wearing any mismatch of clothes they had managed to bring with them. They looked like the cast from a play that had never been performed, Devora thought, with hastily grabbed costumes from a wardrobe room. She'd seen a man wearing tweed plus fours, too heavy for the early summer days, a woman with a fancy straw hat adorned with faded silk roses, foundation and lipstick thickly applied to her tired face.

'I'm afraid Frau Kippenhausen grows loopier by the day,' Vati had whispered, after the woman had insisted on being introduced to his beautiful daughter and then departed for her 'perambulation around the gardens'.

'She's a sad lady,' he explained. 'All alone. We have become her only family but she does annoy some residents. She thinks she can sing but her voice is like a screech owl's.'

In the main reception rooms, rustic wooden tables and cane chairs had replaced velvet divans and fancy antiques, making the space a communal refectory. Four chairs were arranged in a semi-circle near a marble fireplace, above which hung a large, silvered mirror, a crack in one corner, and Vati told her that tonight a concert was to be held by the Oliveto string quartet. The following week a professor of literature was giving a talk about Thomas Mann. 'And Doktor Kempe is giving a lecture soon about medical practices in the Middle Ages,' Vati said, trying to inject enthusiasm into his voice. 'You might be interested, Devora.'

Seeing her grim look, he told her, 'We have to make the best of it here, *liebling*. Otherwise, we would sit around moaning all the time.'

The villa had the strong whiff of institution. Notices were pinned in spots where paintings had been removed for safe-keeping; lists of cooking rotas were pinned to kitchen cupboard doors. Devora had to share a small room with her twin brothers.

There were always people milling around who wanted to chat and share stories of their past lives, women exchanging handy tips on how to make a meal stretch further with sparse ingredients, children shouting in the garden under the blossoming persimmon trees where a couple of swings had been hung. She was corralled into helping with the vegetable plot that some enterprising internee had dug on the gentle slope behind the villa, where early summer sun warmed the soil. 'Make friends, Devora,' her father had said, trying to encourage her. 'We all have to muck in together while we're here.'

He was right, of course he was. But oh, how she missed time

to herself. She should be grateful to be with her family again, she knew that. It should be like old times. But the months apart had been a revelation. She'd had time to grow into herself, think her own thoughts and find her own way. Her parents had changed too in the few months they'd been here. Their Jewishness had come to the fore. It was as if the rituals of their religion had given them a stronger identity and a strength to face the world of war. 'We're in this together,' her father said, frequently peppering his conversations with the importance of solidarity in the face of adversity.

Devora wanted to rebel but she also wanted to please her parents and not make life harder for them than it already was. So she went through the motions, reciting prayers together from the Torah. Rather than giving her a sense of belonging, the recitations made her feel lonely.

She missed her once-ordinary life back in Urbino. Although everything had changed under the anti-Jewish laws, she'd had comparative freedom.

People were basically all the same: two legs, two arms, a brain; they all performed the same bodily functions, whether aristocratic or peasant. Maybe it was her medical training or listening to Luigi's socialist ideals that made her think this way, but religion to her was a prop that most people hid behind. And as for Mussolini's unfair laws that had prevented her from continuing her studies at university, she was determined that her dream of becoming a doctor was not going to be crushed. Somehow, she would find a way and make a difference to the world.

After supper one evening she helped her mother in the kitchen. It was their turn on the rota. Mütti had annoyed her, berating her for saying her prayers without humility in the synagogue room.

'You were gazing around at everybody, instead of bowing your head.'

It was on the tip of Devora's tongue to retaliate and ask her mother how she could possibly notice what her daughter was up to, when she herself should have been concentrating on her own prayers. But she rubbed at the dishes in the sink and ignored the comment.

That seemed to rile her mother even more. 'You are turning into a heathen, Devora. A bad example to your brothers.'

Devora had eventually thrown down the cloth on the counter, unable to contain herself.

'So, Mütti, why is it so very important I say these prayers? What should I feel when I say them?'

'What do you mean, what should you feel? You *say* them. You just say them and you bow your head. That is the way it has always been. These prayers are part of the way we are. Part of us.'

'But have you never thought what would happen to you if you didn't? I mean – do you think you would actually drop dead – or the world would come to an end?'

Her mother tutted. 'You talk such silly things, *Mädchen* – what do you mean, *I would drop dead?* Who's been putting these ideas in your head? I knew we shouldn't have left you alone for months on end. Your head's been turned in the wrong direction. Stop your nonsense – scrub down that worktop. I've got enough worries without you suggesting I drop dead.'

'But, Mütti...'

'Don't you "but Mütti" me, girl. Button your mouth. I'll have to talk to Vati about this. And you definitely need to come to the synagogue again this evening for Shemà Israel. No more excuses of headaches and goodness knows what. We'll talk to Rabbi Caro. He'll set you right. You have forgotten who you are.'

Picking up the cloth again, Devora hurled it into the soapy water in the sink, which splashed on her mother's shoes, and then she rushed from the communal kitchen where a couple of other women were offering sympathetic glances and shrugs to her mother. Devora knew she was acting like a spoilt child.

The only place she could escape was to the middle of the olive grove that lay to the side of the villa's garden. She climbed the wall to get there, scraping her knees in her haste to get away. It was past curfew but she didn't care. What could it possibly matter if one of the guards found her out of bounds? What heinous crime could occur if she sat in the grove for an hour to calm down? The young guard on night duty was probably otherwise engaged, anyway. She'd seen him chatting to one of the young girls in the camp more than once.

Her favourite place was by the oldest, largest tree, its girth wide enough to protect her from being seen from the house as she nestled behind it. This spot was also out of view from the villa's front garden where most of the internees tended to gather now the sun was inviting them to emerge like lizards after a long winter hibernation. Devora had taken to coming here to gather her thoughts. The hollow at the base of the tree seemed to hold her like an embrace that evening.

She hated being interned and, after only these few weeks, didn't know how much longer she could take it. Voices from the villa drifted to her through the curtains of olive branches. The members of the string quartet started to tune up, a woman working through her scales, her voice out of tune. *Dio!* She rose to creep deeper into the grove to distance herself from the massacre of Schubert's 'Ave Maria'.

Perched on the stone wall at the far end of the grove, she gazed on lights from villages on the plain. Freedom beckoned, tantalising her. She imagined herself returning to Via delle Stallacce, living by herself in the little house in the ghetto. But how could she do that to her parents and cause more disappointment in their already miserable lives? She kicked at the wall in frustration. The quartet was killing Vivaldi now and she gritted her teeth. Perhaps if she tried to lose herself in the medical book Luigi had given her and imagine the day when she would be free to practise her vocation, she'd feel better. She jumped from the wall and started to walk back to the villa.

CHAPTER 11

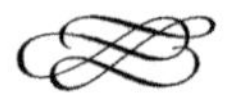

Two days later as she carried a hoe and bucket towards the *orto*, she bumped into the elderly doctor on his daily constitutional walk.

'*Guten morgen*, Doktor Kempe,' she said.

'Ah, young Devora. Your father tells me you are a second-year medical student,' he said, raising his hat to her with old-fashioned courtesy.

He seemed very old to Devora, his face above his white beard wizened like a prune, a stoop to his back making it hard for him to look her in the face.

'Indeed,' she said. 'I managed the first couple of years before the laws came into force, Doctor. I've tried to keep up. But it's been difficult. And frustrating. I don't suppose...' She paused. It was now or never. 'I don't suppose you could do with some help from a medical student, could you?'

He replied without hesitation and her face lit up at what he said.

'You can help me with my patients this very afternoon. I hold a clinic on the second floor. Of course, strictly speaking I am not supposed to practise anymore, in view of the racial laws, but *capitano* Bracciaforte – he encourages me to look after his inmates. In a sense it is easier for him if we are kept healthy and moderately happy. He turns a blind eye to many things.'

She dropped her gardening tools and enveloped him in a hug. 'Thank you, thank you. I cannot wait.'

He chuckled. 'I like to see young people occupied and I'm not getting any younger. You'd be surprised how many people I look after in Villa Oliveto and the village.'

'I hope I can help you out. I still have a lot to learn, Doctor.'

'Well, there's only one way to find out, isn't there? My granddaughter has a spare white overall and you must tie back your hair and wear a scarf. Maybe we can find somebody else to take over your gardening duties. I'll see you at ten minutes to three. We start at three o'clock sharp, Fräulein Devora.'

The sun seemed to shine that much brighter for Devora for the rest of the morning and she even found herself humming a tune: the song Enrico had danced her to a lifetime ago. 'Speak to me of love,' the singer had crooned. Her heart missed a beat as she remembered Enrico's kisses. She hoped he was safe. She'd not heard from him since that night, almost a year ago.

At a quarter to three, Devora knocked on Doctor Kempe's door. It was opened by a teenager whom Devora had noticed laughing and chatting at mealtimes. She smiled as she held out her hand. 'I'm Erma. I was so pleased when Grandfather told me you were coming to help. Now I can concentrate on the record-keeping instead of the sight of blood. I know he'll be relieved not to have me faint any moment.'

The room was equipped with a single bed behind a rudimentary screen that Erma told her Emanuele had rigged up.

'Who's Emanuele?'

Erma blushed. 'The son of *capitano* Bracciaforte. You must have seen him around – one of the guards? Really handsome. He's very kind. In fact, all the Bracciafortes are kind. And very practical. Don't you think their name is so funny? Strongarm? It's quite fitting really. Emanuele is *very* strong.'

Erma was a bubbly girl and extremely attractive, her eyes coal-black, matching lustrous hair escaping from her scarf. Devora could quite see why the young guard would be eager to want to please her with odd jobs.

'Here's my white overall – it should fit you perfectly. Grandfather tells me you're a medical student. How clever. I don't have the brain to study for all those years. And nobody wants a doctor who drops to the floor every time they see a wound, do they? No, I shall be a famous actress one day. I had a part lined up in Rome, where we live, but of course it came to nothing. Mark my words, when this is all over, I shall be well known and sign autographs for my fans and you can come and see me on stage and have cocktails after the performance in my dressing room.'

Her enthusiasm was infectious but Devora didn't have the heart to tell her that the war might last longer than she imagined. If Erma's dream was keeping her happy, then so be it.

'So,' Erma continued, 'you simply have to kind of hover in the background and act as a chaperone – for the female patients. But as you know far more than I do, Grandfather might ask you to help in other ways – medically, I mean. I'll be sitting outside the door, taking people's names and giving them a chit with their number on. Good luck, dear Devora. Maybe we can spend time together after clinic. There aren't many girls of our age in here. You can tell me all about yourself.'

There was a steady trickle of patients during the afternoon. The first was a mother with a crying baby who writhed and screamed in discomfort when the doctor placed hands on his little tummy.

'What do you think, Devora?' he asked, ushering her forwards to examine the child.

His stomach felt very hard and she suggested tentatively, 'Constipation?'

Doctor Kempe beamed at her. 'My thoughts exactly. And what do we suggest?'

'My mother used a tiny piece of warm soap,' she explained to the worried woman. 'Roll it up to make a suppository and then insert it in his little bottom. That should do the trick. Are you still feeding him?'

The woman shook her head. 'My milk has dried up.'

'Make sure he drinks plenty of boiled water,' Devora continued.

'And I shall see about acquiring powdered milk,' Doctor Kempe said. 'Or maybe we can ask Frau Goldenstein to wet nurse your baby. She has plenty of milk. Come back tomorrow and we'll see how it goes.'

The woman had no money to pay for the visit and offered a cotton sheet instead. 'This is patched and old but you could use it for dressings,' she said.

'Keep it, dear woman. And thanks for the offer. For now, we can manage.'

While they waited for the next patient, the doctor congratulated Devora. 'If we can get away with natural remedies, so much the better. It's the very sick patients who need expensive medication and hospitalisation that are the problem. I thought you were very calm and you had the baby gurgling by the time we had finished. Well done!'

'I have twin brothers of eleven. I was ten when they were born, so I'm used to helping with young children.'

As they were tidying up the makeshift clinic, there was a loud rap on the door and a short, stout man came in, supporting a woman, almost bent double.

'*Dottore*, I am desperate,' he said. 'My wife. She's in terrible pain.'

'*Capitano* Bracciaforte, come in, come in,' Doctor Kempe said, ushering the woman to the bed that Devora had laid with a fresh sheet.

'She's had discomfort for a few days now, but, you know, we put it down to women's problems. But today she is so much worse. She can hardly walk.'

The woman was grey in the face, and had brought her knees up, obviously in pain. She bit her hand to stifle her cries and it was apparent she was extremely unwell.

Doctor Kempe made a swift examination, asking only one question. 'Signora Bracciaforte, do you feel any pain in your shoulder?'

The signora, now wringing her hands in distress, nodded yes.

'Signor *capitano*, your wife needs to be taken immediately to hospital. I don't think this is a miscarriage. I shall write you a note to give to the doctor but she needs an operation. I fear this might well be an extra-uterine pregnancy.'

When the *capitano* looked baffled, Devora explained, 'It's when the baby doesn't grow within the womb, most likely within the fallopian tube. She will need to have it removed, otherwise it can be dangerous to her. But try not to worry. The gynaecologists at Arezzo Hospital will be very experienced.'

Devora stayed with the woman while the *capitano* and Doctor Kempe rushed away to arrange transport. She tried to distract signora Bracciaforte from her pain with chit-chat, asking if she had other children.

'Yes, signorina. One son. Emanuele. But he's nineteen. I thought I was too old to bear children. This is such a shock.' She hunched her legs up again and gripped Devora's hand tightly. '*Ahi*, the pain is worse than childbirth.'

. . .

Later on, the doctor and Devora discussed the afternoon clinic.

'Usually, I deal with minor problems. Today was an exception. But, once again, you were a great help to me. I hope the signora will be all right. As you know, if undetected, an ectopic pregnancy can cause death. Remember that question I asked her, Devora? About the pain in her shoulders? It's often ignored – even by the patient. It's a sign of internal bleeding: blood leaking from the fallopian tube.'

Devora scribbled down notes while he talked, eager to absorb as much information as possible. 'I hold my clinics three times a week. I can't offer you a whole range of ailments to study but that is one of the marvellous aspects of the medical profession: we never know who will consult us next or what we will come across. The human body – and mind – is intricate and wonderful. I never cease to be amazed.'

He folded away his stethoscope into his leather doctor's bag. 'I shall see if the *capitano* can acquire more equipment for us. The Red Cross may be able to help too with providing you with your own stethoscope. Or DELASEM – the *capitano* has a hotline to the bishop who deals with financial assistance in these matters. Now, I can't pay you, my dear, but if you are interested, I shall be very happy to have you work alongside me. At least you will be doing something useful while you are in this place. God only knows how long that will be for.'

'I'm very grateful, *dottore*. Thank you so much.'

The hours she'd spent with the kindly doctor had raised her spirits. There'd been a purpose to what she was doing and for the first time in months, Devora felt a sense of optimism.

Some of the cooks were better than others. Tonight was the turn of a Russian-Italian Jewish family, and their repertoire seemed to consist of a variety of ways to cook cabbage. Sour *shchi* was on the menu this evening and not many plates were empty.

'Monday is my slimming night,' Erma said.

'You don't need to slim,' Devora said, eyeing the girl's slender figure with envy, wishing her own curves were not quite so curvy. She was always hungry and she'd scraped the cabbage dish clean.

'So, do you have a boyfriend, Devora?'

There was no time to answer as Rabbi Caro stood to make an announcement, asking for anybody who had carpentry skills to help mend the podium in the synagogue, and then somebody else advertised a bridge evening with tuition for the following week.

Devora fiddled with her cutlery when, after the rabbi had finished, a woman stood up to remind him there was a sewing class the following afternoon for beginners. These people, she thought. Had they forgotten what was going on outside this place? Were they not angry at the injustice at being confined here? Yes, they had freedom to walk outside the grounds during daylight hours. It wasn't a prison as such but all the bridge and needlework classes in the world couldn't paste over the fact that liberty had been taken away from them. They were burying their heads in the sand and the old feelings of frustration poured back, swamping the optimism she'd felt earlier.

Her mother prodded her arm. 'Devora, you should go along to learn how to sew. You never wanted me to show you.'

'I'm helping the doctor. And you know I hate sewing.'

'But it's a useful skill.'

'Medicine is more useful, Mütti.' She shook off her mother's hand and left the table, Erma following close behind.

'Let's go for a walk on our own before curfew,' Erma said. 'It's so stuffy and boring in this place, isn't it?'

They wandered away from the huddle of people chatting and smoking near the entrance and walked towards the little hamlet of Oliveto. Old women sat in their doorways mending and they looked up as the two girls walked past. '*Buonasera*, signorina Erma,' one of them said and Erma went over to kiss her on each cheek.

'*Buonasera*, Nonna.'

The old woman went inside her house and fetched two slices of *pan di Spagna*, a dry sponge cake, yellow from eggs of free-range hens. 'Made fresh today,' she said. '*Mangiate*, eat, both of you. It won't make you fat.'

'*Grazie*, signora,' Devora said.

'Are you new? We haven't seen you around before,' the old lady asked of Devora.

'She's the new medical assistant,' Erma said.

'*Brava, brava*. Tell your nonno my sciatica is much better. He's a saint,' the old lady said.

'I will.' As they moved away, Erma explained the old woman was Emanuele's grandmother. 'I told you that family were all kind.' She wrapped her cake in a handkerchief from her pocket. 'Grandfather will enjoy this. He has a sweet tooth.'

'If I was kind, I would save this for my twin brothers, but they are such pests at the moment.' Devora took a bite from her cake. It was good.

'So, tell me about your boyfriend, Devora. You do have one, don't you?'

'I'm not sure.'

'What do you mean you're not sure? Either you do, or you don't. I *wish* I had a boyfriend. And I know who I wish for. Is it the same for you, perhaps?'

'I suppose so. There is a boy I like. And he's kissed me and—'

'Well, then he's your boyfriend,' Erma said, stopping and clasping Devora's arm.

'Just because he's kissed me doesn't mean he's my boyfriend. A kiss is only a kiss.'

'I dream about Emanuele kissing me. What's it like to be kissed?'

'Like nothing that ever happened to me before,' Devora replied, relieved to chat in a straightforward way. It was a long time since she'd had a heart-to-heart; Sabrina had cut herself off from her in the last weeks before coming away from Urbino and Anna Maria had made her poor opinion of Enrico very clear.

'Is it like in a novel or a film? Like in *Gone with the Wind*? I saw that at the Farnese Cinema in Rome in 1939. I went with a friend who made me up to look older. It was *soooo* romantic. That part where they're at the bottom of the staircase and he scoops her into his arms and carries her up the stairs... Was it like that?'

Devora laughed. 'No! I wasn't carried up the stairs. In fact, our maid decided to open the door and interrupt us. So embarrassing.'

'What was it like? Did your legs go all wobbly?'

'It was a good while ago, but... it was a good kiss. One to remember.'

Suddenly Devora wanted to leave it at that. Somehow, describing Enrico's kisses in detail felt like sharing them and she wanted to keep them to herself.

'That was the first and last time,' Devora said, hoping to bring an end to the discussion.

'Oh, I'm so sorry. Is he... did he... when did you lose him?'

'No, he's not dead, Erma. At least, I don't think so. I would surely have heard if he'd died. But he *is* fighting. And he was in Libya the last I knew. But... I only found that out because he sent a postcard to another girl.'

'Oh, so he's that kind, is he?'

'The girls all like him, put it that way.'

Erma held up her left hand and counted the fingers as she spoke. 'Emanuele is handsome, kind, taller than me, got good teeth, he's strong... but we're never on our own, so he's never kissed me. But I kind of feel he wants to. But it's pointless. I'm Jewish and he's Roman Catholic. I reckon we'll have to run away. Our families would never approve of us getting together. So I have to dream about it and leave it at that.'

She threaded her arm through Devora's. 'Time to go back. They'll lock the gates soon.'

CHAPTER 12

14 AUGUST 1942

A year dragged by. Time weighed heavily on Devora in Villa Oliveto. It was a relief to escape to the clinic and away from Erma and her constant babble and talk of Emanuele this, Emanuele that. Doctor Kempe was pleased with her progress but advised her he could not possibly instruct her in everything she needed to know to become a doctor. When the clinics were quiet, Doctor Kempe took it upon himself to set her a plan of study, loaning her his books to go deeper into topics.

She found she was good at sewing up wounds and wondered how on earth that could ever be. She had hated the embroidery lessons her mother felt she had to give her. Devora was also practising her bedside skills. She would make a compassionate, calm and supportive doctor one day, Doctor Kempe told her. 'You have a skill for listening. When patients come with their anguish, I have no pills, but I always know, despite your young age, you will have empathy for them. Maybe you should consider specialising in psychiatry.'

Devora was not so sure. It seemed to her obvious that the internees of Villa Oliveto would have problems of the mind. How could they not have with the terrible situation they'd all been forced into? Taken away from their homes, trapped here, with no knowledge of how long this would go on for or what would happen to them next.

She attended synagogue to placate her mother, sitting with the women and children, but although she mouthed prayers, her thoughts were elsewhere, dreaming of a day when she would be free. At night she took to keeping herself awake, so that when her brothers slept, she could sneak from the unbearable heat of their shared bedroom and sit in the cool of the garden. But even that small luxury was ruined when she became aware of shadows of others amongst the pines.

It was impossible to be alone in this place and more evacuees arrived all the time so that space grew increasingly limited. With war raging across the seas, the new arrivals were mostly Jews from Libya, or Yugoslavia and Poland. Vati occasionally bought newspapers from the little shop in the village and in the evening, there were heated discussions amongst the mixture of internees.

'Another defeat in Egypt against the *inglesi*.'

'Even though the Italian army is eight times the size of the enemy.'

'Mussolini's quest for his empire has been a thorough waste of life and money. He has no sense.'

Devora was torn as she listened to the heated talk. Despite Mussolini's awful policies, she was born Italian and although upset her country was not doing well, she hoped with all her heart it meant the end of war was approaching and that this strange existence of being cut off from the rest of the world would soon end.

Luigi had only been able to pay a couple of visits but in one of his letters, he mentioned he had caught a glimpse of Enrico on leave in Urbino, wearing his uniform, sitting outside the bar in the piazza, a crowd of friends gathered around him, but they hadn't had a chance to talk. Devora decided to write to him.

Despite over a year going by, or maybe because of this, her yearning for Enrico was as strong as it had ever been. The memories of the time she'd spent with him were as fresh as if they had happened yesterday. Some nights she even dreamt she was fencing with him in the park. Cruel reality hit when she awoke.

Villa Oliveto, near Arezzo, 14 August 1942

Enrico,

Devora had crumpled up three precious sheets of notepaper, unsure of how to start. If she put 'dearest' or 'darling' in front of his name, it seemed too forward. But the kisses they had shared had seemed so much more than kisses for Devora. They were a dream she wanted to become permanently true. And she had felt like an actress in a film when he'd nuzzled her neck and whispered her name, the stars twinkling behind the twin towers of the Ducal Palace, a perfect backdrop. But she hadn't heard from him since that evening, so she feared that for Enrico, his kissing her was likely just another kiss.

Dear Enrico,

There was nothing proprietorial about that, was there? Simply writing 'Enrico' without anything in front sounded as if she was angry. But part of her *was* angry. How come he had sent a postcard to Sabrina last year and not to her? Had he kissed Sabrina too? Or maybe he had sent one and the card had been lost in the post or, maybe because she was interned, the authorities didn't think she should receive a postcard from a serving soldier. She hated that word: interned. It sounded like 'interred'. And sometimes she did feel as if she was buried alive under mounds of earth, gasping for breath.

I would love it if you could visit me here. It's not as bad as I feared and we are allowed visitors. During the day we can walk outside the garden walls of the villa

She had written 'camp' instead of 'villa' originally and then scrubbed it out, but you could still read 'camp' through her scratch marks, so that version of the letter had been torn up too.

and there is a small restaurant in the hamlet where the food is good.

It was apparently far better than the food served up in the camp kitchens but money was tight and she had never actually tried the *osteria* food herself. It was Erma who had told her, because Emanuele had brought her a plate of scrumptious home-made ravioli filled with spinach and ricotta. Devora had had to listen to Erma's childish comments about sharing the same fork as him. But, then again, Erma was two years younger than Devora's twenty-two. *When I am twenty-one,* prefaced most of Erma's sentences.

I have been helping an elderly doctor with his patients and have learnt so much. I study from textbooks too and obviously there has been no chance to carry out dissections, but Doctor Kempe has a lifetime of experience – although some of his methods are rather old-fashioned. Everybody adores him. Even the villagers. And he saved the life of the camp commander's wife by diagnosing her ectopic pregnancy. Do you know, the camp commander refuses to wear his uniform, because he says that most of the people confined here are professionals and far more intelligent than he? He says he cannot understand why we should be imprisoned because of our religion as we do harm to nobody. If only people in government thought the same...

Please, please, please, Enrico, do not tell your superiors about him. I would hate this kind man to be in trouble. I mean, after all, he is right, isn't he? We do no harm to others. You yourself used to say that you didn't think of me as a Jewess. You said, because of my blonde hair, nobody could tell. We are all essentially the same, aren't we, despite our faiths? I truly hope you believe that.

Please write to me and say you'll visit. I'd love to know what you've been up to. Are you using your legal qualifications? Are you allowed to say where you've been? Luigi is coming to see us tomorrow for the Ferragosto feast.

She agonised over how to sign the letter. She wanted to put 'love from your Devora', or at least 'affectionately yours'. But she wasn't his Devora and 'affectionately' sounded like something an aged aunt wrote in a letter. So, after much thought, finally she ended with:

Best wishes from your dear friend, Devora

The letter was disjointed, the ink darker in some parts because she'd had to break off and hide it a few times as she wrote on her bed. Alfredo and Arturo kept asking her what she was doing and would she play noughts and crosses with them on her notebook, and she'd had to tell them she was studying; she needed to concentrate and they should go to sleep otherwise she would tell Mütti.

'Well, put out your torch, Devora. We can't sleep with it on,' Alfredo said.

Arturo added, with his usual lack of tact, 'You're no fun here, Devora. We preferred you when we were back in Urbino.'

So, she'd had to wait until she could hear both boys snoring before continuing the letter. Arturo was right: she'd preferred herself back in Urbino too, when she was free. But she pushed the images of fencing with Enrico and chatting to her friends to the back of her mind. It only made her more miserable to remember those times. When she read over what she had written to Enrico, the letter sounded rather desperate and she almost ripped it up there and then, but shoved it under her mattress instead.

In the morning, she slipped out early and posted the envelope into the letterbox outside the tobacconist's shop in the tiny hamlet.

Luigi turned up half an hour after breakfast, his car laden with gifts: a basket of eggs and lettuces, tomatoes, aubergines, peppers and two chickens he told her he'd bought in the countryside outside Urbino. 'Domenica baked you a cake and *biscotti*,' he said, handing her a traditional sponge cake, baked in a ring mould, and a brown paper bag of the boys' favourite cookies.

He produced a small box from the passenger seat. 'This little cat is for the boys.'

A striped marmalade-coloured kitten extended its paw through the netting serving as a lid. 'I rescued her from the river. She was tied up in a sack. She needs a good home.'

'You're so kind, Gigi. *Grazie.* They will love her. But do your parents mind you not spending the day with them?' She pulled the kitten from the box and the bundle of fur immediately snuggled under her chin, purring like a motor.

He shrugged. 'They're used to me coming and going. And they decided to visit my grandmother instead. How is life treating you? You look well. Better than when I came last.'

A slight rise of her eyebrows, followed by a sigh. 'I shall go crazy if I stay here much longer. If it weren't for the wonderful Doctor Kempe, I would have grown wings and flown away before now. Gigi, can't I hide in your boot and you whisk me away from here? I've been here for far too long.'

He laughed at her suggestion. 'How about I whisk you away in Papà's car for the day? And yes, you've been here a long time: sixteen months and three days to be precise.'

She pulled a face and then grinned. 'Ha ha, you've been counting the days of my life sentence, Gigi. I'd *love* you to help me escape – even if it's only for one day, but unfortunately there are boring, boring rules. "Internees must absolutely not leave the city,"' she quoted. '"Must go to the local command post of the Royal *Carabinieri* on a daily basis; must not return home later than eight in the evening and not leave earlier than seven in the morning; must—"'

He interrupted. 'I know all these rules too. Don't forget I work in the *comune* with facts and figures. There are more: "Internees should not patronise brothels, or keep weapons or act in a suspicious fashion..." Listen! Today as it's a *festa*, I'm sure the *carabinieri* will not have full attention on their job. And we can stretch the rules. Where are we? In Oliveto. *Within* the province of Arezzo... so, if I take you there, you're not leaving the area, are you? And I can get you back before eight o'clock. Where's the problem?'

She beamed at him. 'You have a typical accountant's mind. You know how to massage the truth. Or dilute the broth, as Anna Maria always says.'

'It's useful. Especially nowadays.'

'Let me check it's all right with my parents and go and find the boys. They're probably playing football round the back.'

'Let *me* talk to your parents, Biondina.'

'And use your charm on them?'

'I didn't know I possessed any.'

It was easy to banter with each other. She was already feeling happier in Luigi's company.

Doctor Kempe was chatting to her parents, the three of

them resting in the shade of the lime trees, their blossom fragrant in the sultry August air. There was no clinic today as it was Shabbat and when Devora asked permission to go for a drive with Luigi – not mentioning how far they were going – Mütti's eyebrows almost disappeared into her hairline.

'And what about prayers this evening, young lady?'

Doctor Kempe intervened. 'I know Devora is not my daughter, Frau Lassa, but I know her ways. I'm sure one Saturday won't matter. She's a good girl and has been working so well for me.'

'And you should be resting and not driving on Shabbat,' her mother added, ignoring the doctor.

'*I* am driving, signora,' Luigi intervened. 'It's not forbidden for me.'

'Miriam, leave Devora be for once,' Devora's father added.

'These are for you, signori.' Luigi chose this opportune moment to place his gifts before Devora's parents and, after promising to take care of Devora and ensure to have her back by six o'clock at the latest, they made their way to the car.

Devora tried to ignore the mutterings of her mother as Luigi opened the passenger door. She slumped back against the seat. 'See what it's like? Take me away from this place before I scream it down.'

An hour and a half later, they sat outside a bar in the Piazza Grande. Save for sandbags piled against the back of the parish church of Santa Maria, there were few signs of war. Devora felt plain in her old dress and wished she had at least a colourful scarf to drape around her neck but she also felt marvellous as she lifted her face to the sun, listening to voices of ordinary people at tables around her. A young child scattered pigeons in the centre of the piazza and she smiled as he chased after them, waving his pudgy arms.

'What are you smiling at?' Luigi asked, beckoning to a waiter.

'I was thinking how wonderful it would be to fly away over the rooftops like a pigeon.'

'And then be shot for somebody's dinner. Try to switch off your gloomy thoughts for the day, Devora. Let's look around the art gallery and explore the alleyways. It'll be cooler than staying under this sun. What will you drink?'

'You choose for me, Gigi. Surprise me.'

He ordered two cold beers, pearls of moisture running down the necks of the brown bottles.

She sipped with delight. 'Heavenly! Now, tell me what you've been up to.'

'In many ways, life is equally as frustrating for me,' he told her. He lowered his voice. 'But I'll tell you about it whilst we're walking.' He swivelled his eyes to warn her of the two black-shirted *squadristi* who had seated themselves at a nearby table.

Their beers finished, they walked up to the cathedral and sat on a bench in the park behind the huge basilica whilst waiting for the museum to open after siesta. Save for a man snoozing on a bench beneath umbrella pines, they were alone.

'Why the secrecy?' she asked.

'I'm not the only one who finds our leader idiotic. He's bringing Italy to her knees. And there are more and more of us who feel the same way as time goes by and he loses grip here and abroad.'

'And so? What can be done? There are plenty who still adore him.'

'Most Italians believe in treating others as they would be treated,' Luigi said. 'But there's also an apathy and there are bad Italians too, of course. And the stories we're beginning to hear about what is going on elsewhere in Europe, few want to believe. I fear things will worsen here too. We need to be prepared.'

'I know I moan a lot about Villa Oliveto, but fortunately our camp commander is wonderful, as are the villagers who leave gifts on the doorstep of the villa. Doctor Kempe is a magician for them – and he doesn't charge anything. They pay in kind. Eggs or vegetables from their *orti*. Or an odd job, when needed. In the countryside, we don't see the Blackshirts.'

Luigi looked at her, assessing. 'Then you've been fortunate. It would be wonderful to think it stays that way. But I fear not.'

She struggled to explain. 'We knew about *Kristallnacht* back in 1938. Papà talked about that a lot. How the Hitler Youth helped kill and maim hundreds of Jews. But still I cannot imagine anything like that happening here in Italy. Although we do have new internees from Libya who have told us about bad treatment by the Italian police in their country. Apparently the *maresciallo* in charge of their camp urinated on the food they prepared for the Sabbath. But our *capitano* encourages families to stay together. He even buys gelato and toys for the children. Life is technically relatively good at Villa Oliveto. But really, we're all trapped. I feel I'm... in a stage of nothingness.'

'What do you mean?'

'The way we've been treated, people being taken away from their normal lives, having to be confined there – it's like being caught in the middle of a malevolent spider's web. We Jews are gripped in its vice – Mussolini is doing an arm wrestle against people, most of whom are far weaker physically than he: old people, young, the sick... But I also feel as if I'm trapped in a vice within my own conscience, Gigi.'

As she spoke, her shoulders hunched up, her voice bitter as she explained her dilemma.

'My parents are happy because I'm with them, but I don't, by rights, have to be interned with them as I was born in Italy. I need to be doing something instead of being confined in Villa Oliveto. I was training to be a doctor to tend to my *fellow* Italians. I miss being me and I need to *do* more.'

He looked round to check nobody was listening. 'Biondina, as you well know, I hate the *fascisti* and I've joined a like-minded group in Urbino. We're gathering in strength and numbers as each month passes. Quietly doing our best to undermine the government. We've started to print clandestine newspapers and post them through the doors of every household. And we have Angelo Coen on our side. Unofficially of course—'

'*The* Angelo Coen? Administrator of the university?'

'*Sì*. And what's more, he openly refuses to join the fascist party. He's such a big landowner that they leave him alone. Plus, we've helped with shelter for Jewish evacuees from Lubiana and Pola.'

'It's so confusing. One rule for some, another for others. Where are they sheltering?'

'Many with the Augustinian sisters of Santa Caterina.'

Her face lit up at what he was telling her. 'I'm telling you all this to give you hope,' he said. 'To urge you to hang on. There are plenty of good people on your side and... you never know – you could be useful to us sooner than you think.'

'When you say there are people on our side – what about Enrico? And Sabrina?'

He faltered for a moment when she mentioned Enrico's name.

'I'm not sure about Sabrina. I'm sorry to tell you that. I know you were good friends, once.'

'She's easily led,' Devora said, sadness in her voice. 'And her father's not an easy man.'

'Strong in the fascist party.'

'It became quite obvious she doesn't want to be my friend any longer.'

'We're not all like her.'

She grasped hold of his hand. 'Yes, I know. You're so kind, Gigi.'

She let go of him and stood up.

'Let's walk to the art gallery now,' she said. 'It should be open.'

As they made their way down the hill to the gallery, Devora was comforted by Luigi's words. He'd instilled hope in her again. Hope that Luigi and his resistance fighters would help end the war soon and her family be free again.

CHAPTER 13

OCTOBER 1942

'There's somebody here to see you,' Erma said, rushing into her grandfather's room, where Devora was rolling up bandages from strips of old sheets. 'And, wow, Devora, he's like a film star. He turned up in a red police car and the children are all offering to polish it for him. Where did you meet him?'

'Who is it?'

'He says you'll know who he is. That he has medical notes and books for you.'

Devora dropped the basket of bandages and gave a little shriek. 'It's Enrico. At last! Tell your grandfather I won't be long...'

Before Erma could answer, Devora was out of the room. And then, just as she was about to run from the main door, she stopped. *What do I look like? A sight,* she thought, turning to dash upstairs again to see what she could do to pretty herself up. One of the women in the hamlet had given her a blouse with short, puffy sleeves, embroidered by hand across the yoke and Mütti had adapted it for her, sewing darts to make it fit Devora's new slender figure. She pulled off her white overall and plain shirt and swapped it for the blouse, pulling the sleeves further down, so that her shoulders were exposed. Then, bending to peer at herself in a corner of her cracked mirror, she pinched her cheeks to bring colour and dragged her fingers through her hair. It was lank, in need of a wash, but there was no time for any more sprucing. She ran from her room, the door slamming behind her as she tore down the stairs, pausing only at the bottom to tell herself to calm down, not to appear too eager.

Her heart skipped a beat when she saw Enrico dressed in a police uniform, the buttons on his black jacket shining, and a stiff cap with grey-green bands on his head. On his feet were shining boots and he carried gloves in his right hand. Arturo and Alfredo were seated proudly in the front of the car, Alfredo pretending to drive, whilst another two boys were crouched down, examining the bulletproof protection hanging from the front wheels. Her heart started to pound again as she stepped towards him and he turned to smile and held out his arms.

'Devora,' he said, hugging her. His buttons pressed into the top of her arms, cold and sharp against her bare skin, but she didn't mind. He had come to see her. Her letter had eventually worked and she inhaled the scent of him, thinking she never wanted this moment to stop. Unaccountably, she started to sob and he loosened his grip and put his hand under her chin.

'Hey! You're supposed to be happy, not sad, at seeing me again.'

'Oh, I am, I am. But it's been so long and I never believed you would come and...' She dissolved into sobs again. 'And it's so hard, Enrico. Urbino seems like a city on another planet and...'

'So, don't they treat you well in this place? Do you want me to have a word with anybody about anything?'

'No, no... it's not that. *Capitano* Bracciaforte is a good man. The place is as good as it could be. I mean, if you have to be confined, it's not too bad.'

'Are you going to give me a guided tour?'

'If you want. But... can't you take me out for the day instead? You're allowed to, as long as I'm back by six o'clock, before curfew. You've no idea how cooped up I feel.'

'Right. Well, show me around first quickly. I'm compiling a report about camp conditions in this province, and when I'm done with that, I'll take you for a spin in the Fiat. How about that?'

'Perfect! Wait here and I'll be five minutes while I tell Doctor Kempe and my parents.'

Devora proudly introduced him to a group of old men playing a card game of *briscola* at the back of the villa, in a protected corner where the October sun gave a little warmth. At first they were very wary of this policeman, but he was charming, courteous and they lowered their guard, asking if he would like to join in and play a hand. He politely declined.

She took him to see Doctor Kempe, whose initial reaction at the sight of a uniform was palpably nervous. He looked up from his desk where he was catching up with paperwork in his little clinic and his concerned look disappeared as soon as Enrico asked if he needed more equipment, explaining that part of his work involved checking on medical services for internees.

'Devora needs her own stethoscope for a start. And if you're in a position to get Atabrine for me, that would help enormously. We have an influx of Northern African refugees and a couple of them have malaria.'

'We need Il Duce to eradicate the mosquitoes in our districts too,' Enrico said, 'as he has done in the Pontine Marshes.'

'We need Il Duce to change his mind about us being confined,' Devora piped up. 'And to give us our jobs back. And the right to go to school again, rather than him concentrating on insects and war and playing the violin to his lover.'

'Devora...' The elderly doctor's tone was one of warning.

'You're safe to talk like that to me, Biondina,' Enrico said, lowering his voice, 'because we know each other. But be careful. Conditions here are a thousand light years away from some of the places I've inspected, I can assure you. You wouldn't believe what's going on in Libya and elsewhere.'

The way he had called her Biondina made her wonder how it had come to this: he in his smart military corps *carabiniere* uniform, and she, the prisoner confined to Villa Oliveto, all because she was considered inferior, of an undesirable race. For the first time, she wondered what exactly it was about Enrico that so enraptured her. What did they have in common, after all? His life was so very different from hers.

His voice was even softer as he continued, turning to push the door to. 'There are many who think his time is nearly over. There is a change coming.'

Raising his voice, he turned to the doctor. 'Make me a list of requirements and I shall see what I can do, *dottore*.'

'In the summer, I was able to send two of our elderly friends' – the doctor never used the words 'prisoner' or 'inmate'; he'd told Devora that doing so did nothing to lift the spirits – 'to Bagno Vignoni to take the waters for their bronchitis. If we could have permits to do the same again before the weather turns, it would be of great help.'

Enrico raised his eyebrows but wrote this request down.

'And what about sleeping arrangements here, *dottore*?'

'Space is increasingly limited. If you could talk to your authorities about acquiring another building in the hamlet for the overspill, that would help. Our *capitano* Bracciaforte has tried but if you were to consult someone in higher authority, maybe that would work. There are a couple of places locked up in the village, serving no purpose at the moment.'

Enrico added this to his list.

'I can show you where we sleep,' Devora said. 'As well as the kitchen, where we eat and meet.'

'Show him the football pitch the men have laid out,' Doctor

Kempe said. 'Physical exercise is good for the body as well as the mind. It helps ease our youngsters' frustrations.'

'This place is more like a holiday camp, *dottore*. You have all done well.'

'It is far from a holiday camp, *tenente*. As for conditions, that is mainly down to our excellent camp commander. He has also allowed us a room set aside as the synagogue and tonight our string quartet is performing another concert. Would you like to stay?'

Devora groaned. 'Even the cats run away from the villa when those violins begin to screech.'

'Devora, Devora, don't let them hear you say that. They do their best,' the doctor chided.

She gave Enrico a whistle-stop tour. He was interested in seeing where Devora slept, and looked out of the window at the view over the plain, asking her if they had ever been raided.

'By whom?' she asked. 'Who would want to raid a bunch of elderly men, women and children?'

'The authorities. To see if there were dissidents or deserters hiding in this place.'

'There is nothing like that going on here, Enrico. And, even if there was, do you think I would tell you about it?'

He gave her a strange look as if to test the truth of what she was saying. 'Ever the feisty one, Devora. I've missed you.' He tousled her hair. 'Come on, then. *Andiamo*, I'll take you for a spin.'

Devora longed for him to do more than rough up her hair as if she were a wayward child. Maybe when they were away from the camp, he would kiss her like he had two years ago. As the car purred along the country roads, she stole looks at his handsome profile. The roof of the car was down, her hair blew over her face and she felt cold in her off-the-shoulder blouse. But he was as smooth and debonair as ever in his smart uniform and polished boots. There was something different about him though. He was not the boy she remembered fencing with; he had become a man. That was what it was.

He took the road signposted to Civitella in Val di Chiana and pulled up by a fountain a few minutes later in a small cobbled piazza. A couple of women were washing clothes in the water and they stopped to stare as Enrico opened the door for Devora. She caught her foot on the running board as she climbed out and would have fallen if he hadn't grabbed her.

He pushed back the hair from her face and laughed. 'You always were an untidy ragamuffin, Biondina. When are you going to grow up?'

She narrowed her eyes, annoyed with his patronising air. 'I believe I've done more growing up in these last years than you will ever know about, Conte Enrico di Villanova. If you had been confined and deprived of your freedom as I have, you would understand how much I've had to change.'

She stormed off, not knowing where she was going. Down one side of the street was a portico with doors to a couple of shops and an *osteria*. She turned to shout back at him before entering. 'You can buy me a drink for talking to me like that.'

The gloomy room smelled of stale wine and tobacco. A group of men in the corner turned to stare. The place fell silent and she glared back belligerently as she sat down and waited for Enrico to join her.

'What shall I order for you?' The look on Enrico's face was a mixture of amusement and exasperation. Leaning over the table, he asked, 'Are you really sure you want to stay in here? If it's a drink you want, I'll buy a bottle of wine and we can take it up to the Rocca. Women are not welcome in these places.'

'It seems I'm not welcome anywhere at the moment.' She got up and flounced into the fresh air and she heard laughter from the men as they resumed their card game, slapping down their cards as they commented about the strange ways of *le femmine* and how the world had changed for the worse.

The women had gone from the fountain and she dipped her hands in the water and smoothed down her tangled hair, hating the reflection staring back at her. *You are an idiot, Devora Lassa. You haven't seen the man of your dreams for months and months and you're behaving like a spoilt child and ruining your chances.*

Enrico emerged from the *osteria* with a dusty bottle and two tumblers.

'Come on, *andiamo*, cross-patch. You can let it all out on me and vent your anger. Use me as a sparring partner, without your sword.'

'I'm sick of talking about me,' she said. 'I want to know about you. Where the hell have you been?'

They found a sheltered alcove along the ancient walls of the Rocca. 'Sixth century and still standing,' Enrico said, pulling the cork from the bottle with his teeth. 'Look at that outlook.'

Devora gazed at the view over the valleys, beyond the terraces of olive groves and dirt roads snaking in ribbons towards mountains in the far distance. 'It's like being on top of the world.'

'A brilliant defensive location,' Enrico replied. 'They knew what they were doing when they built these forts.'

'You even sound like a soldier.'

'Not surprisingly.' He poured out the wine and handed a tumbler to her and they toasted each other. 'Although, fortunately, I am not likely to be sent to the front line now. I was injured. The army now require my administrative skills.'

'You always did have an analytical brain when you applied it,' Devora said, thinking back to the annoying way Enrico always came top in science and maths at school without having to put in much revision.

'To my little *amica*, Biondina!'

'To my elusive *amico*, Rico. How were you injured?'

'I was in Libya. It wasn't good,' he said, knocking back a good slug of wine. 'We weren't prepared, despite having plenty of manpower. But the majority of us didn't know what we were doing and fighting in the desert was not fun. I caught an *inglese* bullet in my calf. So I was sent back. Now, I'm a penpusher with the *carabinieri*. Quite different from combat. And I'm based near Urbino too, so my parents have the pleasure of my company from time to time.'

'Luigi comes to see me quite often and he told me you were back. I'm cross you didn't bother to come and see me.'

'I'm here now. Don't moan.'

She held out her tumbler for more wine. It was strong and bitter but she was enjoying the heady feeling that came with the liquid. Or was it Enrico who was the cause? At any rate, the wine was loosening her tongue nicely.

'I long to go back to Urbino to the life I had before. I took it so much for granted.'

'I'm not sure that would be wise. The ghetto is empty now. And there are plenty of efficient *funzionari* milling about, ticking boxes, making sure regulations are adhered to. I'm sure Luigi is finding their interfering very irritating. You would be found and most likely sent elsewhere. You're lucky to be in Villa Oliveto.'

'What do you mean lucky? You try living there. I don't reckon you'd survive one day.'

'There is another camp in Le Marche, nearer Urbino: Servigliano. I can assure you the internees there are not treated half as well as you and your family. And...' He paused. 'That is nothing in comparison with news filtering out about camps in other parts of Europe.'

'So, is it part of your job? To inspect these places?'

'Partly,' Enrico said. 'Because of my legal studies, I am called on to intervene in welfare situations.'

'If women were in charge, had more say, all this rubbish would not be happening. There'd be less trouble. Maybe even no war.'

He laughed.

'Don't laugh. Who is it who starts wars? Men! I believe men are addicted to war. Who is it that makes all these rules? Rules that lock up innocent Jewish men and women, denying the right to work, own property, run a business or study? *Men.*'

'It has always been this way. Ever since the beginning.'

'Oh yes, and that's another thing: in the beginning was the word, and the word was with God, and the word was God... blah, blah, blah! All that stuff. Religion. Invented by a *male* God – the Father – and promulgated by *male* priests and rabbis. Why should it be so? It's unfair.'

'You have grown into quite the philosopher,' he said.

'Don't be patronising, Rico. I've had lots of time to think, that's why.'

He rose to break two sticks from a pile of wood stacked against the walls and handed her one after marking a line in the dirt. 'I think I prefer the old Devora – the one who tried to score points off me when we practised at the Fortezza. This place is quite similar, isn't it? *En garde*,' he said, taking up the ready position, his knees and left elbow bent as he brandished his stick.

It came back to her despite the long gap. She hadn't forgotten the moves, despite Il Duce's racial laws excluding Jews from sport. In fact, she was fitter, the diet at the camp being largely free of sweet stuff. And she was angry. Angry with Enrico and angry with life. Before Enrico knew it, she had scored hit after hit as she moved back and forth, striking at his chest and shoulders and eventually he dropped his stick.

'I surrender. I can see you will do me another injury if we don't stop.'

They both flopped to the ground, panting from exertion.

'Did your fencing help you in battle?' she asked.

'I wasn't involved in hand-to-hand fighting. No swords, Devora. That's only good for pirate films and displays. I'll never forget holding the fencing banner up in front of Il Duce at the Foro Italico...' He paused. 'You and I had fun with the *Circolo Atletico*, didn't we? But... this war...' He tailed off, picking at tufts of grass.

'Do you mind talking about it? I mean – I try to get my patients to talk, to help soothe their minds...'

A single shot cracked the air and three ravens flapped from the castle tower, cawing low-pitched alarm calls. Enrico shot up and, pulling Devora by the hand, raced with her to crouch in the lee of the castle wall. There were no further shots, only shouts from two men in the valley below, one man calling, 'Did you get it?'

'Yes, that thieving fox will get no more eggs from my hens.'

Enrico laughed but Devora had seen the fear in his eyes.

'For one moment I was back in Libya,' he said. 'Time to go, I think. I'll take you back to Oliveto.'

That evening, waiting in vain for sleep to come, Devora tossed and turned on her narrow bed, remembering how she used to survive on the memory of Enrico's kisses. How she had touched herself in bed, her heart racing as she had imagined what it might be like to make love to him, to have his heavy weight on top of her, their hands exploring each other... and how afterwards she used to have to lie on her front, the delicious pain at the pit of her stomach keeping her awake.

But today had been different. Enrico was distant. Their lives had moved on to different places and he had changed. For two years, she'd been marooned here in Villa Oliveto. The years had doubtless made her dull; she'd lost her spark. No wonder Enrico was no longer interested in her. She muffled her sobs, hot tears soaking into her pillow. She simply had to get away from this place. Her parents and brothers were fine in here. But her soul would wither and die if she remained a day longer.

CHAPTER 14

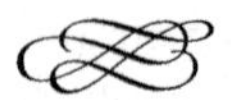

LATE OCTOBER 1942

There were times when Devora felt she was a bird with clipped wings. A bird allowed out of her cage to hop to the hamlet from time to time but who couldn't fly any further than over the fields nearby. The villagers all knew her now and she was often asked for advice as she passed by their houses and this made her feel useful. But by now, if the hateful racial laws had not been enforced, she would be nearing the end of her medical studies, nearer to realising her dream of putting *dottoressa* in front of her name. The future loomed ever bleaker – even her romantic dream of a life shared with Enrico was dwindling to a fading mirage.

'Signorina, could you take a look at my elderly father? He fell yesterday. I think he's broken his arm.'

'Signorina, do you have medicine? It's days since my stomach felt right.'

'Signorina, can I show you this lump in my armpit? It's awfully painful.'

If it was something easy to diagnose, there was no need for Doctor Kempe's advice and he was pleased to have a lighter load. 'I'm not getting any younger, Devora,' he'd say and in truth he looked frailer than some of his patients. She was sure he was not far off eighty years but he never divulged his age.

Under her bed, in her cardboard suitcase, she had placed gifts given to her in gratitude by her patients: a beautifully embroidered pair of pillowcases, a length of ribbon to tie up her hair, an oval plate carved from olive wood, a crucifix handed to her with the comment, 'Your God is the same as our God, signorina.' The villagers were poor but these priceless items were worth more than money to Devora.

Some of her fellow internees had grown used to living at Villa Oliveto and Devora felt guilty for her restlessness but they were mostly elderly, with the best of their lives behind them, she thought. But at least there'd been a wedding to break up the tedium.

Ida and Davide, recently arrived, had been the cause of this joyous occasion. One of the women had donated a pair of lace curtains and helped turn it into a passably pretty dress and *capitano* Bracciaforte had offered to donate a ham, until he was quietly reminded that pork wasn't eaten by Jews. Instead, he procured a turkey. The couple had been treated like king and queen for the week leading up to their wedding and the atmosphere in the villa was joyful for those few days as everybody helped in any way they could. The chuppah, the wedding canopy, was decorated with drapes made from sheets and flowers picked from the fields. Officially, there were no gold rings exchanged, as Mussolini had ordered gold rings to be replaced with steel bands, but afterwards the bride showed Devora the ring she had sewn in a seam of her dress. 'I can't wear this now,' Ida told her. 'But one day we shall be free again and then I'll show it to the whole world and wear it with pride.'

There was a quiet dignity and strength about Ida and Devora preferred her company to Erma, who, frankly, got on her nerves with her incessant chatter and lovesick puppy eyes. 'Emanuele said this and Emanuele did that; if only Emanuele and I could be a couple together like Ida and Davide, we would make a beautiful bride and groom. And I don't think I would look as lumpy as Ida, do you? I wonder if she is already with child?' And on and on. Devora would have told her to shut up ages ago, but as she worked with Erma's grandfather, the situation was delicate. But whenever Erma approached her to ask questions about 'matters of the heart', Devora's own heart sank.

Emanuele's father, *il capitano*, seemed to be all right with his son's friendship with Erma, as he described it. Devora knew it was far more than a friendship. Erma had confided in her that she had let Emanuele go as far with her as was possible to go without being married. 'But I want him to make proper love to me. Can you get me something to prevent a baby?' she had asked one afternoon. Devora had refused. There was no way she was going to ask Erma's grandfather if he could get hold of contraceptives for his granddaughter.

The moon was full, casting milky-blue light on the garden as Devora made her way to her sanctuary in the olive grove. A cat ran in front of her through the shadows and she jumped, standing still to check why it had been disturbed, but the night was quiet and she moved on. The air was far cooler in the grounds than inside the stuffy bedroom she still shared with her twin brothers.

Despite her protests, it had been impossible to find a room of her own. More fugitives had arrived in the last weeks and Villa Oliveto was bursting at the seams. In fact, the doctor had complained to Bracciaforte that if things went on this way, there would soon be an epidemic. The toilets overflowed and there was insufficient water for cleaning. *Il capitano* had shrugged his shoulders in despair. 'I know, *dottore*. But what am I supposed to do? They keep sending me more prisoners. I can ask in the village if there is anybody who can put up your assistant, but she might be worse off, and end up sleeping in the hay with half a dozen *bambini*. Tell her to stay where she is, and to thank the stars.'

The guard by the gate was awake, stamping his feet to keep warm, the glow of his cigarette pinpricking the unearthly twilight, so Devora moved stealthily to the back of the villa and climbed over the lowest part of the wall into the grove. She disturbed a mouse as she scrambled over the stones and stifled a shriek as it scuttled up her skirt. Over the scrubby grass she moved, like a shadow, making her way quietly to the centre of the grove where the old branches of her favourite olive tree welcomed her like open arms. *Peace at last*, she thought, as she settled her back into its smooth hollow. The only sounds here were the gentle rustling of leaves in the night breeze and the hooting of two owls hunting in a nearby meadow. Rolling her shawl into a pillow, she rested her head against the bark and within minutes she was fast asleep.

The sound of crying woke her with a start. She stayed stock-still for a few seconds, catching her bearings before peeping round the shelter of her tree. A young woman, knees hunched to her torso, her head cradled in her arms, was slumped against another tree a couple of metres away. Devora crept closer and bent to touch her arm.

'*No!*' The woman jumped up and Devora held out her hands to show she was not going to harm her.

She was dressed in a long robe, her hair concealed in a scarf, like the women who had recently arrived in the camp.

'Can I help?' Devora asked, in Italian. 'Are you from the villa?'

A nod of the head, followed by a sniff was the reply.

It was hard to tell her age with the scarf covering most of her face, but Devora guessed her to be in her late twenties. Devora brought her finger to her mouth to signify they should be quiet. 'The guard is at the gate,' she whispered, gesturing behind her.

'*Lo so.* I know.'

So, the girl knew Italian. She was probably from Libya, an Italian colony since early in the century, known as Italian North Africa.

'*Mi chiamo Devora. E tu?* What's your name? I'm Devora.'

'Shira,' the girl said, wiping the tears from her face with a corner of her long headscarf.

'Did you arrive recently? I've not seen you before.'

Another nod. 'Three nights ago.'

'Did you come with your family?'

At this the woman started to weep again and Devora let her be for a few moments, until, anxious they might be discovered, she drew nearer to Shira and hunkered down next to her. 'We should go back inside,' she whispered. 'It's too cold out here and if the guard finds us, he will make life difficult. I'll come to find you tomorrow in the villa. Come now!'

CHAPTER 15

On the following morning, after she had helped her mother peel a huge mound of potatoes and carrots for the midday meal, Devora went in search of Shira. She finally found her at the back of the villa, scrubbing sheets at one of the outside sinks.

Shira looked up when she heard her name and smiled shyly at Devora. Her headscarf had slipped and with wet hands, she pulled it back over her head, but not before Devora had noticed her hair shorn close to her scalp. *Scabies or lice,* she assessed. Several of the new refugees turned up with these complaints and it was one of the new problems she and the doctor faced constantly. It was not surprising when you heard about the conditions these new foreign arrivals had endured. It was more infectious with children so the easiest solution to avoid a mass infestation was to shave off all the hair before administering a home-made aloe vera ointment to the scalp.

Devora rolled up her sleeves and set to, helping Shira with the sheets. If she wanted to talk, she would listen.

'How long have *you* been here?' Shira asked eventually as they stretched wet sheets over the lines near the sinks.

'Too long,' Devora replied, wrinkling up her nose. 'Over two years. Where did you come from?'

'Libya.'

So she had guessed correctly. Devora remembered how upset Shira had been when last night she'd mentioned family, so she didn't broach that subject again.

'And you were sent from there to here? To Italy. Why?'

'I am a British citizen. An enemy.'

Devora didn't understand. 'But Libya is governed by Italy.'

The girl puffed out her cheeks. 'Our history is so complicated, signorina.'

'Don't call me "signorina". I'm Devora.'

'Sorry. Devora. Yes, you're correct. But I'm from Cyrenaica and our people have always rebelled against Italian dominance.' She looked up at Devora. 'Are you Italian?'

'*Sì*. I was born here, but my parents are German. They fled to Italy in 1918.'

'Well, I hope you will not be offended if I say Italians have treated us badly for years. Especially us Cyrenaican Jews. We have endured ethnic cleansing in ways you probably don't know about: as prisoners thrown from your aeroplanes, in mass executions, including children.' She lowered her voice. 'Rape of our women, their babies ripped unborn from their bellies. You even used mustard gas against us... and all this on top of being banished from our own lands.'

Devora gasped, her hands to her mouth. She wondered if this young woman was deranged. But the way she was recounting these horrific things, almost dispassionately, as if she'd told these stories before – why would she be saying such terrible things unless they were true?

'It's awful. I can't believe it.'

Shira shrugged her shoulders. 'I can assure you it's all true. In war, nothing is surprising. Nothing is ever black and white. So, you can understand I'm anxious about being here in Italy.

Very afraid. Mussolini tried to cover up all these things. He built new villages and schools for us, but that can never wipe out what he did to us in the past. And what is still happening.'

'But how come you have British citizenship? I don't understand.'

Devora felt very ignorant. She had never heard her father talk about such events in Libya, even though he devoured newspapers from front to back page when he could get hold of them. Maybe these awful things had been censored.

'We have had so many regime changes,' Shira explained. 'The British freed us from racial laws in 1940; life for a short while was good and they granted us citizenship and protections. But one year later, they were pushed out of Libya again by the Germans and Italians. And that is when we had more troubles...'

She bowed her head and Devora waited for her to compose her emotions.

'A British *tenente* befriended our family. He came to eat with us some evenings. He felt at ease with us. But when the British left, our neighbours talked to the Italians and Germans when they took over again and I was accused of whoring, and...' She pulled off her headscarf to reveal patchy hair. 'I was painted with tar and paraded through the souk in front of everybody. By your soldiers. They said I was an example of what happened to collaborators. They hung a notice round my neck to say as such and I was pelted by the storekeepers with rotten vegetables... and other things.'

She broke down, her face in her hands. 'I don't want to talk about it anymore.'

'They are not *my* soldiers, as you put it,' Devora said angrily. 'Mussolini does not include us Jews as his citizens any longer – even though there are men in this villa who fought for Italy during the last war. I was born here but I can't identify with our leaders at the moment. I'm so sorry for your suffering, Shira.'

Devora was horrified that fellow Italians could do such things. Yes, racial laws had devastated their way of life; they faced the injustice of imprisonment each day, but they had not been treated harshly in comparison with what Shira and her people had endured. Here, in the Arezzo countryside, it seemed inconceivable. Enrico had hinted at dark things in the east of Europe but he hadn't talked in any detail. Luigi had talked about resistance and surely this situation would not last forever, but she couldn't make empty promises to this poor woman. Instead, she put her arms around Shira and pulled her close until her sobbing ceased. 'I shall look after you, Shira,' she said. 'I won't let anything bad happen to you.'

CHAPTER 16

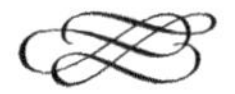

LATE JULY 1943

Over the following months, Devora made sure to sit with Shira at mealtimes and tried to introduce her to other young people. But she was quiet, morose and Erma eventually took a dislike to her.

'She thinks she's superior, always looking down her nose when we try and include her. Who does she think she is? She should be grateful.'

'She's been through a lot,' Devora said. 'Give her a chance.'

'We've all been through a lot. I've tried but it's pointless. She doesn't want to know.'

It was true that Shira kept herself to herself. Devora didn't know where she disappeared to some days but she left the girl to do what she wanted. After all, Devora herself had her own secret spot in the olive grove where she often retreated, especially now the weather was warming up. With the arrival of summer, Shira occasionally walked along the lanes with Devora before curfew but she never opened up again as she had on that first occasion and in fact, Devora enjoyed the silence. Her work in the clinic with Doctor Kempe involved chatting to patients all the time, putting them at their ease by making small talk. It was a relief to stride along the tracks out of curfew hours to escape from the ever more crowded villa.

Early one morning in July as she and Shira rounded a sharp bend on their walk, they had to press back against the stone walls to allow a Fiat Topolino to pass. It screeched to a halt and the smile on Devora's face widened as she recognised not only Luigi in his father's car, but Enrico. Enrico! It was really him. To her annoyance, her cheeks reddened as he waved and blew a kiss. She tried to feign nonchalance but her stomach behaved otherwise, the old butterfly feelings returning with a vengeance.

Both men climbed out to embrace her and she introduced Shira, who looked down demurely as Enrico and Luigi in turn shook her hand. Devora saw how she blushed and bit her lip.

'No need to be afraid of these two,' she whispered. 'They are amongst my oldest friends. We go way back.'

The two girls clambered into the cramped back seats. Enrico kept turning round and Devora noticed how Shira tried to shrink against the leather upholstery, but space was limited in the little car and the gap between them all was slender.

'We thought we'd pay you a surprise visit to see how you are. Have you heard the news?' Enrico asked.

'We're in the middle of nowhere,' Devora answered. 'The only news I have is that hens in the village are laying well, the abscess on Alfredo's tooth is better and I need a new pair of shoes – mine are full of holes.'

'*Spiritosa!* Witty as ever, Biondina. How do you put up with her, signorina Shira?' Enrico winked and Shira turned away, the slightest of smiles touching the corners of her mouth.

'The big news is that the *inglesi* and *americani* have landed in Sicily,' Luigi said.

'So, fighting starts on the mainland?' Devora gasped. 'Is this supposed to be good or bad news? Does it mean we'll soon be free?'

'It depends towards whose side you lean,' Luigi said, nudging Enrico.

'He's trying to tell you I might be open to conversion, Devora,' Enrico said. 'It's obvious our leader's ambitions have overtaken him and Italy is becoming a fumbling sideshow. The list of places where we've failed has grown to laughable proportions: France, Greece, Yugoslavia, Stalingrad, where only two Italians survived out of hundreds, and, of course, Africa... maybe the *inglesi* will rescue us from our shame.'

Devora leant forward, resting her arms on the back of Enrico's seat. 'I cannot believe my ears. What happened to Conte Enrico di Villanova and his ardent beliefs that fascism was the new way? What are you going to do now, Enrico?'

'I don't know. I have some deep thinking to do. One thing's certain: there will be all hell to pay to my father if I desert.'

'I'm working on him, Devora,' Luigi said. 'There are solutions for our Rico. But, with the *alleati* on our doorstep, the *tedeschi,* or *crucchi* as some call the Germans, will now flood into Italy, make no mistake. I fear we shall see much more bloodshed before life improves. Conditions will deteriorate for sure.'

'For now, let's change the subject,' Enrico interrupted. '*Viviamo alla giornata*. Let's live for the day. We shall whisk you both away to a little trattoria I know in Civitella for a slap-up meal. Maybe the last supper,' he said with a bitter laugh. 'You remember the place, Devora? The village you stormed away from? I hope your friend will be happy to join us.'

Shira's smile was the widest Devora had seen at Enrico's chutzpah. Shira's scarf slipped from her head and she draped it round her shoulders. Her dark hair had grown a little and curls framed her forehead, reminding Devora of the popular actress Valentina Cortese and her gamine style. In moments, Shira transformed before Devora's eyes from the traumatised girl she had met months earlier. It was like watching a beautiful creature emerge from a carapace.

Lunching in the company of her friends, Devora enjoyed the brief sensation that war was distant. Shira was not wearing her usual long toga-style dress today, having changed into slacks and a blouse for their walk and, together with Devora's brown-blonde hair, neither girl looked as if they had stepped from a Jewish internment camp. They blended in with the other diners in the trattoria, relaxed and happy.

Shira proved to be a witty storyteller and had them in stitches with her descriptions. Sitting beneath the shade of an awning outside the little eating-place in Piazza Giuseppe Mazzini, they listened as she recounted details of her work for the British in their kitchens in Tripoli. She described the elaborate way of serving tea and cake, how she'd brewed the tea too weak and not boiled the water and the British officers had reacted as if a bomb had dropped. They were eccentric and strange with their pale skins that burned easily under the hot sun, she told them, but they were kind.

Both Luigi and Enrico seemed enchanted by Shira's sparkling repartee and there was much laughter and life between the four of them that afternoon. Devora felt a little left out at times, surprised at Shira's outgoing behaviour, so different from the quiet girl she knew at Villa Oliveto. After a delicious meal, Enrico offered to show Shira round the pretty village and take her up to the castle to see the view.

'Let me show you something of our history, I expect you haven't seen much of our country, signorina,' he said to Shira. 'We'll be back in half an hour, you two.' Before Luigi and Devora could even suggest tagging along, the pair were halfway up the lane leading to the castle.

Devora and Luigi wandered along narrow alleys where swifts screeched and swooped, their cries like high-pitched whistles. Red geraniums basked in the sun in pots on window ledges, scarlet valerian sprouted from the walls and, despite everything, Devora felt as if she was on holiday. They found themselves in the main piazza and sat near the Romanesque church of Santa Maria.

'Devora, I don't want to alarm you but as I said earlier, life is going to get worse for everybody. I want you to be prepared to get away from the camp as soon as the *tedeschi* arrive en masse on our mainland. Because it *will* happen. I think we shall hear soon about big changes in the government too.'

Her holiday mood evaporated as she listened to Luigi. 'How do you know these things, Gigi?'

'I'm not hidden away like you. We have access to information. I've met people who've told me dreadful things. I know a refugee, a young man from Poland who escaped from a cattle train together with other Jews. German guards packed hundreds of them into overcrowded wagons. Dogs bit at them – women, children, the old – if they didn't move quickly enough. A woman was shot for refusing to be separated from her husband. This Polish man's grandfather died standing up and his grandson managed to kick a hole in the side of the compartment where the wood was rotten and he and two others hurled themselves from the moving train. He feels guilty he left his family behind... he has no idea where they were taken but he fears the worst.'

'That's dreadful, Luigi. Where were these poor wretches taken, do you think?'

'There's talk about labour camps, where conditions are bad.' He paused, seeming to choose what to say next. 'The time for ambiguity is over in our country. We have a truly menacing situation when newspapers print such disgusting articles about Jews being rabid dogs and should wear brightly coloured bracelets to warn others against the peril of infection... that is what some of Enrico's friends believed in the GUF too, at university.'

'I know he was a member of that fascist group but I can't believe the Enrico we both know thinks the same way. You heard what he said in the car. He's disillusioned.'

'Let's hope so. But when you're surrounded by others who believe in this kind of thing, when you're drip-fed poison day after day, then it's hard to stand up against it.'

'I think he has lowered his wings a little – he's understood.' There was wishful thinking in Devora's statement.

'I'll keep an eye on him and make sure he's not saying these things simply to please us. Anyway, I came here today to talk to your father and explain my concerns. You really should all be going into hiding and leaving Villa Oliveto.'

Devora leant forwards, her head in her hands. 'Another move will devastate my parents. I hope Papà believes you. He and Mamma are settled; they feel safe. And, anyway, where will we go, Gigi? Back to Urbino?'

'No, no. If the *tedeschi* arrive, the first thing they will do is check the census at the registry and then they'll go to the ghetto to look for any remaining Jews in the city. There are barely forty now that we know of and they'll be easy pickings. Unfortunately, there are people willing to hand them over in return for money. No, no, you can't possibly return. There are three options as I see it: you either go into hiding in the countryside, consider travelling south to where the *alleati* are, or you travel north to Switzerland.'

'*O Dio mio*, Gigi. I can't bear it. When is all this going to end?'

Luigi squeezed her hand. 'I shall help in every way I can. I'm part of a group helping people who need to go into hiding. If Enrico is serious about defecting, then we'll help him too. Talk the options over with your father.'

Devora shook her head in dismay. She had been desperate to escape the confines of Villa Oliveto, but not in this way. Panic seized her and her chest felt tight and she breathed in and out slowly to calm herself.

'Are you all right?' Luigi asked, taking her hand again.

She shook her head and spoke only when her panic began to subside. 'I can't bear the thought of leaving Urbino. Do you think the war will be over soon, Luigi? Now that the *alleati* have invaded?'

A deep shrug of his shoulders. 'We can only pray. And fight... In the meantime, the most important thing is to keep you and your loved ones safe. With *buona volontà*, determination and courage mixed with a generous dose of hope, the war will end. But who knows when? *Chissà?*'

Luigi's question was followed with another deep shrug of his shoulders and Devora's heart sank. Would she and her family ever be safe? And when, if ever, could she return to her beloved Urbino?

CHAPTER 17

END OF JULY 1943

The following week, the main topic of conversation in Villa Oliveto were the newspaper reports that Il Duce had been deposed and was under arrest. King Victor Emanuel had taken Mussolini's place as commander-in-chief and Mussolini had been sent to prison in an ambulance. There was a flurry of excitement in the house: the war was bound to be over soon with Il Duce out of the way. The Lassa family were not the only ones making preparations to leave and routine afternoon and evening activities were abandoned as internees busied themselves with packing.

Luigi's advice had been heeded and during the following weeks, Mütti flitted about their two rooms like a jackdaw, scooping up treasures and belongings from drawers and shelves, preparing for yet another departure. Devora watched her remove chains from the necks of the twins, their precious Chai medallions and Vati's gold ring to add to a modest pile of gold jewellery. She included the earrings Vati had given her on their wedding day and worn each and every day since. Mütti looked somehow different without them. The dainty pearls set in gold had made her seem softer, her eyes brighter. Now she wore a perpetual look of worry, two furrowed lines between her thick brows. Vati's spare reading spectacles were added to the pile. She ordered Friedrich to cut a hole in one of Devora's shoes to hide her wedding ring and earrings. 'The heels on her shoes are sturdier than mine,' she told her husband.

To Devora she entrusted the family's precious candlestick, wrapped in a worn linen towel. 'When it's dark, go hide our menorah. Maybe you can bury it somewhere in your olive grove.'

When Devora opened her mouth in disbelief, her mother said, 'Don't think I haven't seen you steal into the night when you thought we were all asleep, my girl. I'm not stupid.'

She thrust it into Devora's hands, who thought it pointless. Were they likely to set foot in Villa Oliveto again? But she didn't argue. She would do it to appease her mother.

Her mother sat by the window sewing pieces of jewellery into seams and hems on her family's clothes, her stitches tiny. 'So that nobody will detect alterations,' she told Devora.

Of course she didn't ask her daughter to help and Devora didn't blame her either. She might be good at mending people's flesh wounds with sutures, as Doctor Kempe had taught her, but tiny stitches in garments? That was something else.

Devora watched her mother catching the last rays of the day through the small window, her head bent over her work, muttering, 'What shall become of us all? We know nobody in Switzerland.' She wiped stray tears from her face as she worked. 'Merciful God, send your blessings. *Ba-ruch a-tah Adonai...*' she murmured.

After lengthy discussions, the family had decided to escape via Switzerland. Vati refused to hide away in the Urbino countryside like animals in the night, endangering lives of local rescuers. 'We will find work when we are in Switzerland,' he said finally. 'We will pay our way. Devora can finish her studies. We will try to stay in the Ticino area where Italian is spoken.

That way the children's schoolwork will be easier to follow. I shall find work once we're there. It is decided.'

Devora wondered what she should pack for her new life. Did she have anything precious to take, aside from her family? Her medical textbooks and stethoscope might come in useful. The books were heavy but she could carry them on her back. She asked Mütti to sew her a bag with two handles long enough to slip over her shoulders and her mother stayed up to make one from an old pillowcase.

'We must wear all our clothes when we leave,' Vati said. 'It will be cold where we are going and it will be less for us to carry.'

The boys had a dress rehearsal and mucked about, wearing their two pairs of trousers with pyjamas beneath, making them look like fat, well-fed boys. They bumped into each other tummy-first like wrestlers, bouncing off each other before tumbling to the floor. Because of a recent growth spurt, Alfredo's trousers were too short in the leg and the only material Mütti could find to lengthen his worn brown cords was a contrasting green and at first Alfredo kicked up a fuss, until Vati told him to stop moaning. 'There are more important things to worry about, my son, than what you look like. Stop your nonsense.'

Arturo hadn't grown much at all. He was thin and had developed a cough that never seemed to go away.

Luigi visited again and accompanied Devora and her father on a walk along the dusty road leading from the hamlet. When they were sure they were not being observed, Luigi handed over false *tessere annonarie*, ration vouchers. 'Here, you have been fed but once you're travelling, you will need to buy your own food. Without these, you won't get far.' From another pocket, he produced new identity documents.

'You should make sure to practise your new surname. I have amended the census details at the Town Hall to make you sound more Italian. You are now *famiglia* Lassari. It's good that your children already have names that can pass for Italian. I have simply added an "o" to Alfred and Artur on the register – it will be easier for them as they are already known by their Italian names. I've changed the "v" of Devora to "b". But, signore.' He stopped, concern on his face, his hand on Friedrich's arm. 'You and your wife – you must remember you are now Federico and Mariella Lassari. Start to get into the habit today. A slip of the tongue could mean the difference between life and death. And the boys must be made to understand this is not a game.'

Devora examined her new identity documents. With the naked eye, it was impossible to discern the change to her name.

'Can you forge banknotes for us too, Gigi?' she said, trying to lighten the mood.

'I only changed the names on the census, Devora. I stayed late one evening in the *comune*. Your documents were done by somebody else: a friend of mine who owns a tourist shop and has a hand printer. He's done a good job. But...' He paused, as if reluctant to say more.

'But, what, Luigi?' Friedrich asked.

Luigi stopped. 'Forging documents is not without danger. The last man we used was discovered. He was shot on the spot. Keep these papers safe and do not tell a soul about how you acquired them. Or your plans for the future.' He turned to Devora. 'Not even Enrico. Not until I am sure of his intentions. And you need to teach your parents the words of some prayers you learned at school. The *Pater Noster* and *Ave Maria*. From now on the rest of the world must believe you are Christian. Get Alfredo to help. He's a bright boy.'

'When do you think we shall leave?' Friedrich asked. 'And are you sure it's absolutely necessary, Luigi? We are quite safe in the villa. *Capitano* Bracciaforte is a good man. He would protect us, I'm sure,' said Friedrich.

'If I were a husband and father, I wouldn't take the risk. You must leave Italy before it's too late. I've listened to too many reports on Radio Londra about what is happening to Jews across German-occupied Europe. And Italian officers have reported atrocities committed by the Nazis on the Eastern Front and have actively diverted Jewish prisoners to Italy, because they know they'll be treated better here. And the same is happening in Greece, Yugoslavia... the war is getting closer. A brutal episode in our history is on the march. Mark my words, signor Lassari.'

For a couple of seconds, Devora didn't grasp that Luigi was addressing her father with his new surname. How easy would it be for them all to remember their new identities? She resolved to practise writing the new spelling over and over and to make sure Mütti and Vati became Mamma and Papà. Arturo in particular would need reminding that he was a Lassari and not a Lassa. To think such simple changes could be lifesavers was hard to absorb.

'Luigi,' she said. 'Would you be able to arrange one more set of documents? For Shira? I can't leave her alone here. I'm the only person she can talk to. I'm sorry to ask – especially with what you told me earlier about the danger involved. But I promised to take care of her.'

He raised his eyebrows, his expression grim. 'I'll see what I can do.'

They continued walking in silence. Devora thought about how she would bury the family candlestick that evening as well as arranging to meet Shira in the olive grove to discuss their flight from Villa Oliveto. Her stomach churned at the thought of the danger Luigi had put himself in and the seriousness of the whole situation.

There were people out there, Germans and others, who wanted to send them far away, on crowded trains like Luigi had spoken of. Away to places they might never return from. Simply because of who they were. Despite not having chosen Villa Oliveto through free will, for many months they had been cocooned within the confines of the old house. She had yearned to get away, to return to Urbino and her old life. But it seemed there was no going back.

A little before midnight, Devora stepped carefully down the staircase, carrying the menorah out of the unlocked kitchen door. The moon was a fingernail tonight and a refreshing breeze rustled the leaves on the persimmon trees. She stumbled over a rake left leaning against the drystone wall, clutching the candlestick close to stop it from falling.

Even if she'd been blindfolded, she knew exactly how to reach her olive tree. Its vast, knobbly trunk had given her comfort more nights than she could count and this was where she had decided to hide the sacred family heirloom. A hole in the base, wide enough to hide a small child, was too obvious so she ruled that out. Devora knelt down in the spot where she always sheltered and then cursed her stupidity. She hadn't thought about bringing a spade to dig a hole and she retraced her steps to pick up the offending rake. But when she started to scrape the dry earth with the prongs, metal against stone broke the night's silence. She used her fingers instead, clawing at the dust with her nails but the ground was too hard. Devora sat back on her heels, wiping perspiration from her face. The garden tools were all locked up. Maybe there was something in the kitchen she could use.

Back in the kitchen, she jumped when somebody murmured. 'You couldn't sleep either? Would you like some mint tea?'

Ida leant against the sink, her slender fingers cradling a cup.

'You made me jump. I... needed fresh air,' Devora said.

'These are difficult times. Everybody is jittery.'

'Yes.'

'Do you want to talk about it?' Ida asked.

Devora decided to stop pretending. 'I was burying the family menorah, because our plan is to leave soon, but I need something to dig with.'

Ida nodded. 'We can do it together. It will be easier.' She lifted two large serving spoons hanging from the rack above the cooker and they made their way quietly to the grove.

'I sought shelter out here when I first arrived,' Ida whispered as she followed Devora. 'My tears have watered these olive trees.'

'Mine too,' Devora said, wondering how many others the grove had welcomed at night.

They worked together without speaking and when the hole was large enough, Ida uttered a prayer as Devora placed the candlestick beneath the tangled roots that looked so much like hands.

'May it be Your will, Lord, our God and the God of our ancestors,' Ida said quietly, 'that You lead us toward peace, guide our footsteps toward peace, and make us reach our desired destination for life, gladness and peace.'

Devora's face was wet from perspiration. It was the fine summer mist, she told herself. It wasn't tears. She was done with tears. But even so, when Ida embraced her, Devora's heart was full to breaking.

But a few weeks later, in early September, Vati rushed into the communal sitting room waving the *Corriere della Sera* with news that removed the urgency from their escape plans.

'Listen, everybody. Incredible news. Italy is no longer at war with the *inglesi* and *americani*.'

He jabbed with his finger at the huge headline talking up

the front page. '*Armistizio*. Badoglio has been asked by the King to form a non-fascist government. It's wonderful news.'

A crowd quickly gathered round him, excitedly adding their opinions.

'*Baruch Hashem*. Blessed be the name of God.'

'This means the civil war will come to an end, surely.'

'We can return to our homes.'

The twins jumped up and down with other youngsters. '*Evviva, evviva*, the war is over,' Alfredo squealed. 'Can we go back to Urbino now?'

'And return to a proper school?' added Arturo.

'And I can return to university,' Devora said.

'We should wait and see, *Kinder*,' Vati warned. 'But I have to say this is the best news we've had for a long time.' He planted a kiss on Mütti's cheek and she told him to behave, but Devora noted the smile that reached her eyes. She looked almost pretty.

For a few days, there was an air of festivity in the villa and Devora's hopes of returning to Urbino revived. Mamma stopped her frantic packing and joined the women in the kitchen to use up provisions they had carefully stored, pulling flour and sugar from cupboards to make cakes and fancy breads. Portions were increased and beer was drunk at each evening meal. Some of the youngsters unhooked the obligatory framed photographs of Mussolini from the walls of the living room, and stamped on them, breaking the glass and making a bonfire in the middle of the grounds. Mütti started to unpick the seams where she had hidden the family's gold and Papà was his relaxed self again. 'Luigi was scaremongering,' he said. 'Now I can help with preparations for the next concert.'

Capitano Bracciaforte hoisted the Italian flag to hang from the balcony of the villa and made a little speech to his friends. 'My friends, you are free to go whenever you please.' He had hardly ever worn his uniform, stating openly that he could not wear uniform in front of people who were ordinary mortals like him. And professionals to boot, holding more exalted positions than he could ever aspire to, referring to the doctor, industrialists and professors amongst his 'guests', as he preferred to call them.

A handful of families resumed packing their belongings onto assorted transport, and set out for their home towns. They departed in a cloud of dust and cheery waves to various corners of Italy, their few prized possessions piled high on wheelbarrows or home-made carts bodged from planks of wood and purloined wheels. There were even a couple of mules in the train of refugees. Kisses and embraces sent them on their way and promises to see one another soon, in freedom.

Many of the internees decided to stay put, happy where they were. 'Nobody will harm us here,' was the popular consensus. Devora moved into a spare room, revelling in space and privacy.

But it was not long before Luigi reappeared, his dishevelled sweaty state having nothing to do with the hot weather. Devora had never seen him look so agitated and fearful, his eyes wild as he urged them to understand that there was no time for complacency.

'The situation is beyond serious,' he said, holding up a copy of the racist paper *L'Ora*. 'The authorities are now offering five thousand lire for information leading to the immediate arrest of Jews. You absolutely cannot stay here any longer, my friends.'

Devora took the paper from him, utterly dismayed at the theft of their brief period of hope. Were their lives ever going to return to normal? Their dream of returning to Urbino had been dashed again. She turned the page and to her absolute horror read an article about the bodies of fifty-four Jews found floating in Lake Maggiore. She closed the paper so her mother could not read of the bullet holes in necks, and hands bound behind backs. It was too awful for words. How could such hatred exist?

Why? What had they done to deserve such cruelty? Was it really true?

Luigi was showing her parents another newspaper, *Gazette de Lausanne*, a French language newspaper in circulation. 'Primo Levi has an article in here about German atrocities against Jewish people in the east. And he writes that Mussolini knew what had been going on all along.' He read a quote aloud. 'This is what he said: "*Li fanno emigrare... all'altro mondo.*" He knew the *tedeschi* were exterminating Jews and sending them to what he termed *the world beyond this one*. He knew they were being sent to camps in the east, saying they were labour camps when all the while they were travelling to their deaths. And the evil swine did nothing to stop it. My friends, you need to realise what is going on. I urge you to leave this place.'

Devora's mother, her hands to her mouth, cried out and Luigi apologised. Devora moved over to comfort her.

'I'm sorry to frighten you, signora, but you need to know these things. Jews have been murdered in cold blood in Lake Maggiore. Some of the dead in the lake were children, drowned by oarsmen pushing them below the water.'

He turned to Friedrich. 'Signor Lassari, it's high time you left. There are networks of spies willing to identify Jews. Anybody who has a relative in prison has been promised their freedom in exchange for information of the whereabouts of any single Jewish person. Another train left recently from Merano taking Jews to so-called labour camps in the east. They say for reasons of security. Get ready to leave, my friends, and I shall come to collect you tomorrow at seven o'clock for the first stage of your journey. Warn your friends they need to make preparations too. No Jew in central or northern Italy is safe any longer.'

CHAPTER 18

ENRICO

Those were snatched moments we had. Beautiful moments. Clandestine meetings when we could not get enough of each other. Anywhere we could. Out in the countryside, the sun warm on our naked flesh, but never as hot as the passion we shared. In the darkness of alleyways where cats brawled and mice scuttled, the indoor sounds of ordinary lives intensified stolen moments, and we were reckless. On one occasion, a man stepped from a door to light a cigarette and lean against the wall. We turned to stone, my hand within her blouse. I willed him not to turn our way and after a minute or so he cursed aloud, threw down his stub and ground it underfoot before returning from where he had appeared. Our lovemaking resumed. Fierce. As if it might be our last time and I had to still her cries with my hand as I drove into her.

Sometimes we would do nothing but lie and gaze upon one another beneath the shade of an olive tree, its slender branches a silver curtain hiding us, separating us from what was going on elsewhere. Lying on our sides, we drank in the sense of each other. Her eyes were an ocean, her lashes thick and long, her smooth, unblemished skin spicy and oil-scented, her figure voluptuous even beneath her clothes. She traced her fingers down the contours of my face and I caught her thumb in my mouth, sucking on it to watch desire fill her eyes.

Once I took her to eat in a simple trattoria. For an hour and a half, we were an ordinary couple, toasting each other with rough country wine. She invented stories about the diners. The man with the hat was a lawyer. The woman with him was his secretary. I laughed and told her they were father and daughter but she shook her head, telling me no father looked at his child in that way and couldn't I see what was going on beneath the table, her skirt pulled up to her thighs, his hand caressing her? And then, she shucked off her shoe and I felt her toes between my legs and I could hardly bear it: her wantonness, her lazy smile. She told me the proprietor couldn't take his eyes off us and she was right, but I replied it was because he was fearful we would forget to pay the bill, because we were so drunk. Not drunk on wine, drunk on each other. When she chuckled and removed her foot, she threw back her head, her teeth creamy pearls against her olive skin and the man on the table near us threw me a smile of envy. With her thick, dark hair she could have been any woman from that place. But she was every woman to me. The only woman.

She filled my heart, captured my senses. For the first time in my life, I cared for another person more than I cared for myself. My whole aim in life from now onwards was to keep her safe and look after her. For one day in the future, surely, this war would be over and we could live our lives together. I wanted her for my wife. I wanted to make love to her in a proper bed with clean sheets and goose-feather pillows, in a home of our own. I wanted her to bear our babies. I loved her like I'd never loved another human being. Until now everything else in my life had been preparing me for her. I was ready.

I'd laid the ground for our future, wangled a position in the army where I would be far from battle. So far it was working out fine. She knew every single detail of the plans I'd made. We would stay alive to be together, no matter what. I was sure of it. I prayed to the God my mother had introduced to me. God is love, she'd told me. How could He therefore refuse my prayers? Or would He punish us because she was my new religion?

CHAPTER 19

MID-SEPTEMBER 1943

DEVORA

The family were ready and waiting when an ambulance pulled up at the gates of Villa Oliveto just before seven o'clock the following morning, a red cross on the roof of the driver's cab, canvas flaps covering the back. A light drizzle spat at the newly named Lassaris as they huddled together under two worn umbrellas. Shira had refused to leave with them, despite Devora's entreaties in the olive grove the previous night.

'I am not moving anywhere else,' she'd said wearily to Devora as they sat together. 'I'm tired of being sent from one place to the other.'

'But it's growing too dangerous with the *tedeschi* searching everywhere.' Devora had grasped Shira's hands, begging her to change her mind. 'I promised to look after you.'

Shira had smiled. 'You are so kind, Devora. Please don't worry about me. I know how to look after myself. I'll travel south and look for the *inglesi*.'

There'd been nothing she could say to change the girl's mind. Devora kept turning round as they waited in the rain, to see if Shira had relented and would emerge at the last minute from the building, but the large doors to Villa Oliveto stayed firmly shut.

Luigi had warned them they could only bring one bag each as they would eventually travel much of the way on foot and Mütti had muttered they were turning into nomads and would need a camel soon. Friedrich told her off. 'Better nomads than corpses, *mia cara* Mariella,' he said and Devora was proud of his determination to carry this through. It must be hard for him to stay upbeat after yet another setback and have to call his wife with a different name after so many years of being together as Friedrich and Miriam Lassa.

Luigi told them he had another passenger travelling with them.

'She will leave us along the way. There's no need for introductions.'

Devora glanced in the cab where a young woman sat, a scarf wrapped round her head. She was smoking a cigarette and as she turned to flick ash from the window, she made no reaction to the family staring at her. Other orders were quickly issued and Devora marvelled at this new assured Luigi as he handed her a nurse's uniform. 'Put this on and give your stethoscope to your father. He is to be Professor Federico Tommasini for the journey, taking his patients to a clinic in Varese.' He handed fresh documents to Friedrich. 'Keep those papers I gave you the other day in a different place on your person and do not mix them up, signore, whatever you do. You and the rest of the family will travel in the back.'

The twins and their mother were told they were sickly patients. 'You have typhus fever and with any luck, nobody will want to check you out. So, *ragazzi*, no playing about in the back of the ambulance. You have to be as quiet as the night and act your parts. A bit of delirious moaning will be in order, but don't exaggerate. *Mi raccomando.* This is no joke – the lives of your family depend on you.'

He frowned as he noticed a moving bulge in Alberto's shirt and went over to the boy. 'You can't take the cat with you, Alberto.'

'But I can't leave Tigre on her own.' The boy's mouth quivered as his hands lifted out the marmalade cat.

Luigi sighed. 'I'll take care of her, I promise. She'll be fine if you leave her here. Cats are very independent animals. I'll pass by and fetch her. My mother adores cats.'

'You're not just saying that?' Arturo said. 'Like adults always do?'

'I promise.' He glanced at their mother. 'You have appendicitis, signora. You need an operation.'

She would need no urging to play-act. She already looked as pale as a corpse, Devora thought.

Luigi's passenger stepped down from the driver's cab to make room for Devora to shuffle along the seat to sit in the middle. She nodded her head briefly and Devora was struck by the intense blue of the woman's eyes before she closed them and leant back in the seat to sleep. From time to time, Devora stole a glance at her. She was younger than she'd first thought, and very thin, her fingernails bitten right down.

'Who is she?' Devora whispered to Luigi.

He shook his head. 'You don't need to know. And she'll be leaving us soon.'

'But...'

'Don't worry about her. You'll never see her again.'

It was hard not to wonder what Luigi was up to but his tone warned her she wouldn't get any more out of him. It was warm in the cab and before long she nodded off too, tired from a late night of last-minute packing, coupled with the anxiety about what lay ahead.

The journey was to take far longer than the normal two full

days, as Luigi would stick to minor tracks. Devora woke abruptly an hour after they had set off as the passenger door opened and slammed shut again. The mysterious passenger moved to Luigi's window and he wound it down.

'Have you got everything?' he asked.

The girl patted the pocket of her jacket. Luigi leant down to squeeze her hand and she smiled up at him briefly, her smile reaching her eyes.

'Take care. Stay safe and good luck. They'll be here within the hour. Are you quite sure you don't want to wait with us?'

She shook her head. 'You get on, Gigi,' she told him. 'You've a long way to go.'

For a moment, Devora felt something like a pang of envy. Who was this girl who seemed to know Luigi so well? And what were they up to?

Devora watched as the girl crossed the empty track and disappeared into a farm building.

'What's going on?' she asked as Luigi started up the engine and moved off down the track.

Once again, he shook his head. 'I'm sorry, Biondina, I can't tell you. But... it's all good. All for a good cause.' He turned to her and smiled.

She gave up questioning him but she couldn't help feeling there was a whole dimension to Luigi she didn't know.

As evening fell, they stopped outside an austere building on the outskirts of Parma. Devora made out the name above the huge entrance: *Ospedale contumaciale*, a hospital for treating infectious diseases. A young nursing sister greeted Luigi.

'Welcome. I will take your passengers to where they can rest for the night. But you must hurry and nobody is to say anything. Quickly and quietly, please.'

They followed her down endless corridors smelling of beeswax and incense and up three flights of stairs to an isolation ward, a sign on the door warning that only medical staff were permitted to enter. There were no patients in the dozen single beds arranged in two rows.

'You will not be disturbed in here. I shall bring you something to eat in half an hour.'

Devora could not sleep that night and she slipped away from her bed and found herself in the chapel. Dim candlelight flickered before a plaster statue of the Madonna. She sat for a moment in one of the narrow pews, wondering why it was that even now, when they were fleeing for their lives, she had so little sense of spirituality.

The Jewish faith had become a real support for her parents during their stay at Villa Oliveto and there had been far more celebrations than Devora could remember from her childhood. Maybe it was because her parents were living within a Jewish community and maybe because they felt more secure this way. Every Yom Tov Jewish holiday seemed to be followed, as if to imprint on each of their children that they should never forget their traditions and, most importantly, their identity: the fact they were Jewish. Yet in the past, they had only celebrated Pesach and Hanukkah – feasts which she and the boys enjoyed because of special treats prepared and an air of festivity that hung around their home.

Even Anna Maria had joined in with those feasts. Where was she now? Was she safe? Devora wondered as she sat in this holy place where the nuns worshipped every day of their lives, with its stations of the cross arranged around the chapel walls and statues of saints, and oil paintings showing scenes from the Scriptures. Women who had taken vows of chastity, obedience and poverty, cloistered away. To Devora, this need for something to believe in seemed like a denial of life – always thinking about sin, and lining the way to a future eternal existence. What about the present? To her that was more important.

If somebody were to ask her what she was, her immediate reply wouldn't be 'I'm a Jew', or 'I'm a Christian' or even 'I'm an atheist'. Rather she'd reply: 'I'm a woman who wants to make something of her life; I want to become a doctor.' Wasn't that sufficient? Devora wondered. Was she a heretic? No, not even that. She had no strong beliefs about any afterlife or alternative religion. If people felt the need to put their trust in these beliefs, and they did no harm to others, then so be it. As long as that didn't involve narrow-mindedness or persecution. She believed strongly in the here and now. In life. That was sufficient identity for her.

Suddenly the candle in front of the Madonna died with a splutter and she was plunged into almost total darkness, save for a tiny red light on the altar that she knew from scripture lessons at school signified the presence of the Eucharistic host. She grinned wryly. No doubt some believers would take it as a sign: that her thoughts were not good enough, that God disapproved. But her scientific brain told her it was simply because the candle had burnt out. Devora gave up on her contemplations. It was time to grope her way back to bed and grab some sleep.

Luigi joined them again early the following morning after they had said their goodbyes to the nuns. Speaking softly to Devora in the front of the ambulance, he told her about the recent formation of the CLN. 'All of us in the National Liberation Committee are anti-fascist,' he said, 'no matter what political party we belong to.' He told her how they had talked into the night about the situation and Devora felt envious about his purpose, his involvement in the war effort to topple the *fascisti*.

'DELASEM has had to fold,' he continued, 'but our new freedom organisation is taking up from where they left off to help with the displaced. We are intent on delivering our country to liberty. At last we're heading in the right direction,

Biondina. This truck we're using was provided by a sympathiser in the police who invented an excuse to requisition it. They're not all bad, you know. And when more people understand the strength of our opposition, they'll join in. Too many have remained silent for too long. But there are still too many Blackshirts and Mussolini sympathisers rattling about.'

'I want to stay here in Italy, Gigi. I feel cowardly escaping like this from my country. I want to help and join in with the opposition. That girl in the truck is obviously involved and I could be useful too – with my medical training.'

He turned to look at her, ignoring her remark about the passenger. 'Don't you think your family needs you?'

'Papà is still a fit man. Alfredo is almost a man. Arturo will do what they tell him.'

'And your mother? Does she not need her daughter?'

Devora fell silent. Luigi had a point. It was an impossible choice to make: to support her family or abandon them to join the cause for freedom. Her mother was not as strong as she used to be and despite theirs not being the sweetest of relationships, she was still her mother. Devora felt torn. Freedom came at a price. But one day when all this horror was over, she vowed to do what *she* wanted: follow her own path, pursue her medical career and become a useful member of a free society. She felt heavy clouds settle on her shoulders like a shawl dragging her down.

Sensing her despondency, Luigi tried to reassure her. 'I've heard that anybody studying medicine will be allowed into Switzerland. You will be considered *accolta*, welcomed. And that in turn will help your family. And when all this is over, you can safely return to Urbino and look after us all.' He fell silent as he navigated a series of bumps in the road. When the truck was on an even course again, he said quietly, 'Do not think I want you to go, Devora.'

He was courageous and kind, she thought, risking a lot to

drive them all this way and put his life on the line with his political involvement. She valued his friendship and she smiled at him and whispered, '*Grazie*, Gigi.'

On the outskirts of Milan, they were stopped at a roadblock where a couple of young men wearing black shirts and tricornered caps stood up from chairs where they'd been lounging.

'*Squadristi. Porca boia.* Blackshirts. Bloody hell,' muttered Luigi. 'All we need.' He knocked four times on the panel behind that separated them from the passengers. A signal in particular to the boys: a warning to behave as sickly patients.

'*Documenti!*' the burlier of the two youths commanded, thrusting his head through the window to peer suspiciously at Luigi and Devora.

Her heart hammering, Devora delivered as sweet a smile as she could muster and fumbled for her identity papers.

'And yours, signore?' he demanded of Luigi. 'Where are you going?'

'To a specialist clinic in Varese. With patients in the back.'

'And why are you not sitting with them, signorina—' The Blackshirt paused to look at Devora's papers, adding, 'signorina Debora?'

The change in her name sounded for one second strange to Devora but she didn't falter. 'We have a specialist doctor travelling with them behind. Our patients are very infectious, suffering from typhus fever and he advised me to limit my contact with them.' She pointed at her stomach, arching herself slightly forwards in the hope it would make her stomach appear round. Lowering her eyelashes demurely, she said, 'You see, I'm in the early stages of pregnancy.' She sniffed and pulled out a handkerchief. 'My husband doesn't know yet. He's a soldier.'

'Where is he fighting, signorina?'

She noticed his gaze fall on her fingers but she already had an excuse for the absence of a wedding ring. She would tell him she had given it up for the cause, as Mussolini had ordered, to raise money for the war effort, and was still waiting for her metal government replacement. Thankfully he seemed happy enough with her statement, especially when she told him her husband was stationed not too far away, guarding the Beretta factory, near the Republic of Salò.

When the second *squadrista* made his way to the back of the ambulance and went to lift the canvas covering, the first one shouted, 'Leave it, Paolo. Unless you want to catch typhoid.'

He waved Luigi on, who tipped his cap and Devora gave a flutter of her trembling fingers.

'*Che attrice!* What an actress, Devora. I never knew. *Mamma mia!*' Luigi laughed when they were at a safe distance, changing up a gear. 'You could be useful in sabotage.'

'Well, I won't be any use to you in Switzerland, will I? Unless you come and fetch me back. Stop!' she added. 'My waters have broken. I'm going to have my baby.' She sniggered when he pulled a look of horror, his foot slamming on the brake. In reality she desperately needed to find somewhere to relieve her churned-up stomach.

How could laughter follow moments of terror? she wondered as she crouched behind a tree. How did spies control themselves in difficult situations? How much training did they need and how much luck was involved? Maybe Luigi was right and it was best to stick to being a dutiful daughter. But for those few agonising minutes when she had successfully duped the two men and plucked an excuse of pregnancy from who knew where, she had enjoyed being in control and feeling useful.

Luigi had lied to the *squadristi.* Their destination was not a clinic in Varese. As daylight faded on the third and final day, Luigi took a winding secondary road that led away from the city, a fast-flowing river gushing over stones alongside the bumpy dirt track. 'Our passengers will have an uncomfortable ride from now on,' Luigi said. 'Thank heavens they're not really sick.'

Devora heard the occasional squeal from the boys as the ambulance jolted over bumps and she wondered how her mother was faring. 'Could I not let Mamma sit here more comfortably in the front instead of me?'

'Best not. If we're stopped, I don't think her acting skills would match yours,' he said, turning to her with a smile. 'I'm really going to miss you, Biondina, but I have to return this crate by tomorrow morning. I have a long drive ahead of me.'

She stretched her hand to touch his arm and he took one of his off the wheel to cover hers. She would never know what he had been about to say because the truck skidded towards the road's edge and the river below. Swearing, he straightened the vehicle. 'We've come all this way and right at the end I nearly drowned us through carelessness. It would have been a cold drowning too.'

Devora kept quiet, not wanting to distract him, but she too was going to miss Luigi. He had been amazingly kind and she hoped his journey back to Urbino would be without mishap. When the road straightened out eventually, she resumed their conversation.

'It's such a long way. How can you possibly drive four hundred kilometres without rest?'

'I'm not taking the ambulance back to Urbino. I'm delivering it to Torino. It's needed there for a similar mission. With a different driver.'

'Still a long way. How will you return home?'

'Don't you worry about me. I have plenty of acquaintances who will help. You concentrate on your family and getting to safety. Lie low once you get across the border. Don't attempt to send me a message. Nobody must trace any connection between us. I may have to make this journey again for others. My contacts will inform me how you all are.'

It was cloak and dagger and highly organised. Devora felt like a rat abandoning a ship she wanted to be sailing with, but she kept this to herself. She had already made it plain to Luigi about wanting to remain in Italy.

He stopped the engine outside a large house beside a stone church. The air was fresh, the grass damp underfoot as she climbed from the cab to help her family from the back. When she dragged open the main flaps, she was greeted by not four passengers, but nine. In absolute astonishment, Devora saw that she recognised the extra travellers, hidden away beside her parents.

CHAPTER 20

'Erma, Ida, what on *earth* are you doing here?'

She turned to look sternly at her parents. 'Mamma, Papà? How could you travel all this way without saying anything?' Devora was shocked at finding their friends from Villa Oliveto: Doctor Kempe, his granddaughter Erma, alongside Emanuele – what would his father, the commander of the camp, say? And Ida and Davide, the married couple, stared back at her too.

Luigi jumped from the driving seat to join her. 'Keep your voice down, Devora. The whole world—' He broke off when he saw what she had discovered. '*Porca boia!* Bloody hellfire. What the devil are you all doing? How did you manage to slip past us like this? Where have you been hiding all these days we've been travelling?'

'It's my fault, Luigi. I'm sorry.' Devora's father held his hat in his hands, his fingers worrying at the rim as he turned it round and round. 'They begged me to let them come with us. How could I refuse? We hid them under our blankets at the back of the truck and let them come out while you were driving. If the situation is as dangerous as you warned, then how could I leave them for the *crucchi*?'

Luigi swore again. 'We have to trust one another, signor Lassari. Without trust, nothing can work for the better in this war. Now, I shall have to see if the guide we've arranged is willing to accompany more travellers.' He ran his hands through his hair and expelled a long sigh, shaking his head. 'Did you know anything about this, Devora?'

'I had no idea. I'm so sorry.' She held out a hand to help Doctor Kempe descend. He stumbled, his legs crumpling beneath him, and Luigi moved quickly to offer support.

'It will not be an easy journey crossing the border,' Luigi said. 'You might have to delay your departure until you're stronger. *Mannaggia*, damnation!'

They were high in the mountains here – the zigzag peaks of the Alps outlined against the horizon, already covered with a thick mantle of snow. The penetrating air bit at their faces and hands. Devora gazed up at the sheer mountainside, wondering how on earth her mother and Doctor Kempe could possibly manage to navigate those peaks. Maybe they shouldn't have embarked on this crazy journey.

A woman and a priest emerged from the house by the church and they both shook hands with Luigi. 'Come in, all of you. Out of the cold. My housekeeper prepared soup,' the priest said. 'Come in. *Entrate!* Luigi, park the truck in the barn and make sure to close the doors. You never know who might pass by.'

He patted Luigi on his back. '*Dio buono*, but it's good to see you again, Michelozzi. How long has it been?'

A couple of hunting dogs bounded over from a kennel at the side of the porch and Luigi bent to make a fuss of them. One fell on his back in submission as he tickled the dog's stomach.

'I reckon the last time was three autumns ago, Andrea. When we went to look for mushrooms on Monte Nerone.'

And then Devora recognised him from university days. She'd had no inkling he'd been destined for the priesthood. He'd been popular with the girls, like Enrico, but even back then he must have been studying towards his vocation. What a turn-up.

'Andrea?' she said tentatively. 'Andrea Ricci?'

He pulled her into a hug. '*Sì, sono io,* Devora. Yes, it's me. Luigi explained your predicament. And he knows I've helped others along this route, so of course it was natural for him to bring you all this way. We'll sort you out. Don't worry.'

He ruffled the boys' hair and asked them if they were hungry.

'They're always hungry,' Devora said ruefully. 'They have hollow legs.'

'Luckily my housekeeper is a magician and she can rustle up filling meals. She has a healthily stocked *orto* that she zealously guards. Woe betide any porcupine or badger that dares to steal her potatoes!'

The housekeeper, a plump woman of an age hard to fathom, bustled over with a tray of piping hot milky coffees laced with grappa and told Andrea to stop exaggerating, but her smile was a beam of pleasure as she chastised him.

Don Andrea moved to the far side of the kitchen where a large bookshelf stood beside a terracotta woodburning stove. He slid the shelving to one side to reveal a doorway and he beckoned the group to follow.

'This will be your hiding place for the night. The group is larger than I was expecting, but we shall find a way.'

Luigi explained Doctor Kempe was not feeling well and might have to wait a couple of days to build up his strength.

The frown on the young priest's face was fleeting before he said, 'Nothing is impossible, Luigi. God will help us. He's on our side.'

That evening they ate hearty dishes of polenta and mushrooms, accompanied by jugs of strong country wine. Don Andrea had insisted Luigi sleep at least a couple of hours before setting off again to reconnoitre with his contacts from Turin.

'We don't want you as another casualty,' Devora had overheard the priest say. 'You're too important to us.'

Yet again, she realised there was more to her old school friend. When she woke in the early hours, Luigi was already gone from the heap of straw where he had slept and in one way she was pleased. Partings were always difficult. But in another way, she would have liked to have thanked him properly and wished him well. She wondered if he was on his way to meet the girl in the cab. He had told her he would see her soon. What were they up to?

The group had to wait another three days until leaving on their final trek across the mountains to Switzerland. The weather was wet and freezing and Devora worried about how they would cope, especially when don Andrea warned them of the difficult paths, pointing to her mother's footwear, asking her if she had anything sturdier. He returned with a worn pair of rubber boots and a thick pair of socks to make them fit better. The boys laughed at her and the priest promptly found them a job for their cheek: mucking out the cows. When her father tried to pay the priest for Mütti's footwear, he waved the money away. 'There may come a time when I can't help future escapees, but while I can, please accept what I am able to freely offer, signore.'

Devora wandered into the kitchen to help the housekeeper in an effort to take her mind off the trek ahead. But she was shooed away.

'Her kitchen is her kingdom alone,' don Andrea explained. 'Nobody will ever be able to perform in there to her standards. Don't worry, she's quite happy.'

'But how are you managing with extra mouths to feed?'

'I receive funds from *cardinale* Schuster in Milan. He has

urged us to help as many refugees as possible. Please don't worry. Now tell me about yourself and our Luigi.'

She frowned. 'He's a good friend. A very good friend, Andrea, but that's all.'

The young priest was silent for a moment. 'Yes, he's one of the best friends anybody could have. You were studying medicine, weren't you? Before the racial laws? How's that going?'

'I managed to eventually take a couple of papers a while ago now. The authorities made me sit in a corridor outside the university *aula* with three other *racially impure*.' She stressed the last two words with sarcasm. 'Doctor Kempe has been helping me as much as he can. At our camp he used me as his assistant. But I can't wait to resume my studies properly.' She sighed. 'If that will ever happen.'

'Have faith, Devora. There are a couple of Italian students in our group who help with the crossings of the border who are enrolled at Lausanne University. The Swiss look favourably on students following vocational courses in particular. Once you're successfully over the frontier, the students can point you in the right direction.'

'That would be wonderful.' It was a mixed blessing, however. Yes, she could resume her studies to become a doctor, but in a country whose culture she knew little about. She wondered if there would ever come a point when she stopped resenting the way she and her family had been treated by the *nazifascisti*. She hated them so much.

'Would you mind if I offered a blessing to your family and friends before we leave?' The young priest broke into her simmering thoughts with his question.

'Andrea, I wouldn't mind and neither should the others. I believe we follow the same God, after all. But ask them yourself. Best to ask my father. Mamma is extremely traditional – as I have discovered over the past two years.'

'When we are frightened or lost, we always turn to our Maker in the way we know best.'

Devora didn't pursue that comment. She didn't want to disappoint him with her doubts.

During the couple of days before leaving, Devora had observed how Erma tried to ingratiate herself with Ida and Davide. She was full of questions as to how they had gone about arranging their wedding. When they'd been at the camp near Arezzo, she had hardly paid them any attention.

'I enjoyed your wedding in the villa. But Grandfather wouldn't let me marry. However, I plan to celebrate in style once we get to Switzerland and are more settled,' Erma said. 'We shall plan a big wedding, won't we, Emanuele?'

'*Sì, cara.* Yes, dear,' was Emanuele's reply as he ignored Devora's look.

She wondered how many times he would use that phrase in his new life with Erma. He needed to wise up, in her opinion.

They were woken at two o'clock the following morning. Don Andrea blessed them as they bowed their heads. The Catholic blessing was so similar to a Jewish *brachah*, Devora couldn't for the life of her see why her mother's lips remained pursed whilst everyone else responded with the universal 'Amen', their breath adding to the early mist.

Above the Alps, the high moon lit a frosty way through the woods. They traipsed in single file, tall shadows in the eerie light. Don Andrea walked in front with one of the young scouts from the *Aquile Randagie* group who had joined them, whilst a third scout called Doriano brought up the rear to keep them safe.

This might be the last time she and her family walked across Italian soil and each step was like a long goodbye as Devora put one foot in front of another.

CHAPTER 21

Devora walked behind her mother as the group filed upwards along a narrow path above the river Tresa. Don Andrea had urged them to speak as little as possible. Despite the noise of the gushing waters, their words would carry, he'd warned. Progress was painfully slow and at one stage, they stopped stock-still, don Andrea holding up his arm in warning. While they waited, Doriano handed his alpine sticks to her mother and as they set off again after the false alarm, he whispered to Devora not to be afraid, that the noise they had heard had probably been a deer bounding into the undergrowth, but at this stage of the path, smugglers had been known to hold travellers up and demand money. 'It's not named the *passo dei ladri* without reason: the thieves' pass,' he muttered.

Minutes later, a man jumped from the shadows, his rifle raised, and Devora leapt to hold on to her mother, who swayed and cried out, stepping dangerously close to the steep riverbank.

'*Mani in alto,* hands up,' the man shouted, the bottom part of his face concealed by a black scarf. 'Hand over your money and valuables. And be quick!' He spoke in Italian, his accent strange, his words muffled.

Don Andrea stepped towards the intruder, his hands raised in surrender. 'These good people have no money, my friend. They have nothing. They've been hounded from place to place and lost everything. Shame on you.'

The thief stepped forwards. 'I don't need lectures from you, *padre*,' he said, moving closer to the priest.

And in that moment while he was distracted, Emanuele sprang forwards and tackled the thief to the ground. A glint from a steel blade in the light of the moon was followed by a gurgle as his throat was slit. Automatically, Devora ran over to the prone body, her medical instinct to save life foremost in her mind, but it was useless; blood gushed from his wound, soaking into her slacks. There was nothing she could do.

Doriano pulled her away. 'We have to leave him,' he said. 'It's possible he's not alone and they'll come looking for him.'

She watched as the three scouts dragged his body towards the riverbank. Don Andrea made the sign of the cross over him before they pushed his corpse down the slope, his body rolling round and round to splash below them and float away in the fast current.

Erma and Devora's mother were crying and were told to hush. 'We need to move out of this area as quickly as we can,' don Andrea commanded.

Death had come from nowhere and Devora wondered why the man had needed to thieve. What had brought him to this point? Did he have a wife and family to feed? His life was gone, from one minute to the next. And then she pushed these thoughts away and concentrated on helping her mother as they trudged onwards through the chill dawn.

Daylight appeared slowly: a grey lifting followed by a spectacular sunrise that in ordinary circumstances would have brought gasps with its palette of reds and pinks, but it was the signal to stop and rest for the next hours. It was too dangerous to travel by day. They huddled together in bunkers left over from

World War One, trenches lining this stretch of the Linea Cadorna, nibbling on bread and cheese that don Andrea distributed from his rucksack. There was an apple each too and he urged them to try to sleep while he and the scouts took it in turns to keep watch.

Doriano came to sit next to Devora.

'Are you all right?' he asked. 'The first time you see death is always the hardest.'

'I've seen dead bodies before,' she replied. 'I'm a medical student.'

Devora chatted on about her medical studies, how she had dissected bodies in anatomy classes, and Doriano reinforced don Andrea's suggestion of continuing university once she was in Switzerland. He himself had been studying chemistry there but had moved nearer the border when the armistice was announced.

'I'm not Swiss. I'm Italian, brought up in Varese but I was given the opportunity to study in Lausanne before this war started,' he told her. 'I've returned to join up with one of the newly formed scout groups from the area. We are passionate about helping prisoners-of-war escape to Switzerland, as well as your people.

'It's early days,' he continued, 'but so far we've helped over a hundred people along this pass since the start of September. More and more will come with what is happening. At Merano we heard twenty-five Jews were arrested and deported. It's shameful and we've vowed to do everything to help restore freedom. Mussolini banned our scout movement in the 1920s but we are proud to be assembled again, with even more purpose.'

Doriano lowered his voice to tell her that don Andrea was a wanted man, labelled *traditore di capestro* by the *nazifascisti*. The threat of the gallows hung over him.

Devora looked over at the priest on guard, rifle in his hands, with even more respect than before. The boy she remembered from their group at university had found his vocation in more ways than one. The only sign today of his priesthood was his dog collar. Corduroy trousers and a woollen jacket instead of a soutane made him look almost ordinary, she thought. But he was extraordinary. He carried a knapsack and a thick coil of rope on his back and wore an air of quiet authority. More and more stories of horror were emerging with the people she was meeting along this journey and Devora felt yet again frustrated at not being more active in the cause.

Doriano touched her gently on the shoulder, suggesting she try to sleep. He moved away to join the priest and scouts.

Her mother opened her eyes. 'That boy is soft on you,' she muttered. 'Stop flirting and encouraging him.'

Devora shook her head. 'Mamma, you call that flirting? Don't be ridiculous. Try to get some sleep. We still have another night's walk ahead of us.'

'If I'm not dead from exhaustion and cold before then.'

'Mariella, stop your nonsense,' her father said. 'Only a few more hours and we shall be free. *Coraggio*, my dear.'

Before dusk, they were on the move again. Maybe because she was tired and apprehensive, Devora felt the cold more keenly. Knowing her mother was struggling too, she removed her scarf and wound it round her neck.

Her mother squeezed her hand. 'You're a good girl,' she breathed, offering her daughter a rare, sweet smile.

They reached a shallow point of the river where the remains of a bridge spanned the water and they sheltered beneath the arches for a few minutes, sharing water from a bottle. Icicles hung from above and for a while, Devora stared at the dancing reflection of the moon, distorted in the current.

Don Andrea handed the rope to Doriano, who secured one end to a metal stake protruding from the brickwork of the bridge. Then, he removed his boots and tied the laces together to hang them round his neck before rolling up his trousers and wading slowly across the fast-flowing waters to secure it to the sturdy trunk of a fir. He gave a thumbs up to the waiting group.

'We have to cross the river now,' don Andrea announced and Devora's heart sank. How would the elderly manage? She waited for her mother to protest but before anybody could say anything, the priest continued with his instructions.

'My scouts and I will carry anybody who can't manage. Everybody else, remove your shoes and do as Doriano just did, but hold tight to the rope as you cross. The water's ice-cold but shallow at this time of year. Any later in the season and it would be impassable. But I assure you this is the easiest way to get to Switzerland, my friends. We're nearly there.'

The twins treated it as a game, Arturo wagering with his brother: 'I'll give you my catapult if you beat me across.'

'And you can have my ammonite if I'm last,' Alfredo said.

'*Ragazzi!* If you fall, you'll not only get very wet and cold, but you'll be swept down river. No wagers,' don Andrea pronounced severely, 'just get on with it. With care. However, I *might* have a piece of chocolate about my person if you both manage to cross slowly *and* remain dry.'

The temptation of chocolate worked and Devora waited until the boys had safely crossed, followed by Papà, her heart in her mouth when at the middle of the river, he wobbled. But he managed to keep hold of the rope, Doriano encouraging him to hold fast and aim his focus on the opposite bank and not on the flowing water. Mamma clung to the back of the priest, looking like the shell of a tortoise, her eyes squeezed shut. Don Andrea made her seem as light as a bag of feathers and as soon as he dropped her gently on the other bank, Papà embraced her and man and wife held on to each other fast.

Devora watched how her father tenderly rubbed her mother's hands, trying to warm them, wiping tears of fear from her cheeks, kissing her gently, murmuring words of encouragement.

It was rare to see her parents share such an intimate moment and it brought a lump to Devora's throat.

One of the scouts carried Doctor Kempe across and don Andrea returned to carry Erma on his back, as she'd protested that she couldn't possibly manage on her own. He warned her to keep as mute as a fish and not to shout in his ears. Devora smiled wryly. Three days in her company and the priest had the measure of her.

Davide and Ida followed and next it was Devora's turn. She made sure to tie her shoes securely round her neck, remembering the precious cargo stashed in the heels. The water was colder than anything she'd ever experienced and halfway across she could hardly feel her feet. It was Doriano who helped her replace her socks and shoes when she fumbled with numb fingers and she thanked him, ignoring the looks from her mother, who had miraculously mustered enough strength to return to the warpath.

The only person remaining was Emanuele. He stood at the edge of the bank while they waited. Don Andrea urged him to hurry because they needed to get to the frontier before the changing of guards.

'I'm not crossing,' he said, his words carrying to them across the water. 'I'm sorry, Erma. I'll wait for you. I promise. Your life will be better in Switzerland but I'm staying in Italy to fight the *crucchi*. I love you but I can't run away like this.'

He untied the rope from the bridge and didn't wait for a reply, turning to run down the path they had traipsed. Despite Erma's wails, he didn't stop.

Devora wanted to applaud him and shout '*Coraggio!*' She heard the priest mutter, '*Bravo,* Emanuele, *bravo, ragazzo,*' as he reeled in the rope from the river, while she bent to offer what sympathy she could to the distressed girl.

'He loves you, Erma,' Devora said. 'Be brave for him.'

'If he truly loved me, he wouldn't leave without me,' Erma sobbed. 'He's ruined everything.'

It was her grandfather who reprimanded her. 'Stop your crying, *mein Kind*. You'll wake up all the guards in Switzerland.' He pulled her to him, not unkindly. 'You are both very young. There's plenty of time. *Komm*, Erma! Buck up! Devora is correct. You need to be brave.'

CHAPTER 22

Devora and Doctor Kempe walked either side of Erma, supporting her as she sobbed silently for the next hour. She'd tried to run back down the path a couple of times but her grandfather had told her he needed her to look after him. They were the only remaining members of the Kempe family, and they had to stick together.

Devora felt sorry for the girl and encouraged her to keep up her spirits. 'Emanuele told you he'd wait for you. As your grandfather said, you're both very young, Erma, and he wouldn't have been happy going against his principles. You need to hang on to thoughts of a better future together.'

'Yes, but he might be killed before then. Then what future do we have?' Erma said with a sniff and another fit of sobs.

'We all have to do what we have to do in these times. Nothing is straightforward in war.'

She couldn't help feeling she was describing herself with those words. She was doing her duty by sticking with her family, but was it the right thing? A grey storm continued to rumble in her head.

After an hour of steep climbing, they reached the summit and don Andrea held his finger to his mouth, speaking softly to the group. 'Crouch down, all of you. We are very near the perimeter fence of the border. One of the guards we know has cut a hole near those trees but we have to approach with stealth. They'll change the guards soon and our friend will be going off duty. We can't count on the new watch being sympathetic. I have a couple of the bottles of olive oil they so love in my knapsack but it would be best not to have to bargain at all. Once you're safely through, I'll leave you. Stay hidden and move as far away from the border as you can. A group from Bern is expecting your arrival and they'll look after you. God speed and good luck, my friends.'

'Thank you, *padre*,' Friedrich said. 'I speak on behalf of all of us when I say we shall be eternally grateful to you.'

Don Andrea shook his head. 'I am only one person in this chain. There are plenty of others involved in the planning. Now, I suggest Doctor Kempe and Erma go first, then the boys and their parents, followed by you three.' He pointed to Devora and the young couple. 'Keep as low as possible and do not speak while you cross.'

He checked there were no sentries patrolling and then told Erma and Doctor Kempe to keep low and head for the trees. Once they were safely across, he pushed the boys and Devora's parents to leave.

Her heart pumping like mad, Devora crossed her fingers as she watched the people most precious to her in the world crouch right down and move across the meadow to the trees.

'You go first, Davide,' Ida said. 'I'll watch carefully to see how you do it.' She kissed her young husband and once he was on his way, she put her hands to her stomach and whimpered, clutching hold of Devora. 'I can't go... *ahi*, the pains. I have such pains.'

'It's the fear,' Devora said. 'Come with me. We'll find somewhere for you to relieve yourself.'

'But hurry, signorine,' don Andrea said. 'We have very little time.'

Devora found a rock and Ida approached, holding her belly; her face was wreathed in pain.

'It's the baby,' Ida said. 'I think it's coming. But it's too early,' she muttered as she bit her lip. '*Ahi, mi fa male.* It hurts.' She collapsed to the grass and Devora pulled up Ida's wide skirts and gasped. She was indeed with child. Her pregnancy had been well concealed beneath her voluminous clothing. Devora kicked herself for simply thinking, even with her experience, that Ida had gained weight.

'I can't go on, but don't stop Davide from leaving. *Please...*'

Devora hurried from her to explain to the priest. 'She doesn't want to hold her husband back. Could you tell him I'll stay to help her and as soon as we can, we'll join them in Switzerland. She can't travel in her condition. The baby's arriving any minute now.' Worries about her parents and brothers approaching the border swirled around her head but delivering Ida's baby was more important now.

'He won't want to leave her, you can be sure of that. Leave it with me, Devora. Will you be all right? Can you manage?'

'I've helped with a couple of births in the last months. But we need to find shelter.'

'There's a shepherd's hut nearby. We've used it in the past in storms. I'll help you get her there and then I'll go to Davide. Oh, my dear Lord! Why didn't she let us know about her condition?'

He sighed as they joined their hands to make a seat to carry Ida halfway back down the slope and into a meadow where a stone hut was partially hidden within a tangle of brambles. They set her gently down and Ida drew her knees up to her stomach, moaning.

With a last anxious look, don Andrea left the two girls alone.

There was no need to examine Ida to measure her cervix. She was already trying to push out her baby.

'Ida, listen to me. Don't push yet. Look at me. You need to take this more slowly,' Devora said, trying to instil authority and calm into her voice. She didn't want Ida to tear. She had absolutely no equipment to deal with that. She'd had to leave her stethoscope and textbooks behind at the priest's house for this stage of the journey. Neither did she have any idea of Ida's blood group or anything with which to measure her pressure, but there was no time to worry about details. The birth was happening.

Hunkered down in the mercifully clean and dry hut, Devora thanked all her stars that Ida's delivery was a simple one. As the baby was pushed out Devora felt a glow of purpose, knowing that whatever happened, Ida had brought new life into this world. Then while Ida's baby girl suckled at her breast, Devora gently placed her hand on Ida's tummy and pulled out the placenta, using her shoelace to tie off the cord.

'How I wish Davide were here to see his daughter,' Ida said, a tear trickling down her cheek. 'We agreed to name the baby Nechama if it was a girl. It means "comfort".' She looked up at Devora, her eyes beseeching her. 'Can we say a *Kaddish* together? Will you recite a prayer of thanksgiving with me?'

Devora wiped mucus from the baby's head with a clean headscarf she had packed in her rucksack. 'I'm not so good with the prayers, Ida. If you say it, I'll join you with my heart. Our family – we never celebrated much – not until we came to Villa Oliveto. My mother would know one, but I don't. Sorry.'

'You have no need to say sorry. If you hadn't been with me

today, I don't know what would have happened.' Ida gazed down at her baby, her words faltering at first, stronger as she went on.

'Welcome, welcome to this breathtaking world. Daddy and I have been waiting for you, little Nechama. Waiting to see your beautiful face, to hear the sound of your cry, to kiss you, hold you, rock you. You are the fruit of our love...'

Ida stopped, her voice cracking. She bent her head and Devora watched tears splash down on the baby's head, like water from a rabbi's hands at a *mikvah* ceremony.

Devora was moved to tears herself as she listened to Ida's soft voice, the scene before her timeless, represented by artists of all faiths. Urbino's own famous painter, Raffaello Sanzio, and his images of the holy mother and child came to mind.

Making sure Ida was comfortable, covering mother and baby with her own shawl, Devora left them for a few moments to step outside. Delivering the baby on her own had been both terrifying and wonderful and she was shaking. She wrapped her arms across her chest and breathed deeply to restore calm. The sky was red, a shepherd's morning warning of bad weather, a scarlet backdrop to the mountains all about. In the distance cowbells clanged and birds chirruped in the trees over where she had last seen her family disappear. She crossed her fingers, praying they had successfully passed through the border. Don Andrea would surely come to find them soon in the hut and take Ida somewhere to recuperate and then Devora would be on her way, following her family into neutral territory on a journey of hope.

She found a tree laden with apples beside a shallow stream tripping over stones to the valley below. Ida needed to eat and drink to restore her energy and feed her baby. For the first days, colostrum was all that baby Nechama would need. Her name meant 'comfort' in Hebrew, Ida had said. There was small comfort in their world at the moment, but there was nothing as strong as life itself. With any luck, Ida would be on her way in a couple of weeks to join Davide in celebrating the little miracle they had produced.

A shot rang out as she reached to pick an apple and she ducked to lie prostrate on the grass, her heart racing.

CHAPTER 23

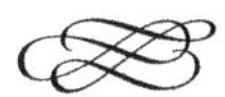

Footsteps approached and she raised her head to see a middle-aged man, a rifle slung over his back. There was no escape and she sat up, raising her hands. 'Don't shoot. *Non sparare,*' she said.

'Leave my apples alone. There'll be none left to store for this winter.' The man's Italian accent was sing-song.

'*Scusate!*' she said, kneeling up slowly, her hands still in the air. 'I'm sorry.'

'Are you alone? There've been so many of you passing through my meadows these past days. I have to guard what's mine, you know. Those apples are for market. They're not ready to eat. They'll give you stomach ache.'

He bent to pull her to her feet. He seemed harmless enough and she decided to take a risk. He could possibly hand them over to the authorities but she reckoned he had only used his gun in warning. Whatever way she looked at it, she needed help with Ida and the baby. Don Andrea should have returned by now. Something must have happened and she couldn't wait forever for him to come back. Ida needed food and somewhere clean to stay to avoid infection.

'I'm not alone, signore. I've helped a woman give birth this morning.' She pointed to the hut. 'Is that yours too?'

His eyes wide, he nodded. 'Show me,' he said. 'But this had better not be a trick.' He pulled his rifle round to his front again as he followed her.

When Devora pushed open the rickety door to the hut, the grin on the old man's face was almost as wide as the river they had crossed. 'Well, well, well. If it's not Mary and Jesus,' he said. 'But where is Joseph?'

Signora Madlaine Zanzi was as round as her husband Alvaro was skinny. She immediately set to when he brought his new visitors to their home, making up a bed for Ida and ordering her husband to clean up the wooden cradle immediately and to bring it downstairs to set by the fire. Then she told him to go and milk their cow and bring in a jug for the new mother. He bustled here and there and Devora thought that he was likely so skinny because his wife had him constantly on the go.

Signora Zanzi wore traditional dress: a white, embroidered blouse and a full skirt, her grey-blonde hair wound around her head in two fat plaits. Round her generous waist, she wore a red-striped linen apron tied in a neat bow at the back.

'We never had children of our own,' she told Devora, rocking little Nechama against her pillowy bosom as Ida went to relieve herself in the outside privy. 'So, I never expected our cradle to be used. Thanks be to heaven it has no woodworm.'

There were no questions asked in those first hours. The middle-aged couple simply accepted their unusual guests, opened their home and hearts to them and made sure they had everything they needed. An embroidered nightdress in soft lawn cotton was produced by signora Zanzi from a chest perfumed with sprigs of lemon balm. 'I never stopped making a trousseau for a future child, but that future never arrived.

Best you use this, Ida, rather than the moths make a meal of it.'

They learned that Madlaine Zanzi was Swiss and had met her husband when he had brought his sheep to sell over the border at the market in Ponte Tresa. 'Alvaro was handsome back then. I wasn't the only girl who set eyes at him. He might be small, but he's very strong. Still is!' She winked at the girls over the dough she was kneading on her floured kitchen table.

Within hours, they were all on first names and Madlaine kept producing food to 'bring strength back to the new mother'. Little cakes stuffed with preserved fruits, apricot biscuits, a hearty stew with dumplings, raw eggs whisked up with honey from their beehives, with fresh cream added, 'to help bring in your milk', and so many cups of fresh milk that Ida protested she was beginning to feel like a cow herself.

On day four when Ida's milk had come in with a vengeance, her breasts swollen fit to burst, little Nechama sucked and dozed peacefully next to her mother. There was a knock at the door and Devora and Ida looked at each other.

'Might it be Davide?' Ida said, her eyes full of hope. 'I can't wait to see his face when he meets Nechama.'

Devora went to look through the little guest bedroom window that looked out over the farmhouse porch, but she couldn't see anybody. She held her finger to her mouth as she turned back to Ida. Whoever it was, it was highly unlikely to be Davide. How could he have found them in the Zanzis' farmhouse, tucked away as it was in a fold of the alpine meadows? It was more likely guards, searching for fugitives. By now, her family would be safely in Switzerland, waiting for her to join them and once Ida and her baby were settled, she planned to cross the border too. She prayed Nechama wouldn't wake and cry. She'd started to be colicky, Ida's milk flowing too fast for her at times and Madlaine had shown Ida how to massage Nechama's tiny tummy and bind her sore breasts with cabbage leaves. For a woman who hadn't given birth, she knew a lot about babyhood, and Devora had said so.

'I keep lambs and ewes, my dear,' Madlaine had replied. 'It's common sense. When they cry it's either because of hunger, pain or because they want their mother's attention.'

The two young women heard heavy footsteps climb the wooden stairs and Devora's heart hammered. There was no escaping the bedroom. The window was too small to squeeze through and, anyway, she would never leave Ida to fend for herself. She picked up a chair and tiptoed to the side of the door.

Ida's eyes were round with terror as she watched her friend poised, the chair raised above her head.

Upon hearing Madlaine's voice, 'It's only me, my dears,' and seeing her plump hand pushing the bedroom door open, Devora's shoulders slumped in relief and she lowered the chair.

'There's a priest to see you, Devora. Come, child. He needs to talk to you.' She went over to Ida and straightened her pillows, touching the baby's peachy cheeks, and Devora hurried downstairs.

Don Andrea stood with his back to her, warming himself at the stove and when he turned, his hands outstretched, the expression on his face made her stop with a sharp cry.

'What's happened?' she asked.

'Come and sit down,' he said. 'I've been scouring the countryside, searching for you. This place was my last resort.'

'We couldn't stay in that hut. Ida needed food and better shelter. She's had a baby daughter. But what's the matter? Tell me.' She lowered her voice, the floorboards an insufficient buffer to the carrying of sound.

The priest sighed. 'It didn't go to plan. There was...' He paused. 'A hiccough.'

'What? Tell me, Andrea.' She resorted instinctively to the Christian name she knew from the past. Her heart filled with fear. What about her parents, the twins?

'When we got to the fence, the usual guards were not on duty. I'm afraid it happens like this sometimes. The Swiss guards intercepted your family and the others. They weren't convinced by your father's story, that they were Jews escaping. They demanded to see their identity documents and, of course, they only had false papers. I tried to argue for them, but none of the guards were sympathetic. They wanted proof they were Jews but your parents didn't have their original papers with them.'

'Of course not. They've hidden them in our house in Urbino. I can go and get them. Prove to them—'

'That's not necessary, Devora. The Swiss guards wouldn't let them pass and they handed them over to the Italian *guardie di finanza*, who sent them back to sort their Jewish documents at the Consulate in Milan. They were taken to the station under guard and escorted onto a train.'

Her head in her hands, she cried out, 'I should be with them. How will they cope?'

'They won't be abandoned, Devora. We have contacts everywhere. Try not to worry. And *cardinale* Schuster in Milan, he will do his best to help. I'm not too concerned about them, but...'

'What? What more? Tell me.' She grabbed at the priest's hands.

'Davide. He... tried to escape. My contact told me he jumped from the truck on the way to the station and... he was shot... in the back. He died immediately.'

With a deep intake of breath and a look of horror, she indicated the ceiling. 'Ida... what am I going to tell her?'

There were a few seconds of silence before he replied, his voice low, anguished. 'Maybe don't tell her for the time being.

Let her concentrate on the new life she's brought into the world.'

'I have to go and find my family.' Devora stood up and he blocked her way.

'What is the good of putting yourself in danger too, Devora? It helps nobody. Your family is being looked after. You should stay here and wait for them to return and then travel to Switzerland together. In the meantime, I'll sort new guides and a different crossing point. Your task for now is to stay and look after Ida.'

He pulled her into an embrace. 'Try not to worry. Your parents and brothers will be back with you before you know. I'll personally bring them to you. With their new documents.'

'And how shall I get through? Without mine?'

'We have other ways. Rest easy, Devora. I have to go. *Arrivederci*. God be with you.'

She stopped herself from asking why God wasn't with her now. Where had He ever been during these past years of persecution? Why had He taken Davide from Ida and denied Nechama a father? What was the use of saying 'God be with you', if God wasn't there in the first place? But don Andrea was already shutting the door behind him and she needed all the energy and calm she could muster for waiting to see her family again, as well as caring for Ida. Poor Ida. She lowered her head to her hands on the table and silently wept.

She hadn't heard footsteps on the stairs but she felt soft hands stroking her hair and looked up through tear-soaked lashes to signora Madlaine's look of concern.

'What has happened, my dear?'

In a whisper, Devora told her about her family's failure to cross the border and Davide's death and the kindly woman took her in her arms, saying nothing until Devora's crying subsided.

Eventually, Devora drew back and Madlaine handed her a clean kitchen cloth to wipe her face.

'I have to keep it from Ida for as long as necessary,' Devora said, looking anxiously towards the ceiling, the baby's crying now muffling their conversation. 'She needs to be strong before I tell her. Her milk could dry up.'

'I will help. Let *me* spend more time with the dear girl. You might give away the terrible news. You're too close to her and she'll read it in your eyes. While you wait for your family to return, go for walks, help my husband gather our fruit. Try not to be alone with Ida until your spirits are calmer. You have enough to worry about.'

She wrung her hands. 'These are terrible times but they cannot last forever. We have to cling to that.' She rose from her chair and went to move a pan, opening the stove door to throw in another log. 'I shall prepare Ida my special dumpling soup tonight. We'll build her up and make her strong to face what she has to face. Go and find parsley for me from my kitchen garden. The fresh air will dry your tears.' She handed Devora a small knife and encouraged her out of the door.

'*Grazie,* Madlaine.'

A few days earlier, Madlaine and Alvaro Zanzi had been complete strangers. Now they were like family and for that at least, Devora was grateful. She wandered into the gated vegetable garden where bees from hives in the far corner buzzed on scented thyme and marigolds. Fennel was ready to be harvested, delicate pale-green fronds waving in a slight breeze. A few borlotti pods remained hanging from supports, the beans drying for next year's sowing seeds. Next year. *Who knows what will happen next year?* she wondered.

Here, in the middle of the lush green countryside, war seemed distant. But for how long would that last? She gave a shiver as she bent to cut a handful of flat parsley, her thoughts turning to other friends caught up in this terrible time. Where was Shira now? Had she stayed at Villa Oliveto or started on her journey south? What would she wear to make herself blend in? She spoke excellent Italian but how would she know which route to take? She had never been to Italy before. She wondered if they would ever meet again and if she should have tried harder to persuade her to come to Switzerland. She felt responsible for her, but it had been enough to cope with her own family. Her mind full of questions, she tapped on the kitchen window and Madlaine came to the door and took the herbs.

'I'm taking your advice and going for a walk with my thoughts.'

'*Brava!* Well done. Supper will be ready in one hour.'

Devora took a track that led past a meadow where two cows munched on the grass, their bells clanging like musical notes as they bent to find the next fresh clump. In the near distance, Alvaro was busy chopping logs and he waved as she took a narrow path leading upwards. Her shoes were wearing thin on the soles and she tried to avoid stones but it was almost impossible. She would ask Madlaine if she had an old pair of clogs to lend her for the time being. The last thing she wanted was for her shoes to fall apart, and to lose her mother's precious jewellery hidden in her heels.

Over the following days, she felt almost guilty as she tramped the countryside, her cheeks rosy from the warm October sun. As she walked, her mind seemed to untangle, her worries decrease and she became convinced that everything would be fine in the end. In a couple of days' time, Papà and Mütti – why was it that Mamma never sounded right when thinking of her mother? – and her two scamps of brothers, would be back from fetching their documents. With don Andrea's help, they would all cross into Switzerland together and their troubles would be over. Then when the war was finished, and the *fascisti* were conquered and dispatched, they would return to Urbino and resume their lives. She had to believe that or she would fall apart.

She helped harvest baskets of apples and pears, wrapping each one in straw to store for the winter months in one of the outbuildings. It was only one week since her parents had left, but the muscles on her arms and legs were growing stronger from the physical work. Alvaro was easy company. A gentle man of few words and ready smiles of encouragement.

She pushed the problem of when to tell Ida about Davide right out of her mind. For the time being she seemed content enough in Madlaine's cosy home. The two women could almost be mother and daughter, so close had they become, sharing recipes for stews and cakes. No, Devora had too many other worries to contend with: the welfare of her parents, her twin brothers, and although she was beginning to think him a lost cause, her thoughts strayed to Enrico too. When would she see him again? And did he ever think of her? Her former life in Urbino seemed so very far away.

CHAPTER 24

SUMMER 1943

ENRICO

I'd never made love in a barn before – the stuff of bucolic Boccaccio stories, brimming with bodily delight. The sweet scent of hay, her sweet scent, her skin paler, more tender in those places veiled by clothes, her most private parts. Her nipples dark, her hair darker, arms thrown back behind her head as my mouth travelled down her body.

To tell the truth, we decided not to repeat the romps in the hay, the stubble scratchy and full of tiny insects that irritated our bare skin. She smothered giggles as she picked stalks from my hairs. Outside, we heard peasants at work in the meadows, folding round the city edges like patterned skirts, the striking of workers' hoes in rhythm with their songs. They were so near I could make out every word of their verses and the fact we could be discovered any moment heightened our passion.

We did it anywhere we could. One afternoon we came across a stream with rock pools, deep within the woods, the water ice-cold. Our skin prickled with bumps as we waded in. *Pelle d'oca*, I said. Goosebumps. It was an expression she'd never heard and she couldn't understand until I tweaked at a hair in her groin to show her the raised bump and then she slapped me, jumped on me, pinned me to the bank with her thighs astride mine. So then, naturally, one thing led to another and our groans of pleasure washed along with the water that played over the boulders.

As we lay afterwards on our backs on a flat rock, drowsy from our efforts, we heard the drone of an aeroplane high above the canopy of beech leaves dancing shadows on our skin. Half a dozen silver shapes like fish swam across the sky. British Flying Fortresses. They would not drop their bombs upon Urbino. A huge red cross had been painted on the roof of our Ducal Palace from when the *alleati* and *tedeschi* had agreed not to touch our city of art. These planes were likely bound for Milan or Bologna.

'They're not interested in us, *amore*,' I told my lover. But the mood was broken and we pulled on our clothes. I drove her back to where she was staying, reminding her to wait for messages about our next meeting.

It wasn't easy to get away. The war had intensified. But then I was sent to Ferrara as part of a team investigating a massacre. Eleven citizens had been picked out by *squadre fasciste* in reprisal for the assassination of one of their leaders. The city was up in arms – the massacred were innocent, the citizens claimed, and we'd been sent to calm muddy waters.

I took her with me. Dangerous, but in another way, not. For, thankfully, the citizens of Ferrara were mostly sympathetic to their many Jews.

We stayed in a hotel that time. An upmarket *palazzo* near the centre where *tedeschi* dined. I told the proprietor we were newly-weds; we did not wish to be disturbed. She wore one of my mother's gold rings, 'borrowed' from Mamma's overflowing jewellery box in her dressing room. The proprietor couldn't do enough for us, bringing food and wine to our suite, turning the sign on the door to *non disturbare*.

She loved the bath, the luxury of hot water, perfumed soaps and clean linen towels a new experience. I joined her and we soaped each other, spilling water as we slipped about in the tub. I took photographs I look at even now: her hair sleek, wet and straight, covering her breasts like black weeds. Another where she stands, her hands concealing herself, unwittingly striking the pose of a dark-haired Botticelli's Venus. One where she sits on the side of the bath, her robe slipping off her shoulders to reveal a glimpse of full breasts. And in every image, her laughter and unashamed joy sound through these fading prints that I have kept all these years. I could have sold them to the photographic studio along the portico, where many men in Urbino, and no doubt many wives, know of the special room at the back. Behind a door hidden by a black velvet curtain is a snug lined with a gallery of erotic paintings. And a magic lantern, where for fifty lire, a man can dream as he views women he will never know, his greedy gaze following their saucy poses. But I would never show my photographs to another soul. She belonged to me.

The investigation at Ferrara added another layer to my disquiet. We interviewed relatives of civilians who had been lined up against Castello Estense and it was plain to us all that none of them qualified as *partigiani* or rebel rousers. My misgivings about the direction in which the *nazifascisti* were heading intensified. So, what was I doing amongst their ranks?

CHAPTER 25

OCTOBER 1943

DEVORA

In the distance the Alps were mantled with white that crept further down the peaks with each passing day. Crossing into Switzerland would be more difficult from now on. It had been over two weeks since don Andrea had left and with each day Devora grew more anxious for news about her family. The initial respite at the Zanzi farmhouse began to pall.

When the priest came to find her, Devora was pegging out Nechama's nappies on the line, the towelling squares dancing in the October wind. She turned to see Andrea, dressed once again in his long black soutane that flapped against his legs. There was no smile on his face when she greeted him.

'Come and sit with me, Devora,' he said, leading her to an old bench patterned with lichen.

'Why do I have to sit?' she asked, the empty basket cradled against her hip. 'People are asked to sit before bad news.' She remained standing and so did he.

'I'm afraid...'

At those words, she dropped the basket and clasped her hands to her mouth.

'I'm very sorry, Devora, but your family...'

'Not dead,' she screamed. 'Not that...' She crumpled to the ground and he bent to pull her up.

'No, not dead. I'm afraid they were picked up by the *tedeschi* in Milan when they returned to sort their documents. There was a raid, *un rastrellamento.* Many Jews were arrested that day. And they were put on a train and taken away. I'm so sorry...'

'Where? Where have they been taken? I have to go after them. I told you I should have gone and helped them and now look what's happened.' She pummelled at his chest. 'It's your fault. I should have listened to myself. You said they'd be looked after. Which prison have they taken them to? Can't you arrange something with one of your contacts?' Her questions were thrown at him like stones and before he could answer, she picked up the basket and strode towards the house and he chased after her.

'They've been taken away from Italy, Devora. We're not sure where to. A labour camp in Germany, we think.'

She turned with a look of disbelief. 'Labour camp? Germany? But my parents *left* Germany to come here. It will kill them to return. What labour can two young boys and an elderly couple possibly do for anybody? Why? Why have they been taken to a labour camp? It doesn't make sense.'

'We've been trying to find out but it's not easy. All I can tell you is that hundreds of people, old and young, were packed into wagons and taken north. It was impossible to get near them. There were guards shooting at anybody who tried to intervene. And they had fierce dogs. But we're trying to find out where they've gone.'

She tore the apron from her waist. 'I can't stay here one moment longer. I have to go to Milan to find out for myself. I knew it was wrong not to go with them. They need me...' She tore at her hair, her voice hysterical.

He caught hold of her. 'Devora. You must not. You cannot. Milan is crawling with *tedeschi* going from house to house, turning places upside down to hunt for Jews. In Rome, over one thousand have been arrested in the last days. The Republic of Salò has issued orders for the capture of every single Jew in the land and increased the bounty from five thousand lire to nine thousand. The situation is dire. It won't be long before they come looking for you here. You're in great danger.'

She shook her head. 'And Ida? And the baby? Are they to flee like rabbits too?'

He held out both hands with a touch of resignation. 'Even babies were forced onto the train. Some...' He paused, lowering his voice. 'Some were dragged from their mothers' arms...'

Devora was momentarily speechless at the horrors he was describing. But Andrea pressed on.

'We have somewhere you can hide. There is a hospital in Viggiù. We've already taken others there who are trying to cross into Switzerland. That too is growing riskier. And Heinrich Rothmund, the head of the Swiss police division, he's issued a statement decreeing that any foreigner, whether civil or military, who tries to cross into Switzerland from north Italy is to be stopped. More than ten thousand fled across on one single day last month and the authorities are clamping down. They can't cope with the influx and are demanding what they call onward migration.'

'What choice do I have, Andrea? What choice? It seems no matter what happens, we never have a choice.' She paced the grass, wringing her hands. 'What can I do? Tell me. But this time, don't spin me empty promises.'

'If you were my wife or daughter, I would advise you to come away with me. Hide until the danger is over.'

. . .

The Zanzis did not want Ida and the baby to leave. They showed Devora and don Andrea a hiding place in their attic.

'We keep our most precious things up here,' Madlaine said as she climbed the ladder to a storage area in the eaves. 'But what does precious mean to us now? We have no children to pass on my gold jewellery and my mother's dinner set. More precious to us now are the lives of Ida and her child.'

The space was dusty; cobwebs hung like curtains from the rafters where an assortment of clutter was stored: two large trunks, odd chairs that needed mending and an ornate mirror frame, its glass badly spotted.

Madlaine moved down the attic space, crouching low to avoid banging her head. Behind a box of used bottles draped with cobwebs stood a cupboard riddled with woodworm.

'They can hide behind here if necessary. But I doubt anyone will come to search this farm. It's so out of the way.' With that she pushed the cupboard aside to reveal an opening to a further space in the eaves.

'We can put a mattress down and make Ida and the baby as comfortable as possible. Surely she will be better up here than in a town? I can sweep the place clean. What do you think?'

'And what if the baby cries, signora?' don Andrea asked. 'In the hospital, there's a maternity wing. If your place was searched, one squeak from baby Nechama and they would be discovered. And you would be punished for harbouring them. Severely punished,' he added.

Devora watched as joy seeped from Madlaine's eyes.

'We are old. I don't care what happens to us. But the baby, Ida... I couldn't bear it if anything happened to them.'

A single tear trailed down her cheek and splashed onto her embroidered blouse.

'You are right,' she said, her voice resigned. 'I'll prepare a basket of food for the journey,' she said, lifting her apron to wipe her eyes.

Later that evening, they left. Devora could hardly bear to witness Madlaine's brave sorrow as she hugged mother and child to her bosom. 'There will always be a home here for you,' she told Ida. 'Always.'

'Davide and I will return as soon as we can,' Ida said. 'Thank you, Madlaine. And when we baptise Nechama, will you be her *Kvaterin*?'

At Madlaine's puzzled look, Ida explained. 'The person who brings baby to a *simchat bat*.' She turned to Devora for help.

'It's like a baptism, Madlaine. She's asking if you can be like a godmother to welcome Nechama,' Devora explained. 'It's an honour.'

With that, Madlaine reached to undo the gold chain with a Madonna medallion from round her neck. Without words, she nodded her head and pushed it into Ida's pocket.

Ida watched the woman age years in those last minutes. Another embrace and then Madlaine turned back to her house and shut the door.

Don Andrea had borrowed a horse to carry Ida and Nechama, bound close in a shawl to her mother, down the steep mountain path that night. He carried a kerosene lamp to guide the way and the light jerked back and forth across the stone-strewn path.

'Did you know, don Andrea, this is a very special night for us? Eighth of October?' Ida asked. 'The holiest of the year? When we traditionally refrain from pleasure and repent for what we've done wrong. It seems apt, don't you think?'

'Yom Kippur,' he replied. 'Yes, I do know.'

'It seems to me,' Devora said resentfully, thinking of her parents and the twins, 'there has been no pleasure for far too long. And why should we repent, Ida? Others should repent. Not us.'

'*Shh!* Devora. I know you like to be controversial,' Ida replied. 'Tomorrow is the start of a new year for us. Everything will work out, you'll see.'

Devora had to bite her tongue to stop herself from arguing. What good did it serve? Ida was sweet, trusting. Her faith was important. But she would need every hectogram of faith she could scrape together once she heard about Davide's fate, Devora thought, bitterness mounting in her heart. Nothing was going right.

She trailed after the horse led by the priest, like an actress in a ghastly biblical scene, willing herself to stay strong and positive. Where were Mütti and Vati? And the boys – were they behaving themselves? What were they eating? Where were they sleeping? How was Mütti managing? She tried not to torment herself with worry. It wouldn't help anybody. But it was hard. So very hard.

The hospital was as safe a place as any for the time being. Ida settled in with her baby in a ward for premature babies, run by a formidable nun: tall and imposing, rosary beads on her belt clicking as she walked. The hospital was also used for wounded German soldiers but Suor Chiara seemed to ignore the fact they were the enemy and bossed them about as if they were tiresome young boys. No man was allowed to set foot within the baby wing, with their big feet and uniforms that smelled of cigar smoke, she said. One German grumbled she was like his mother. He had travelled and fought all the way down Europe only to meet up with another dragon. Devora understood everything they said, but did not let on.

Ida and Devora wore nuns' habits. Another change in identity, Devora thought bitterly. She was losing herself a little more every day.

Ida sang as she washed nappies and Devora had to warn her

not to sing '*Durme, Durme*', a Jewish lullaby she'd crooned since Nechama's birth. They had also changed her baby's name to Benedetta.

'Benedetta fills my heart as much as Nechama. After all, blessed is what we've been,' Ida said, translating the Italian name.

On the second evening, tasks completed, Devora knocked on Suor Chiara's door.

'*Avanti!* Enter!' The nun closed the notebook on her desk and replaced the top on her fountain pen.

'Yes?'

'Sister,' Devora began.

'Is there a problem, signorina?'

Despite the woman's formidable gaze, Devora dived in. 'I'd like to do more than empty bedpans, Suor Chiara. I'm medically trained. Not qualified yet, but I've had lots of experience in the past months, helping our camp doctor.'

The nun leant back in her chair, her hands clasped. 'But this is marvellous. Why did you not say so before? There's *plenty* you can help with. In fact...' She opened her book and consulted a list.

'There is a particular patient I would like you to help. We keep her isolated from the other patients. The girl has terrible injuries all over her body, but it's her mind that will take longer to heal. I shall entrust her to you. In confidence,' she added.

Devora followed her from the office. The nun rapped on the door of a room at the end of the corridor and entered immediately. The room was stuffy, the windows tightly shut and Devora went to open them but Suor Chiara stopped her, shaking her head. 'Lisa doesn't like them open.'

All that Devora could see of Lisa was a thin form under the bedcovers, turned towards the wall, a sheet pulled up above her shoulders.

'*Buonasera*,' Suor Chiara said, her voice raised slightly, her tone calm as she moved to the woman's bedside to adjust the bedcovers. 'How are you this evening? Do you fancy a bowl of vegetable broth? I made it fresh today with greens and potatoes from the cloister *orto*. And it's very good, though I say so myself.'

A shrug was the only response.

'I have a new nurse. She'll be looking after you this evening.'

Another shrug. The woman did not turn to acknowledge Devora's presence.

'She will need to change your dressings.'

Another shrug.

Suor Chiara indicated the tray of linen strips and instruments on the bedside table and left Devora to cope with the patient.

Gently, gently does it, Devora thought as the door closed, leaving her alone with her difficult patient. She turned up the flame on the oil lamp to better see and the woman croaked at her. 'Go away. There's no point in changing my dressings. No point.'

'Suor Chiara tells me they haven't been done today. Your wounds will become infected.'

'Suor Chiara can go to hell. And she will join me there.'

Devora sat down by the bed. 'What makes you think you're both going to hell? I dread to think how the devil would cope with that nun. She's quite something.'

'There's no point either in trying to make me laugh. Don't waste your time on me. Go and nurse someone else who needs you more.' Lisa turned slowly in the bed and Devora nearly dropped the dish of instruments. She knew this girl. She had pulled a mask from her face to reveal a mess of scars. Her nose was broken. Her left eye socket was empty, oozing yellow pus; the other eye was closed, purple and black bruising circling the socket. But Devora knew that if she were to open her damaged eye, it would be forget-me-not blue. She was Luigi's mysterious passenger. Her arms were bandaged and fresh blood had seeped onto the sheets. She opened her mouth in a ghastly snarl of missing teeth.

'What happened to you? Oh my good God. Were you involved in an accident?'

'If you want to call prolonged beating of a woman tied to a chair with wire by a bastard *fascista* an accident,' Lisa replied through broken teeth, a slight lisp to her words. 'And of all the nurses to come across...' She bit her lip. 'Luigi's friend. What are the odds?'

Devora had suspected something covert had been going on between Luigi and this girl. She'd asked Luigi to tell her, but he'd promptly said to forget about it. Shocked, she asked, 'And Luigi? Was he hurt too?'

'Luigi knows nothing about this.'

Lisa winced with pain and Devora automatically reverted to carer, her patient's condition of primary importance. 'Let me wash you and then I'll deal with those soiled bandages,' Devora said.

'And if I tell you I don't want you to? That I won't let you? That there's no point? That I want to be left alone to die?'

'Then, I'd have to answer that I don't want you to die,' Devora said, reaching out to dab tentatively at the woman's face with saline solution. 'And I'm damn sure Luigi wouldn't want that either. This might sting.'

'A sting is nothing,' she said. 'Nothing.'

Nevertheless, she grimaced as Devora gently cleaned pus from what looked like cigarette burns on the girl's cheeks.

'*Brava*, you're doing well,' Devora murmured as she cleaned her patient, who had turned back to the wall. Easing up the girl's nightdress, Devora frowned when she saw livid bruises on her back and thighs. When she encouraged her to turn over, Devora saw more bruises and circles of cigarette burns round her nipples. Every part of the poor girl's body had been attacked. 'Whoever did this to you is a monster,' she said, tears stinging her eyes.

'Because I didn't tell him what he wanted to know.' Her voice trailed off after she spoke another two words. 'Not everything...'

'What do you mean?'

But that was all she got from the girl called Lisa that evening. Suor Chiara returned a few minutes later with a small bowl of soup and nodded her head with approval when she saw Lisa had allowed herself to be treated.

Devora fed her half the broth but that was all she wanted and she shook her head, refusing adamantly to swallow more.

'*Sei stata bravissima*, Lisa,' Devora said. 'You've done really well. Thank you for letting me help you.'

She left the room and leant against the door, steadying her shock at what she had seen. Another victim of this war. She was collecting them as she went along. When was it going to end? And how could she get a message to Luigi to tell him about his friend? He had warned her not to contact him.

That night she tossed and turned, unable to sleep, torturing herself with thoughts of her parents and brothers, hoping they were safe. What man was capable of doing to man, defied belief. Surely nothing would happen to a middle-aged couple and two innocent boys? Surely not. Lisa's damaged face kept superimposing on images of her beloved family's faces, no matter how hard she willed sleep to come.

She was still awake when the birds began to chorus and creeping out of bed to let Ida sleep on, she made her way to the kitchen in search of coffee.

CHAPTER 26

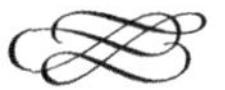

NOVEMBER 1943

Suor Chiara delegated tasks to her small band of nurses at the daily morning meeting. 'Ida, you need to rest today. Otherwise, your milk will dry up and we have neither wet nurses nor spare powdered milk.' She handed the young mother a pile of old sheets. 'Sit in the nursery and tear these into even strips. But no rushing about. You're doing more than enough.'

Turning to Devora, she said, 'Devora, I need a word. Everybody else, you may start your work. God, be with us on this day.' She made the sign of the cross and Devora mumbled an 'Amen' along with the others.

After the women had left, Suor Chiara told her to sit.

'You did well last night with Lisa. I know she's hard to cope with. She's isolated because she needs special rest,' Suor Chiara explained. 'And nobody need know anything about her.' The nun looked over her spectacles at Devora, like a schoolteacher not wishing to be disobeyed. 'She's been through a tough time and there's no need for the other patients... or indeed nurses... to be upset by her. Any problems, you come straight to me. And make sure to wear your mask while you tend to her.'

'*Certo, suora,*' Devora replied. She had said 'of course' but her heart was sinking. She felt out of her depth with Lisa but she resolved to confront the challenge and do her best. There was no need to tell the nun she had met her in the past.

'Not you again,' was Lisa's greeting as Devora pushed open the door.

'Yes, you're stuck with me, I'm afraid,' Devora replied. The room was stuffy and she went to open the window.

'Leave the fucking window closed.'

'We need fresh air in here. And it's not too bad outside. The sky's blue, the birds...'

'Shut the fuck up, will you? I don't need a running commentary about what is going on with the birds and the bees. And shut that bloody window too.'

'Bad night, was it?' Devora said, coming to sit by the bed.

'Every night is bad.'

'I have nightmares too, you know. You're not the only one. And I'm exhausted this morning. I didn't sleep one wink. So don't make it hard for me.'

This last comment was met with silence and Devora rose to pour water into the bowl by Lisa's bed.

'Shall we get washed?'

'*We* won't do anything. *You* can do what the hell you want. Shut the door when you leave.'

'I'm not leaving. And as you won't be leaving for a while either, at least not until your broken legs have mended, you'll have to put up with me. So, let's not waste more energy on fighting.'

A deep sigh was followed by Lisa shuffling round to face Devora. 'Why couldn't you sleep?'

'Are you sure you're interested?'

'For fuck's sake. Now who's being difficult?'

That brought a hint of a smile to Devora's face. 'Fair enough.'

'I get to sleep by cooking up my revenge,' Lisa said, grimacing as she tried to sit up.

Devora went to help her, moving the pillows to support her back and gently easing her to a sitting position. Lisa was skin and bone and she thought how easy the bones on her legs must have been to break. She would take a long while to heal. 'You should eat more if you want to build yourself up to avenge the man who did this to you.'

'Who said it was a man? Anyway, what's happened to you to keep you awake at night?'

Devora found it surprisingly easy to talk to Lisa, despite her attempts to put up barriers. It was a release. The girl wasn't going anywhere very soon. She couldn't open up to Ida in case she revealed about Davide and there was never time to talk to Suor Chiara, even if she'd wanted to.

'My family is Jewish.'

'I actually knew that. Luigi told me. But, in any case, it's not difficult to see you're playing a part.'

'What are you talking about?'

'It's as clear as daylight you're hiding your identity. You've not got that... piety about you that nuns have. You don't kind of glide along in your habit. I notice how you scratch at yourself. You're not used to wearing that thing.'

Devora grinned. 'This habit is the most uncomfortable, scratchy garment I've ever worn in my life.'

'Well, take heed of what I say. If I can tell you're not a nun, then the bastard *tedeschi* will if they barge in here on a raid. And they're bound to at some time. Make yourself look more... humble. Cast your eyes down, that sort of thing. Don't stride. Take smaller steps. I bet you're a runner, good at sports. Am I right?'

'What are you? Some kind of detective?'

'No. I'm... an observer. Leave it at that. Anyway, this is not about me. Why couldn't you sleep?'

'My family were taken away a couple of weeks back. I don't know where they are. I should be with them.'

'Taken away?'

'Put on a train from Milan. I think they're in Germany. In a labour camp. But what sort of work do they want two young boys for? And my parents are not young... and my mother not in the best of health... I feel so bad being here. Not helping them...' Two tears funnelled down her face and she swiped them away with the backs of her hands.

'*Maledetti bastardi*. Damn the bastards to hell. That's not good.'

The words were blunt. Very different from don Andrea's reassurances. Devora's heart sank.

'Was the train packed?' Lisa asked.

'Apparently. I wanted to go and find them. Maybe I should have, but I was told it was pointless. Too dangerous. That's what's tormenting me. I feel useless stuck here, not knowing what's happened ...'

'You're not useless, Devora. And whoever told you it is dangerous is correct,' Lisa said. 'You'd end up on a train too and there's no guarantee you'd be sent to the same place as your family. You're better off here and you're good at what you're doing.'

Her voice had lost its belligerent tone and a chill ran down Devora. 'What do you know about these trains?' she asked.

'We tried to intercept one going north. Faces squashed up to the slats, children crying. The stench... We set up an attack at one of the fuel stops, but... we'd miscalculated how many guards were on the train... we lost good men and women that day.'

'We? Who are you, Lisa? What are you and Luigi up to?'

Lisa shook her head. 'I can't tell you. I'm tired.' She shuffled down from the pillows and closed her eyes.

Devora shook her and Lisa yelped. 'Ouch! Leave me alone.' She breathed in and out, her face contorted with pain as she laboured for breath. She flicked open her eyes and her words were chilling to Devora.

'You need to prepare yourself for the worst, Devora. Just do what you have to do to me and then leave me alone. Maybe we'll talk later. If you have something to ease the pain, then give me extra. I need it today.'

Devora hurried through the rest of her rounds, tending to a woman with pre-eclampsia, changing dressings on a burnt toddler's legs. He had fallen into a campfire his mother had lit in the ruins of their bombed house and he screamed as Devora worked on him. Afterwards, she found him an apple from the kitchen and sat with him, telling him one of her brothers' favourite childhood stories about the hare and the tortoise. She stroked his damp little head as his eyes drooped and his face became the faces of Alfredo and Arturo as he drifted off. She couldn't bear to imagine what they were doing. To stop herself from going crazy, she squeezed her eyes tight and told herself that worrying would do no good. *Bury yourself in your work, Devora. Work, work, work.*

Later, she sat by the bedside of an elderly man with dementia, listening to his same accounts of the past over and over until he too eventually fell asleep. And although she desperately tried not to, she thought of her own family and what Lisa had said: *you need to prepare yourself for the worst.* What did she mean? Where was her family? Where had the train taken them?

At nine o'clock, at the end of a long, difficult day, Suor Chiara sent her with a tray of food to feed to Lisa.

'I'm cold. Close the bloody window.'

'*Buonasera*, Lisa. Nice welcome you always give me! How was your day? Mine was pretty shit, dragging myself round with your comments earlier of doom and gloom. I haven't been able to concentrate on work.'

Lisa was quiet, her eyes following Devora all the while as she set down the tray of food, straightened her sheets and finally closed the window.

'You need to wise up,' Lisa said eventually.

Devora dropped the spoon that she had picked up to feed her patient, splashing soup onto the sheets. She set the tray down with a thump on the bedside table.

'Don't you tell me I need to wise up. Just don't,' she said. A medical professional should stay calm and dispassionate. Devora knew that. Her patient should come first and her own feelings be put to one side. But Lisa's last comment had tipped her. How dare she?

'Do you actually know what we Jews have had to endure these last years in this country that welcomed us once upon a time? How slowly our rights have been peeled away, one by one? Do you know what it is like to be looked at in disgust? To see that people think you are dirty, evil and infectious? To be refused access to shops and places overnight that you frequented all your life? What it is like when your father loses his job, his dignity and sense of worth? To have to stop your studies and all the things you loved doing? Fencing, athletics, going to the theatre, walking freely with your friends? Having to hide away like a terrified animal expecting a beating for something it hasn't done? I can't begin to describe how awful it is, so how can *you* even imagine how awful it is? You don't know a thing. So, don't you dare tell me I have to wise up.'

She was shaking, waiting for some kind of apology but she didn't get one.

'That's nothing compared with what others are enduring,' Lisa said. 'No fencing, no theatre visits. Pah! If things are so bad, then why are you hiding away and not doing something about it? You need to get out there and act, my friend. Before it's too late.'

'I think whoever beat you up did something to your brain. How could life get worse than it is now? What can *I* do against an army?'

'You're very naïve. Just because you're Jewish, it doesn't mean you have to hide or allow these things to continue to happen. Where's your thirst for acting against all these injustices instead of accepting them? Leave this cloistered place and get out there and fight, girl. Fight for a free Italy.'

Devora sat down on the bed, the anger knocked out of her. 'How? I don't even know how to use a gun.'

Lisa lowered her voice. 'There are many ways to fight. There are groups of freedom fighters springing up all over the country. You would be of great use to them with your medical knowledge. They can't bring their wounded to hospitals but if you were with them, you could use your skills. The *tedeschi* are stupid, as are many of the *repubblichini*. Women can get away, literally, with murder. They don't suspect us as we *staffette* go about our missions. If I had counted the times I've passed through their checkpoints with a hand grenade between my breasts, or carried messages hidden in the seams of my clothes, you wouldn't believe me.'

She started to cough and Devora went to her aid.

'We... need... more...' Lisa gasped.

Devora noted with dismay the spatters of blood round Lisa's mouth. 'Rest now,' she said. 'No more talking.' She wiped away the red drops and held Lisa's hand as she closed her eyes, her breathing steadying a little. When she was sure Lisa was asleep, she lifted the tray of untouched food and went to find Suor Chiara.

'How can I help you?'

Suor Chiara looked up from writing her notes by candlelight as Devora knocked and peered around the door.

'Lisa is struggling. And I believe she needs surgery. She's bleeding internally, I think. Whoever beat her up most probably stamped on her stomach.'

The nun looked at Devora, concern clouding her eyes. 'Sit down, my dear.' She placed her pen neatly by the side of her register.

'Lisa is dying. She was already ill before she fell into the hands of Mussolini's *repubblichini*. We can only make her comfortable. I asked you to look after her because I can trust you. We're hiding her here. And nobody must know. *Nobody*.'

Devora spent another sleepless night thrashing over poor Lisa's words. The truth had stung. For all her anguishing over what to do, Devora realised she had not actually *done* much during this war. Even hiding the truth from Ida could be considered a form of cowardice. She was living like a tortoise in its shell and Lisa was right.

By the time dawn's dim, pearly light heralded a new day, Devora had resolved she would heed Lisa's words. Her first duty was to Ida. She had to find the right moment to tell her about her dead husband. But was there ever going to be a right moment?

CHAPTER 27

LATE NOVEMBER 1943

ENRICO

The bordello was housed in an ordinary palazzo in Via Piave beyond the cathedral square, metal handrails along the walls of the street to help when treacherous snow and ice fell. No sign outside but two heavy doors with a tarnished brass knocker shaped like a woman's torso, the only hint at what lay behind. I'd been there in my late teens to lose my virginity and never returned to the sordid place since. It had been a hurried, furtive affair, the woman working on me old enough to be my mother. A smattering of blackheads across the end of her nose, a stale smell of perspiration wafting from her greasy body, made worse by cheap perfume sprayed between her sagging breasts, had made me want to heave.

But I believed it to be the perfect hiding place. After the *tedeschi* occupied Urbino towards the end of September, they began to frequent this establishment. I negotiated a special price with the signora for a studio room on the top floor. At first, she thought I was bringing her a new girl, and rubbed her hands with glee. '*Bellissima*,' she said, her gaze travelling up and down my loved one's body. 'I shall increase my price. Where did you find her?'

She got the message soon enough. If any man so much as caught whiff of her, I warned the old bag, then I would have the place shut down. And to her complaints about how the other girls would react if they found out she was not working, I simply dangled an extra wad of lire in front of her greedy eyes to increase the rental money, telling her they need never know. She should keep her mouth shut, I threatened, and invent something if they asked. Tell them she was sheltering a niece. That her visitor was her future husband.

I hid her under the very noses of the people she was hiding from. Which *tedesco* or *nazifascista* would ever search for a Jewish girl in the brothel they used? For a while, it was perfect. She had time on her hands and she busied herself transforming the attic space into a comfortable nest. The windows overlooked the mountains and as winter tightened its hold, with the stove lit and curtains I'd stolen from my parents' house drawn tight across the panes, we were snug.

Our lovemaking grew less frenzied and she was less abandoned. When I asked her why, I understood the arrangement I had thought so perfect was perfect only in my eyes.

'Enrico,' she said, one afternoon as we lay curled together, the first flakes of snow stroking the casements, her words hesitant. 'I'm grateful you rescued me. I truly am.' As she spoke, she traced her fingers down my chest and I caught hold of them and brought them to my lips.

'You are going to add a "but", aren't you?' I replied. 'You're not happy here, are you, *amore mio*?'

There was a pause as she searched my eyes, the tiniest of frowns between her own. I bent to kiss her concern away and with her head snuggled against my neck, she mumbled a reply.

'Something happened to make me change my mind about this hiding place. It would only take one drunken soldier to blunder up the stairs and find me.' She turned her face from me and I sensed something had already happened.

'Tell me,' I said, grasping hold of her arms.

'*Ahi*, Enrico, you hurt me.' She rose from the bed, rubbing her arms. 'If you promise to stay calm, I shall tell you...'

'What?' I jumped up, turned her round, searching her face for the truth. 'Has anybody touched you? I'll kill anybody who—'

'*Shh!* Keep your voice down. Sit.'

My fists clenched at my side, I listened.

Two days earlier, she had been leaning from the window, she told me. 'It is so dark up here. The sun was shining. A sparrow hopped onto the sill and I put crumbs out and it was wonderful to feel fresh air on my face. I stayed there a while longer. And then, across the way, a soldier appeared at the window. He was shaving and he saw me and waved... I thought nothing of it... I didn't wave back, I promise. I shut the window and moved away quickly.

'That afternoon the signora hammered on the door, told me there was a *tedesco* asking after me. She had told him I wasn't working for her but he insisted, despite her telling him I was family. He wants to come to me tomorrow. It's impossible to hide here now... and... although I love it when you manage to come, I spend the rest of my time worrying something might happen to not let you come anymore. And then I will be marooned up here. Like a cat stuck up a tree with nobody coming to rescue me. Where would I run to? Who would help me? For sure I could not go to your parents. You've told me often enough about them.' She shuddered.

I lifted her face to look into her eyes. 'I will think of something. I promise. But keep away from the window, even when it's dark.'

At the time of uttering those words, I had absolutely no idea what to do. Wherever I hid her, she wouldn't merge in. And if I took her to an empty house in the countryside, that wouldn't work either. There were raids all the time: searches for men who refused to fight, searches by the Todt organisation for labour, searches for *partigiani* and escaped prisoners of war. Nowhere was safe.

Of course I couldn't keep away. The next day I came to her again. When I heard heavy boots on the stairs, I hid to the side of the wardrobe. She opened the door a crack but the *tedesco* barged in. Even from where I hid, I smelled the reek of alcohol. He was young, slight, his cheeks red and he spoke terrible Italian: '*Tu baciare me*, you kiss me,' he slurred. '*Io pagare*. I pay.' He held out two bars of chocolate and stumbled towards my love, grabbing at her breasts.

Without thinking twice, I picked up a paring knife from the sink and lunged at him. My left arm round his neck, I plunged in the blade. Blood soaked my sleeve and with a gurgle, he slumped to the floor.

'What have you done?' Her eyes wide with terror, she backed away.

'It had to be done.' I was calm as I spoke.

She wouldn't let me take her in my arms. She pointed at the blood, shaking her head, her body trembling.

'Pack a small bag of warm clothing. Wear those boots I bought you. Find a shawl to cover your head and shoulders. We have to leave this place before they come looking for him.'

I dragged his body across the floor, his boots scraping trails of blood across the boards, and shoved him under the bed. Then I fetched a cloth from the sink and clumsily dabbed at the stains and she took over from me, muttering things I didn't understand as she worked, scrubbing frantically as she knelt.

I looked at my watch. Three o'clock. From past visits I knew the signora and the girls rested at this time of the afternoon, in readiness for the night's work. With fortune on our side, we could leave without anyone noticing.

On the second-floor landing, a door opened as we passed. A girl in a petticoat emerged, curlers in her hair. She nodded sleepily as she slapped over the floor in her mules towards the toilet and we continued down the stairs uninterrupted. There were few people about outside, icy wind funnelling through the alleys. She slipped once and I pulled her close. In her shawl pulled across to conceal her features and with me carrying her bag, she could have been my grandmother. I kept hold of her as we hastened towards the car parked at the foot of the hill.

The only place I could think of was my father's hunting lodge near Cesana. He had stopped using it since the *tedeschi* had rolled in. For the time being, it would do.

CHAPTER 28

DEVORA

Don Andrea paid a visit to the hospital on the following evening, bringing another family to hide. Devora found him in the convent kitchen where he was eating a bowl of broth, dunking a hunk of dark rye bread, a half bottle of red wine beside him. He looked tired and pale.

'Are they looking after you?' he asked.

'I'm being treated almost too well here, but I worry constantly about my family. Everything feels wrong at the moment.'

'These are hard times. So many uncertainties for us all. Talk to me, Devora. I'm a good listener.'

While he finished his simple supper, she told him how she felt redundant, despite knowing she was of some use in the hospital. 'But I could be doing much more. Time is passing me by.'

She paused, weighing up how much she should divulge about Lisa. Hadn't Suor Chiara told her nobody was to know about her? Was don Andrea meant to be kept in the dark too?

Or had he brought Lisa here too, rescued her as he had done so many others?

'I want to leave. Go back to Urbino and do what I can in an area I know well. And be there for when my family returns.'

He paused, stretching his long legs under the table and leaning back in his chair. 'Devora, have you thought they may not—'

Before he could finish, she blocked her ears. 'Don't say it, Andrea. Just don't. Don't take away my hopes.'

He paused and she averted her eyes from his look of sympathy. 'Perhaps it might be a good move to go back to Michelozzi? Join up with him?'

'So you know what Luigi does? He hasn't spelled everything out to me, but he's hinted enough.' She pushed her finger up inside her veil to scratch her head. 'Life is too short. If I were to die without having done anything more for the cause of liberty than pottering about here, then my life will have been wasted. Something a patient told me yesterday—'

He interrupted, picking up a crust to mop up the rest of his soup. 'Something Lisa said?'

She stopped. 'You know about her? Luigi knows her too. Who is she?'

He nodded. 'A brave woman. She's done so much for us and the *fascisti* know it. They tortured her to an extent that even some of the republican guards were shocked. It didn't take much persuading to smuggle her out of prison.'

'I've done nothing compared to her. We only have the present moment, don't we, Andrea?'

He looked at her. 'That's not what I believe. I'm a priest. I believe in the afterlife, but I understand what you're trying to say.'

'I find it difficult to believe in any of that stuff. In a God who permits such suffering.'

'God never burdens us with more than we can bear.'

'How can you say that? I can't bear to think what is happening to my parents and brothers. I have no idea where they might be. I try to keep it locked up, but...' She broke off, tears she was sick of swilling her eyes. 'It's easy for you to come out with these...' – she searched for words – 'these nuggets of wisdom and scripture, but to me it's a way of... winding bandages round life. It doesn't cure anything. And Lisa, *poor* Lisa! Talk to *her*. Don't tell me *she* hasn't been burdened with more than she can bear. She's destroyed. God has abandoned her.'

'If God brings that thought to your mind, then it is a reflection of how you see yourself.'

'You're talking in riddles. Why do priests and rabbis always talk in riddles? As far as I'm concerned, as long as a person leads a good life, then it doesn't matter what they believe. They don't need religion.'

'Having these doubts shows you're alive. That you're searching for truth. You think that God has abandoned you but maybe it's you who has abandoned Him. Or... you've abandoned life.' He paused, his fingers laced together on the table. 'What you said before about feeling useless. Have you not thought God might be dropping these thoughts into your conscience? Act upon His divine messages, Devora. Leave the hospital. Follow your instincts. This life is only on temporary loan. You're right about that at least.'

He rose, his chair scraping across the tiles. 'But you will need fresh documents again. This time, you can travel as a different nun: one journeying back south to care for her sick mother in Calabria. With the allies down there, it's impossible to check records now and nobody can prove a southerner's identity. Leave it with me, Devora. Is there anything else I can help you with?'

'I need to tell Ida about Davide. Will you be there with me? We've put it off for too long.'

• • •

Suor Chiara let them use her study. Don Andrea sat behind her desk and Devora chose to remain standing. At first, Ida refused to believe what they had told her.

'I shall only believe it if I can see where my husband is buried,' Ida said, rocking Nechama so fiercely that the baby started to scream. She fumbled at the buttons on her blouse and let Nechama suckle, covering her bosom from the priest with her shawl. But because she was agitated her milk didn't flow and Nechama screamed louder.

'We know where he lies,' don Andrea said. 'When I can, I'll take you there and we shall bury him properly. But at the moment it's not safe.'

'*Please...*'

Devora couldn't bear the expression in Ida's eyes. She took Nechama and tried to pacify the baby but it was as if the infant knew what was happening and she continued to bunch up her little legs and cry.

'You could take me there in the dark,' Ida entreated. '*Please...* I need to say goodbye to Davide. To pray over the place where he sleeps and place a stone there. I wish I hadn't sent him ahead of me at the border. If I'd let him stay with us, then he would still be alive. Please let me go to him.'

No tears fell from Ida's eyes. Devora understood why. It wasn't courage, it was numbness. And disbelief, mixed with guilt. What she herself felt most of the time, separated from her own loved ones.

The priest shook his head. 'It happened near the station. There are guards everywhere; it's impossible. You need to stay alive for your daughter.'

Pale as marble, Ida paced Suor Chiara's study whilst Devora tried to calm the baby. She had no words to make it easier for Ida. What could she come out with but a load of platitudes? Words would not bring Davide back.

'Would you like me to pray for you here, Ida?' she heard

don Andrea ask.

A nod from Ida, who reached out her arms for her baby. 'For both of us.' She sat down, Nechama settling against her and Devora watched as the priest laid his hands on Ida's head and spoke gently.

'Mother of God, enfold this precious mother in your loving grace. Grant her comfort, ease her pain. You who suffered the loss of your only son, intercede for her. Protect mother and child from future harm, I beseech you in God's name. Amen.'

Ida's 'Amen' was a whisper. Andrea's words seemed to soothe her a little; her eyes shone with tears but she blinked them back as she thanked the priest and left the study.

It was Devora who broke down. 'I can't bear it. How can *she*?'

'Because she has a faith. Because deep down she believes that nothing that God has created is in vain,' don Andrea replied.

Devora left the study, slamming the door behind her.

She was still awake when Ida slipped into her cell later that night and climbed beside her into the narrow bed.

'I can't get warm,' Ida whispered.

Devora spooned herself round Ida. She understood that listening was sometimes the best medicine. She'd learned that from bedside vigils at Villa Oliveto and so she waited for her friend to talk if she needed.

'Nechama took a long time to fall asleep. She's been on my breast ever since we left the priest. I'm sore,' Ida said.

'Baby will be all right. We'll hear her next door if she cries.'

The two girls spoke in whispers. The nuns' cells were close together. You could hear coughs, sneezes, the rustle of mattresses as women turned in their sleep. The rule was strict silence after last prayers and right through the night until first morning prayers.

'Why did you let me believe Davide was alive?'

Devora paused. 'I'm so sorry. I thought it for the best.'

'It's such a shock. The thought of living our lives without him. Him not ever knowing our baby. Thinking we would be together again kept me going...' Her voice trailed away.

This was the hardest conversation Devora had ever had to negotiate. Would anything she said help Ida in any way? She hadn't been straight with Ida, this was true. But she would be from now on.

'Ida, I've decided to leave this place. I... life is passing me by; I want to do more and follow my conscience. I want to fight against this crazy war.'

Ida sat up. 'Where will you go?'

'Back to my home town. Urbino. I know somebody there who will tell me how I can help.'

'I want to come with you.'

'It's impossible, Ida. You have to look after Nechama.'

'I've been thinking about that too. Madlaine can look after her. I'll wean her. She'll be loved and safe in the mountains. If I'm not there and there's a search, nobody would take a baby, surely? And at the end of this war, I'll go back to fetch her.'

'And what if this war lasts months? Years, even? And you're killed. Then your baby would have neither mother nor father.'

Ida flopped back on the hard mattress. After a few moments, she spoke, her voice devoid of emotion. 'Tell me where you live in Urbino, so I can picture you there. I shall miss you when you've gone. Tell me.'

So Devora described the little house in the ghetto at the foot of the Ducal Palace where she, her family and Anna Maria used to live.

'It's not big, our home. You enter it through a low door at the bottom of two steps, but once you're inside, you're in your own world. Mamma made it cosy and comfortable with a few precious dishes brought from Germany from her own mother that she kept on a dresser and used for special occasions. The kitchen is the hub of the house, with gingham curtains at the window overlooking the rooftops and a view of Monte Nerone. A simple house. But a home.'

'My parents lived in a grand house in Ferrara. Papà managed a bank, you see,' Ida said, 'and he was well respected. He was enrolled and active in the fascist party. He'd fought in the Great War and was awarded a medal for his courage. It is so unjust how he was treated. At first, he thought it was a mistake when they came to tell him we had to leave and refused to do so. He sent me to Davide's and my father and mother were taken away and shot. Now, when I think of how I used to moan about my parents, how strict they were with me, I want to weep. If only I hadn't taken everything for granted...'

And as the two girls continued to share details about their homes, their families, their favourite foods and subjects at school, the pranks they had played, Devora also told Ida about her feelings for Enrico. 'I've known him since we were tiny,' she said. 'For as long as I can remember, I always had a crush on him; I wasn't the only one. But... I've hardly seen him lately. Sometimes I wonder if I'm more in love with the *idea* of him. It's difficult to explain.'

'My Davide was my childhood sweetheart too. I used to stare down at him in the synagogue from the women's balcony. Instead of praying.'

The two young women were quiet for a while, finding comfort in sharing their stories from the past.

'I am determined Nechama shall have a happy childhood like mine,' Ida said, breaking the silence, her voice sleepy. 'My parents are gone but they gave me a wonderful childhood. I want my daughter to have a future without hiding and moving from place to place. Come and find us when this is all over, Devora, and in the meantime, I shall pray for you every day.'

Devora squeezed her hand, still cold as stone. '*Grazie*, Ida. I need all the good fortune anybody cares to send my way.'

When Devora woke to the sound of the prayer bell, Ida was gone from her bed.

CHAPTER 29

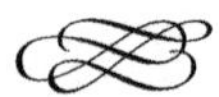

LATE NOVEMBER 1943

I am Suor Rosa. I don't hear very well, so please speak up, Devora practised in her head, moving the rosary beads between her fingers as she sat on the train, pretending to say her prayers. She cast down her eyes, as Lisa had advised when she'd been to say goodbye, and tried to think herself into the part. Lisa had been very weak but she made her say her lines over and over, interrupting her with suggestions, her voice laboured as she struggled to catch her breath: 'Act dense, Devora. You're not the brightest nun. Make mistakes with your grammar. You sound too educated. Remember your mother sent you away to a convent when you were eleven years old because she couldn't afford to feed you. You've been away a long time from Calabria so you've almost lost your southern accent. Don't attract attention to yourself. If people talk to you, pretend you're deaf.'

Suor Chiara had given her a basket of food to last the journey: pears from the little orchard in the cloister, rye bread, two hard-boiled eggs and a slice of cheese. On her feet she wore open-toed sandals, despite the November chill, and at the bottom of the basket she had packed her old shoes, the heels still concealing her mother's jewellery. She would hide them in Via delle Stallacce as soon as she could. To complete her disguise, Suor Chiara had shaved off Devora's thick blonde hair, in case she was properly searched. 'Best be safe than sorry,' the nun had said as Devora watched her waves fall to the kitchen floor. When she'd gazed on her reflection in the only convent mirror, even she hadn't recognised herself. Lisa had told her she needed a spirit of fire to succeed. Cutting her hair was a small sacrifice to make. It would grow again.

'At least you won't be called upon to flirt,' Lisa had told her, a thin smile on her face. 'Not looking like that, at any rate.'

When Devora had bent to kiss her on the cheeks, Lisa had pushed her away. 'Don't go sentimental on me, girl. Fight for me instead. *Viva la libertà*,' she'd said, holding up her bandaged fist. Devora knew she would never see her again.

At Milan, half a dozen German soldiers pushed into the carriage. There was room for only five and she rose to vacate her seat.

'*Nein, nein. Tu stare*,' one of the older men told her in pidgin Italian, ordering the youngest of the troops to stand. The youth looked daggers at her and mumbled it wasn't right she sat and he stood. 'The stupid bag is our enemy,' he complained.

Of course Devora understood every German word he uttered. Her parents had brought their children up to speak both languages. She smiled sweetly at the young soldier. *If only you knew, you lot. That you have left your seat to a Jewish girl.* It gave her a feeling of control. The older soldier nodded his head at her and she lowered her gaze and listened intently to what they were discussing.

The older soldier was complaining about a shooting he had witnessed by republican guards. 'They're depraved. They shot children and women in the village. Because they were harbouring an injured partisan.' He shook his head. 'I can understand warnings are necessary, but to shoot children? This is not why I signed up.'

'You're too soft, Hans,' another soldier replied. 'This is war, man. And Italians can't be trusted. Look how they changed sides. At least it will make them think again about sheltering bandits.'

She listened to them as they argued about the rights and wrongs. The *crucchi* were the enemy, Devora thought. But not all of them were bad. War was war, orders were orders and if a soldier disobeyed a command, then there were punishments. She thought of Lisa. A woman who had stood up to the aggressor. She'd told Devora she hadn't acted alone. And she thought of Luigi too. And wondered about Enrico. The last time she'd seen him, he was wavering, doubts creeping in about Il Duce.

Alfredo and Arturo liked to play dominoes and to arrange them in a line on their ends, so that when one fell, it brought the rest down. She wanted to be a part of a line of dominoes that felled the enemy. Sitting in the corner of the compartment on the hard seat, listening in to the German soldiers' conversations reinforced an idea.

Medicine was not the only way she could help. She would offer her fluent knowledge of German to help the *partigiani* operating in the Urbino area and pick up any information she could.

She had to change trains at Parma. The guard who checked her documents and ticket smiled broadly at her and said something in a dialect she couldn't understand. She looked at him blankly, pointing to her ears. '*Sono sorda*. I'm deaf,' she said, trying to make her words sound like a deaf girl in her class at school. The guard pointed at her place of birth and spoke slowly, opening his mouth wide to say that he was from Acri too. Her heart skipped a beat. What if he started to ask more questions? She had never been south of Urbino. Fortunately, there was a queue behind her and the train was about to leave and she slipped away, breathing a sigh of relief. Certainly, she needed her wits about her in this game.

It was late when she alighted at Fano to take the connection to Urbino. 'Curfew soon, *suora*,' the guard at the station told her. 'You'll have to hurry if you want to catch the last train.'

He gave a piercing whistle to attract the driver, shouting there was one more passenger and she picked up the skirts of her habit to dash over the platform, remembering in time to drop them demurely to the ground and take smaller steps. Oh, but it was hard to keep up pretences and she was tired. *Concentrate, Devora*, she chided herself. *Don't fall at the last hurdle.*

Once in Urbino, she kept to the shadows, breathing in the familiar smell of woodsmoke sifting in the night air. Once she reached the ghetto alleys, there was silence, broken only by the eerie sound of wind gusting leaves and litter to skitter along dark passages. No smoke, no lights filtering through shutters, no sounds of families within their homes preparing for the night. Dead plants in pots wilted outside doorways and a couple of scrawny cats jumped from the wall and disappeared through a gap in the base of a door as she passed. For a minute, where in daylight the alleyway opened to offer a view of the marketplace and, higher up, the Fortezza Albornez, she stood to catch her breath as well as memories. But she had returned to a place of ghosts. No lights anywhere. Windows were blacked out to deter fighter aircraft from locating their positions. Even though Urbino had been declared a *città aperta* – an open city, exempt from enemy attack – mistakes happened.

She heard footsteps approaching and the laughter of a man and woman. She froze, pressing herself into a doorway, praying they wouldn't detect her. For what could a nun be doing out at this time of night? If they asked her, she'd say she had to nurse a dying patient, that she'd taken a shortcut back to the convent. *Think on your feet,* Lisa had urged her. The man and woman stopped walking and she had to endure giggling, the man murmuring, '*Dai! Dammi un altro bacio*. Go on, give me another kiss.' Then silence and, after a while, gasps as they finished what they were up to in the shadows. A few more agonising moments and they hurried away, the woman's heels clip-clopping over the cobbles. In the silence, Devora continued to the little house in Via delle Stallacce, descended to the low front door, fumbled for the key that was always kept in the niche above the door and let herself back into her home.

Even in the dark, she knew it well. Devora felt her way around the rooms like a blind woman, checking the shutters on the insides of the windows were secured against the night and when she was sure, she stepped carefully back to the kitchen, groping for the cupboard door, her fingers searching for a candle and box of matches. It took three before she struck a flame, the box being damp. The candle flickered, giving a mysterious glow to the room. Despite the chill, everywhere looked clean. She shivered and carried the candle upstairs to the chest at the end of her bed, the mattress rolled up. The scent of lavender hit her as she lifted the lid and retrieved the woollen ski sweater Anna Maria had knitted her. The lavender was fresh and she offered up a thank you to their faithful servant who must have been keeping an eye on the place.

As she passed the bedroom doors of her parents and brothers, she couldn't resist pushing them open. The sight of her parents' bed, where she and the boys had fought with pillows that had scattered throughout the house, broke her. Her tears started to fall as she made her way down to the kitchen.

Stop it! This will do no good. You said you wanted to come back. What did you expect? It was as if Lisa was talking to her, trying to make her see sense. She set the candle down on the table and, fisting away her tears, she pulled out Suor Chiara's picnic. At the bottom of the bag, next to her shoes was a crumpled piece of paper wrapped round a withered apple and she pulled it out, not remembering having seen it before. Smoothing it out, she deciphered lines written in shaky handwriting.

It will be hard but I know you can do this. Do it for me because I know I have little time left. I want you to complete something I cannot finish. Tell Luigi when you see him that he must go to Pesaro to collect his mother's shopping.

As soon as I met you, I knew you had a thirst to act inside you that needed to be turned on. We women of Italy are stronger than we believe. Over the last years we have lost our freedom. Mussolini and his nazifascisti want us to be piccole donne. But we are not little women; we are mighty. It's time to rise up. In the resistance, you can be anybody you want to be. Yes, you will have to run and think, think and run, but you will achieve great things, I know. Do it for all who have fallen. Be a rescuer, a liberator, believe in what you have to do with the greatest of passion. You will surprise yourself at how brave you are. Help bring freedom back to our country. Be a part of this victory.

Viva l'Italia,

Lisa

She read the letter over and over, digesting each of Lisa's words before taking the note to the candle. It burnt with a rush of flame and she dropped it to the floor, stamping on the ashes. It would not do to be caught with this in her possession. Thank God she hadn't been searched on her journey. It seemed strange to Devora that such a note should have been inserted by Lisa into her bag. Maybe the drugs for her pain had clouded her thinking. No matter the reasons, the message must be very important for her to have taken such a risk. It could have well been the last act of a dying woman, Devora thought; the last act of a remarkable, courageous woman.

The candle burnt down and she found another stub in the cupboard, noting that only one remained. She wasn't hungry but she forced herself to eat some of Suor Chiara's bread and cheese and one of the pears. Maybe tomorrow night she would light a small fire in the kitchen hearth. Nobody would see the woodsmoke in the dark and she needed something warm in her stomach, if only hot water. And after that, she would go to Luigi and deliver Lisa's message.

She slept long and deep, dreaming of Mütti's breakfast pancakes and sweet *Kugel*, imagining the aroma of hot chocolate served in one of her mother's porcelain cups, but when she woke, she was alone and a thin layer of frost streaked across her bedcovers like a snail trail. She had no watch but she heard the city bells strike the midday Angelus. Eight more hours of daylight until she could make her next move. Devora snuggled under the blanket, covering her head, trying to sleep but sleep refused to come. She forced herself to stay where she was and make no noise. No passer-by should be able to tell there was someone inside the house. At one stage she tiptoed from the bed across the floorboards, bundled in a moth-eaten shawl and Papà's darned socks from the chest, and opened the shutter a fraction to see if night was approaching, but a strip of daylight stole in. Having to wait meant there was time to think. She concentrated on remembering happy times spent here: noisy card games played with Arturo and Alfredo, her father's accordion playing, the southern dances that Anna Maria had shown them, her feet tapping on the polished kitchen tiles as she whirled and twirled. Devora refused to be gloomy. Lisa had told her she must be brave. There would be happy times together in the future. She had to believe in that.

Then she remembered her father's hiding place under the table. Six tiles by three. Eighteen: the lucky Jewish number. She fetched her shoes from upstairs and prised apart the heels with a kitchen knife. Out tumbled her mother's wedding ring and earrings, the tiny diamonds glittering in the candlelight. Devora breathed in, controlling her emotions, as she picked up the jewellery, the gold scratched and worn. She found a piece of cotton material and wrapped her mother's precious jewellery carefully and crawled under the table to push them into the hole.

'They are there for when you return, Mütti,' she whispered, using the name she knew her mother preferred.

CHAPTER 30

At two fifteen the following morning, it took a third handful of pebbles against Luigi's bedroom window to make him stir. He opened the window, his hair tousled. '*Chi c'è?*' he hissed. 'Who is it? What do you want at this ungodly hour?'

'*Sono io*. It's me. Devora.'

'*Per Bacco*. What the... go and wait for me in the grotto,' he whispered. 'I'll be there in a moment.'

The grotto was a folly Luigi's mother had designed after visiting the Amalfi Coast on honeymoon. She was a passionate gardener and as a child Devora had often played in the wonderland she had created.

'What on earth are you doing here, Devora?' Luigi whispered, buttoning up his shirt as he approached across the dew-silvered grass. He looked her up and down. 'I wouldn't have recognised you if I'd passed you in the street.'

'That was the idea. Good disguise, no?' She did a twirl for him in her nun's habit and he smiled. 'I've even shaved my hair off.'

He pulled a face. 'It's wonderful to see you.' He pulled her into a hug. 'But... why are you here?'

They sat on a bench next to the fountain, trickles of water covering up their whispered conversation.

'I have a message for you,' she said. 'From Lisa.'

She heard his sharp intake of breath. 'Lisa? What...?'

'I treated her in hospital. She's...' She put a hand on his arm. 'They tortured her. I'm so sorry, Gigi. I think you knew her well. She was the girl you gave a lift to, wasn't she?'

He nodded. 'What's the message?' He lowered his voice and she leant in to whisper what Lisa had told her.

Luigi slumped back against the bench. 'I need to go to Pesaro first thing tomorrow. Devora, thank God you didn't turn up here two days later. The *tedeschi* have requisitioned our home and given us until Friday to get out. We're having to move out of Urbino to Papà's country house in Castel Cavallino. The *Kommandant* has promised Mamma he will look after our place, but she's distraught so I came back to help her pack. God knows who you might have woken if I hadn't been in my room.'

'Well, I've been lucky then.'

'No such thing as luck in war, Biondina.' He hugged her again and Devora sank into his comforting embrace. 'I really can't believe you're here,' he said. 'Tell me what's been going on with you.'

'A lot has happened and nothing has happened, Gigi. But what does Lisa's message mean? What did she mean about your mother's shopping?'

'I can't tell you.'

At that she jumped up from the bench. 'Don't keep saying that to me. I want to help. For Christ's sake, stop treating me like a child.'

She began to pace up and down, filling him in about her parents and brothers being taken to Germany, of where she and Ida had ended up with Madlaine, about the baby she'd delivered, about don Andrea's help and finally Lisa. There was much to tell and he listened intently.

'So, don't treat me as if I don't know what's going on. I can be useful here, I *know* it. I couldn't stay north any longer, Gigi. I *must* have more to do. Apart from my medical knowledge – I've come on a lot in that respect – I can speak fluent German. Don't you see – there must be some way of using that? I want to join in with whatever you're doing. And you *can't* send me away.' She bent to grab hold of his arm, her fingers digging into him.

He shook his head. 'Of course I won't send you away. I won't do that again. But... it's dangerous for you here. There are *tedeschi* everywhere. And besides that, you're an *urbinate* – you could be recognised by locals. There are a couple of nasty *fascisti* in Urbino who would pounce on any opportunity to turn in a Jew. Most citizens here are sound but it only takes one informer. They've put up posters everywhere offering rewards. It's disgusting.'

'You said yourself *you* wouldn't have recognised me, Gigi. I thought I'd stay disguised as Suor Rosa from Acri.' She pulled out her identity papers from the pocket of her thick habit and waved them under his nose.

He took them and flicked on his lighter to scrutinise the details. 'These are poor quality. I'll see what I can do to improve them,' he said, folding them and stuffing them into his shirt pocket. 'In the meantime, you'll have to lie low until they're ready.'

'I've been hiding in Via delle Stallacce. But I've no food left, Luigi.'

'I'll go and fetch something from the kitchen. Wait here.'

While she waited, she sat back against the bench. When he was a little boy, Luigi's mother had often arranged parties for his school companions in this grotto. She remembered the squeals of laughter as they played games of hide-and-seek around the bushes of roses and lavender, the treasure hunts, fishing for coins and little gifts in the fountain. There were always freshly baked cakes, biscotti and dishes of sweets. In Urbino there were a handful of gardens behind the high walls of some of the *palazzi*, strands of wisteria falling over the stones to hint at what lay behind, but none as enchanting as signora Michelozzi's. And yet, in a few days' time, the enemy would be using this garden and taking over Luigi's home. The thought appalled her.

'I'll walk you home,' Luigi said as he returned with a small sack of provisions. 'We'll stick to the back ways. I know where the sentries are posted.'

'If we're stopped, I'll use my usual story of having to visit the sick.'

'You'll have to vary that excuse in future, Biondina.'

'And you'll have to call me Suor Rosa,' she said. 'I've no blonde hair anymore.'

Luigi came to her two nights later, tapping gently six times on the door in the signal they'd decided on. He'd brought half a roast chicken, hard-boiled eggs, a twist of paper with real ground coffee, bread, a small pot of jam as well as a bottle of Sangiovese wine.

Her eyes widened. 'What a feast.' She sniffed the coffee and asked from where on earth he had procured it. 'Did you go to Pesaro?'

'Don't ask,' he said. 'Where's your corkscrew, Suor Rosa?'

'I don't know.' She added with a twinkle in her eye, 'I've given wine up for Lent.'

He smirked. 'Well, you've had an extremely long Lenten fast then, seeing as we're in November and Lent stops at Easter.'

'I always knew I would never make a good nun,' she said. She had taken off the uncomfortable habit and was wearing one of the dresses she'd left behind and pulled on her ski jumper for extra warmth. On her head she had tied a scarf round her stubbly hair. As it grew, her scalp itched and she constantly scratched at it through the material.

Luigi had found the corkscrew and he pulled out the cork with a satisfying pop. 'You no longer have to be Suor Rosa,' he said. 'I've re-christened you as Elena from Siracusa. I'll give you the papers in a minute.'

She sighed. 'I am Devora but I'm also Debora, then I've been Suor Rosa, now Elena. How shall I remember... Tell me about me now. Who is Elena?' She scratched at her head again.

Luigi handed her a cup of wine and she took a swig, reaching for the chicken to tear off a piece.

'Elena from Siracusa, Sicily,' he said, pausing before he added, 'Elena who has nits.' He eyed her with a grin as she scratched again.

'I have *not*. You try shaving off your hair. *Porca Madosca*,' she said, pulling off her scarf and scratching at her scalp with both hands.

Her eyes looked enormous with her stark haircut and she had lost weight so that her cheekbones were more pronounced. Luigi stared at her.

'Don't look at me like that, Luigi. I know I'm ugly.'

'Never,' he said, still staring at her so that she looked away, embarrassed.

She offered him a slice of chicken breast but he declined. 'All for you. I've eaten this evening. I think Mamma thought it would be our last decent meal and she went to town. We move to our country house tomorrow morning.'

Her mouth full, she said. '*Grazie!* I'll save the rest for later.' Wiping her greasy hands on a cloth, she asked, 'Have you thought about what I should do next?'

'*Sì*.' He pulled clothes from his rucksack: a long skirt of thick woollen material, woollen socks, a cap and scarf, a coat and a pair of scuffed boots. The clothes were darned, the coat had odd buttons and patches at the elbow. 'You need to look poor, ordinary, so that nobody gives you a second glance. Until your hair grows again, keep the cap firmly on. You can say you were infested and had to shave off your hair.'

'Or I could say my hair was shaved off because I was a collaborator, and was punished for sleeping with a *tedesco*,' she said.

'No, Devora. No need for such an active imagination. You mustn't draw attention to yourself. Before you know it, that bit of juicy news would be all round the city and they'd hunt down the whore. You know what people are like. They love a scandal.'

He lowered his voice. 'You're actually needed tonight for a nursing job. I'll take you there now. One of our boys was snatched from hospital but he needs further care.'

Her senses alert, she sat up, eager to start as soon as possible and then she slumped back again. 'I don't have any medicine or equipment with me, Luigi. I left all that behind.'

'Don't worry – we have supplies. A doctor at the hospital gives us what we need – he's one of us but he has to keep up the pretence of being a *fascista* so it would be too dangerous for him to tend to Raffaello himself. There are snoops at the hospital. If you've finished eating, then we'll go now. He's in a bad way. I'll bring you back here afterwards but it will be your last night, so pack up what you need to bring for your new life, Biondina. Or should I say Elena?'

It was only a short way to a small house built into the walls on the northern side of the city. Raffaello was lying on a soiled mattress in the attic and when Devora saw his injuries, she wondered how on earth they had managed to carry him up the ladder to the tiny space in the eaves. He had been shot in the back, the bullet narrowly missing his vital organs. His bandages were stained with fresh blood and after washing her hands carefully, she removed the bindings. The wound wasn't infected but he needed more stitches. As Luigi had said, there was a bag provided containing fresh bandages and alcohol to clean the wound, as well as sutures and needles.

'Is there any grappa or something for him to numb the pain?' she whispered to Luigi.

'Don't worry, signorina,' Raffaello muttered, opening his eyes to stare at her. 'If somebody gives me something to bite down on, I'll manage.'

He was brave, lying still as she worked on him, his rolled-up red partisan's neckerchief between his teeth, gripping Luigi's hand when she inserted the sutures, her fingers steady. She sewed by the flicker of candlelight, thinking how different it was from a sterile hospital environment or even Doctor Kempe's tiny, pristine clinic room.

'You're an angel, signorina,' the boy muttered as she told him, 'All done,' and began to apply a fresh dressing to the wound from the provided package.

He was very young, not much older than her little brothers, his body gangly, not yet fully developed. Fourteen maybe, she assessed. Too young to be shot. But war was war. The young and frail were not spared.

'You have to keep this dressing clean,' she told him. 'And rest as much as you can, Raffaello.'

'I'll try,' he said. 'Luigi, can you get a message to my mother to tell her I'm alive and safe? Please.'

'*Certo*, Raffaello. Sleep now and when you wake there'll be something to eat.'

'I'm not hungry,' the boy mumbled, his eyes already closing.

They stayed by his side for a few minutes until they were sure he was asleep.

Downstairs, Devora again reiterated the importance of keeping the wound clean. 'I'll come and change the bandage in a couple of days' time. We don't want it turning septic.'

'Time to go,' Luigi said, 'it will turn light soon.'

As they walked, he told her how Raffaello had been acting

as lookout for a job he'd helped with. They'd been busy inserting dynamite on the road to the city, knowing more *tedeschi* were on their way. Raffaello had seen two women approach downhill on bikes and ran towards them to warn them not to go any further and one of the *partigiani* had shot at him by mistake in the confusion. 'These things happen,' Luigi said. 'A mistake was made. *Grazie a Dio* he wasn't killed.'

'But he'll bear that scar forever,' Devora said. 'Isn't he too young to be involved? It's not a game.'

'You're right. We have all kinds of men... and boys in our group... But we shall learn from this. We need to be more organised.'

'You need women too,' she said with determination and Luigi nodded slowly.

'We need more women like you.'

Her heart swelled with pride at his words. And gratitude. At last she felt useful.

They spoke quietly, aware of early risers behind closed shutters as they made their way down steps past terraced houses and crossed the wide marketplace. As they reached the edge of the ghetto area, two dark green trucks turned in to Borgo Mercatale, braking hard to let soldiers jump from the back.

Luigi grabbed her hand. 'Run,' he urged.

It was fortunate they were already at the very edge of the marketplace and they dashed through the arches and pelted up the stairs towards Via delle Stallacce. Luigi pushed open the unlocked door, Devora close behind him and they both leant, hands on knees to catch their breath, the sound magnified in the tiny space.

'Do you think they saw us?' Devora panted.

'No. But a couple of minutes earlier and we would have been in the open. It's still curfew. It shows how careful you will have to be, Devora. You can't stay in the ghetto any longer.'

CHAPTER 31

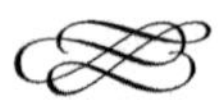

CASTEL CAVALLINO, NOVEMBER 1943

Anna Maria had hung the stolen salame from the roof of the pigeon house so ants would not find it but today there was a thick black line marching along the dirt floor, up the mud and stone walls and across the ceiling towards the precious sausage.

'Pesky things.' She followed this with a ripe curse: a satisfying, blasphemous oath against the saints and the Madonna, and wrenched the sausage from the string. Where to hide it now? To tell the truth, this place had outlived its usefulness. With November gales whistling through the slats of the pigeon cages and into the space behind, where she had made her refuge during the last months of the summer, she was ready to abandon this hidey-hole. On one of her recent forages, when she had picked a sack full of apples from the orchard behind a country house near Castel Cavallino, she'd come across a single-storey building hidden in a dense thicket of olive trees. She'd waited at a safe distance for most of that day, watching, but nobody had come near. There was a chimney, she observed, thinking it would be good to cook indoors instead of over a campfire at night. The roof was half-covered with planks and patched with lengths of sacking but the shutters at the windows, although paint-blistered and slightly rotten, were not too bad.

After the Lassa family had left, she'd tried living in Via delle Stallacce but, without them, the house had given her the heebie-jeebies. She'd popped back once or twice to check nobody had broken in, but she couldn't bear the memories of happy times now crushed. Her life was already sprinkled with too many ghosts. Living with the family had been the happiest period of her life. They had welcomed her into their hearts but she feared for them now. The stories she'd heard, scraps of news she'd heard didn't generally bode well for Jews. The Lassas had been good to her. It was a crying shame.

She moved into the building three nights later. It was easy enough for her to travel about the dirt tracks. The peasants working in the meadows, yellow and green patches beneath the hilltop village of Castel Cavallino, knew she wasn't local, but the countryside was full of refugees these days, desperate for food and shelter. Nobody took notice of the middle-aged peasant woman with a face as weathered and burnt as their own.

She'd been stopped at checkpoints once or twice. On the last occasion, a bored uniformed youth had lifted the cloth covering her basket with the tip of his bayonet and speared one of the bunches of grapes she'd pulled from a vine near the road. He'd laughed as he pulled it out and popped the fruit in his mouth.

I'd like to take a bite out of you, Anna Maria had thought. *And stick that bayonet up your skinny arse.*

Her heart was filled with weary hatred of these hooligans ruining her country and this hatred was mixed with a tiredness of life, a resignation that nothing good was ever going to come her way. She sensed there were rumblings, that people were weary of the past twenty years of exploitation and stupid ventures far across the seas that Mussolini and his henchmen had dived into, bent on making Italy into a mighty empire, but what could *she* do about it, a simple country woman from the south? Mussolini had been arrested but he'd been rescued from his prison on the Gran Sasso soon afterwards. It seemed evil always won the day.

Naturally she didn't speak her mind to the spotty young guard or to anybody else, for that matter. Apart from her time with the Lassa family, her life had been a constant round of being told what to do, of hearing what a failure she was, how ugly she was, how nobody would ever love her. She'd thought her priest had loved her when she was just a girl, but that too had been another huge helping of disappointment. Since then she'd learned to keep quiet and swallow her seething thoughts, assuming a bovine look, an acceptance of her lot, as she survived from day to day.

Cobwebs, like strips of soiled petticoats, adorned the beams of the hut and rickety sticks of furniture were layered with dust. Rodents had made their home in a soiled mattress on a rusting metal bed, so she slept on the floor that first night. In the morning, she would pull the mattress outside to beat it and leave it in the fresh air, if the rain kept away.

She lit a fire in the grate from sticks gathered from a pile at the back of the house, chewed on the remains of the salame and slept.

Next morning, she woke with the crows and heated a small pan of water in the still-warm embers to brew herself a cup of chicory coffee. She had enough scraps of food to last a couple of days, but soon she would have to forage again. The country house nearby was her best bet. There were usually jars of preserves or a tin or two left in kitchen cupboards in these abandoned places. Unless, of course, some other refugee had already moved in. City dwellers had staked claims on the countryside since the bombings had started. And then there were the army conscripts in hiding and other poor wretches like her own

Jewish family. Her soul was best in the countryside, where she felt free. Moving back to the city was a choice she would make only in the last instance. Bombs seldom fell on the countryside and this place was far from major routes. She was lucky to have come across it. Maybe her luck was changing.

Anna Maria spread the counterpane over a juniper bush to air, the berries black and ripe for picking. She harvested a handful and dropped them into her wide skirt pocket, her poacher's pouch, she liked to call it. If her luck was truly in, she might scrounge a roaming chicken to stew. Juniper berries, a handful of wild carrot roots and a sprig of rosemary to flavour would make a feast to last days. Feeling optimistic, she startled herself by beginning to hum a tune and then stopped dead as she heard voices and moved quickly to shelter behind a large olive tree.

The voices stopped and she peeped from behind the knotted trunk. A young man, a rifle raised to his shoulder, and a scruffy youngster behind him, stood facing the open doorway to the place she had hoped would become her home – at least for a while.

'*Chi c'è?*' The man's voice was authoritative, assured. 'Who's there? Come out,' he called. 'Whoever you are, you're trespassing.'

She watched as the speaker gestured to his companion to hide and, to her horror, the youngster scampered in the direction of her olive tree. *Porca boia*, but her luck was out after all. *Nothing changes*. She tried to hide herself by moving farther round the large girth, but it was pointless and she shouted out, stepping into the open, her arms raised. 'Don't shoot. *Non sparare*. I'm coming out.'

And then the youngster shrieked: 'Anna Maria, *ma non e' vero*. Is it really you?' The man rushed over to Anna Maria, his rifle pointing at her head – and the scruffy youngster was Devora in dreadful clothes. It really was Devora and Anna

Maria shrieked too and then Devora's arms were round her, and Anna Maria swore softly, '*Porca miseria. Ma che culo, che culo!* It really is my lucky day, after all.'

Devora was crying, her arms still tight about her waist and the man, who Anna Maria vaguely recognised, was urging them to keep their voices down and to come inside before they were discovered. The two women disentangled themselves and the three of them hurried indoors.

'Is there anybody else with you?' the man asked, his rifle still at the ready.

'No, signore. I'm alone – except for the mice,' she added, with a rueful smile, good humour seeping into her heart at being reunited with one of the members of her beloved adoptive family.

The man put down his rifle and shook her hand – actually shook her hand, *per Bacco*. Good heavens! *Dio buono!* First, Devora's loving welcome and now this taking of her hand: the first physical touches from another human in months.

'This is Luigi, Anna Maria. You remember him, don't you? From school days?'

Anna Maria had sensed something about him, but this young man was not the awkward boy she remembered. He had filled out, the muscles on his arms obvious through his shirt sleeves. Thick stubble shadowed his face. But as he removed his glasses to rub his eyes, she remembered that gesture of old: the same tic from when he used to come round to study with Devora at the kitchen table in Via delle Stallacce. Anna Maria nodded slowly, a smile beginning to move her mouth.

'Signor Luigi. *Sì. Mi ricordo bene*. Yes, I do recollect.' Then, as if remembering her place, she wiped her hands down her skirt as if it was a pinafore and said, 'I'm very sorry, I have nothing to offer you.'

They laughed at her then and Luigi lifted the rucksack from his back and patted it. 'I have a good twist of coffee in here,' he said and, as if he knew the place well, went to the cupboard above the cracked sink in the corner of the hut and pulled out a pot. 'Will you do us the honour of brewing it, Anna Maria?'

He produced a small bottle of grappa too, as well as dark bread and a wedge of pecorino cheese wrapped in a fine linen serviette. 'Borrowed from my mother's larder,' he said with a wink.

'This place belongs to my family, you see. It's the old caretaker's quarters. We're staying in our country house nearby since the *tedeschi* decided they fancied our Urbino home. Nobody, except for bats and mice, has used this for a long time because of the roof.' He pointed upwards.

'And so, Luigi brought me here to hide,' Devora added. 'But who would have thought to bump into you, Anna Maria? Oh, I can't believe it. We have so much to talk about. Tell me what you're doing here.'

'First, signorina, you tell me what's happened to you. Where are the rest of the family? The boys? What are they up to, the little rascals?'

'Don't call me "signorina", Anna Maria. Don't even call me Devora. You mustn't anymore. My name has changed so many times since we last met. You must address me as Elena now. And...' She paused, looking for confirmation from Luigi. 'If anybody asks you who I am, tell them I'm your young cousin. And I'm from Siracusa and want to return to Sicily as soon as I can. Explain that you're taking care of me until then.'

Luigi nodded his head. 'Not such a wild story,' he said, adding with a chuckle, 'I like this version.'

There were tears shed by both women over the next half hour as Devora shared accounts of events since they had last been together.

'I wish I could find out where the boys and Mamma and Papà are, but at the moment it's impossible. The only way for me to cope, Anna Maria, is to concentrate on one day at a time.

And each day from now on will be spent helping restore liberty to our country. Then I can go in search of my family and bring them home.'

Anna Maria listened, sadness again weighing her down. Her fear for Devora was an invisible presence but it was there: she felt the weight of it from Devora too. But she didn't voice it. What was the point of dragging others down with her pessimism?

'If I can be of use,' she said, 'I will. How can I help?'

'I should be happy simply knowing you are here to look after De—' Luigi corrected himself. 'After Elena. Making sure she eats and sleeps. I can bring you food. And then we shall think what to do for the best.'

Anna Maria nodded slowly. Her eyes were brighter than they had been for many days and when Devora clasped her hand in hers, it was a gift that made her eyes spill over with emotion.

CHAPTER 32

ENRICO

For me, it was the last straw. News came in about the massacre of villagers ten days earlier in the Apennines, near Stia. It sickened me to the core: an entire village wiped out in reprisal for the death of two *tedeschi* who had tried to infiltrate the local band of *partigiani*. One hundred and nine dead civilians, including women and babies.

I watched in growing horror now as events looked set to repeat themselves. Half a dozen men were being selected by a small group of National Republican guards I'd been accompanying, to line up in the piazza outside the trattoria where I'd eaten so many times. I recognised the butcher's son and the sickly elderly father of the chemist. He was still in his nightshirt. There were a couple of skinny boys with the soft complexions of girls. The officer's black uniform was immaculate, the stripes on his lapels showing his rank of *maggiore.* He barked out questions one after the other. 'Where are you hiding them? Tell us or you will all be shot. Who can give me the name of the *partigiano* who injured my sergeant?' He thwacked his whip against his rubber-soled boots as he strutted back and forth over the cobbles and I watched in pity as a stain spread down the trouser legs of one of the boys.

'*Maggiore*,' I said, stepping forward. 'If you leave it with me for five minutes, I'm sure I can easily extract the information. I know these people personally,' I said, exaggerating the fact I only knew them by sight from times I'd lingered at a table outside the trattoria. I'd watched the world go by in this little town as I sipped after-dinner *liquori*, viewing the village as a theatre stage, admiring the pretty girls as they washed their baskets of clothes at the fountain and tossed looks at me from under their eyelashes. I'd even had one of the girls in the shadows of the fortress walls, back when I was single and had a roving eye. In the past.

'Very well, *tenente*. I'm feeling generous this morning. You can have ten minutes, while I take my coffee.' He turned on his heel, a couple of Republican henchmen following, the tassels on their berets swinging jauntily as they stepped after him to leave the line of terrified civilians to me.

My voice stern, I instructed the hostages in no uncertain terms to move to the edge of the piazza, next to the church, where a low wall divided them from a steep drop down the hillside. 'Move it. Quickly!' I ordered, my handgun raised as I told them to quick march. With my back to the bar where the *maggiore* had retreated to an outside table, I lowered my voice. 'Listen carefully. On the count of three, I shall raise my gun and shoot.'

There were murmurs from the group. 'Signore, I beg of you...'

'I have a family of six to feed...'

'Shoot me, not my father,' the pharmacist said, pushing his elderly father, dressed in his nightgown, behind him.

My voice still low, I continued. 'I promise not to harm you.

When I shoot, you are to disappear behind the wall. I shan't aim at you, I promise. Run away as fast as you can. Save yourselves.'

I had already taken in the vehicle parked in the shade by the church, the key left in the ignition, the insolent, fascist slogan *me ne frego* daubed on the windshield. If I timed it perfectly, I could use the car to get away.

From the corner of my eye, I noticed the door to the priest's house slowly open. Nodding at me and whispering that I was a good man, that he had heard everything, a priest stepped over to the group and stood by the side of the boys and the elderly man. He pretended to bless them, interspersing his Latin words with local dialect. '*In nomine patris*,' he began, holding up a small crucifix as he spoke, '*et filii*... and when he shoots, you three follow me into the church,' he said. '*Et spiritus sancti*... and the rest of you, scatter into the *macchia*. And don't try to come back for at least one week. *Amen*.'

He finished his warnings, nodding discreetly in my direction and then I aimed my weapon slightly to the right of the group and shot, the hostages scattering as I did so. The door to the church slammed shut during the volley of bullets, the three hostages safe inside, and I was left standing alone. I moved towards the vehicle but it was too late. The shots had alerted the *maggiore*'s troops and they bounded over, firing as they ran.

The *maggiore* strode from the bar, followed by his two guards. '*Che succede qua?* What is going on here?'

'They threatened to overpower me. One of the hostages pulled a gun before they ran off. I couldn't stop them.'

'*Imbecile!* Take his weapon,' the *maggiore* shouted.

'But I've done nothing wrong. My gun jammed after the first shots. I could do nothing to stop them,' I shouted, hoping that the hostages had managed to disperse.

'Search for those *banditi*,' the *maggiore* barked. 'Alive or dead, I want them back.' Turning to me, he said, 'I'll question you back at barracks. You've made fools of us and prevented the gathering of information.'

A crowd of villagers appeared and a woman approached. 'Where are our men? When shall we see them again?'

'Most likely never,' the flustered *maggiore* answered, shoving her aside. 'And if I find out any of you are sheltering them, there will be consequences.'

Twenty-four hours later, I was still in solitary confinement at the barracks when I heard news from my guard.

'There's been an incident at that village where you cocked up. One of the boys you let go crept back to his home and was discovered. He was shot on the spot, his mother too.'

'*O Dio mio!*' I exclaimed, despair filling me in the realisation it was my fault.

'But it didn't end there. The SS are on the rampage now. They surrounded another village at dawn and went on a killing spree.'

The guard moved further into my cell, crouching down to leave a metal bowl of coffee and bread on the floor. 'I want out of this, *tenente.* I have a wife and four children in a village up in Casentino and I'm frightened for them with these crazy reprisals. Who wants to be associated with these thugs? This *maggiore,* from this new *ufficio politico investigativo* – the UPI, or whatever they like to call themselves – he's a swine. And the young soldiers involved in these killings – they have no heart. Their heads have been stuffed with nonsense.' He indicated the bread. 'I've left you something extra this morning. Don't eat it all at once. Half past ten is the best time,' he whispered. 'Be careful.' His knees creaked as he stood up. 'Good luck. *In bocca...*'

I waited until the guard's footsteps receded, puzzling at his enigmatic words. What was he trying to tell me? Was it a trap?

When the only sounds were the voices of other prisoners through the walls, complaining about the stale bread and watery coffee, I picked up my crust, wiping a layer of mould from it, before dipping it in the tin bowl of liquid. As the bread softened, something hard protruded and I cursed. Something extra, my arse. A stone to break my teeth.

I fished into the soggy dough with my fingers. A key had been shoved into the bread and my spirits lifted. Ten thirty, the man had said. I didn't have a watch but could listen to the tinny chimes of the church bells and count. It was early still. I'd heard six o'clock chime recently. The waiting was agonising, the passing of minutes like the passing of hours.

Four and a half hours later, while the chimes of half past ten clanged, I sang an aria from *La bohème* as I inserted the key, my voice covering up the sound of metal on metal.

I have a terrible voice. The words were wrong and one of the inmates in another cell jeered, 'You can't sing. Shut up and leave it to the best.' The man continued the aria perfectly and cheers rang out amongst the inmates: '*Bravo*, Dino. *Bravissimo!*'

The man did indeed have a wonderful singing voice and I offered up a silent prayer for his unwitting distraction. I pushed open the door as it scraped on the metal frame and peered out, fully expecting to see a guard poised with his rifle: a trap set by the *maggiore* with the guard to give an excuse to legitimately kill a fellow officer. But the coast was clear. The guards were on their coffee break.

I kept to the wall, ducking each time I passed the bars on the doors of the cells and got as far as the guards' room. Another gift in the form of a jacket and cap hung from a hook and I slipped them on, turning up the collar. The cap was large and for that I was grateful as I pulled it further down my brow to conceal my features. I could hear a man holding forth from the canteen, his voice loud as he told a story, followed by ribald laughter at the punchline. 'You're a filthy pig,' somebody shouted. 'What will you give me for not telling your wife?'

The man who had slipped me the key was standing guard at the main gate. He nodded, beckoning at me to make haste, before opening the wide door. Together, we slipped outside.

'Follow me,' he said. 'Olinto is my name. Quick!'

Never had a cold, grey November drizzle felt so welcome as I hurried away with my new comrade from the barracks. Soon I would be warm again, in the arms of my beautiful girl.

CHAPTER 33

MAY/JUNE 1944

DEVORA

Luigi had not taken long to find useful employment for Devora in Urbino. He'd wangled a cleaning job in his parents' requisitioned home in the city centre. Her task for the *partigiani* was to listen in to the officers' conversations and generally see what information she could pick up.

On her hands and knees, Devora emptied the ashes from Luigi's mother's prized fireplace in the grand house. On her first day at work, Colonel Karl von Wentzling had asked her, in his strange Italian, to make up the fire. He had hair like snow, razor short, the thinnest man she'd ever seen. She cleaned round him in the sitting room. He was folded into Luigi's mother's armchair, his almond-green greatcoat over his legs. He pronounced his Italian like Papà: the stresses on some words exaggerated or in the wrong place and he liked to practise on her.

'I studied Classics at university,' he'd told her on the first occasion they'd met, pointing to the volumes of Dante's *Inferno* he'd extracted from the library shelves and piled up to use as a drinks table. He'd quoted the opening lines of the *Inferno*: '"*Nel mezzo del cammin di nostra vita...*" I'd always dreamt of coming to Italy in my mid-life,' he said, 'but not like this.'

He'd stared at her and taken another swig from his glass, slurring his words. 'But, being mute, you can't discuss this with me, can you, Elena? Never mind... *non importa...*'

Likes his drink, Devora had assessed, wondering if she could slip something into his glass in the future – maybe Luigi could get hold of a strong sleeping draught. *If he sleeps, then I can snoop.*

During the six months she had worked as a cleaner and general skivvy for these officers, she'd been useful to the *partigiani*.

As she laid the fire this morning for the colonel, Devora thanked heaven Luigi's mother couldn't see the state of the room. Candle wax had dripped down the frieze along the mantle and the velvet covers of the settees bore scorch marks from cigar ash carelessly allowed to drop where officers sat in the evenings. The polished chestnut-wood table between the fire and the sofa, where Luigi's mother used to arrange her glass sweets from Murano and her collection of miniature silver birds, was scratched from boots and marked with permanent rings from drinking glasses.

I bet the swine wouldn't treat their own homes like this, Devora thought, as she rescued the remains of a volume of Ungaretti's poetry from the ashes, used no doubt to start a fire. *Schweine*, she wanted to mutter. But she kept her mouth firmly shut. Luigi had told her German employers she was mute. She could hear but she would never answer, he'd told them.

It was a strain to remember and check herself. Especially when the officers billeted here, who knew no Italian, barked instructions at her in slow German, as if the speed of the words would make them more intelligible. She had to pretend she didn't understand when they were asking her to make up their beds with clean sheets or to fetch them a cup of coffee as she stood there looking blank, thinking acid thoughts about the occupiers.

The colonel's head had dropped to his chest and he'd begun to snore. She coughed to check how deeply he slept. He didn't flinch so she stepped quietly to the desk by the window.

A map lay open, a red line stretching all the way from coast to coast, from Pesaro to Pisa. There were crosses marked along the way and she memorised the names and as many of the scribbled notes as she could. A telegram lay to one side: *MOTHER DIED LAST NIGHT*. It reminded her that the enemy had family too. Or was it a code? The enemy was enemy, no matter what.

Papà had always told his family that the world was made up of love and hate. 'Choose which one you follow,' was his counsel. Hitler and his followers had chosen hatred. She steeled herself to discover more details and opened a brown folder, her brain taking in as much as she could, thanking the stars she'd had to learn the skill of scanning notes during her medical studies.

A shuffle of feet, a sneeze and she froze before flicking her duster over the ugly Gothic lettering on a German handbook and stepped back to lay the fire as the colonel stirred and stretched his bony arms above his head.

Luigi was pleased with the information when she'd recounted what she had observed. 'Well done. *Brava*, Devora. They've renamed the Gothic Line the Green Line. We'll need to communicate this to our radio operators. *Brava*. And they're obviously building more emplacements along the Foglia river. Your information will help us.'

'There was a letter from Kesselring in the file but I didn't have time to read it all... something about diverting materials from the Gustav Line to the Apennines and an order to evacuate civilians from the construction area.'

'That means there will be more reinforcements coming.

More opportunities for sabotage. This is gold dust. See what else you can glean... but take care.'

She'd been able to warn Luigi of a night raid that was to take place in a village at the foot of Monte Nerone. Luigi had sent word immediately to the fighters hiding in an empty house so they could flee to the woods higher up the slopes. She absorbed information either from listening in to the officers' conversations as they drank brandy round the fire or from reading notes carelessly left on the bureau in Luigi's father's office as she cleaned, the portrait of the Führer watching her.

Devora made sure to make herself look as unpresentable and as dim-witted as possible, wearing an unwashed blouse and an old scarf pulled low over her forehead. She trained herself to walk with a stoop, like an old woman, straightening up only when she had put sufficient distance between the house in Urbino and her refuge in Castel Cavallino, stretching her arms then to the sky and breathing in relief before she pedalled away along the dusty track on a rusty old bicycle Luigi had acquired for her. So ancient was it, she was forced to push the machine uphill, sitting down only for straight or downhill sections. By now, she knew where the sentries set up their blocks and managed to avoid most, making her way home across the meadows or through woods to divert from the main route. If they set up a new roadblock, she immediately reverted to her hunched, mute condition, listening to the vulgar comments about her tossed out either by young, bored *tedeschi* or fascist militia. The militia were worse, with their comments, to her mind. Her own people.

'She looks as if she's full of disease, leave her be' or, 'You'd have to be desperate to poke that one,' or 'Don't the peasants round here know about soap and water?'

It was hard not to react but her life depended on it and she had to keep alive to do everything she could to support the *partigiani*, as well as seeing her family again. During these past months, despite Luigi's best efforts, he'd been unable to trace her loved ones and the only way to survive the anguish had been to immerse herself in this new routine, satisfied in the knowledge she was finally doing something useful.

The winter of '43 was cruel, cold penetrating every crack in the hut, snow lingering on the ground until April, and most evenings had been spent huddled by the fire. Anna Maria knitted warm socks for Luigi and the boys, as she called them, up on Monte Nerone, while Devora studied from medical textbooks that Luigi procured for her. Once or twice she'd been called to care for a sick *partigiano*, the first case far too ill to survive. His wound had turned septic and he hadn't lasted the night. She'd tried her best, cutting gangrene with a knife, disinfected as best she could in the flame of a candle, but he was too far gone. She'd stood with the others on the hillside to bury him, a couple of whom she recognised from Urbino: Luigi's companions from the bar – Franco and skinny Gianni, who smiled shyly at her as he fiddled with his cap.

'Devora,' Luigi had said. 'Make a note of where we've buried him and keep it hidden in a safe place. After this war is over, we shall bring his mother to where he rests. There will be others. Can I entrust you with this task too?'

She did it unquestioningly. And, as the last sods of earth were placed over the young *partigiano*, she'd added a pebble, the Jewish way, surprising herself with her pursuit of this tradition. She remembered Mütti's explanation of how a stone kept the soul safe, preserved the memory of the dead person and stopped it from wandering and haunting. *Stones do not die*, she'd said. *Flowers wither, but not stones*. It gave a kind of permanence to the lost.

Once back in the hut near Castel Cavallino, she hid her note with the burial details in the base of an empty beehive at the edge of the property's boundary, which also housed a radio transmitter used by the *partigiani*. Anna Maria had captured a swarm back in the summer. She'd arranged a white sheet beneath the branch where the swarm hung and an upturned crate on the ground and Devora had watched in amazement as the bees slowly made their way into the crate: their new hive. When it was dark, Anna Maria had fashioned a smoker from an old metal pot, adding hot ashes to subdue the bees in the crate and carry them over to one of the two empty hives.

'Is there anything you don't know how to do?' Devora had asked from a distance, wary of being stung.

'When you are poor,' Anna Maria answered, 'you learn through necessity. These little creatures will provide us with sweetness. And you will thank me for it when our sugar runs out.'

'I sometimes think you're a wizard,' Devora said. 'You're so clever.'

'Pah! Clever? Me! I can't even read or write.'

'Knowing how to read and write doesn't make a person clever, Anna Maria. There are academics who write thousands of pages but who wouldn't survive a week if left to their own devices.'

'They would manage eventually. People in need learn how to survive through desperation.'

Such conversations usually ended with Anna Maria turning her back on Devora and she learned to understand this was her way of coping with emotions. Devora abandoned the talk and left Anna Maria to what she liked doing best: providing something from nothing.

Anna Maria kept them well fed and Luigi dropped in occasionally, especially if he knew she had hare stew on the go. With the shutters closed and the fire lit, evenings passed pleasantly enough.

'Guess who I bumped into the other day?' he had asked on his latest visit.

'Surprise me,' Devora said, closing her medical book.

'Enrico.'

Even after the years that had passed, her heart had missed a beat at this news and she'd avoided Anna Maria's narrowing of eyes by prodding at a log in the fire, sparks crackling up the tar-blackened bricks as she waited for her cheeks to stop burning.

'Oh yes?' she said, feigning indifference. 'And what did he have to say for himself?'

'He asked after you, actually.'

She looked up, her eyebrows raised in surprise.

'Of course I told him I had no idea where you were or what you were doing.'

'Of course,' she replied.

'He was a little cagey, actually. Said he didn't want to be in Urbino for long. He wants to come and see me in the Town Hall. I suggested he come late, when most people have gone home.'

'I wonder what he wants?'

'He briefly told me he's disillusioned and was not going back to the *carabinieri* and did I think there was a place for him with the CLN? But...' Luigi removed his spectacles and rubbed his eyes before polishing the lenses with his handkerchief. 'I need to check on him first. Make sure he's not trying to infiltrate. It's not the first time he's said things like this, as you and I know. Words don't mean anything to me until they're followed by action.'

'*Humph!*' The snort had come from Anna Maria, whose knitting needles clacked faster, her feelings about Enrico plain enough.

Devora's heart beat a little faster knowing that Enrico had asked after her. Maybe tomorrow she'd take a different route to work and pass through the piazza to see if he was around. She hardly heard what Luigi continued to talk about, her mind full of Enrico. So much time had passed since last seeing him, and she knew she was being foolish, but he still occupied a corner of her heart.

Another visitor had started to drop by earlier in the winter, much to Devora's horror. A furious row had erupted between the two women after he left.

'I can't believe you're allowing that German to visit. Don't encourage him.' Devora had spat words at Anna Maria after the soldier had gone, swaying a little from the glasses of home-made grappa that Anna Maria had plied him with.

'He's harmless.'

'He's *tedesco*. The enemy. Stop encouraging him.'

'I can't force him not to come. He was walking past and saw the beehives. He told me he kept bees, back in his country. He stood watching them for ages but as it was cold, none of the bees came out. He suggested I placed a dish of sugar to feed them next winter, but where can I get sugar? He told me he'd try and get me some.'

'And so you now speak fluent German, do you? What else do you get up to while I'm working my socks off as a cleaner?'

Anna Maria had stormed out at that, saying she was going to shut in the hens. But she didn't stop the *crucco* from calling.

The next time he'd visited, Devora sat, her headscarf covering her dark blonde hair, the farthest away she could and observed how the two engaged with each other.

Anna Maria had arranged her hair into two long plaits and wound them into a topknot. It was obvious the middle-aged soldier had taken a shine to her and she didn't seem averse to his attentions either. He'd brought along sugar and a bar of chocolate, which he handed to her with a bow and a click of his heels.

A cup of barley coffee had been offered and a slice of

ciambella cake that Anna Maria had baked from flour he'd supplied on an earlier visit. Devora moaned afterwards, saying they were most likely eating flour stolen from their own people and Anna Maria shrugged.

He'd pulled a photo from his wallet and showed them three smiling children: two boys, one with his front teeth missing, the other about twelve years of age, dressed in a smart uniform. The little girl wore a dress, not unlike the traditional Swiss costume Madlaine had worn: a colourful, striped skirt and a white, embroidered blouse with puffy sleeves.

Anna Maria had smiled and nodded her head. Devora had listened to him telling her they were his children but Anna Maria didn't understand.

'*Belli, belli!* They're beautiful. Aren't they, Dev... Elena?' Anna Maria had corrected herself.

Keeping to her part, Devora had frowned, nodded but said not a word.

The man was obviously homesick. He'd explained he'd been conscripted to work on building the Green Line to stop *die Englische* from advancing, and was billeted in the village with Todt engineers and construction workers. He'd talked in German to Anna Maria, as if she would understand every word and she'd nodded and smiled at intervals.

'I miss my children,' he'd said. 'I hope you don't mind that I come and sit with you from time to time. I won't harm you. I like to get away from the men.' He'd looked at his photo again. 'I fear I won't see these little ones again.' With a shake of his head, he'd replaced the photo in his wallet.

'This place. It's a bit like my homestead in Wesel. I keep cows and goats. And we eat the beef. Chickens too. Your chickens have mites, did you know? I could take a look and see what I could do. Garlic works. You have some in your vegetable garden.'

Anna Maria had risen to pour him more barley coffee and

he'd thanked her in the only Italian word he knew, pronouncing it badly: 'Grutsy,' he'd said. 'Your coffee is bad. I shall bring you some, in return for your charming company. You look a little like my wife, with your plaits. But hers are blonde. She's very lovely. Not beautiful. But lovely.'

Devora had begun to feel slightly sorry for the man. Yes, he was their enemy, but he was ordinary and different from the arrogant officers she cleaned for. Before he'd left, he'd asked if one night he could sleep beneath the cherry tree at the back of the hut. 'Not tonight, because it will drizzle,' he'd said. 'But another night I should love to sleep under the stars and forget about this war for a few hours.'

As he was leaving, he'd stopped before lifting the latch. 'And, by the way, you should hide any precious things. Your olive oil, your eggs, anything of value. Because as soon as our work is finished here, we are leaving. And the soldiers who follow us will not be good men. Not good at all.'

And with another click of his boots and a deep bow, he had gone.

Devora had waited a while, listening until she could no longer hear his footsteps. 'You shouldn't encourage him, Anna Maria. You really shouldn't. Before long, he'll bring a friend and then the locals will think we're fraternising. There'll be trouble.'

'You understand his language. Does he seem a bad man to you? I can't understand a word he says, but he's... gentle. He does no harm. He's simply a long way from home and he misses his family. I can tell a good man from a bad man.'

'That's not what you told me before. What about your priest?'

Anna Maria had risen to sluice their coffee cups, her back to Devora. 'That was a long time ago.'

She'd turned round, pointing a finger. 'And surely anything you can pick up from him when he speaks will be useful to Luigi. He talks such a lot. Isn't it useful?'

'All he talks about is how he misses his wife – he says you're like her – and he goes on about bees and animals. Nothing of any consequence. Except... he said that more soldiers are coming and they will not be good men – that's what he said. And we should hide anything precious.'

'Ha! Anything precious? What does he think we own?'

'Food mostly. I think we should do as he says. How about hiding more inside the beehives? Nobody would dare to look there. Most people are frightened of getting stung.'

Nevertheless, she'd taken on board what Anna Maria had said. You never knew what might come in useful to Luigi and the others.

CHAPTER 34

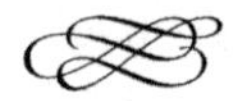

LUIGI

The pass in his pocket, his fascist *tessera* and his recent swearing of loyalty to the party, *il doppio gioco*, the double game, felt like a huge betrayal to Luigi and yet don Cecchetti had drilled home the importance that Luigi kept up this front.

'You're more use to us like this. I know you want to proclaim to the world your disgust of the military command, but keep your head down, *compagno mio*. Go about your daily business quietly. Be a mole. Keep your ears to the ground and pick up anything useful you can for the committee. Keep aloof. And keep safe. By the way, the new password is *ovo*. Memorise it.'

The registrar's office where Luigi worked was on the second floor, its large window looking over the piazza and, from his desk, he was able to observe the comings and goings in Urbino centre. When he worked late, which was often, as it was easier for him to alter information in the ledgers when the office was empty, he'd observed Sabrina.

She'd started sitting with German officers for *aperitivi* in the early evenings, laughing and flirting with them as she drank cocktails and passed round plates of appetizers. She was not the only young local woman who clinked glasses and shared laughter with the occupiers as the sun went down, and he felt disgust at their connivance. *Even if times are desperate, there are other ways to survive,* he thought, in his straightforward way. One of the officers was an accomplished pianist and the singing of German songs echoing round the portico made Luigi curl his fists into two balls of fury.

He unlocked his drawer and pulled out documents he needed to alter. The sergeant of the militia had asked for addresses of certain young men from Urbino, suspected of being *partigiani*. There were three and Luigi removed the cap from his fountain pen and wrote in neat handwriting in the official register: *deceased*, or, *deported to Germany*. He blotted the ink dry and was about to write a letter to the sergeant when there was a tap at his door and he quickly covered the documents with a folder.

'*Avanti!*' he said. 'Enter!'

Enrico stuck his head round the door. 'Is it safe to come in, Gigi?'

'I'm alone in the office. Come!' He rose to shake friends with his old school friend. 'You look well, Rico.' He indicated the chair on the other side of his desk but Enrico shook his head.

'I prefer to stand. I shan't keep you long.' He lowered his voice. 'I've taken a risk returning to Urbino but there are a couple of things to sort. One is a request of you, my friend. Can you alter my details to say I'm dead?'

Luigi frowned. 'What's up?'

'I left the *carabinieri*. I'm in a spot of trouble. Escaped solitary confinement and they'll find me if I stay here.'

He ran his hands through his hair and squared his shoulders. 'But it's more than that. I want out, anyway. And... I wondered if you could introduce me to the Pesaro contingent of the *partigiani*... the Fifth Brigade... I want to help.'

'How do I know you're not a spy?' Luigi's question was frank; he was ready to scrutinise Enrico's reaction.

'Hah! Well, I suppose you won't, will you? But... you know me from way back, Gigi. If I give you my word... surely that's good enough?'

There was a look of desperation in his eyes. Luigi was still uncertain but when Enrico continued, his voice full of emotion, he made up his mind.

'I'm sickened by what is happening, Gigi. I... don't want to be associated with monsters who kill innocent children, women and old men. I tried my best to save a handful, but I want to do more... these massacres... they've gone too far. The new guard are depraved.'

'Leave it with me. How can I contact you?'

'I'll come to you. At the moment, I'm moving about and I don't want to put my various hosts at risk.'

'I'm staying with my parents at my mother's old house in the countryside. The *tedeschi* requisitioned our place in the city.' Luigi removed his glasses to wipe them, stalling for time as he thought how to proceed.

'I tell you what,' Luigi continued. 'Let's meet at the fortress tomorrow morning first thing. By then, I'll have changed your details. No sense in turning up at my place if you're supposed to be dead, after all. What are you going to tell your parents?'

'I'm planning on not telling them for the time being. They'll have to think I'm dead. I'm sorry to put them through this, but you know what Papà's like. Son or not, he would hand me over for being a deserter. When all this is over, I'll turn up on their doorstep.'

The two men shook hands again and Enrico slipped out of the door.

Luigi was not far behind. Could he trust Enrico? He was riddled with doubt. It was as if certain details of Enrico's story had been invented on the spot. He'd been cagey about where he was staying. If he was indeed being hunted, why return to his birthplace – the first location any investigator worth his salt would search? And asking him to alter the records felt suspicious. The penalties for discovery of this were harsher than harbouring Jews or escaped prisoners of war. Something stank.

Luigi decided to follow Enrico. He was not prepared to put lives of fellow *partigiani* in danger by recommending somebody who might be setting up an elaborate trap. There had been several cases like this already. Rewards for information were tempting for the desperate.

Daylight was fading rapidly in the narrow streets. There were no lights and Luigi struggled to make out Enrico as he hurried up the hill. Luigi backed into the doorway of a closed shop as Enrico turned, checking before climbing the steps to the cathedral and slipping inside.

The huge doors were open. Mass was being celebrated, the early evening congregation of mostly women chanting a hymn to Maria. Luigi dipped his hand in the holy water font and made the sign of the cross as he entered and went to stand in the shadow of a column, scrutinising the crowd of worshippers. Enrico was metres away, sitting close to a woman in a back pew. Despite the woman wearing a veil that covered her head and shoulders, Luigi recognised the clothes and shape of Sabrina immediately. He watched as Sabrina dropped her missal to the floor. Enrico leant to pick it up and, after lifting her veil to drop a kiss on her lips and slipping the prayer book into his pocket, he rose, genuflected and left the church, Luigi not far behind.

Enrico was in a hurry as he strode towards the southern quarter of the city, Luigi attempting to match his footsteps to mask the sounds. Once or twice, Enrico turned and Luigi froze, convinced this was the moment he would be detected, his heart thumping from exertion as well as adrenaline. Enrico made his way down Via Piave and Luigi heard the rap of the knocker on the door to the city brothel.

You haven't changed, Enrico. You haven't changed.

But Luigi was puzzled. Why had Sabrina given him a missal? What was the significance? Did it contain some kind of message? It seemed Enrico was not the only one he had to keep tabs on.

The nights in May still had a nip, and a chill wind funnelled along the alley. Luigi was reluctant to hang around and wait for Enrico to finish with whatever harlot he had chosen for the night. Coiling his scarf around his neck, he stuck his hands in his pocket and trudged his way out of the city and into the countryside, wishing he had Tuffo by his side to keep him company.

One thing was sure. He would not tell Devora that Enrico was frequenting the city's brothel. As much as it might help his own cause, he would not do that to her.

CHAPTER 35

ENRICO

Sabrina still had the hots for me. She'd do anything to get in my trousers and I squeezed her hand and kissed her on the lips, to the tutting of the woman in the pew behind. Over the months, I'd kept her sweet with the occasional postcard, keeping her hopes alive. That madness I knew she felt in her heart was familiar to me. We were both, in our separate ways, obsessed.

I've always known how to appeal to women and I'll admit, I strung Sabrina along. Her parents' apartment in Fano was in my mind as I wooed her. I remembered how they occasionally spent a month in August by the coast before the troubles began. The place had been empty for the past two years. It would be perfect. In the past, she'd shown us photographs of the view over the canal, the sea within walking distance and restaurants where you could eat plates of fresh fish for almost nothing. She'd willingly handed me the key and I'd enjoyed the cloak-and-dagger of it all. Even though there really had been no need to hide the thing in a missal, like a second-rate thriller. When she whispered that she might even visit, I'd smiled but I hadn't encouraged her. Of course I hadn't. If she turned up, I would cross that bridge. But right now, I had to get myself and my girl away from Urbino. And fast.

It honestly gave me the creeps returning to that hole in Via Piave. Why I had ever thought of trying to hide her in a brothel was madness. I hadn't reckoned on German soldiers being billeted opposite and the city was teeming with the bastards now.

The signora was at her desk, puffing on a cheroot, a dingy red shade in the lamp on her table doing little to hide the deep lines on her horrified face. She half rose from her chair as she stubbed out her cheroot. '*Che cazzo fai qui?* What the fuck are you doing here?' she asked in her usual charming way.

'What have you done with her things?' I snarled at the old bag. It was insanity to return but everything was mad at the moment. My lover had left the only thing that linked her with her past: a gold chain that once belonged to her mother's mother. Only a trinket but I knew she wanted it and, in my crazy state, I was prepared to do most anything to please her.

The woman put her hand to her neck. Stupid bitch was wearing it and I yanked it from her. She yelped, just as a *tedesco* stumbled from the room near the desk, fumbling with the buttons on his trousers.

'*Problema?*' he asked, his eyes adjusting to the light as he squinted at us.

'No, no,' the signora replied. 'The signore was just leaving. *Nessun problema.*'

'I need more wine in the room,' the soldier barked, swaying a little and winking at me, man to man.

With a thumbs up, I was out of the place. Curfew would start soon and I increased my pace, threading through the alleyways, wondering if I would ever return to my place of birth.

I regretted not being totally honest with dear old Luigi but I didn't want to meet him tomorrow. Yes, I'd lost heart in the fascist cause that I'd followed all those years, but did I have the courage to sacrifice my life for an alternative when all I wanted was to enjoy the love of my woman? For the time being, the answer was no.

What I needed was a severing of all links with the past. A fresh start.

CHAPTER 36

LUIGI

Luigi laughed at Tuffo's antics as he tried to jump up at the swifts that swooped high and low round the fortress walls. Nature was largely unpeturbed by war, he thought. It was good to watch these birds on their return from Africa as they circled, weaving through the air to catch insects. Whenever everything got too much for Luigi, nature was his solace.

Only last week, on a fine sunny afternoon, he'd taken a rare walk with Devora and Tuffo up towards the abbey of Castel Cavallino, its bell tower protruding like a castle turret beyond a row of lime trees. In a meadow, he'd suddenly fallen to his knees, sunlight glinting from the lens of the magnifying glass he'd pulled from its permanent place in his pocket.

'Are you trying to start a fire, Gigi?' she'd asked him. 'Like we learned back in the day in the Scouts? When they were allowed to exist,' she'd added ruefully.

'*I'm* being set on fire by the amazing flora,' he said, looking up at her with a shy smile. Her hair had grown a little. Still short, her dark blonde curls were nevertheless escaping from the dreadful scarf she insisted on wearing. He'd had an urge to pull it from her head and run his fingers through them. Instead, he'd told her gruffly it was best to cover up; you never knew who'd be working in the fields and might recognise her. She'd looked around, terrified, and adjusted the material and he hoped he hadn't broken the spell of the afternoon.

'Come and take a look at what I've found,' he'd said, tugging at her sleeve, wanting the reminders of war to disappear for at least this precious hour.

She'd bent down, her hands on her knees, and her distinctive scent had made him lose his train of thought for a moment.

'What can you see?' she asked, her breath on the back of his neck.

'*Ophrys speculum*. A mirror orchid. I nearly stamped on it. It won't flower for much longer. Look at the colours and its furry petals.'

'It's beautiful,' she'd said as he passed her the glass to see better.

'The other day I found a woodcock orchid in this meadow. *Ophrys scolopax*.'

'You love everything about the outdoors, don't you, Gigi?'

'I never used to as a boy. I hated it when Papà dragged me up the mountains to hunt with his friends. I wanted to stay at home and hide my nose in a book instead of watching grown men kill boar and deer. And all those tiny birds... There's no meat on their bones... What is the point? It's simply the thrill of the kill.'

He had bent to observe another orchid in the scrubby grass and then continued. 'Discovering the intricate beauty of flowers and plants – somehow it softened those killing days. I found an old botany textbook in the bookshop in the piazza and started to collect names...'

'Latin names,' she'd said. 'The medical terms were so hard

when I started to study.' She'd rattled off a few: *quadratus femoris, subscapularis...*

'So I turned them into spells to remember them by but of course there's a logic too, if you think of the Italian: *polmoni* for *pulmones, cervello* for *cerebrum, capo* for *caput.*'

He'd smiled, happy in the knowledge they could chat so easily. 'We're lucky at least that our language stems partly from Latin,' he said.

Yes, it had been good to switch off from the war for a while.

Now, while he waited for Enrico to turn up at the Fortezza, he threw a stick for Tuffo, watching his silken ears stream behind him as he raced about. Below him, the timeless view of the city spread like a picture postcard, the twin towers of the Ducal Palace the main landmark, a cross painted on its roof to signify the ancient city was a no-bomb zone. He loved this panorama in every season – subdued browns and beiges that followed the fire of autumn colours, snow-laden roofs like a Christmas scene later on and soft pinks and oranges of terracotta roof tiles baking in the haze of high summer.

He threw the stick again for Tuffo with greater force, angry that his city was occupied by the *tedeschi*. 'It's *our* city, our nation,' he muttered aloud. 'And we shall vanquish you and get it back for ourselves.'

He turned away from the view, the barbed wire and a couple of German tanks parked on the greening grass rubbing in the presence of the enemy. A soldier wandered over and tickled the dog behind his ears.

'*Cane – bello*,' he attempted. 'Nice dog.' Followed by, '*Documenti, per favore*,' and the ubiquitous '*Verboten hier*.' Forbidden here.

'*Heil* Hitler,' the young soldier said after he had flicked through Luigi's papers and told him to leave, his arm raised in the grotesque salute.

Luigi copied him, his head brimming with hatred. He had to conform for the time being but it made him sick to the stomach.

Enrico was late anyway. It had been a stupid location to suggest. Of course the *tedeschi* would be using the fortress as a vantage point, but he hadn't been up here for a while, and he hadn't registered. Feeling foolish, he whistled to Tuffo to come to heel and then trudged down the alleyways to his work in the Town Hall. With each step he took, a mantra rang inside his head in sync with the striking of his hobnailed boots on the cobbles: *Viva, viva, viva la libertà.* He had to believe the allies would arrive soon to liberate the city and that one day soon, Italy would be free again.

There were a few babies to add to the list of new births that morning. In the early years of his posting as registrar, he had frequently written out the names Benito, Addis, Romolo and Remo on birth certificates. The fact that he hadn't had to do this for months reflected the disenchantment of the populace for the *fascisti*.

At ten o'clock sharp, Sergeant Gelsi of the republican militia strode up to his desk.

'Michelozzi. Show me the census again.'

Luigi's heart began to hammer as he reached for the file on the shelf.

The sergeant removed his glove. 'Where are the classes of 1919 and the nearest years?'

Luigi turned the pages slowly and carefully, hoping that the alterations he had made would not be detectable. He had used an eyeglass and worked carefully at scraping away the original script. The class of 1919 had included half a dozen Jewish names and he had changed their religions to Roman Catholic. Other details, such as deaths or transfer to a different city or country, had been easy enough to write in the margins in his careful calligraphy.

Luigi watched the man run his grubby fingernail down the page.

'And where are the death certificates for these men?' he asked, pointing to two names.

'They died in action, *sergente*. I have no certificates yet. How could I? Such details will take a while to properly record and confirm in these difficult times. That is why I've only pencilled them in.'

The sergeant straightened up. 'Suspicious, is it not, that both these men have been reported to me as *partigiani combattenti*, active partisans?' He pulled on his gloves again. 'Michelozzi. If I find any inconsistencies here in the future, I shall deal with you severely.'

Luigi's mouth was dry but he stared directly into the man's eyes. 'I am sure you will find nothing wrong with my work. Ask my manager, *ingegner* Torricci, if you have doubts.'

The man left, after saluting Luigi and, for the second time that day, Luigi was forced to reluctantly retaliate with the same grotesque gesture. He slumped back in his chair until his heart stopped beating like a drum in a mediaeval jousting tournament. He would have to lie low for a few days until the odious man returned to his headquarters in Pesaro. The *sergente* was obviously suspicious of him and he knew where he stayed at his parents' place. Don Cecchetti would find him refuge somewhere else in Castel Cavallino, he was sure.

He pulled a couple of blank food coupon forms from his desk drawer as well as his fountain pen and magnifying glass and slipped them into his briefcase. Knocking at his manager's door, he told him he needed to visit the family of a recently deceased soldier to complete details for his death certificate. 'His mother is infirm and lives alone. She can't come to the Town Hall, sir.' Bending down, he muttered that, in reality, he had to steer clear of *sergente* Gelsi for a while and would be away from his desk for three days. 'Can you cover for me if Gelsi drops by again and also let my parents know somehow? They'll be worried when I don't return tonight.'

Ingegner Torricci nodded at his diligent registrar. '*Va bene, Michelozzi. A più tardi*. We shall see you later.' He added sotto voce, 'Comrade.'

The pair had a complicit hatred of the *fascisti* and no further explanation was needed. Luigi never confided in what he was actually involved in and Torricci didn't ask. It was better that way.

Don Cecchetti was kneeling at the altar when Luigi pushed open the door to the abbey out in the country one hour and a half later. The priest turned as Luigi stepped up the aisle. Making the sign of the cross, he rose slowly from his knees.

'Is anything the matter, Michelozzi?' he asked, his hand on Luigi's arm. 'It's unusual to see you here in daytime.'

'Can I stay for a couple of days? *Sergente* Gelsi is suspicious about my register. He's looking for Mari and Bacchielli. I marked them as deceased but I don't think he believes me.'

The priest sighed. 'You take such risks, my son.'

'We all take risks these days.'

'True, true. Follow me.'

The priest took him down the narrow steps that led to the crypt. It had been kept locked for years due to subsidence but don Cecchetti took a large key from his pocket and turned it. 'This will be where you can sleep for the next nights.' He turned to add, 'Along with my other guests.'

It took a while for Luigi's eyes to adjust to the gloom. In the far corner, at the only place where feeble daylight seeped through a grating, sat a huddle of figures.

'It's only me and a good friend. *Un amico*,' the priest reassured them.

A man rose and approached. He was middle-aged, his hair

close-shaven. Behind him a woman nursed a small baby. Four young children leant with their backs against the cold walls of the crypt, their eyes round from fear and malnutrition. They were bundled in blankets and assorted garments, some too large for their skinny frames.

'Don't be afraid of my dog,' Luigi said, noticing how the children shrank nearer their mother when Tuffo padded in. 'He's very gentle.'

'*Buongiorno*,' the man said in Italian, extending his hand to Luigi in a firm handshake. He too was skinny, fatigue lining his face. 'The children are terrified of dogs, signore. They've been chased too often by them.'

'Let me keep him for the moment, Luigi.' Don Cechetti took hold of Tuffo's collar. 'And I'll bring you all soup later,' he said. 'Do you have everything you need?'

The man hesitated.

'Tell me, my friend,' the priest encouraged.

'You've done so much for us already, *padre*.'

'If I'm able to help, I shall.'

'My wife,' he lowered his voice. 'She's ill. Women's problems.'

Luigi interrupted. 'I have a friend I can ask, *padre*. She's training to be a doctor. She's staying not far from here.'

'You'll have to wait until dark,' don Cecchetti said. 'There are guards posted further along the road. But you know the footpaths round here, Luigi.'

'I'll slip out later.'

The priest showed him where a few thin blankets were stored on a shelf and left Luigi to sort himself out. Luigi stroked the dog, telling him he would see him soon. Tuffo licked him on the nose and went obediently with the priest. The sound of the key turning in the lock echoed round the chilly crypt. Luigi noticed the grating was too small for even the tiniest child to squeeze through. For a slender moment, he felt panic but he willed himself to calm down and breathe deeply. It was not that he didn't trust the priest but if anything were to happen to the old man, they would all be trapped. The door was solid, its oak panels at least ten centimetres thick. It would take a battering ram to break it down. He resolved to ask the priest for a spare key.

Luigi spoke for a while to the family. They were Jews from the port of Ancona where the bombing had been fierce.

'We have moved so many times. My wife gave birth to our new son in a stable, shared with the farmer's goats. We hide here by day and during the night the priest opens the door for a while so the children can step outside for fresh air. It's not good for them, signore. But what is the alternative? They've forgotten how to play and they jump at the slightest noise. This war... it has taken childhood away from the innocent. Our new baby cries all the time. He's hungry – my wife has hardly any milk. And we worry his cries will betray us.'

He lowered his voice to confide something that shocked Luigi. 'I have to watch my wife does not do anything... two days ago she tried to smother him.'

Luigi bit his lip. 'My friend will help. Stay strong, signore.'

CHAPTER 37

True to his word, don Cecchetti unlocked the door to the crypt not long after ten thirty that night.

Luigi was greeted rapturously by Tuffo. The dog pinned him to the wall, his front paws on Luigi's shoulders, tail wagging furiously as he licked his owner's face.

'Woah, Tuffo, my friend,' Luigi said, the children behind him sharing his laughter. 'I don't need a bath from you. *Padre,* why don't you make a sign to say it's dangerous to enter the crypt? That there is severe subsidence. Paint a skull and cross-bones on the door. Write *Pericolo* and *Achtung*.' He pointed at the shininess of the escutcheon, where the key had so obviously been used frequently and recently. 'And you should render this dull. Cover your tracks. Have you a spare key? What would happen if we needed to escape and you were somehow not available? I've heard churches have been set alight by the *tedeschi*.' He kept his voice low for this last piece of information.

'Excellent suggestions. I could do with a practical man at my side, dear Michelozzi.'

'Unfortunately, I can't be in two places at once. If I'm to

remain at the *comune* to be of use there, then I can't be at the abbey as well.'

'True, true. But we do need to recruit more young people.' He ushered the children and their parents outside, warning them not to stray too far and to be very quiet. 'Half an hour,' he told them, 'and then it will be time to return inside. Michelozzi, come into the presbytery with me for one moment.'

Two clean sets of vestments hung from hooks on the wall of the musty room next to a small bookcase containing Bibles and hymn books. Don Cecchetti reached behind the books and pulled a handful of papers from their hiding place. 'These leaflets need to be distributed in Urbino, wherever you think fit. The words were written by a young *partigiano* called Mirko, just before he was shot. Compelling, you'll find.'

Luigi adjusted his spectacles. It was a call to arms to disillusioned young soldiers.

> Dear companions, it is up to us now. You know what you have to do. I am going to die, but I know I shall die for a better future: brighter, bigger and more beautiful. These days from now on will be like the last days of a life ruled by a terrible monster whose aim is to make victims of as many people as he can. Don't allow him to do this. Fight for our freedom. Don't hide yourselves away. Present yourselves to the *partigiani* and join in the fight for our country's liberty. The militia of the *Repubblica Sociale* will hunt you down where you are hiding at home and send you to Germany or labour camps. So, escape to the woods and fight with us. We shall greet you with the happiness of finding lost brothers.
>
> *Sui nostri corpi si farà il grande faro della libertà.* Our bodies will create a huge beacon to freedom.

'Moving indeed. *Che coraggio.* I'll see what I can do, *padre.* Now, let me fetch my friend. That woman is in a bad way.'

. . .

A harvest moon lit the countryside with a dim yellow glow and Luigi kept to the hedges as he crossed the meadows towards Devora and Anna Maria's simple dwelling. Tuffo stopped at one point, lifting one paw to point as a hare streaked across his path. Luigi had him on his lead and he placed one hand on the dog's head. '*Zitto*, Tuffo. Quiet.' If he barked, then all the sentries in the area would be on alert. He shouldn't really have brought him along, but the dog had been tied up all afternoon in the priest's house. He had trained Tuffo well, and despite the animal's trembling and thwarted instinct to hunt, he remained quiet. Luigi pulled a tiny piece of sausage from his pocket and tossed it in the air. Tuffo swallowed it with a snap of his jaws.

A faint telltale light emerged through the shutters. The gap needed to be repaired and he would warn the women. He tapped gently on the door three times, followed by another three and noted how the light was almost immediately extinguished. Again, he tapped and called gently, '*Sono io*. Gigi. Let me in, it's me.'

The door opened a crack.

'Why the bloody hell are you calling on us at this hour?' Anna Maria asked. She held a stout stick and Luigi had no doubt that it would have been used effectively. 'You gave us both a fright.'

'You need to patch up that front shutter. Light is filtering through.'

'So you came all this way to tell us that?'

She pulled him in and bolted the door.

Devora was sitting by the stove, drying her hair. She wore a nightdress and Luigi averted his eyes from the flimsy material revealing her figure.

'Can you get dressed, Devora? I need you at the abbey. There's a sick woman hiding who needs your help,' Luigi said.

'*Certo*. Of course.' She moved to the far side of the room where a rudimentary curtain-screen made of sacking separated the bed from the living area. 'Give me one moment.'

'Your hair is wet, girl,' Anna Maria said. 'You'll catch a chill. Wear a hat or your thick scarf.'

Within five minutes, after reassuring the older woman that, yes, he would take good care of Devora and, yes, she would be back before daylight and, yes, they would be really careful, yes, he knew there was a war on and so on and so forth, Luigi and Devora were on their way.

'She's an amazing woman,' Devora said, when they had left the hut behind, 'but she's turned into my surrogate mother.'

'I'm pleased somebody is looking after you.'

'I've put on weight from her cooking.'

'Nothing wrong with that,' he said. 'Best not talk anymore until we get there, Biondina.'

The woman was in pain, that much was obvious to Devora, her face pale and drawn. As the baby suckled, she kept her shoulders hunched and winced.

She was reluctant at first to speak and it needed all Devora's bedside skills to coax her to open up.

'*Mi chiamo* Elena,' she said, keeping to her disguise. It was best that way. 'I'm a medical student. *Shalom*,' she said, recalling words she'd heard her parents use so often. '*Ma nishma?* What's up?' Luigi had briefly filled her in on what little he knew about the family.

At that, the woman's expression altered slightly and she responded with a weak smile.

'I'm Haddie. *Shalom*.'

'Let's move to a quieter corner,' Devora suggested. A little girl had climbed onto Haddie's lap, sucking her thumb, trying to pull the baby from her mother's breast. The poor woman would have found it hard to cope in ordinary circumstances, Devora thought, let alone on the run, hiding who knew where in the past months, likely exhausted from a difficult birth. The mental and physical trauma was huge and anger filled Devora's heart. But she remained calm and asked her husband, Adamo, to please keep the children busy while she examined his wife.

'When did you give birth, Haddie?'

'Ten days ago. In a stable. My two nurses were goats,' she answered, her words laboured, but trying bravely to inject spirit into them.

Not the most hygienic of situations, Devora assessed, thinking back to the similar birth of baby Nechama. But that infant and Ida had been immediately cared for by Madlaine in a pristine and comfortable mountain home. Most likely Haddie had picked up an infection or had retained products. She tested her forehead with her hand and, yes, she was clammy and burning.

'Are you still bleeding?' Devora asked.

'Yes, signorina.'

'I'd like to examine you.'

She told Haddie to lie down behind one of the thick columns and, shielding her with her back to the family, Devora helped raise the woman's skirt. She knew what was wrong almost immediately. The woman's rags were drenched with blood and smelled. If she had a puerperal infection, she needed a hospital, not a cursory examination in a dark crypt. It would not help to show her patient her concern but Devora feared sepsis had already set in. It could lead to multiple organ failure and in the worst cases, death.

'Haddie, my dear, I'm going to talk to the priest. We need to get you to a hospital. Don't worry,' she said, clasping the woman's hand. 'We'll look after you.'

She hurried from the crypt to find Luigi and don Cecchetti.

'*Le suore!*' don Cecchetti said after she'd explained the

predicament. 'The nursing nuns at Santa Caterina. But... how to get her there?'

'If we could get hold of transport, *padre*, I can accompany her to the convent hospital,' Devora suggested. 'The woman is extremely sick. It really is a matter of life and death.'

'I only have my mule,' the priest said.

'My parents' Fiat,' Luigi thought aloud. 'My plan was to lie low for a few days. The *sergente* has his suspicions about me. But... if I was to disguise myself in some way...' He paced the room, thinking on his feet and then stopped, punching one hand into the other palm. 'Maybe, just maybe, Enrico might help. What do you think, Devora? When we last spoke, he talked about his disillusionment. If he lends me his police uniform, I could drive Haddie. How ill is this woman? What's the urgency?'

'Like I said: urgent. If we're going to save her, then it has to be now.'

'Twenty-four hours?'

Devora's face was grim. 'No longer than that. Sepsis is insidious. She's already burning up with a fever. We have to save her. Do what you can, Gigi, but do it fast.'

CHAPTER 38

Luigi took the route to the city in a sprint. The sky was turning pearly grey as he stopped at the main gate to show the sentries his documents.

'Where have you been?' a pimply *repubblichino* guard asked as he flicked through Luigi's papers.

Luigi feigned a sheepish look. 'Let's just say I was keeping a farmer's wife company while her husband is away.'

The youth gave a dirty snigger and ushered him through the barrier. 'Can you let me have her address?' he called after Luigi. 'In exchange for a couple of cigarettes?'

The piazza was empty save for a couple of stray dogs that bounded over to Luigi, tails wagging. They knew him well. He always had something good in his pocket and he tossed them each the remainders of Tuffo's sausage supply before making his way to Sabrina's apartment. He was certain Sabrina knew of Enrico's whereabouts. Why else had they met so furtively in the cathedral? His watch told him it was ten to six and he was counting on the fact that, as it was a working day, Sabrina would be already up and making herself presentable. Her appearance was important to her. No doubt she needed more effort than a splash of soap and water on her face to prepare herself. For her new German friends. He swallowed disgust as he thought of it.

The maid opened the door at the second ring.

'I need to speak to Sabrina. It's urgent,' he told the woman.

'She's not ready to receive visitors, signor Luigi.'

Luigi put his foot in the door. 'Tell her I have a message from Enrico. And it's important.'

Three minutes later, Sabrina came to the hallway, where the maid had told him to wait. Her hair was in curlers and she was pulling a silk dressing gown round her ample figure, her slippers slapping over the parquet floor as she hurried towards him.

'What on earth's the matter, Luigi? Is Enrico hurt?'

'No. But I've been asked to give him an important message.' He lowered his voice. 'Sabrina, it's a matter of life and death. He's in trouble. Where can I find him?'

'How do I know you're not tricking me?'

He stamped his foot, his impatience real. 'Why would I do that? How could you possibly think it? Haven't we been friends for years? I've tried his parents' house,' he lied, 'but he's not there. If you have the slightest idea of where he is, then you have to tell me. You'll be saving his skin. I beg of you.'

She grabbed a notepad from the hall table and scribbled down an address. 'He's staying in Fano, at one of my parents' apartments. He told me he needed somewhere to hide for a while.' She grabbed hold of Luigi's arm, lowering her voice. 'Please let me know he's all right when you find him. Tell him I'll come and visit as soon as I can.'

'I don't advise that,' Luigi said, opening the door and peering out slowly as if checking he hadn't been followed. 'For the safety of you and your family, do not – on any account – try to meet with him. He's a wanted man. There's a warrant out for his arrest.'

Luigi hoped he was injecting the right amount of drama to

make Sabrina worried. Then, leaning in to give her a kiss on each cheek, although he would rather have throttled the fickle girl, he turned on his heel and ran down the wide marble staircase to the courtyard below.

His mind full of Haddie, the sweat on the sick woman's brow and the concern in Devora's voice, he let himself into the Town Hall, relieved that nobody had turned up early for work. In his office, he pulled a couple of files from his shelf, stamped with *Comune di Urbino*, before continuing his way out of the city again. If questioned at the road stops, he would produce these and say he was on urgent business for the military command.

The grey light of dawn had already disappeared as he left the Town Hall, keeping to the alleyways at the edges of the wakening city. The same sentry was still on duty, half dozing, but he perked up when he saw Luigi. 'Can't keep away, eh? *Dio mio*, but she must be a goer. I hope you can keep it up for her.'

'I'll give you her address next time I see you, *amico*,' Luigi said.

He broke into a jog when he was out of the sentry's sight. Haste was of the essence. He needed to get to his parents' country house and beg use of Papà's car. Fano was a good two hours' drive away. With luck, he could be there and back in the day. *If*. One small word that carried huge weight. *If* everything went smoothly. He avoided the main road, knowing the *tedeschi* had dug themselves in, taking advantage of sweeping views of the surrounding countryside, and he kept to the footpaths he knew so well from his walks with Tuffo.

His father's sympathies were broadly the same as his and, without needing to go into too much detail – simply telling him it truly was a matter of life or death and that his conscience would not permit him to ignore the problem – his father showed him where he had buried a couple of cans of petrol and handed over the keys to the Topolino.

'Your need is greater than mine,' he told his son. 'But be careful. Fano is occupied by the *tedeschi* and there'll be many roadblocks. Take dirt tracks whenever possible. There's a spare wheel if needs be and a detailed map in the glove compartment.'

The two men embraced. 'I'm proud of you, *figlio mio*. But make sure you come back to us.'

As he skirted round Fossombrone, the sky turned black as hordes of Lancasters appeared from the clouds. Seconds later, there was a huge explosion in the valley, a volcanic eruption of smoke and flames that mushroomed into the heavens, destroying a munitions depot. The Pesaro partisans must have been successful in relaying information to the *alleati*, he thought, with elation. But it shook him up to think that if it had not been for the dirt track he'd taken, he'd have been driving next to where the bombs had exploded.

His hands began to shake on the wheel and he pulled up under the shade of an oak tree for a few minutes, taking a swig from the bottle of grappa his father kept under the driver's seat. Breathing deeply, he continued on his way. The bombing had diverted sentries from roadblocks and the rest of the journey was smooth. He stopped to give a lift to an old woman wearily carrying a goose tied up in a basket and was rewarded with a brown paper bag containing two eggs when he set her down at the next village. '*Buona fortuna*, signore,' she said, her smile showing gaps between her brown teeth.

'*Grazie*,' he said, thinking how much good fortune he really did need if this plan was going to work.

Luigi had spent a couple of summer holidays with his parents by the sea in Fano as a teenager and knew the layout of the town. He drove alongside the railway line, parts of it buckled from recent bomb raids, gangs of men working on repairs, guarded by German soldiers, and parked not far from the canal. Within three minutes he had walked to the address Sabrina had scribbled.

The palazzo of apartments was two doors away from a seafood restaurant. He hoped Enrico was at home and not lunching out. If he had to search for him along the many eating establishments along the beach, it would be like looking for a needle in the proverbial haystack. And the place was crawling with *crucchi* in their grey-green uniforms. He had to get through today without trouble. The image of Devora flashed into his mind again, telling him Haddie would die if their plan did not work. The children huddled forlornly in the crypt with their father was a compelling reminder that there were already too many orphans because of this damn war. He would do his best to make sure their mother lived.

CHAPTER 39

After knocking for ages, Luigi heard footsteps on the other side of the door, just when he was about to give up.

The door opened a crack, Enrico's voice asking, '*Chi è?* Who is it?'

'It's me. Luigi. And I'm alone.'

The door opened wider. Enrico stood there, a revolver in his right hand.

'If this is some kind of trap, my friend, I swear I'll blast out your brains.'

'*Sciocco*. Stop acting the idiot and let me in.'

Enrico pulled him inside. The place was in semi-darkness, all the doors off the hallway shut, and it took a while for Luigi's eyes to adjust.

'What are you doing here? How did you find me?' Enrico asked, his gun still in his hand, pointed at Luigi.

'Put that blasted thing down and listen to me. I need your help. Sabrina gave me your address.'

'*Porca boia*. The bitch.'

'Can't we sit somewhere and talk, Enrico? I've come a long way and I'm thirsty.'

'I'll take you to the bar I go to,' Enrico said, replacing his weapon in its holster round his shoulder.

'No. I need to talk in privacy. A glass of water from your kitchen is fine.'

'Wait in here,' Enrico said, pushing open the door to the room nearest the entrance and hustling Luigi in. The shutters were closed but shafts of sunlight streamed through the slats to show it was a single bedroom, unused, the mattress bare, dust coating the top of a fancy chest of drawers. Enrico shut the door behind him and was away for a couple of minutes. Luigi wiped sweat from his brow. The temperature was stifling in the room and he went to open the window. Sounds from outside poured in and the delicious aroma of grilled fish. He realised he hadn't eaten all day.

Enrico returned with a bottle of water and two glasses, setting them on a small table by the bed. He tutted when he noticed the open window and closed it.

'Tell me why you're here.'

Luigi downed a whole glass of water and held it out for more. 'Do you have something to eat? A roll or something?'

'For fuck's sake, Luigi. Don't tell me you drove all the way from Urbino to eat a fucking panino with me. Spit out what is so urgent, man.'

'I need your help. Do you still have your *carabiniere* uniform?'

'Yes. Why?'

'I need to borrow it.'

He filled Enrico in with a few details, explaining how he needed to get a sick woman to hospital. If he drove like a maniac into the city, dressed as a *sbirro*, then there was a good chance he wouldn't be stopped. There was nobody else he could ask.

'You've obviously gone AWOL, Enrico. Why else are you holed up here? Now's your chance to do something useful for your country. You told me yourself you've had enough of the *nazifascisti.* It's taking you long enough to do something about it...'

The two friends stared long and hard at each other and then, with a scrape of his chair on the tiled floor, Enrico rose to leave the room. He closed the door, so that Luigi wondered if he was maybe harbouring somebody else, another disenchanted fascist, perhaps. It was a waste of resources if there were other fit men hiding themselves away in this apartment. *Carabinieri*, like Enrico, who knew how to use weapons and who could usefully swell the numbers of the *partigiani*. They would not be the first to have changed sides. The dilemma was always how reliable and trustworthy new candidates were.

The door opened again, Enrico carrying his uniform over his arm. 'It will be too large for you. You'll look like a carnival character.'

'That's my problem to worry about. *Grazie*, Enrico. I won't forget this.'

Enrico handed him his revolver too. 'I have another. This might come in useful, my friend.' He pulled Luigi into an embrace. 'In return for this, Gigi, promise me you won't tell my parents you've seen me. For the time being, they don't need to know I'm alive.'

There was no time to argue about Rico's odd request. Luigi nodded agreement but just before leaving, he threw in, 'By the way, Sabrina told me she'd come and visit you soon.' Luigi grinned. 'Better prepare yourself.'

'Well, maybe you could pass on the sad news to her too, *amico*. I really do not want her turning up here.'

The look of horror on Enrico's face was a picture. Sabrina had always had a crush on him. *Una cotta*. But it had also been plain, from their discussions, that he didn't fancy her at all. Devora, on the other hand, had definitely caught Enrico's eye. Luigi knew that well enough but tried to quash his resentment.

There were more serious concerns to deal with right now, he told himself.

He let himself out of the door, carrying his precious cargo to the car. As he pulled out the choke, he offered up a prayer that his return journey would be as smooth as when he'd driven here.

Once he'd left the view of the Fano suburbs behind in his rear-view mirror, he pulled in along a lonely stretch and changed into Enrico's uniform. Time to practise being *tenente* Luigi Michelozzi. If he was asked for his documents, then he was a goner. Unless he used Enrico's revolver. It sat next to him on the passenger seat and he hoped he wouldn't have to use it.

The uniform proved invaluable from the start. He was waved through three road checks. At the fourth, when it became apparent the guard was not sure whether to let him pass, he wound down his window and shouted, 'I'm in a hurry, man. If I'm late for my meeting with the *maresciallo*, I'll hold you personally responsible.' He revved his foot on the accelerator in impatience and was waved through, the guard saluting him as he accelerated away, his words bringing a grin of relief to Luigi's face. '*Va bene, signor tenente. Mi scusi, mi scusi.*'

Luigi was starving when he pulled in at the abbey buildings after dark. Adrenaline had kept him going, but he swayed as he got out of the car and grabbed hold of the open door to steady himself. Nervous exhaustion, he presumed. He could hardly believe he'd made it. When the priest opened his door, he took one look at Luigi and immediately ordered him to sit.

'You need refuelling, my son. Eat!' He bustled about the kitchen and found bread, cheese, a dish of tomatoes and a tumbler of wine. Luigi handed over the goose eggs and the priest scrambled one. While Luigi set to, the priest went to unlock the crypt.

. . .

Devora had bound strips of bandages round her own head. Don Cecchetti stopped short when he saw her.

'Have you injured yourself, signorina?'

'No, *padre*. The car can have two sick patients. Why else would I be accompanying Haddie?' she said.

'Good thinking, signorina. Luigi's returned but he's exhausted. We should let him rest for an hour before leaving.' He lowered his voice. 'How is she?'

Devora bit her lip. 'She's deteriorating. Her fever is worrying me, *padre*. The sooner we get her to hospital, the better.'

Adamo knelt by the side of his wife, sponging her head with a damp cloth. The children sat in a huddle nearby and the priest crouched down to talk to them. 'Be good for your mother. Tomorrow morning I'll sit with you for a while and tell you all the stories I know. Time will pass quickly that way. My stories are very funny, you know.'

They nodded, their eyes large with fear and Devora smiled wanly at them. She wasn't going to offer false hope but the children deserved none of this. They had been through too much. She pulled a pencil and paper from her medical bag and handed them to the oldest child. 'Draw your mother pictures for when she returns.'

Her greatest wish at the moment was that their mother would pull through. In the meantime, the children needed distraction and she was impressed by the priest's understanding. He was a people's person and not a lofty preacher, like some of the priests she had met.

Adamo handed Devora the baby and then carried his wife to the car where he arranged mother and baby on the back seat, before kissing them tenderly goodbye.

A few minutes later, Luigi came out, refusing to rest any longer. He was still recognisable as Luigi, despite the uniform.

'Wait,' Devora said, turning to the priest. 'Do you have charcoal? Anything I can use to make Luigi look different?'

By the time she had painted on a moustache and stubble and darkened Luigi's eyebrows, even his own mother would not have recognised him.

'Now pull on your cap and let's get going,' she said, climbing into the car.

'One more thing. *Un attimo.* One moment.' Picking up the skirts of his hassock, don Cecchetti rushed into the church and reappeared again with a white altar cloth. 'When you reach a roadblock, hang this out of the window, put your hand down hard on the claxon and shout that it's an emergency, that you need to get to the hospital as soon as possible. It will be no lie.' He pushed the cloth through the car window at Devora and moved his hands in a blessing.

'God be with you,' he prayed over the car and its passengers.

The next hour was the craziest Devora had ever passed. The hullabaloo they created with the car hooter blaring as they drove up to the sentries at the gates of Urbino; their being waved on without hesitation, the echo of the car's engine through the narrow alleys that Luigi drove along like a racing driver, scraping the rear wing at one stage, swearing that his father would have his guts when he saw the scratch; Devora holding on tight to the baby and the slippery leather seat to stop herself sliding into Luigi; her car sickness as she turned frequently to check on her patient moaning on the back seat. If they were stopped, she and Haddie would be identified as Jewish women and this added to the indescribable tension.

When the nuns hurried from the convent doors to greet them and take over, calmly and efficiently, Devora almost collapsed from relief but she forced herself to remain professional and briefly explained to the nursing sisters what was wrong. Haddie and her baby disappeared with the nursing sisters on a stretcher into the bowels of the convent and for a long moment after Haddie had gone from their care, Luigi and Devora clung to each other. Then Luigi slumped down on the steps, his head in his hands.

'Sweet Jesus, Devora. We managed it. We pulled it off. Can you believe it? *Per Dio.*'

'*Sì, tenente* Michelozzi. I can believe it. But...' She disintegrated into a fit of giggles. 'Your face, Luigi. The charcoal has run and you look like a *carbonaro* from the mountains... a real charcoal maker.'

Her laughter was shrill as she sat down by him, holding her sides in agony as relief, adrenaline and hysteria swamped her. And then, he joined in too, laughing at her laughter, the pair of them rolling about on the steps, until a window above them opened and somebody shouted, 'Hey, you down there. Don't you know there's a war going on? Pipe down and go home. Disgusting drunkards!'

Devora didn't dare to look at Luigi as he pulled her up. She would have dissolved into fits again. But inside she was proud of herself. She'd given Haddie a chance to live and the feeling was indescribable. There was a purpose to her being on this earth after all and she knew without a shadow of a doubt that she wanted to help more. Exhaustion hit her after the adrenaline rush. Her hands began to shake and her legs turned to water as she collapsed against Luigi.

'Let's get you home, Biondina,' he said, holding on to her. 'I think we know only too well that there's a war going on. *Cristo*, what a day.'

CHAPTER 40

EARLY AUGUST 1944

DEVORA

Despite Devora's deep misgivings that Anna Maria should allow a German soldier to visit, Kurt still dropped by occasionally during the hot August evenings. Anna Maria had almost stopped thinking of him as a *crucco*, a German soldier, but Devora was unable to rid herself of the fact that his army was the cause of the misery inflicted on her and so many other families. She noted an edginess to him these days and he talked often about bad things happening, how he only found peace when he visited them. He'd received no letters recently from his wife and was worried. 'How will it all end?' was one of his constant refrains. Once, Devora had let down her guard and responded to something that Anna Maria had said and Kurt had glanced at her questioningly.

'She only speaks with me, signor Kurt,' Anna Maria explained, miming and using simple language that Kurt had picked up from their evening vigils together. 'She's had a bad time.'

Kurt had nodded and placed his finger in front of his mouth

to signify he would not say anything. He sat there, staring at Devora for a long time, one of his legs jigging up and down.

Devora had wanted to bite off her own tongue at her stupidity and from then on, she made sure to keep well in the background when he visited so she didn't make the same mistake twice.

Anna Maria had taken to serving him up a portion of whatever they ate in the evening. He was a bulky man, his legs like two tree trunks, and when he rose from the table one evening after a simple meal of polenta, there were two grease marks on his trousers. He had brushed against the last precious joint of prosciutto Anna Maria had hidden, tying it to the underneath of the tabletop. He had frowned and rubbed at the stains, bending under the table to investigate. He rose with a broad smile on his face and a wink. '*Sehr gut, meine Damen*... but do not worry. I will not tell.' He made a cutting motion across his throat with his right hand and Devora shuddered inside. Could he be trusted?

Anna Maria rewarded him with a generous slice of ham and no more was said. The *crucchi* generally loved pork products and seemed to sniff them from afar. It was not unusual for a group of soldiers to barge into a farmhouse, roll up their sleeves and fry themselves vast omelettes, cutting up greedy lumps of *lardo*, demanding wine be set before them, drinking the peasants' supplies dry. It was hard for the *contadini* to deny them when they were faced with the barrel of a loaded gun. They took to hiding food, wrapped well, in manure heaps or buried in orchards.

Kurt told them when the war was over, he would return to visit with his wife and children. And they must travel on a holiday and find him in Wesel to picnic by the river Rhine flowing past his farm.

'Peace must return one day,' he said, raising his glass to the two women.

Devora found the situation bizarre but for Anna Maria it was simple. 'He's a good man, on the wrong side. I do not believe he will do us harm. And don't tell me he's not dropped useful titbits...'

Devora helped Luigi when she could, rolling up his recruitment leaflets and clandestine papers to smuggle under her skirt in large pockets sewn by Anna Maria. She distributed them discreetly around the city after she had finished her cleaning job. This evening, she stopped in the piazza to read the latest poster issued by the fascist command. The tables outside the bar were full of soldiers drinking jugs of wine. More than once, Devora had glimpsed Sabrina talking to them and she had hurried by, pulling her scarf around her face, altering her gait and crossing her fingers that her old school friend would not recognise her.

On her way to work, Devora stopped to read another bulletin, still sticky and wet from fresh glue, posted next to recent death notices. Her jaw clenched at the words. All deserters were required to present themselves to the *carabinieri* from immediate effect. Lists would be sent to the Town Hall of those soldiers absent without leave. If families did not hand over their sons, brothers and husbands, ration cards would be confiscated from the head of the family forthwith; all benefits to families would be cancelled and licences to work suspended. Devora knew that in the most serious of cases, the head of the family would be arrested. She wanted to tear down the bulletin and rip it to shreds but what good would it serve? It was broad daylight and she'd be arrested on the spot. But it was hard to swallow her resentment. The atmosphere in Urbino was tense. She'd seen a vicious, discriminatory article in the paper, *L'Ora*: 'Jews are a public danger... Jews let loose amongst the population are a poisonous virus... We must hate them and above all isolate them. Isolate them morally and materially.' A generous reward of several thousand lire for information leading to their arrest was temptation indeed to a starving people: a substantial amount of easy money, but it didn't justify it.

Minutes later, as she cleaned windows in Colonel von Wentzling's study, rubbing vigorously at the panes to rid herself of some of her anger, Devora heard news that turned her cold. He was shouting into the phone and she found herself rubbing the same pane over and over as she listened.

'*Ja, Freitag um neun uhr*. Nine o'clock. The orders are to round them all up. We know they're hiding in the contamination ward. Mostly Jews, but also a handful of *Partisanen*.'

There was a gap in the conversation as the colonel listened to the speaker at the other end. Devora hovered with the rag as she waited.

'We already found thirteen of the bandits hiding there last July,' he continued. '*Bestimmt*. Two trucks, *ja, ja*. To Fossoli, via Pesaro. *Am Bahnhof*. The station.'

She continued to clean, memorising details with each rub. The colonel tapped a pen on the desk as he listened again.

'*Jawohl*. If anything changes, let me know as soon as possible. I'll ...'

Devora stepped back and knocked over her cleaning bucket, water spreading over the rug at his feet.

He held the receiver away from his ear and swore at her. '*Trottel!* You idiot, take the rug outside to dry.'

She couldn't get out fast enough. How to let Luigi know? Would the colonel notice, in his agitated state, if she disappeared for half an hour? The name Fossoli conjured fear in everybody's hearts – a place from where nobody returned. Word had spread about the transit camp for Jews and dissidents, described as 'undesirables'. It was situated further north, near Modena and run by the dreaded German SS.

Her heart pounded as she flung the rug over a wall in the

courtyard to dry and, glancing up at the study window, she hurried into the street towards the *comune.* She lowered her head as she strode past the bar. Sabrina was there again, sipping a coffee, her giddy laughter echoing along the loggia, her companion a German officer. Devora altered her gait slightly, sticking to the opposite side of the piazza.

Tuffo was asleep in the shade of the *comune* stairway but he opened one eye and rose to greet her with a wagging of his tail as soon as she entered the wide doors. She ignored him and took the stairs two at a time, almost knocking over a clerk descending with a pile of documents in his arms.

'I need to speak urgently to signor Michelozzi,' she told the woman at the desk outside the registry, plucking a reason from the air. 'About my grandfather...'

'He's busy. Someone is registering a birth. May I help you, signora?' The woman scrutinised her over her glasses.

'*Grazie*, but no. He knows our family situation. I can wait.'

The woman indicated a bench on the landing outside the office and Devora sat, willing herself to calm down as she clasped her hands to stop them shaking, hoping whoever was with Luigi would hurry. Whenever any of the office workers passed by, she lowered her gaze, her heart thumping unreasonably.

After what seemed a lifetime, Luigi emerged with a young couple, bidding them good luck with their new child. He frowned when Devora rose.

'The office is shut, signorina.' The look on his face was a mix of puzzlement and anger but he acted as if she were a stranger. 'No more business today. I'm sorry.' He put his head round the door and Devora heard him tell the receptionist he was going for lunch.

'*Buon appetito*, signore. Enjoy your meal.'

Devora followed him down the stairs and along a couple of

alleyways until they were in the quiet of Via dei Fornari. The bakers finished work early each day and so they were alone.

'What the hell are you doing? Are you mad? Coming to find me in the Town Hall like this.'

She took his arm. 'The bastards are planning another raid. This Friday. On the hospital.' The words spilled out of her in her panic. 'I overheard von Wentzling on the phone. They're taking them to Fossoli via Pesaro Station. Haddie, her baby... and our injured comrades are there. Oh God, we have to do something, Gigi. I wanted to tell you as soon as possible. Friday is only three days away. We need to act fast.'

He swore. 'I'll come to you tonight. Now, get back to work. Try to act as normal as possible.'

The colonel was gone when she returned to fetch her broom and rags from his study. His desk had been cleared and the drawer was locked when she tried to search for further information about the raid. He had said Friday, without specifying a date. Was it this Friday? What time was the train from Pesaro?

The photo of his attractive blonde wife holding a chubby baby sat in the same place it always did. How often had she dusted that glass, wondering about his family and how he, a husband and father, could reconcile what was happening to thousands of innocent families across Europe because of the war his crazy leader had started? She wanted to smash the photo in its frame against the marble fireplace today and stamp on it. But she had to behave as she always did. As a humble cleaner who couldn't speak.

Devora took a deep breath and moved into his bedroom, carrying mop, bucket and dusters with her. The door to the vast wardrobe was open and she gazed on his clothes hanging neatly from the rails: his tailor-made white summer uniform, his field-grey combat shirts as well as formal crisp-white shirts with stand-up collars. A steel helmet rested on the top shelf and suddenly she knew what to do.

Luigi had driven all the way to Fano to borrow Enrico's policeman's uniform to disguise himself. Here, under her very nose, were uniforms for the taking. Maybe they could be of use in a rescue of those poor people bound for Fossoli camp. She had taken the colonel's jackets to the laundry in the past. If anybody stopped her, she had a legitimate reason for carrying items of uniform. The steel helmet was another matter. She rushed down to the empty kitchen and chose the largest basket from the shelves, knocking a casserole dish down in her haste. She kicked the pieces under the table and hurried back upstairs. There was no telling where the colonel had disappeared to and how long she had before he returned.

The helmet went at the bottom of the basket and she covered it with a couple of field-grey trousers and a jacket. If she was caught with these on her person, she would also be sent to the camp. But she had to risk it. There was too much at stake.

CHAPTER 41

That evening Devora and Anna Maria were sitting outside the caretaker's half-ruined house, waiting in the cooler air, when first Luigi, then don Cecchetti pushed through the vegetation. Luigi cupped his hands to his mouth and twice imitated an owl's cry and not long afterwards, four more shadows emerged from the gloom. They made their way inside, Franco taking up guard at the window, his rifle poised, while Anna Maria handed out rough wine to the group.

Luigi spoke, his voice so low they drew nearer to listen.

'No more meetings at the church. Nowhere is sacrosanct and now the Camilluccia militia are in Urbino, things have turned vicious.'

'Four *partigiani* shot at Porta Lavagine. My mother was there at the fountains and she witnessed it. *Bastardi*,' Gianni said. 'Excuse my language, *padre*.'

Don Cecchetti shrugged. 'The truth is the truth, young man. They also shot Branco. Ex-police. Accused of desertion.'

'The fact is,' Luigi interrupted, taking charge of the discussion, 'we have barely three days to plan how to thwart this raid.'

He turned to Devora. 'Are you absolutely sure he means the hospital of Santa Chiara and *this* Friday?'

'Yes, Luigi. You *know* I'm fluent, but I can't one hundred per cent vouch it's this coming Friday. I didn't hear a date mentioned.'

'We shall take it as this Friday. There's no choice,' Luigi said, running his hand through his thick hair.

Devora moved to the back of the room to retrieve the basket she'd hidden under a pile of sacks. 'I took these from the colonel's room. They could be useful, don't you think?'

A low whistle from one of the men followed when Luigi held up the German jacket. 'You took a risk.'

'My whole life is a risk at the moment,' she said. 'I only hope it's worthwhile.'

Franco turned from his position at the window. 'You've done well, *ragazza*. We'll be sure to make it worthwhile.'

Encouraged, Devora spoke. 'What about disguising ourselves as *crucchi* to create a roadblock to divert the prisoners' trucks after they've left the hospital? I can be there to help you with the correct German—'

'Too dangerous,' Luigi interrupted.

'She's making sense,' don Cecchetti said. 'I have a smattering of German. There was a young novice from Bavaria at our seminary and I helped him with Italian in exchange for some lessons.'

'You could teach me basic phrases, Devora,' Luigi suggested. 'But I don't want you on the scene. You'll jeopardise the mission. You've already done enough by taking these uniforms.'

Devora fumed but kept quiet as she listened to Luigi and the others discussing details. Her idea had been taken on board by Luigi but she was annoyed he wanted her excluded from the plan. Did he not think she could be useful? Yes, it was dangerous, but it was dangerous for everyone.

'I think a hijack away from the hospital is good,' Luigi said, glancing at Devora and then back to the others. 'It will minimise loss of life, but we need transport to carry them to safety. Best not to use the *crucchis'* vehicles either, so we need to get hold of our own transport. If the *crucchi* are using two trucks, that's a lot of people.'

Questions were fired at him by the men.

'Where do we find extra backup? Plus extra weapons?'

'Do we have enough time to plan this?'

'Two trucks or a lorry should be sufficient, and I can arrange for the men and guns,' Luigi said. 'Leave that with me. But can you think of where we can take them afterwards, *padre*? Your abbey is too near Urbino. Too obvious.'

'We need to get them as far south as we can, from where the *tedeschi* have moved. But for the first stage, I suggest Volponi's brick factory at the edge of the city,' the priest said. 'We've used it in the past. There's plenty of space in the warehouse. The manager is a good man. His son, Paolo, he's one of us. And the *crucchi* will never imagine their prisoners are still under their noses.'

While Luigi jotted down notes, don Ceccchetti picked up the colonel's jacket and tried it on. The sleeves were too long and Anna Maria moved over to take hold of one arm, folding the hem up.

'You look... quite different,' she muttered as she fetched a needle and thread and returned to the priest to tack the thick material.

Luigi produced a map from his pocket and jabbed his finger at a spot east of the city. 'As for the route we take after the rescue, there's a junction here on the Pesaro road that takes a back way to Urbino.'

'No good – the bridge is gone,' Franco said, handing his rifle to Gianni to take up position at the window. He leant over the map and pointed to another route. 'I drove down here last week to fetch supplies for my bar. It was clear then. And there's a shortcut through a vineyard.'

'Then I'll entrust you with driving,' Luigi said. 'Tonight, I'll contact our friends on the mountains for extra manpower and we'll meet here same time tomorrow to finalise plans. I'd prefer more time, but it is what it is. Leave here separately and – not a word to anybody. Not even your wives or *fidanzate*.'

Everyone knew what was on Luigi's mind. As the allies fast progressed northwards, Germans and Italian *nazifascisti* alike were jittery and news of atrocities were commonplace. It was best to keep your head down, best not to get involved, many citizens believed, and it was important for discretion and secrecy amongst the group.

It was therefore not surprising when Gianni piped up with, 'Sure as eggs, there'll be reprisals.'

Luigi's response was immediate. 'No risk, no gain. We can't stand by and do nothing.'

Don Cecchetti nodded. '"Even though I walk through the valley of the shadow of death, I will fear no evil, for thou art with me." God will look after us, my friends. Trust in Him.'

Luigi and don Cecchetti stayed behind after the others had left.

'Use the sacristy to transmit with the radio to the archbishop, Michelozzi,' the priest said. 'He will send us what we need and put out word for extra manpower. And we need to warn the factory manager.'

'But is it still safe for everything to be delivered to you?'

'So far, so good. No raids on me as yet. We have to take this chance. And a friar arriving with a cart full of clothes and blankets will not be stopped.'

'They are more thorough now in their searches. The weapons must be well hidden.'

The priest tapped his nose. 'The cart has been fashioned with a false bottom. Calm yourself, Michelozzi. *Calmati.*'

Devora listened to all this in astonishment. She had known Luigi and the priest were involved with the liberation committee, but not to this extent.

Before man and priest left, Luigi turned to thank Devora. 'You've done well, Biondina. But don't turn up for your cleaning work. It's not safe now.'

'Don't you think it's going to look suspicious if I don't turn up tomorrow? I should stay at least until Friday is over.' He was treating her like a porcelain doll and she felt resentful. She wanted to help but he kept vetoing her suggestions.

'I don't think you should. What if the colonel realises his stuff is missing?'

'I can say it needed cleaning.'

'I think Devora is right,' don Cecchetti said. 'We must carry on as normal and not stir the hornets' nest until Friday. But you must in no way return after then, signorina.'

'And naturally you'll need to make yourself scarce from the city afterwards,' Luigi added.

When the men had gone, Anna Maria continued to alter the jacket, leaning into the light cast by the kerosene lamp on the table. 'So, we move again,' she said, hemming the final alteration to the sleeves, her rough work-fingers remarkably deft.

'Yes,' Devora replied, her voice small and weary. 'Where to next, do you suppose?'

'Further south where there are no *crucchi* now the *alleati* have taken over. We can travel to my house in Lucania and I'll show you around. We can eat *fichi d'India* and pick fennel from the wild. The winters are warmer too. I reckon it won't be too bad.' She bit the thread from the jacket sleeve and folded the garment carefully. 'Pity you didn't pinch another of these.'

Devora said nothing, her mind full of the injustice of war. Why should she be pushed out of the city she loved so much, again? She wanted to wait for the return of her family. And it would mean being far away from Enrico too if she travelled south. Luigi had mentioned he'd been in town recently. If she had to leave, then she wanted to say goodbye first. And tomorrow she would steal another jacket. If she was working there for only a couple more days, she might as well take full advantage.

CHAPTER 42

Thieving was easier than she'd imagined. She scooped a jacket and a pair of trousers from the bedroom of the colonel's orderly and pushed them into her empty bucket, covering them with a floor cloth. Downstairs, the kitchen was clear and she stepped outside to stuff them beneath a pile of rubbish, to collect later. Cook returned from the privy just as she finished concealing her loot.

'I'm missing a basket, Elena. And was it you who broke my casserole dish? If I report you, your wages will be docked. But if you stay behind and peel this pan of vegetables, I'll not say a word. My *fidanzato* is taking me to the cinema this evening and I need to get away early. Bring my basket back tomorrow too or there'll be trouble.'

Devora nodded meekly, although she was seething. Where was solidarity when you needed it? Cook's *fidanzato* was a nasty piece of work too. A Blackshirt with wandering hands. He'd pinched her behind when she was scrubbing the kitchen floor on more than one occasion. The two were rotten. They deserved each other.

An hour and a half later, with the last of the potatoes peeled and a couple stored in her pockets to take back for supper with Anna Maria, Devora let herself into the cooler air of the courtyard. Two soldiers were sitting by the fountain, smoking, making it impossible to retrieve the stolen goods. She decided to return later when they'd gone.

To kill time, she wandered into the main piazza and sat on a low wall to observe the customers at the bar under the arcade. Sabrina was not there for a change, but there were other young women in smart dresses entertaining German officers. The clink of glasses, music from an out-of-tune piano and the sound of laughter jarred on Devora. The last time she'd laughed properly had been after she'd accompanied Luigi in the ambulance to transport Haddie to hospital. She wanted to laugh again until her stomach hurt, to enjoy freedom, wear a pretty frock and sit at a table drinking cocktails with her friends. But there was no place for frivolity in her life. And soon, if everything worked out, Haddie would once again be spirited away in a truck. Maybe there would be time to laugh and celebrate afterwards.

She smacked at her ankles as a mosquito stung her and then, on a whim, she decided to while away time until she could collect the hidden uniforms. As she was going to be absent from Urbino for some time, she would say farewell to her home in Via delle Stallacce. She would fetch her mother's jewellery and stout shoes to take with her down south. But more than anything, Devora wanted to spend an hour in her old home, fill her heart with memories, feel the presence of her family without distractions.

The key wasn't in the niche above the doorway and she felt along the frame, thinking it had been dislodged by an animal. They had been bothered by *glis-glis* in the past: furry edible dormice – squirrel-like creatures, thieves of stray food morsels, capable of squeezing through tiny gaps in roofs and shutters. But there was no key. Devora slumped down in despair on the step, leaning against the door, and found herself tumbling backwards into the house. She yelped in pain and uttered the filthiest of oaths – regularly used by Franco and the other *partigiani*. '*Porca puttana, porca Madonna, cazzo, cazzo, cazzo...*'

And then she heard a chuckle and she turned round, her nerves jangling. '*Chi c'è?* Who's there? Get the hell out of my house whoever you are, *porca puttana*.'

'Your swearing has improved exponentially.'

A man was sitting at the kitchen table, his outline dark in the light sifting through the open window. She couldn't make out his features, but she recognised the voice. Oh yes! That unmistakable soft drawl, rich with sarcasm and something else she could never fathom.

'So, you've finally put in an appearance, Enrico. Where've you been all this time?' she asked, collapsing into the chair opposite.

'I might ask the same of you.' He peered closer. '*Dio*, you don't look a pretty sight. Your dress sense has deteriorated even further.'

'What are you actually doing in my house?' she asked wearily, removing her cap and scraping her fingers through her short hair.

He shrugged. 'Not safe at my parents' place. I've never got on with them anyway, as well you know. And... as I've been reported missing, presumed dead, I don't want to give Mamma a heart attack by turning up out of the blue. So, I've been hiding here for a while. I hope you don't mind. I knew your place was empty and, frankly, I didn't know where else to go.' His words were indistinct and Devora spotted an open bottle on the table.

'That's so cruel, Rico. You can't not tell your parents.'

Following her gaze, he asked, 'Won't you share this excellent wine with me?'

'I'm not thirsty.'

He pulled a brown paper bag from a knapsack slung over the back of the chair and proceeded to cut bread and cheese.

'Food always brings on a thirst. Sure you won't join me? I need to sober up and you look half-starved. You've lost weight. Doesn't suit you. Where have your curves gone?'

She ignored this last comment and nibbled on a slice of cheese. It was a mild, soft pecorino. It was hours since she'd eaten and the wine that he poured her was good. Very good. When he topped up her glass, she didn't stop him. It had been a hard day. Annoying and elusive as Enrico was, she was pleased to be in his company again and she stole a glance at him, ruing the fact she looked a sight.

He sat back in her father's chair and stretched his long legs beneath the table so that they nudged hers. She moved slightly and he laughed.

'Don't worry, Biondina, I'm not going to molest you. Not in that get-up, anyway. Why in God's name are you looking so drab? I hardly recognise you.'

'It suits my job,' she said, reaching out for another top-up, enjoying how relaxed she felt despite his comments. Enrico really was a good-looking man, even though he needed a shave. She imagined what it would feel like to have his rough skin on hers again. It had been a long time.

'What job is this?' he asked.

The strong wine loosened her tongue. She told him about her work for the colonel and how she pretended to be dumb and eavesdropped. And as he smiled encouragingly, she began to tell him more and it was as if she had no control over her words. He laughed as she described how she had stolen uniforms from the colonel. The look of admiration on Enrico's face was stronger than that distant part of her brain telling her to shut up.

He lit a cigarette, offering one to her, which she declined. Nicotine filled the kitchen and she bit her lip, an image of her father puffing on his pipe before her, a stern expression on his face, listening to her blab.

Leaning forwards, grabbing Enrico's hands, Devora's words

were now slurred. 'I shouldn't have told you any of this. You won't tell a soul, will you, Rico? I beg you.'

'Why would I do that?' He squeezed her hands before letting go. 'You know, I do admire you and Luigi. When I think about it, what good have I done in this fucking war? Bugger all.'

'Never too late. Help us. Luigi would be so pleased to have you. They're short of manpower.'

She hiccoughed and pushed her glass forwards again.

He shook his head and tipped up the empty bottle. 'All gone, little Devora. And... I think you've had enough anyway.'

Rising from his chair, he began to pace the room. 'What are the uniforms for? What has Luigi planned?'

Devora bit her lip, uncertain of how much to tell. But he was one of her oldest friends and no longer a *fascista* from what Luigi had said. She stood up. The room span. Enrico's face, his lovely, stubbly face, was reachable if she stood on tiptoe. She wanted to kiss him to show how grateful she was and tell him how much she'd missed him.

He caught her as she staggered. 'Woah, steady,' he said, a chuckle in his voice. 'You never could handle your wine, could you?'

'Signor Conte di Villanova,' she said, stumbling over his title, looking up at him from the comfort of his hold. 'I'm going to tell you what we've planned. But you have to promise me on your life not to tell a soul. Can I trust you? You're a good man. Despite what they say.' She reached up up to kiss him on the mouth. She said the last words again and this time they didn't come out in a tangle.

Enrico didn't respond to her kiss and he removed her arms from round his neck.

'I can't do this when you're tipsy,' he said, fetching water to fill up her glass. 'I'm going out to buy some more food and then, when you're sobered up, we'll talk more.'

She watched in dismay and embarrassment as he left,

wondering if he would bother to return. She followed one glass of water with another and then she climbed the stairs. In her parents' room, she caught her reflection in her mother's dressing table and grimaced. 'Devora Lassa, you are a mess. And an idiot,' she said out loud. She dragged her fingers through her untidy short crop and sat on the bed for a few moments. Her home was a shell without her lovely family and she lay down, hunching her knees to her chest, biting back tears.

The sound of the door opening a while later and Enrico moving about downstairs brought her back to the kitchen.

'Freshly baked *crescie.* Let's eat while they're hot,' he said, tearing a piece off the traditional Urbino flatbreads, watching her as she ate.

'How can I get you to trust me, Devora? I honestly want to help, you know.'

Feeling more sober now, she stared at him. They'd known each other since they were toddlers. He wasn't a traitor, was he? She focused on his eyes. The same smile in his eyes and yet—

'I *want* to help,' he repeated. 'Listen, I can understand why you're holding back. I promise. How can I make you believe me?'

'You tell *me*...' His answer was so important. She scrutinised his face as he spoke.

'I suppose I'm ashamed of what I haven't done and ashamed at what I *have* done. We were all strung along with promises of a better future, weren't we? And for a while, life *was* better with Il Duce. But Luigi is so... very honourable, isn't he? He's always stood up for what he believes is right. I've never done that. Maybe this is my chance to redeem myself, Biondina.'

She took a chance. It was a risk but there was something earnest about him tonight. She believed him and so she told him of their plans to rescue Jews and dissidents from certain death and when she had finished, he promised immediately to find them a vehicle, more weapons and to deliver them personally.

And Devora had a hunch everything would turn out right – that she hadn't made a mistake.

'Where is it happening?' he asked.

'I'll take you there,' she said, contradicting Luigi's orders for her to stay away. 'Pick me up at the Cavallino crossroad.'

She rose from the table. 'I've got something else I need to do now, Rico. You can sleep here tonight in Anna Maria's bed and I'll see you Friday morning, six o'clock,' she said. 'Don't be late. And... thank you.'

He gave a little wave as she let herself out of the door. It was dark; curfew had started and she crept along the alleyways like a cat to retrieve the hidden uniforms. She'd missed Luigi's final meeting but it didn't matter. She couldn't wait to see his reaction when she and Enrico turned up for the ambush.

CHAPTER 43

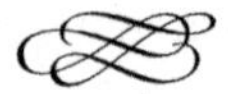

ENRICO

Olinto, the guard who had helped me escape from prison, owned a farm truck. I waited a couple of hours after Devora had left, choosing my route carefully to his farmhouse. It was after midnight when I arrived. A dog chained by the door barked as I approached but, used to my father's hunting dogs, I crouched down and spoke gently to the animal. I held out my hand and the dog whined, before settling down. But it was enough to wake the occupants and the door opened suddenly. Olinto's wife stood on the step, rifle aimed at me.

'One step nearer, and I'll blast out your brains.'

'Maria, it's me. *Il conte*,' I said, hands in the air. 'I need to speak to Olinto.'

She lowered the weapon. 'Unsociable hour to come calling. He's in the usual place, Enrico.'

I smiled to myself as I moved over to the pigsty. Maria is a feisty woman. Prone to throwing her husband out of the house for the most minor offence.

'Banished again?' I asked when Olinto opened the door.

From behind a wooden partition, a large pig poked out its nose and I guffawed. 'What have you done this time, Olinto?'

'It's not what I did – it's what I can't do,' he told me sheepishly. 'She's always wanting it. I can't do it twice a night. Not at my age.' He grinned. 'You can't help me out, can you?'

I roared with laughter. 'Sounds as if your life was easier in the *carabinieri* barracks, my friend. Listen, I need to borrow your truck. For a couple of days.'

'You can have it for a price. For one day only.'

'I don't think so. It would be the easiest thing in the world for me to push a note through the barracks door to reveal your whereabouts on my way back to the city.'

'*Porca miseria*, you wouldn't. Half the men have left anyhow. They know the *inglesi* are on their way. They've had enough.'

'That still leaves the other half to reckon with, *amico mio*. Frankly, you don't have a choice.'

'She'll skin me alive, so you'll have to take me too. What do you need it for anyway?'

It was after four o'clock when I let myself back into the little house in Via delle Stallacce, having parked up the truck by a mill on the outskirts of the city. Olinto wasn't with me. I'd sped off while he was taking a piss; I don't trust the fellow. Devora had gone and I decided to stay one more night. On Friday, I'd do the right thing and help my friends. It would serve to massage my conscience.

Italy is a mess. There's nothing to keep me in Urbino anymore. Devora is sweet but that is all. Sweetness is not enough in a woman. But I shall do this one last thing for my old friends before leaving.

CHAPTER 44

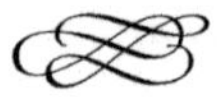

LUIGI

In his altered jacket, steel helmet on his head, don Cecchetti struck an imposing figure. Luigi, practising the phrases Devora had made him repeat a dozen times, murmured over and over in passable German, 'Turn left. The road has been mined.' The whole team, including Franco and Gianni, dressed as Blackshirts, had been practising their salutes. After their crash course they knew how to say, '*Halt!*' and a couple of other phrases such as 'hurry up', 'watch out' and 'good luck'.

A dented green truck with a ripped canvas cover, requisitioned from a ditch after a skirmish, was parked in a copse a few metres along from the junction. A couple of partisans, mechanics in their other lives, had got it running again. It was smaller than Luigi would have liked but that was all they had been able to get their hands on at short notice.

'Keep the engine going. The battery's knackered,' the partisan had told Luigi as he wiped his oily fingers on a rag. 'There's spare fuel in the can in the back. *In bocca al lupo*,' he'd said when he handed over the keys. 'Good luck.'

Nine men from the mountains waited in hastily dug trenches, including a couple of British POWs, dressed in an assortment of gear, ranging from patched British Army shorts, to fatigues and ragged shirts. The Italian *partigiani* wore red scarves around their necks. One wore the green of the *Brigate fiamme*, symbol of Catholic resistance fighters.

'I can hear a motor,' Luigi said.

'Wait until I give the order to fire,' Franco said. 'Gianni will whistle if it's what we're waiting for.'

Luigi's heart was pounding. It was one thing forging documents in the offices of the *comune*. Quite another huddling in a ditch, rifle cocked, stones digging into his belly, and bowels churning uncomfortably as he waited to shoot to kill. He glanced through the trees towards don Cecchetti, looking one hundred per cent the part as a German officer, flanked by a burly youth. Farmer turned fighter, young Marcello, a companion from his schooldays, was also disguised in part of Devora's purloined German uniform, helped with Anna Maria's home-made attempt at dyeing ordinary trousers with nettles. Luigi prayed Marcello wouldn't need to open his mouth. No matter how often don Cecchetti had made him repeat the German phrases, his friend couldn't get them quite right. But his ginger hair and stocky figure had got him the part this morning.

The truck that pulled up was not the one they were expecting. Neither was the driver. Nor the passenger.

Enrico leant from the window. 'Shall I park this down the road, next to yours? It's surprisingly fast for an old—'

'What the fuck are you doing here?' Luigi shouted, clambering from his hole and making his way the short distance to the checkpoint. 'And... you! You shouldn't be here...' His eyes wide with alarm, he watched as Devora, dressed in trousers and grey-green shirt, jumped from the passenger seat. She wore a flat cap on her head and, with dismay, Luigi took in the ammunition belt slung round her shoulder.

'Well, I *am* here. And you can't send me back now,' she replied.

She marched over and Luigi watched as she spoke to Marcello and don Cecchetti, before crouching down behind the simple barricade of sand-filled sacks positioned a few metres beyond the diversion. A sign warning of mines, bearing a crude diagram of a skull and crossbones, had been nailed to a tree. *Achtung! Minen.*

There was no time to confront her. A piercing whistle from Gianni sent Luigi scampering to his trench. Rounding the bend, two dark-green German army vehicles filled with prisoners slowed to a stop with a screech of brakes.

It had begun.

Luigi's heart hammered as if it would burst through his ribcage. Don Cecchetti, in the commanding voice he used so well during services, kept his words to a minimum, ordering the soldiers to make haste, pointing to the side-road diversion, and the trucks reversed slightly, the drivers saluting in response to don Cecchetti's extended arm and sonorous '*Heil* Hitler!'

The shooting that followed sent crows flapping and cawing from the trees. Windscreens on the drivers' sides shattered almost simultaneously on both German trucks and the air was rent with screams, bullets and the animalistic roar of attack.

Luigi looked on in horror as a *crucco* jumped from the back of the truck, dragging a child as a shield but a single shot to the German's head felled him, the child running off, screaming in terror. Luigi jumped from his trench, Franco warning him to stay down but Luigi yanked the child and ran to the shelter of the copse, dragging the child with him, bullets whistling past as they zigzagged their way.

They were not alone in the trees. An injured German, blood oozing from his leg, aimed his handgun at Luigi and instinct took over. Luigi kicked out viciously, his heavy boot making contact with the man's wound and the German, whimpering, dropped his Luger and held up his hands in surrender. Luigi remained, for the rest of the skirmish, as mayhem ensued around, his gun pointing at his prisoner, his other arm around the little boy shivering and snivelling in his charge.

In all, seven Germans and two *partigiani* lay dead when the shooting stopped. One elderly Jewish prisoner had suffered a fatal heart attack and another younger man had been caught in crossfire as he attempted to join in the battle. Four *partigiani*, seventeen Jewish prisoners who had been hiding at the convent and Luigi's captured German were hustled into the partisans' two waiting trucks. The tyres on the Germans' trucks were slashed and the keys thrown deep into the woods.

Of Enrico there was no sign but Luigi breathed a sigh of relief to see Devora emerge from where she had been hiding near the barricade. After returning the little boy to his grateful mother, Luigi grabbed Devora by her arm and made her sit next to him as they sped towards the brick factory. The partisans' repaired truck had not started, as warned, and anxious moments had ticked by as Franco tried again and again and, eventually, everybody was packed in Enrico's truck, three of the rescued *partigiani* electing to make their own way back to their villages.

'What in the devil's name made you believe you could help today? I can't believe how irresponsible you've been,' Luigi shouted at Devora, shaking with anger as they sped away.

'Hey, Michelozzi, leave off. She was *amazing*,' young Marcello interrupted. He was already divesting himself of his hot disguise, his face dripping. 'She was there all the time, whispering German words to us. I'd have been in a right panic without her. Isn't that right, *padre*?'

Don Cecchetti sat as red as a Lollo Rosso lettuce, his helmet at his feet. 'My soutane can be uncomfortable in August weather, but not as much as these infernal outfits.' He mopped his brow and began to unbutton the thick German jacket. 'Yes, signorina, you were our guardian angel today.' He made the sign of the cross and wiped his face again.

Devora inched away from Luigi across the truck floor towards a mother struggling to hold on to a baby and child as the truck bumped over ruts in the dirt track.

Luigi continued to rant. 'And what was Enrico doing here? How did he know about today?'

To his annoyance, Devora ignored his questions, retorting, 'He brought us another vehicle. Just as well, as the other one didn't start. Is that not good enough for you? We'd have been sitting ducks if it hadn't been for him.'

Devora lifted the little girl onto her lap and turned her back on Luigi, peeved at his strange attitude.

'Signorina?' The woman touched Devora on her arm.

'Haddie!'

Haddie smiled back, her face pale, eyes filled with fear. 'My family? Are they safe?'

'Oh, Haddie,' Devora said, her eyes glistening. 'They're safe. Don Cecchetti is here too.' She pointed at the priest. 'Look, over there! He'll take you to them as soon as possible.'

The little girl in Devora's lap reached her arms towards Haddie, wriggling to escape from Devora's hold.

'Let her come to me, signorina. She's clingy.' She lowered her voice. 'Her mother... she didn't survive childbirth. I'm looking after her. One more won't make much difference.'

The little girl moved over to Haddie and hid her face in her skirts and Devora had to check back more tears. Haddie had endured so much evil in this war but her heart still brimmed with kindness. She concentrated her gaze on the mother and children, forcing away the memory of the dead German soldier she had shot. The shot she had fired to save the life of a child. She had killed a man but she was training to save lives. And yet, her reaction had been one of instinct. It was justifiable. But the reality of war was shocking. Her hands began to shake and she sat on them.

Paolo Volponi was waiting at the entrance to the brickworks' tower. As the packed vehicle entered the gates, two workers ran to padlock them. The Jewish families were hurriedly led to a stock room where a narrow gap in bricks stacked roof-high led to an empty area behind. Mattresses had been arranged on the floor; a basket of food and demijohns of water waited on a makeshift table. While Luigi was busy talking to the remaining rescued *partigiani*, Devora embraced Haddie and slipped away. She wanted no more of Luigi's rebukes.

CHAPTER 45

DEVORA

Devora crossed the parched countryside, stepping through fields of waving corn and keeping to hedgerows whenever she could until the twin towers of Urbino came into view. Enrico had saved the day by turning up with his vehicle but Luigi was so hopping mad. Well, he could stew on it. What was done was done. Better to think of what they had achieved and pin hopes on the future safety of all those they'd rescued than waste anger for the wrong reasons.

She was looking forward to seeing Enrico again. She'd taken a huge risk in sharing details about the mission and she knew that drinking too much had made her drop her guard. But the risk had paid off, hadn't it? What was it Luigi had once said? Something about nothing being achieved without stepping out of line. She'd proved his theory to the full today.

A hare bolted from a hollow and startled her, reminding her to pay more attention. Anybody could be about. As a result of what they had done, there would be patrols scouring the countryside. She was still wearing her boy's outfit but she'd have to be extra careful once she entered the city. She had no forged documents for this disguise. She began to regret having left the shelter of the brick factory and decided to rest up in the shade for a while and make her way to her old home after dark. Anna Maria would be frantic with worry and wonder where she had disappeared to, but she would make her way to Castel Cavallino once she had made one last visit to her home. If she managed to see Enrico again, then that was a bonus.

She slept fitfully in a hollow below a towering oak. The stubby grass was flattened, probably by wild boar or deer, she presumed. No doubt she would discover ticks on her body later, but at least she was completely hidden from view. In the distance, the rumble of heavy vehicles on the main route and an occasional burst of gunfire reminded her of danger. She tried to still her fears, which conjured images of *fascisti* troops advancing across the fields searching for her and the others. It did no good to worry about what had not yet happened, she told herself. And she squeezed shut her eyes.

When darkness fell, she slowly made her way up the hill towards Urbino, still keeping to the hedgerows, cursing the full moon. The Ducal Palace was silhouetted against a spread of stars and she needed no torch to find her way. Inside the city walls, it was surprisingly quiet, and soon after the clock struck ten, she slipped down the steps towards Via delle Stallacce. The key had been replaced above the door, which told her she had missed Enrico. She wondered where he had disappeared to this time, in whose place he was sheltering. Maybe he had listened to her and gone to placate his parents. She felt for the matches in their place on the shelf and lit a stub of candle in its enamel holder on Mütti's mahogany sideboard.

On the kitchen table, propped against Enrico's empty wine bottle, was a note in his scrawling handwriting.

Thanks for last night, dearest D. Don't tell my parents I was here. See you when I see you.
Rico – *baci, baci*. Kisses.

Why did I think he would ever change? she asked herself. *Elusive and mysterious as ever.*

It was lonely in the house. She carried the candle upstairs to fetch an old pair of boots that Alfredo had outgrown. Although too large, they would do for the journey south if she stuffed newspaper in the toes. She opened the door a crack to her parents' room, dismayed at the dust and cobwebs everywhere and when she caught sight of a stray feather, she choked back a sob. How they had laughed that day with their pillow fight, she and her young brothers. Where were they now? Had they managed to stay together? How was Mütti coping without Anna Maria's help? She dreaded to think what kind of work they were being forced to do in Germany. She straightened the counterpane, hoping Mütti at least had somewhere comfortable to sleep. Pulling the door to on her sadness, she slipped downstairs. Careful not to make any noise, she moved a chair and crawled under the table to remove her mother's jewellery from the hiding place beneath the tile. As she pulled out the cloth bag she'd placed there on her first visit, a couple of bank notes dislodged themselves and she pocketed those too for the journey south.

Devora wasn't sleepy. She'd dozed on and off in the ditch during the day, and sitting alone in the kitchen, no ticking of the clock or family to keep her company and memories of happier times besieging her again, she felt claustrophobic. Nobody would be about in the middle of the night, surely. Who knew how long it would be before she could return to her beloved birthplace? What harm would it do to drift along the quiet alleys while the city slept? She would keep away from main thoroughfares and city entrances and visit the quiet corners: the places where she, Enrico, Luigi and Sabrina had played hide-and-seek in tiny *piazze*, finding secret corners in innocent childhood. She would inhale her city and swallow it like a tonic to keep her going.

Urbino belonged to her as she stepped outside, a warm breeze caressing her face. She lifted her head to the stars, searching for the Plough and Venus, the goddess of love. Could her loved ones possibly be staring at this very moment at the same stars? Papà had taught his children their names and told them stories about these beacons of light. Where were her parents now? Were her brothers learning at school? Had they found somewhere comfortable to stay?

She wandered closer to the centre, past university buildings where she had once studied. A large poster on the wall gleamed white in the moonlight and she made out the words: *EBREO NEMICO DELLA PATRIA*. Jew. Enemy of the motherland. A line had been drawn by some protestor across it in black paint, but that wasn't enough for Devora. She reached up and tore at the poster, using her fingernails like the claws of a cat.

'Caught you at last, you bastard.' A young Blackshirt appeared from nowhere. He held her fast as she shouted at him to take his filthy hands off her. He was joined by another. Together they dragged her, kicking and screaming to the *questura*. As she thrashed and struggled, Devora saw two women on their way to the bakery stop and watch. She wanted to cry out to them to help her, but her mouth was clamped fast by the Blackshirt holding her. It was pointless anyhow, their words revealing where their sentiments lay.

'That's not a boy,' one of them said when Devora's cap fell to the cobbles, revealing her stubby blonde curls.

'I've seen her plenty of mornings on her way to work, that one. She's a cleaner to the German officers. She never speaks, but listen to her now. Fancy cleaning for the enemy. I've always wondered what else she does for the bastards.'

'She's nothing but a whore.'

The older woman hushed her. 'Keep your voice down, Armida. God be with her. We're all in this together, aren't we?'

'No, we're not! Some of us try to keep our noses clean. I reckon she's one of them protestors, those so-called *partigiani*. All they do is make a heap of trouble for ordinary people like us. And what about all those mass killings in the villages? Why do you think they happen? Because of protestors like her. If that girl's been causing trouble, then she deserves trouble back from them in charge.'

'Hush. Keep your voice down. And hurry now, *we'll* be in trouble if we don't have the bread baked in time.'

The Blackshirt loosened his grip on Devora's mouth as the women hurried off and Devora took satisfaction in biting his finger, but she was rewarded by a sharp blow to her stomach and her knees buckled under her.

A paunchy, middle-aged police sergeant glared at Devora as he spat out his words. She concentrated on the patterns in the cracked cell wall behind him rather than his ugly face disfigured with frustration. He had tried gentle persuasion at first but there was anger in his eyes now.

'Signorina, you can be out of here within the hour once you've told me who you're working with.' He pushed a pencil and a piece of paper over the table and she stared at him with defiance before spitting on the floor and brushing the paper away.

That met with a slap on the face, the unexpected force whipping her head back, tears of pain springing to her eyes. She swiped them away with the backs of her hands.

The *sergente* nodded to the *squadrista* standing behind Devora and the young bully seized her arms, wrenching them back, tying them with thick rope.

She stared at the bulging nose of her interrogator, at the tinge of yellow in his eyes, his bulging belly bloated no doubt from black market goods. 'I can tell you're a drinker,' she said. 'You have the beginnings of cirrhosis. The stench of alcohol on your breath and your jaundiced skin is a giveaway. I recommend you stop drinking, otherwise you'll be lying in the cemetery before the end of the summer. And your behaviour today will do nothing for your blood pressure either.'

Her spirited medical talk was rewarded with another heavy blow, this time from his young accomplice, delivered to her chin with an upper cut. Blood spurted from her mouth and she wiggled with her tongue at a loose molar. She hung her head, pretending to faint, and listened as the *sergente* reprimanded his accomplice, warning they would get no information out of her if she was knocked out.

She jumped when icy water was thrown over her head from a bucket. 'That's so refreshing,' she managed after she had coughed back her breath. 'August in the city is so hot.'

'If you want more refreshment, you shall have it, you sarcastic bitch.'

The younger man's voice was cruel, his eyes cold, unfathomable. He was more of a challenge than the older *sergente*. She wouldn't be able to reason with him, she knew. He was a typical product of a young mind warped by fascist teachings. Most likely one of the *Arditi*, addicted to war, she assessed, not particularly bright but an unquestioning follower of rules. Best not to ignite his ardour.

Before she could finish her theorising, which she was doing to keep calm, her head was plunged into a second bucket of water and held down while she fought to hold her breath. But, bent double on the chair, her lungs squashed against her thighs, shoulders and arms restrained, the pain was excruciating. She started to panic, her mouth opening as she tried to shout to stop, water filling her nostrils, burning at her throat in the agony of drowning. When she thought she could bear it no longer, her hair was tugged, her head yanked from the bucket as she coughed and spluttered, gasping for air. The pain was like nothing she'd ever experienced.

'Tell us!' the *sergente* shouted. 'Who are you working for? Who hijacked the trucks this morning? Names, addresses, and we'll let you go. You can stop this, you stupid girl. Very easily.' He leant back in his chair, tapping his fingers on the table while Devora breathed in the delicious air, willing herself to stay calm, concentrating on a crack shaped like a bird at the corner of the ceiling. How she wanted to be a bird at this moment: a tiny sparrow to fly up from where she was bound and slip through the bars of this awful place and escape over the twin towers of...

Her head was yanked again and thrust into the hateful bucket and at that moment, she decided the only way out of this nightmare was to let herself sink into death. That way she would reveal no secrets, suffer no more torture and her soul would flutter freely with the wings of a sparrow. She forced herself to stop thrashing about, not to give in to the instinct of survival. She saw Mütti and Vati and her two adored brothers standing before her, beckoning her to come. She felt herself floating above the fat, oily *sergente* and his automaton assistant, as she hovered over them and their evil work. She was edging towards the bars of the tiny window and nothing mattered anymore: she was as light as a sparrow's feather and she would float through, spread her delicate wings and soar free.

Yet again her head was viciously pulled from the bucket and despite herself, she gulped in delicious lungfuls of air. The *sergente* was on his feet.

'Leave us,' he shouted at the *squadrista*. 'Take a break.' He threw the youngster a packet of Ambrosiana. 'Take a smoke. I'll deal with her. It isn't going to work this way.'

Devora slumped in the chair, shattered, despair seeping in

where she wanted courage to remain, wondering how to keep silent and protect her comrades.

'We know where you live, signorina. With that old woman who pretends to be a simpleton. She's one of yours. And we know who you are too. We know you're Jewish and you try to disguise yourself. And we're certain you were involved early this morning with the skirmish on the Pesaro road. You have an enemy out there who squealed. I'll leave you alone for a while to stew. A pretty girl like you with her whole life in front of her. Think on it. When I return, you can tell me where exactly those prisoners have gone.'

Before he left the cell, the sergeant thumped her hard in the chest. The chair fell back. As Devora was wondering who her informer might be, her head smacked against the stone wall, knocking her senseless as the chair crashed to the ground. As her head made contact with the floor, a trickle of blood seeped from Devora's mouth. She lay still.

CHAPTER 46

LUIGI

Once again, Luigi lay flat on his stomach. This time in a copse on the Cesana ridge outside Urbino. A message had come through to the brick factory that earlier that morning, a small partisan group of the Fifth Garibaldi Brigade had flushed out a stray group of *crucchi* hiding up in the trees. More help had been called for and Luigi and the others had offered their services without a second thought. The countryside was crawling with Germans, some of them willing to fight to the bitter end, others disillusioned and wanting to surrender and join the *partigiani* now the *alleati* were drawing nearer.

Luigi looked at his beloved countryside. The *contadini* had been unable to harvest their wheat during the skirmishes. Pink and golden stalks lay crushed where tanks had rolled over crops. In a crater, in the middle of the dirt road, a German Semovente, seized from the Italian army soon after the Armistice, lay twisted, a helmet perched on top of the assault gun, spent shell cases littering the parched grass around. A dead cow lay in the hot sun, its stomach bloated, legs in the air. Luigi listened to flies buzzing in the distance, feasting on its rotting flesh. A barn smouldered on the horizon, smoke curling into a perfect blue sky, mingling with battle fire in the distance. *A perfect sky in an imperfect landscape,* Luigi thought ruefully, the days of wandering freely over his beloved meadows with Tuffo, looking for flora and insect specimens, a distant memory.

He shifted his position. God, it was hot. What wouldn't he give to plunge into a clear mountain stream at this moment? But nowhere was safe to wander these days and he hadn't walked with poor Tuffo in a long while. There were defectors from the German army holed up anywhere they could hide: nervous, trigger-happy, knowing the *alleati* were approaching. Those *tedeschi* more than ready to surrender were shit-scared of being shot as traitors by their own men. Some of them were infiltrators, wearing bogus red scarves, symbols of resistance. You needed eyes in the back of your head to check each movement and Luigi was bone-tired.

He and the others had arranged themselves in a circle in hastily dug trenches round the copse for this reason, near enough to communicate and warn each other of an enemy approach from every direction. On retreat, the *crucchi* were dynamiting anything they could to slow down the *alleati*.

In the distance towards Fossombrone, dust clouds screened the horizon's edge.

'Vehicles approaching. Lots of them,' Franco muttered. '*Dio mio,* there are too many for us to tackle.'

'No need to commit suicide if we're outnumbered,' Luigi said. 'We stay down. Let them pass and then take the back road into the city to join the others and attack then.'

He picked up his binoculars, careful to shade them from the glare of the blistering sun's rays. In the early days, positions had been given away from the bouncing of light from lenses and they had learned this lesson to their cost. He checked twice, assuring himself of the vehicles' markings.

'*Alleati*,' he whooped. 'It's the *alleati*. Hundreds of them, *ragazzi*.'

A grenade lobbed from nearby landed near the trench, showering the *partigiani* with dust and stones and the men ducked. When they looked up, the line of tanks and jeeps were almost upon them. Luigi stepped warily into the road, hands in the air, his men waving grubby white handkerchiefs on the ends of their guns, red scarves, anything they could use to prove they were not enemy.

'*Non siamo tedeschi – siamo partigiani – viva l'Italia*,' Luigi called.

A young man astride a lightweight motorcycle stopped and answered in perfect Italian. Luigi and his comrades listened nervously.

'Stay where you are. I'm coming over to talk. One false move, our men will shoot to kill. Lay your weapons on the ground.'

Luigi put his rifle down in front of him, signalling to the others to follow suit. The moment they had all been waiting for had arrived. The *alleati* were here at last and with their help, surely the war would quickly be over and the *crucchi* banished from their land.

The slim, dark-haired man parked his Enfield at the side of the road and strode over to the *partigiani*, extending his hand to Luigi in a firm greeting. He asked for confirmation of identities. His Italian was good. His smile seemed genuine. Luigi took an immediate liking to this fellow and explained how the group had been busy sabotaging the *tedeschi* as they retreated from the area.

'They're everywhere,' Luigi said. They flinched at the crack of nearby gunfire, ducking automatically to the ground and as soon as they could, Luigi and the Englishman ran, hunched, towards the copse as the *alleati* responded, the *takka takka* percussion of their machine guns loud in their ears.

'*Sono* John Magrath,' the British soldier shouted above the guns as they crouched in the hole where Luigi and Franco had waited only minutes before. '*Interprete per generale* Holworthy. The major general wants to know the locations of all German positions in Urbino before he advances. And I need to get into the city to take a look myself.'

Luigi's eyes widened as he watched the interpreter remove his uniform cap and khaki army shirt, pulling a plain shirt from his knapsack. 'Lend me your cap,' he told Luigi as he changed, adding, 'you're to accompany me. You look light enough – you can perch on the back. I need to speak to your mayor. Your men wait here.'

It sounded a crazy idea but Luigi trusted this assured fellow. He perched on the luggage rack of the motorcycle, his hands resting on the shoulders of John Magrath, and directed the young intelligence officer along rutted paths towards the city's walls. Even from a distance, they could see huge chunks of the ramparts had been recently destroyed, blocking gateways and roads into the city, dust still settling from the explosions.

'Bloody hellfire! So much for Urbino being a *città aperta*,' John swore as he cut the engine and they dismounted.

'We'll leave the motor here,' he said, pushing the Enfield behind a gorse bush. 'Now take me to your mayor.'

The acting mayor was a lawyer, a member of the fascist party, but Luigi was not too concerned. There were many *urbinati*, like himself, who were nominal fascist party members. It was expedient for the job and Luigi knew that *avvocato* Giorgio Pagi would be willing to cooperate. The German army would with any luck be gone from Urbino very soon, their place taken by the allies. The mayor would doubtless be happy to change sides.

Midday had barely passed, the sun a scorcher, and Luigi knew Pagi would be at home for his meal. They took a circuitous route round his city. Many doors were wide open, showing signs of hasty withdrawal. An abandoned chest spewed assorted contents onto the cobbles: two brass candlesticks, a silk shawl, bottles of olive oil, flasks of red wine. A sewing machine had been placed outside another door. Soldiers' spoils. Gifts for their German women back home.

The door to the mayor's home was opened by his daughter, startled at the sight of two dusty men standing there. She would have slammed the door on them had Luigi not barged in.

'Don't be afraid, Giovanna. This man needs to talk urgently to your father.'

Avvocato Giorgio Pagi, a crisp linen serviette tucked into his collar, was about to insert a forkful of spaghetti into his mouth as they entered his dining room.

He jumped up, his fork clattering onto the plate, hands raised. '*Che diavolo volete*? What the devil do you want?'

In fluent, concise Italian, John Magrath explained what he needed and the mayor called to Giovanna to bring paper and pen, adding she should serve up two more plates of pasta for their visitors. He sketched a map of the city, showing major landmarks and principal areas where *tedeschi* were positioned.

Two glasses of wine and dishes of spaghetti were produced and within half an hour, Luigi and Magrath were en route again.

'Almost as good as my own mother's pasta,' John said with a grin over his shoulder as the compact motorbike bumped along the track. 'She's Italian. That's why I can speak your lingo.'

'I can't remember the last time I ate spaghetti,' Luigi replied. 'Rare indeed. Our mayor obviously has his contacts,' he added wryly. He couldn't wait to catch up with Devora and the others to share in the celebrations once this was all over.

In the late afternoon of 28 August, Luigi and his small band of *partigiani* joined up with a handful of Polish and British soldiers from the Fourth Indian Division. They accompanied the *alleati* into the city, sitting wherever and however they could upon jeeps and huge tanks, greeted by citizens handing out bunches of grapes to their saviours, offering tumblers of wine, flowers, hugs and kisses from some of the women – both young and old. Luigi noted with disgust Sabrina standing outside her parents' tailoring business, waving a starched handkerchief, welcoming the *alleati* as she had welcomed the *tedeschi*. She would not be the only one to change sides to suit her needs.

Moving stealthily over fallen debris along the narrow alleys, Luigi joined in with flushing out remaining *tedeschi* snipers left in the city. As the band of *partigiani* moved up Via Raffaello, an old woman emerged from her house and told Luigi the last of the *tedeschi* soldiers had disappeared an hour earlier up Via Raffaello. 'I gave one of them smelling salts, poor lad; he'd fainted onto the road. He was very young. Younger than my own grandson, bless him. I couldn't help myself. He revived and I've never seen anybody scarper so fast. Did I do wrong, signore? They went that way.' She pointed up the hill past the house where Raffaello had been born in the fifteenth century, rubble and tiles strewing the incline.

Luigi preferred this woman's attitude to Sabrina's. She hadn't been thinking of herself, after all. She'd treated a fellow human being with dignity and an *etto* of kindness. If all people were like this, if there was more humanity, maybe there would be fewer wars in the first place. He squeezed the old lady's hand, reassuring her. 'You did no wrong, signora. You did no wrong at all. Just be grateful the *alleati* have arrived. Life will improve from now on.'

It was after midnight when Luigi, light-headed from swigging wine with his friends to celebrate the liberation of Urbino, approached Anna Maria and Devora's simple dwelling.

'Wake up, you two. It's time to celebrate. Urbino is free,' he shouted, a bottle of grappa stowed in his pocket, ready to share with his two ladies.

The front door is as skewwhiff as my head, he thought, swaying as he stood, observing the flimsy door hanging from one hinge.

He sobered up quickly enough. Candles dotted about the place spluttered in the draught and he took in Anna Maria lying on the mattress, hands clasped in prayer, petals of wild chamomile scattered around her body. She was clothed in a white nightdress and her hair was covered in crudely plaited straw, so that at first sight Luigi thought her dark hair was dyed blonde. Like a ghastly red jewel, a bullet hole pierced her forehead, her eyes closed as if in sleep.

Stretched on the floor beside her, slumped in final slumber, was a squat German soldier. He wore grey-green army trousers, but on his torso was a white shirt spattered with blood and brains. *Suicide,* Luigi surmised, bile rising as he took in the gun protruding from where the man's mouth should have been. Arranged neatly next to him in a circle, a candle in the centre, were photographs of a comely woman. In one, her blonde hair was braided around her head and two young children leant against her, another seated on her lap. The candle had burnt down and wax had spilled onto the sepia images.

He rushed from the hut, vomiting wine and food greedily swallowed during his earlier street celebrations. What had gone on here? And where the hell was...? Panic seized him. Where was Devora? He called, over and over, 'Devora, *dove sei, dove sei?* Where are you?'

Back in the hut, he scrabbled to light a lamp with trembling fingers, swinging it into all corners of the room, searching for her body. But she wasn't there. His mind whirred with horrific possibilities: she'd gone off on her own after the raid. Had she been picked up? Taken from here by the *nazifascisti?* Was she dead too? He cursed himself for not following her after this morning's mission, but, *Dio mio*, he'd been angry. Was she with Enrico? Had Enrico handed her in? Had he duped her? He tortured himself with questions and then ordered himself to stay calm.

He hunted outside the building, startling a fox lurking near the hen coop, calling out Devora's name repeatedly, wondering what in hell's name had gone on in this place. He turned when he heard a scuffle in the bushes, his free hand feeling for his Beretta. And then Tuffo emerged over the dry grass, limping towards his master and Luigi fell to his knees. The dog licked his cheek and Luigi buried his face in his faithful friend's fur. 'Help me find her, Tuffo. Help me.'

In all the revelries, he'd mislaid the key to his parents' country house and he pummelled at their door, yelling at them to open up.

It was their servant Domenica who opened it, her hair bound in curling rags, a shawl over her long nightdress, his parents following behind on the stairs.

'What on earth is going on?' his father asked.

'Is Devora here?'

'Luigi, it's the middle of the night,' his mother said. She looked him up and down. 'What do you mean is Devora here? She left Urbino two years ago. Are you drunk?'

He pushed past his parents and sank to the bottom stair and Tuffo hobbled after him. For the first time, he noticed a gash on the dog's front right paw and he pulled out his handkerchief to dab at it. Domenica took over, speaking softly to the animal, leading him to her kitchen where Luigi knew he would be cared for. This small act of kindness, a recognition of goodness after the horror he had witnessed, the knowledge that he was with people who loved him, brought a lump to his throat.

'Urbino has been liberated,' he explained to his parents, 'but... the *tedeschi*, in leaving, have done despicable things... Devora has been here for a while... she came back... but I can't find her and her servant has been murdered... I have to find her...'

'I'll dress and we'll take the car and look for her, *figlio*,' his father said.

'I'll make you coffee, Gigi,' his mother said, pulling him up from the stairs into an embrace.

He let his parents fuss over him, his mother repeating her favourite saying, 'Help is worth a hundred words.' But he didn't want coffee; he wanted to find Devora. If she was dead, he would never forgive himself.

CHAPTER 47

DEVORA

A tap dripped somewhere and as night fell, disparate sounds from the city drifted in through the bars of the cell window: the call of a mother to her children, hobnailed steps of soldiers hastening down the cobbled street, a phone ringing deep within the *questura* building. It rang on and on and nobody answered. In the corner of the room, there was a scuttling. A mouse. It sat on its haunches and observed the girl on the floor. She stared back and when she wriggled her arms in the ropes binding her and the chair moved, it disappeared into a hole in the wall.

Luigi had owned a pet mouse at elementary school he'd insisted on carrying everywhere. He'd smuggled Topo into school one day. It had escaped and caused havoc in the classroom, *maestra* Berenghini jumping onto her chair, clutching her skirts and screaming. How innocent they'd been back then.

Devora's stomach rumbled. She hadn't eaten since leaving Anna Maria in Castel Cavallino. How long had it been? More than one day? Devora's head pounded as she tried to think. Anna Maria would be worrying why she wasn't home. How long would she leave it before going for help? Devora had landed on her left side but her right wrist was bound less tightly and she could wriggle it about. If she could work against the back of the chair, maybe she could loosen her bindings further.

While she chafed the rope against the rough wood, she thought about who had informed on her and then pushed away that concern to think more positive thoughts. Her life brimmed with enough negativity. She pictured her loved ones instead and the people who might miss her if she were never to get out of here. Mütti, Vati, the twins. Were they thinking about her like she was thinking about them? Of course they were.

She bit her sore lip and winced. What about her school friends? Enrico. Where was he now? Why had he disappeared so quickly? She'd seen him run off shortly after parking the truck. Sabrina. Well, she had shown her true light, hadn't she? What sort of a friend was she? She pulled a face, yelping as the muscles screamed.

Luigi. He'd been furious. How long had she lain here unconscious? Was it only this morning or had days gone past? Dear Luigi. He'd been her staunch friend throughout: kind, brave, principled. Yes, that was the right adjective for Luigi. True to himself, true to the cause of liberty. Her forehead puckered as out of the blue, she realised she would miss him more than she would miss Enrico. Enrico had been the elusive one and she'd been... what had she been? She'd been a child. That was it. Thinking she was in love with him. But she wasn't a child anymore. Childhood did not flourish in war; she'd learned that.

When the twins returned and this awful war was over, she would make sure she prolonged their childhood: she'd accompany them to the Fortezza to fly kites together whenever they asked. She'd even play football, even though she was useless at it. Yes, all those occasions when she'd been too tired to play with them filled her with regret. 'Later, boys. I'll play later,' she'd said so often to her brothers. And later had never happened. She'd always found an excuse. She vowed to change that. While she thought, she continued to chafe against the chair, pausing every now and again to gather her strength.

Her brain rolled back to friends made at the internment camp at Villa Oliveto: Shira, so mysterious and melancholy. Where had she ended up? Ida and baby Nechama? How were they? And dear old Doctor Kempe? She owed him so much. How patient he'd been with her hundreds of medical questions, sharing the benefit of his experience. She hoped he was able to relax in his new life in Switzerland. Even Erma, besotted with the prison commander's son, Emanuele. She was so annoying, but even she felt dear to Devora in this cheerless cell while she waited for her torturers to return through the locked door and devise other ways of extracting information. *Bastardi.* She said the word aloud, wincing again at the pain, and the mouse, who had advanced again over the floor towards her, fled, tail in the air, to the safety of its hole. *If I were Alice in Wonderland and had a magic potion, I could follow you,* she thought. But life was no fairy tale.

She tried to shake her head to rid herself of bitter thoughts, like a horse that shakes away pesky flies. But she couldn't even do that, her head rammed against this damp, filthy cell floor. *Never mind, Devora. Take your mind off this hellhole.*

Her mind swam with people: the Zanzis, Haddie, Adamo and their poor children in the crypt, battered and forlorn from their constant escapes, hiding in the dark instead of playing in the open air like children should. Because of this damned, fucking war... But Haddie was free now. She'd sat near her in the truck. Soon she'd be reunited with her husband and children. She damn well hoped so.

And Luigi's men: Franco and Gianni and many others, their numbers growing all the time. She called them Luigi's men, although she knew he wasn't the leader of that band of *parti-*

giani. They took their orders from don Cecchetti, who in turn passed them down from the *partigiano capitano*, Emo Cartellucci. These names were best not remembered, she chided herself, saying *basta* aloud. Enough. Yes, *basta* to everything. And *basta* to all the names she'd assumed over these past months: Devora, Debora, Suor Rosa, Elena and now, disguised as a boy. A boy without a name, on a floor, in a cell...

She thought about the battle names assumed by the *partigiani* she'd met. If she had to choose a battle name for herself, she would choose Basta. Because she'd truly had enough and if she ever got out of here, she was going to damn well continue to fight against the evil men and women ruining her country. *Basta* to the whole lot of them. Enough! They could rot in Hell. She realised she was clenching her jaw and she told herself to breathe evenly, to save her anger for when it was needed.

And then, of course, there was her second mother. Her darling Anna Maria, who could be so annoying at times in the way she fussed, making sure she ate, clasping her tight in an embrace against her pillowy bosom every morning when she set off to her cleaning job in Urbino and clasping her even tighter when she returned. How worried she must be. There was always something inviting to eat on the table when she returned: a *minestra* made from wild plants and roots from the meadows, a *frittata* from her free-range hens, or her famous hare stew... A single tear trickled down Devora's cheek as she thought how much she had taken Anna Maria for granted. She would make it up to her too once she was free.

The remaining strands of rope snapped sooner than she'd expected and she brought her thoughts to the present. Her shoulders ached where they had been wrenched back for so long and as blood returned to her hands, she flexed away pins and needles.

An explosion of heavy gunfire bounced into the cell from outside and she jumped at the *ra-ta-ta-ta* of machine guns, followed by the boom of canon fire and whistle of bullets, far too close for her liking. She crawled towards the door. If the building were bombed, she knew the safest place was the door frame if the ceiling collapsed. There was panicked shouting from the guards as they raced down the corridor. Other prisoners shouted, 'For the love of God, let us out. Take us with you to the cellars.'

But nobody came to unlock the cell doors and Devora remained, slumped, her back against the heavy door, flinching every time a gun fired outside. The shooting in the city went on all night as she listened to men calling to each other from the cells.

'It's the *alleati*,' one said. 'They're chasing the *nazifascisti* away. We'll be out soon, you'll see.'

The pessimistic response from another was shouted down. 'Yes, *porca Madonna*, we'll be out of here in coffins when they've bombed the *questura* to smithereens.'

'*Ma vai all'inferno*, Enzo. Go to Hell. Always looking on the dark side. Hell will suit you fine.'

She must have dozed off, because some time before the glimmer of dawn, a key turned in the lock and somebody entered. Instinctively she curled into a ball and then she heard someone shout in English, 'There's another one in here, sarge. A girl. Beaten up bad.'

A young soldier in a British tin hat bearing a red cross, and wearing light khaki uniform, touched her gently on the shoulder and she stared up at him. He was followed by two more, carrying a stretcher. Crouching down, the first soldier reached for her hand, shaking his head at the sight of her bloodied face. He spoke in Italian, his accent the way Stanlio and Olio talked to each other in the *Laurel and Hardy* films she'd seen before the war and she began to laugh.

Doctor Kempe had told her laughter was the best medicine, but being lifted into the arms of a strong young man and carried out of the *questura* into daylight by kindly stretcher-bearers was the best tonic she'd had in a long time.

'*Grazie*,' she muttered through her swollen mouth.

'*Prego*, signorina. You're very welcome.'

She laughed again. *He probably thinks I'm a mad woman with my hysterical laughter*, she thought. *But who cares?*

CHAPTER 48

Her face cleaned up and minus a back tooth that the British medical orderly had suggested was better out than in – 'You'll end up swallowing it otherwise, miss,' he had said – Devora limped through the streets of Urbino back home to Via delle Stallacce. Urbino was one big party: bottles of wine carefully hidden away over the past lean years were being shared between neighbours and soldiers. A couple of elderly men played on accordions and as she crossed the piazza in front of the cathedral, couples were dancing. A soldier called to her, inviting her to join him, but she shook her head and pushed her way through the dizzy throng.

Her first task on entering the kitchen was to hide her mother's jewels again. Thank God they hadn't body searched her at the *questura*. They would have found the pouch in her undergarments. The Blackshirts had searched her pockets in the street and taken her bank notes, *bastardi*. She climbed the stairs wearily. All she wanted to do was lay her head on her own pillow and sleep away the horror of the last hours. She would only celebrate the liberation of Urbino once she was surrounded by her cherished family. When that would be, she had no idea. Urbino might no longer be occupied by the *tedeschi*, but the war was not over.

It was almost midday when she woke. At first, she didn't know where she was as she turned on the mattress, expecting to see the stout shape of Anna Maria beside her. Sunlight filtered through broken slats in the shutters and angelus bells rang out in the city: a sound she hadn't heard for months. She made out the outline of the wooden desk where she had toiled over school homework and later her first year of medical studies. Through the walls came everyday soothing sounds: the beating of a carpet, a chair scraped across a tiled floor, a child crying. The neighbours were back. It was safe at last for inhabitants to creep back to the ghetto. But the everyday sounds in her own house were absent. How wonderful it would be to hear her father knocking his pipe against the edge of the fireplace again before loading the bowl with his morning tobacco, and inhale the spicy scent as he lit up. Her mother would sing again as she cooked, moving sizzling pans about on the blackened stove, shouting upstairs to remind her children it was time to get out of bed and dress for school.

She sat up, her head swimming, body aching, and gingerly she made her way downstairs, clinging to the rope handrail, counting the thirteen wooden steps in the same way she always had done in the past. A cobweb brushed the top of her head. The house would need a good spring clean before Mamma returned. When she felt stronger, she would roll up her sleeves and make a start with Anna Maria's help. She hated housework but she would ensure the windows sparkled, furniture gleamed with polish and bed linen was laundered for her family's return.

Devora reached for Mamma's shopping bag from the back of the door and let herself out in the midday heat. If she tried to hurry, despite her aches and pains, she might catch the shops before they closed for the afternoon. She was as hungry as a wolf. It felt good to climb the narrow steps to the long portico leading to the piazza without having to disguise herself. Still sore, she nevertheless held her head high as she made her way towards the store.

Someone grabbed her from behind, lifting her, swinging her round and round as she screamed for help.

'Devora, darling Devora. *Carissima.* I've been searching for you all over,' Luigi shouted.

'*Ahi,* Gigi! You're hurting me. *Stop...*'

When he set her down, he looked at her bruised face and agonised expression.

'What has happened to your face? Where have you been? You left without saying anything.'

The look on his face was of tender concern, his anger gone.

'I'll explain everything. But not here in the street. Come with me to shop first. We can talk back home.'

He insisted on paying for everything and she was grateful. She only had a few coins rattling in her pocket. The *bastardi* hadn't bothered with those. Goodness only knew how she would manage until Papà returned. Half a loaf, eggs, a couple of slices of cheese and a handful of figs would have been more than enough to keep her going but Luigi added a bottle of wine, a kilo of potatoes and a dozen tomatoes grown in the shopkeeper's own vegetable garden. There were no other customers waiting and he told them, as he wrapped up mortadella sausage and pushed it in her bag, that he wouldn't do this for everybody, but wasn't it grand to see signorina Devora back again and wasn't it wonderful that life might return to normal now the *crucchi* had left and the *alleati* would set life back on a correct footing?

'It won't happen overnight,' Luigi told him. 'But I've seen already there's good cooperation between the *alleati* and *partigiani.* Things should indeed look up. Hopefully, with Giorgio Fanelli at the helm of the CLN, life will start to improve.'

The shopkeeper added half a dozen courgettes to Devora's

shopping bag. '*Buon appetito*, signorina. You look as if you need feeding up. Come to me each day at this time and I'll see you right.'

On their walk to the ghetto, Luigi was quiet, wondering how to break the devastating news about Anna Maria. Devora hadn't uttered a word yet as to how she had received the bruises to her face and body. He couldn't take his eyes off her. Her features were so angular and he could have circled her wrists twice with his hands. Oh, how he wanted to hold her, look after her. She was limping and his heart filled with rage. Of course there were hundreds of people who looked frail now, who had suffered unspeakably during these past months. But Devora wasn't a number amongst hundreds; she was Devora. Unique. The most precious person in the world, if only he could pluck up courage to tell her.

He decided they should eat before he told her – get sustenance into her and then break the awful news about Anna Maria. It was a mystery what had happened. Maybe the German had received bad news about his family and it had turned him crazy, hence the photograph shrine? He'd seen many men fall to pieces with what they'd witnessed and carried out. It could have been the last straw.

Devora had mentioned this German soldier came frequently to visit Anna Maria; he seemed to have a soft spot for her and maybe he'd been riven with guilt. Perhaps Anna Maria and her German friend were murdered by the SS in retaliation for the rescue... The new intake of fascist GNR, the Republican guard, were awful. He'd heard even the *tedeschi* thought they were depraved. Whatever had gone on, the pair were dead and he was dreading telling Devora.

In the kitchen, he placed the shopping bag on the table and caught sight of a note, immediately recognising Enrico's scrawl.

He scanned the message, his heart plummeting to his heavy boots.

'Enrico was here?' he asked, forcing himself to sound nonchalant, when in reality jealousy twisted his guts. Enrico had asked to be part of the *resistenza*. Yes, he'd turned up at the ambush with his truck, but he hadn't been part of the original plan and he'd done very little else for the cause. He had a habit of disappearing for days on end. 'I'm on something hush hush,' he'd say to Luigi. 'Best not to ask too much. It's top secret, *amico mio*.'

Luigi knew not to ask. It was second nature in this game. Even the best of fellows had succumbed to interrogation. The less you knew, the safer for everyone. Husbands kept secrets from wives, friends from friends. It was accepted. But it was suspicious the way Enrico had disappeared so suddenly after the ambush. Luigi clenched his fists at a suspicion that wormed into his brain. Had Enrico had second thoughts and informed on them? Was he ultimately responsible for what had happened to Devora? And where was he now?

'Rico was here when I arrived a couple of days ago,' Devora said. 'He's been sheltering in different places and I let him stay the night. But he's disappeared again.'

She didn't seem angry or hurt. His misgiving increased: Enrico sleeping in Devora's house. Had they shared the same bed? Was she still holding a torch for him? And when was she going to tell him what had happened to her? It was driving him crazy, but he kept quiet, waiting for her to open up.

He watched as Devora broke four eggs into a pan. They hissed and spluttered as they met the fat, and he went over to cut bread and slice tomatoes. The remains of a heel of cheese lay on the draining board and an empty bottle of wine. Had Devora and Enrico enjoyed a romantic supper together? Devora never could handle her drink. Had he got her drunk to get her into bed? He cut into the tomato fiercely and the knife slipped, slashing his finger and he swore. '*Dio cane...*'

She laughed. 'You too. Enrico commented on the language I've picked up.' She moved nearer and pulled his hand close to examine the cut.

'You will live, signor Gigi. I don't need to stitch you up.' She pulled a cloth from a drawer and tore it into strips.

'This might sting, but I know you're a brave soldier,' she said with a smile, dabbing alcohol onto the cut and winding the strip round his finger.

He breathed in her wholesome scent. Her hair had started to grow again, a couple of dirty blonde curls curling at the nape of her neck and he wanted to bend to kiss her there. His hand began to shake and she looked up at him.

'You don't feel faint, do you?'

'Of course not,' he said, dragging himself away to sit again at the table. 'Tell me what happened to you.'

'Let's eat first. I'm ravenous.'

He watched as she munched greedily on their simple meal, wiping the last traces of egg from her plate with a corner of bread and licking her fingers after.

'That was the feast of feasts. *Grazie*, Luigi. Maybe life is not too bad after all.' She pushed her plate away and fiddled with scattered breadcrumbs, sweeping them into little piles with her fingers.

Still he waited. Waited for her to be ready to talk.

Eventually she spoke. 'I had the most awful time at the *questura*.'

Her sentences were halting but she spared no details – as if wanting to expunge the experience.

Luigi listened as patiently as he could, but he was horrified. He wanted to hunt down the bastards there and then, but first he had to tell her about Anna Maria and shatter her faith in human nature all over again.

'But I didn't reveal a thing, Gigi. Not a thing,' Devora continued, in the same matter-of-fact tone that worried Luigi. 'But... if they had returned to work on me, I hope I'd have found the courage to keep quiet.' She looked up at him, anger flaring in her eyes. 'I kept telling myself that if I died, I'd have at last done something good. Something to make my life worthwhile...'

He took her hands, cradling them in his, where they sat opposite each other, and she frowned.

'What's up, Gigi? You do believe me, don't you? I didn't blab. I *promise*. I know you're angry with me about Enrico turning up. But it was just as well in the end, wasn't it?'

When he told her about Anna Maria, she screamed, pulling away her hands to cover her mouth. He felt wretched for adding to her anguish, but it had to be done. At least he'd saved her from coming across the scene herself.

'I can take you to where she is,' he told Devora, her face wreathed with such sadness he couldn't bear it. 'Her funeral is this afternoon.'

She nodded. 'Now!' she said. 'Take me now. Please.' Anger in her eyes was replaced with bleakness. He couldn't bear it. This time, when they walked down through the city, they no longer scuttled along alleys like rats. They took the main route. Life had returned to the streets. Children played. Women chatted at the fountain as they pounded their laundry. British soldiers on guard next to jeeps smiled as they passed. They had to show documents at the city gate but the young men were courteous, saying *grazie* with their round-vowel accents as they handed back their papers. When they passed a group of *alleati* outside the city, clustered bare-chested around a tank, one of them looked up from plucking a chicken. '*Pollo tedesco*, German hen,' he said, with a cheeky grin, a cigarette dangling from the corner of his mouth as he worked. Some unsuspecting free-range hen had been taken prisoner, they joked. But Devora said nothing. She set one foot in front of the other, her head down, and Luigi too stayed silent, always at her side.

He remained at the back of the church to let Devora say goodbye. She approached the simple coffin slowly and bent to kiss the dead woman's face. Don Cecchetti rose from the pew where he had been praying and Luigi heard him ask Devora if there were any particular prayers that she wanted him to say for Anna Maria.

She shook her head. 'I'll leave that to you. But... she tried to be a mother to me, *padre*. And much more... let them be special prayers.'

Franco, Gianni and a few other young men and women she didn't recognise let themselves into the church later, together with the priest's housekeeper and a couple of women from the village. The small group of mourners walked with the priest to the cemetery after a simple requiem service, the women fanning themselves under the afternoon sun, the screeching of cicadas like a chorus of lament.

'When this is all over, I want to take her back to Lucania,' Devora murmured to Luigi as they trod the dusty white track towards the cemetery. 'Her baby son is buried there. I want to make sure they're beside each other in death and I'll pay for a memorial stone to remember them by.' She picked up a piece of quartz stone, glistening in the sunlight at the side of the road, and placed it in her pocket.

And when the simple coffin, which Luigi told her had been hastily cobbled together by Franco from the boards of an old table, was covered with the last sods, Luigi watched Devora place the stone at Anna Maria's feet in the Jewish tradition, and crouch to lift a handful of dusty earth, letting it sift through her fingers.

'Life is so fleeting, isn't it, Luigi?' she murmured. 'But Anna

Maria made more difference than she realised. She'll forever be part of my family.'

He swallowed back his emotion as Devora touched the fresh earth.

'I'll never forget you,' he heard her whisper. 'Never.'

CHAPTER 49

ALMOST ONE YEAR LATER, JULY 1945

'Devora, can you look in on that new patient this morning? I think you'll be of more help to him than I. And – that exam you're sitting in September. If you want me to go over anything at lunch, then come sit with me in the *mensa*.'

'*Grazie*. I might well take you up on that. It's anatomy... so many tricky muscles to remember.'

Dottor Goffredo Minghotti, assistant director of the main Urbino Hospital, had been attentive to Devora from the first day she'd been offered a post in the department of psychiatry. Despite not yet being qualified, in the immediate aftermath of war there was a shortage of medical staff and with a severe outbreak of scabies and influenza in the city, extra help was needed in all departments.

Goffredo was older than Devora and had been briefly married, but his young wife had left for Canada at the end of the war, having been whisked off her feet by a soldier more attentive than her husband. He'd asked Devora out for dinner a couple of times, but she felt her heart had run dry of feelings nowadays.

She'd accepted the first invitation from him, ground down by his persistence, and he'd taken her to a restaurant in Sassocorvaro, snaking up the winding road in his Lancia Aprilia, carefully avoiding craters waiting to be repaired. She wore the two-piece Anna Maria had lovingly adapted for her before the war, but it hung from her frame, the colour faded, the new fashion for wider skirts in contrast with the slimline, austere style. She felt dowdy and the food was too rich. He had ordered a second course of loin of pork with truffles without consulting her and, although she had never bothered too much about eating kosher meat, she had grown used to dishes concocted from vegetables and pulses and she lifted her plate and swept her over-seasoned meat onto Goffredo's. He had drunk a couple of glasses of Verdicchio and waggled his finger. 'You need to put more flesh on, Devora. If you're going to bear children, we must get you healthier.'

Her eyes had nearly popped out of her head at his bald statement. 'Whoever said I wanted to have babies, Goffredo?'

He'd looked perplexed. 'But all women want babies, don't they? And Italy needs to build a healthy new nation after what we've been through.'

She declined all invitations after that, preferring to keep their relationship on a work footing. He was kind, generous but not somebody she could spend time with outside of hospital work, let alone a life as a wife and baby-machine.

Sabrina had stopped her in the piazza one day. 'I never see you these days, Devora,' she had said, trying to link arms but Devora withdrew hers, thinking Sabrina was like a dandelion releasing its seeds whichever way the wind blew. She remembered how her so-called school friend had been unwilling to have anything to do with her from the very start of racial laws, how she had milked the German occupiers for what she could get and then cosied up to the *alleati* when they had liberated Urbino the previous summer.

'I have a lot to do, Sabrina,' Devora had said as she'd walked off down the portico.

Sabrina hadn't tried to follow her but called out, 'Do drop in and have tea with me and Mamma some time. She'd love to see you again.'

'My arse, she would,' Devora had muttered under her breath. 'No bloody way.'

She kept the house in Via delle Stallacce clean, discovering she was more domesticated than she'd imagined and she couldn't wait to see her mother's reaction when she returned. She refused to add the proviso, *if* she returned. That was out of the question, despite unbelievable reports of extermination camps in the newspapers and horrific snippets of information gleaned from newly returned Jewish neighbours. She preferred to push all this to the back of her mind. Her parents had been sent to a work camp in Germany. That was it. Despite Luigi doing everything he could to track down the whereabouts of her family, there'd been nothing to report so far. It was torture not knowing, her life in limbo.

'Of course there are bound to be huge administrative problems tracking the displaced,' she told Luigi when he occasionally popped round to Via delle Stallacce and she'd ask yet again if he had news. 'It will take time to find them,' she'd say, ignoring the niggling question as to why Papà had not thought to put pen to paper and send a letter.

Luigi had kept away for long weeks but lately he'd started to turn up on her doorstep and she was always pleased to see him. Each time, he bore gifts: bunches of perfumed roses from his mother's garden, pots of Domenica's home-made jams, a dozen eggs bought from the *contadini* in Castel Cavallino. Occasionally, they'd wander to the piazza to enjoy an ice cream or a coffee. He was easy company and she had begun to look forward to spending time with her childhood friend.

Friday was her study day, when she allowed herself to stay

in bed a while longer, listening to the city stir for work, turning over to bury her face in the pillow and sleep in until she felt the need for a good, strong cup of coffee before settling down to her notes. Coffee was one of the miracles of life now that food supplies were very slowly returning to normal.

She tutted when somebody rapped at the door. Sometimes the little boy from the house at the end of the alley did this as he passed by on his way to synagogue. He was a spoilt child, pampered by his grandparents who had lost everybody else at Auschwitz. They never told him off and he grew fatter by the week. As a trainee doctor, she had taken it upon herself to warn them he would develop diabetes if they didn't cut down on sugary treats.

'He is all we have left, Devora dear, but we shall try. We do love to pamper him, poor child.'

The child knew Devora was responsible for his grandparents' denying him chocolate and biscotti and he had taken to sticking his tongue out at Devora and knocking at her door before running off. She accepted it for what it was: another bizarre effect of war.

The knocking continued and she jumped out of bed and rushed down the stairs. *Enough is enough. I'll give him a good boxing round the ears this time, spoilt little brat.*

She flung open the door to see Luigi and a gangly boy hovering at his side. It was not the boy from the end of the road. This boy was too big for his clothes: his trousers were short, patched at the knees. His hair was long and greasy but there was something about him. Where had she seen him before? And then she staggered forwards and he put out his arms, tentatively. He had wispy down on his top lip but it was her little brother. Definitely. Not so little anymore. Fifteen years old. Almost a young man. Almost.

'Alfredo?'

She pulled him into the house, Luigi following. She was full of questions but didn't know what to say. She kept touching him. 'Is it really you?' Hugging him, running her fingers over his face as if to assure herself he was real. He was stiff in her arms. Tears ran down her cheeks while he, on the other hand, remained strangely calm.

'Are you hungry, Alfredo? I'm quite a good cook now, you know. What shall I make? What do you fancy?'

And then came the question she had been putting off.

'Where are the others? Artur? Mütti, Vati?' She used the German names her mother always preferred. 'Are they coming later?'

Alfredo shook his head, turning to Luigi, an expression in his eyes she didn't want to read.

'Let's sit,' Luigi said, taking her arm, guiding her gently to her chair.

And Devora knew in that moment she was about to hear news nobody ever wanted to hear.

'Let me make us all coffee,' she said, moving towards the stove, delaying the moment.

'No, Devora. You must listen,' Luigi said.

He looked at Alfredo. And Alfredo nodded again. So far, he had uttered not one word.

'I'm so sorry, Devora,' Luigi started. 'Alfredo is the only one to come back.'

She shut her eyes as if shutting them would blot out the words Luigi had said. She felt his warm hands on hers and she let them rest there. 'In my heart I knew it. I just knew,' she whispered. 'It's been too long.'

Luigi continued. 'Alfredo, are you able to tell your sister what happened?' He spoke to the boy with such tenderness Devora could almost not bear it.

She couldn't take her eyes off her younger brother. He was Alfredo and yet... he looked different: his face pinched, his eyes... his eyes had lost their sparkle; they were the eyes of an old man. A shiver went down her spine as she asked, 'What happened to the others? Mamma, Papà? Arturo?' She used the Italian names for her parents this time. She was all of a muddle; she couldn't think straight.

He looked at her, his eyes black brimming pools, and shook his head, staring at her.

'Tell me, Alfredo. What happened?'

Another shake of his head and the words she had dreaded to hear spilled out. Three words she'd feared.

'They are gone.'

Alfredo seemed to shrink further within himself after that, his shoulders hunched. His voice was deeper than the last time she'd heard it. 'I'm sorry, Devora. So sorry. They're not coming back. I should have gone with them too. But...'

She moved to sit and he let her pull him onto her lap. He was shaking and she found herself instinctively rocking him. He was too big for his body, too big for her lap, his wrists poked from his too-short shirtsleeves, his breath was bad, he smelled hungry. She wanted to fill him with love but she didn't know where to start.

'Papà pushed me from the train when the guards were distracted and told me to get away. I thought they would follow, but they couldn't. There were so many people, Devora. Babies crying, people screaming. I saw a guard shoot a mother and baby because the mother fell down and didn't climb fast enough onto the train. I watched it pull out from Milan Station from where I was hiding behind the wheels of a stationary train...

'A cleaner found me when it was dark. He took me to his house. He was a kind man. But his wife wasn't. She hit me when he was at work, told me I ate too much, that she didn't have enough food to feed her own children and so, I ran away...'

He stopped talking and slid off her lap. 'But I'm home now. Home.'

She watched him walk round the kitchen. He moved over to

the menorah on the chimney place, his fingers touching the candlestick that Devora had retrieved from the olive grove at Villa Oliveto. Driven there by loyal Luigi at war's end, he had helped her dig it from the dry soil. She'd gone to fetch it for Mütti. And now Mütti would never have it.

Her bottom lip trembled as her eyes fell on the only photo of her parents she'd found in the house. Taken on their wedding day: Papà with his wiry hair tamed back, shining like patent leather, Mamma wearing a wide straw hat decorated with cloth roses, her waist tiny, her precious earrings peeping from her ringlets. Both looking so young. So serious.

He made his way up the stairs and Devora listened to him moving above her: sounds of drawers being opened, something falling to the floor. His cough, rattling, unhealthy.

'He was picked up in Ancona,' Luigi explained, his voice hushed. 'Stealing from a market stall. He's been living on the streets. He... he wasn't fully aware the war was over.' He looked at Devora, narrowing his eyes as Alfredo returned to the kitchen, clutching a pair of trousers and a shirt. 'We'll talk later but...' He tapped Alfredo on his arm and the boy flinched. 'Nobody is going to hurt you now, Alfredo. Are you hungry?'

'Pancakes. I should love a pancake,' he said, holding the clothes to his body. 'These don't fit me anymore.'

'I'll make you as many pancakes as you want, Alfredo. I even have honey to pour on them,' Devora said, tying her mother's apron round her waist. 'Your favourite. And then afterwards, I'll find you some of Papà's clothes, and you can have a good wash. We'll fill the bath with warm, soapy water. Your bed is made up.' She was talking to him as if he was much younger, talking to him like a mother would a child, but she didn't feel old enough or wise enough to be a mother figure. Her hopes had been crushed and she felt the weight of responsibility pressing on her shoulders.

She could not break down. She would not. Alfredo was her

family now. He needed her to be strong. Her brother was ill. She recognised trauma when she saw it and he would need patience. Healing of the mind took time. Sometimes mental wounds never healed but she would try her utmost to help him recover and listen when he was ready to talk.

'Luigi, thank you. How can I thank you?' she said as she broke eggs into a bowl containing flour, slowly adding milk as she talked.

'I'm sorry I couldn't bring you home the rest of your family, Devora. So sorry.'

Tears glistened in his eyes as he spoke but even if they hadn't, she knew he was truly sorry.

'At least we know something now. That at least,' she said. 'Do you think we will ever know the details?'

He bit his lip. 'We're hearing things all the time, but... maybe it's best not to know, Devora.'

She sighed and straightened her back and shoulders. 'Stay and eat with us, Gigi. Please stay.'

When Alfredo had grabbed at his food as they sat together, shovelling it in as if it might be his first and last meal, she'd tried not to look shocked. He'd grabbed three slices of bread as soon as she'd sliced the loaf and shoved them in his pocket, giving her a furtive look as he did so.

It will take time, she told herself. *Time and patience.* Her heart bled a little more at the suffering they had all endured.

CHAPTER 50

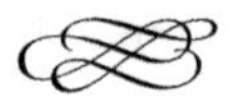

Two weeks later, Luigi visited again, carrying a small crate.

'It's for you, Alfredo. Open it.'

Devora had cut her brother's hair. Washed and tidied up, he looked almost presentable, save for Papà's trousers and shirt, too large for his slight frame and the haunted look he still carried.

Two small paws reached up through slats in the lid and Alfredo's face was a picture when he saw two kittens: one ginger striped, the other black as soot.

'They are descendants of Tigre,' Luigi said. 'I'm afraid Tigre is no more, but I thought you might like to look after these two.'

Alfredo picked them both up and the black cat immediately nestled into his neck like a fur collar. The ginger cat was braver and clambered inside Alfredo's roomy shirt, where he moved about before settling at his waist, the shirt tucked in, like a bag.

Alfredo laughed. 'It tickles. They are... sweet,' he said. '*Süsser*, Mütti would have said, wouldn't she, Devora?'

Devora nodded. 'But she never let us keep animals in the house. I think Papà would have allowed it. But not her. She liked everywhere to be spick and span.'

It was important to talk about their parents, to keep them

alive through memories. Devora glanced up at their photograph on the mantlepiece and promised them she would forever provide safe shelter for Alfredo. She tried not to think about what their last moments might have been like.

Luigi had found Red Cross records of her family's deaths. Arturo and Mütti had not made it past the first day at Auschwitz but Papà had apparently been selected to work in the latrines and showers as a *Bademeister*. He had survived until the end of the war and ended up at Katowice where the Russians sent him on a six-day train journey bound for Odessa to catch a ship back to Italy. He died on the train and unfortunately nobody knew where he had been buried. Hastily, no doubt.

Devora didn't like to dwell on this, but her imagination crept to that place. She supposed it might have been at some isolated station stop or even dropped from a loaded cattle truck into the night. Jews had been transported to Auschwitz like cattle and rescued like cattle. When darkness pushed at her mind, she willed herself to imagine her family as eagles soaring over the mountains, their wings outstretched, free at last.

'Do you fancy coming for a walk with me and Tuffo?' Luigi asked Alfredo. 'He's getting on now but he's still up for a wander on the mountains. We can see if there are porcini mushrooms after the rain.'

Devora was grateful to Luigi. It would be a relief to have time on her own. While Alfredo was near her, she was forever checking on him, worrying about his state of mind and it was good to share the load.

There was a knock on the door as she was playing with the kittens. They were a happy distraction, although she had a research paper to read. Four more exams to sit and she would be qualified to start her final year's studies as a doctor and then hopefully go on to complete in her chosen field of psychiatry.

Her next-door neighbour handed her the letter delivered in

error. 'The address wasn't quite right, Devora,' she said, loitering at the door. 'And how is your brother? How wonderful he turned up. So many haven't. How is he?' She made as if to come in and Devora indicated her books open on the table.

'I'd invite you in, Bela,' Devora said, 'but I have to study for an exam. Alfredo is... better than when he arrived.'

She had no wish to explain how hard she was finding Alfredo's behaviour: about her embarrassment when they were out walking and he picked food from the gutter, his head constantly down, scavenging for whatever he could find. He'd stolen apples from outside the greengrocer and she'd made him take them back to the shop and pay. Tomorrow, she planned to dig out his old kite and take him to the Fortezza. She longed to see him lift his face to the sun instead of walking stooped, like an old man. Hopefully, he would enjoy today's walk with Luigi.

The stamp was marked Helvetia. Switzerland. Intrigued, she shut the door so that the kittens wouldn't escape and went to sit by the light of the kitchen window to open the envelope.

Casa della Strega, Viggiù
2 July 1945

My dear Devora,

I hope this finds you well. I often think of you – my saviour, the girl who helped me give birth to my darling Nechama. As you can see from the enclosed photograph, she has turned into a beautiful child. In fact, she looks a lot like Davide, don't you think? Madlaine's pastries and dumplings – in fact all of Madlaine's tender care has helped us flourish. She is such a dear. Nechama calls her Oma, and that is fine. We are family now.

I left the hospital, you see, and returned to the mountains to be with the Zanzis after a bomb flattened the nuns' dormitories. Poor Suor Chiara... she didn't deserve to die like that.

Despite all our concerns, we were never bothered here in Viggiù. At first, I thought about coming down to Urbino. Do you remember me asking you to describe where you lived? I needed to memorise it in case I had to come one day. But then, I heard your city was still occupied by the tedeschi and I changed my mind. And in the end, it didn't feel right to burden you with us again...

I'm writing to give you my news; I never believed I could open my heart to another man, but – can you imagine, Devora, my dear... the local postman literally knocked at the door a few weeks after we returned to the Zanzis and he never stopped knocking. He's a good man and he loves Nechama. What's more he is Jewish, although like you he doesn't practise his faith. But it is a start. Maybe I can bring him back to God.

We married in a simple ceremony two weeks ago. Primo has no family in Italy. They left for Palestine at the start of the war and we are thinking of joining them next year. Madlaine and Alvaro will be devastated, I know, but we need a fresh beginning.

Wish us luck, dear Devora, and if you write to me, then you'll make me very happy.

Your loving friend,

Ida

The kittens pulled at her hem as she sat in the cool of the kitchen, smiling at Ida's news. As she fondled the heads of the little cats, Devora wondered if Nechama would one day be joined by brothers and sisters. She herself had no maternal feelings. The world seemed too cruel a place to introduce children. In danger of becoming maudlin, she replaced the letter in the envelope and leant the photograph of Nechama on the mantle-piece, next to her parents.

Alfredo and Luigi returned with a basket of mushrooms collected from the slopes of Monte Catria.

'We couldn't walk some of the paths,' Alfredo told Devora as he carefully laid the assorted fungi on the table. 'Some fields need clearing of mines. A farmer lost his leg last week, apparently.'

Yes, Devora thought. *The war might be over but repercussions will last a long time.* Alfredo had caught the sun and was more relaxed than she had seen him. Luigi's company was obviously good for him.

Later that evening, after the three of them had enjoyed mushroom risotto at the kitchen table and Luigi had left, Alfredo asked, 'Why don't you marry him?'

She nearly dropped the bowls she was carrying to the sink at his question.

'What a blunt thing to say, Alfredo!'

'Luigi obviously likes you. A lot.'

'We're good friends. We've known each other a long time.'

'Can't friends be married?'

She laughed. 'What's all this about, Alfredo? You're embarrassing me.'

'It would be wonderful to have him as a brother. I like him too.'

'I can't marry a man because my brother likes him.' She laughed. 'What an idea! Now come and help me wash these plates.'

That night in bed, she went over and over what her brother had said. Marry Luigi? The thought had never occurred to her. He was a wonderful friend but did he set her heart on fire? Did a heart need to be set on fire? It seemed to have happened for

Ida. How she wished she could talk to her old friend. It took her a while to fall asleep, the idea of sharing her life with Luigi filling her restless thoughts.

Devora heard Alfredo tiptoe down the wooden stairs early the following morning and when she came down later, the kitchen table was covered with kites and tangles of string.

'I found Arturo's kite,' he told her. 'It needed patching...' He held it up and Devora's eyes glistened at the sight of the little home-made kite Arturo had spent hours making. She remembered how, when he concentrated, his tongue would rest on his upper lip.

'I thought we could fly it this morning. Together. Luigi told me he was bringing his old kite along too.'

The wind was ideal: sufficient breeze to lightly fan the face and rustle leaves on trees as the three of them stood on a patch of land overlooking the city of Urbino. They were alone, the grass choked with weeds and wild flowers. The barbed wire skirting the fortress, left by the soldiers, had been neatly rolled up, waiting for collection.

Alfredo reeled out the string from Arturo's kite. 'Arturo and I often talked in the camp at Villa Oliveto about flying these together once we returned to Urbino,' he said.

The string spooled out and caught the wind, and Devora watched as Luigi's kite joined Arturo's, never tangling. Both young men let their kites fly away a little, then pulled in the lines as the kites pointed upwards, so they would climb further. They repeated the action again and again until they gained altitude and danced beneath the clouds. Then, Alfredo took a penknife from his pocket and cut the line. '*Addio, fratello mio,*' he said, shading his eyes with his hand as he bid farewell to Arturo's kite. It was tugged further and further into the currents of warm air on high and soon it was out of sight.

Devora stood in the middle of the two young men and as she put her arm round her brother's shoulders, her other hand crept into Luigi's and remained there as they stood in silence, gazing above, lost in their own thoughts.

Her fingers stayed entwined in his as they walked back through the alleys to Via delle Stallacce. While Devora prepared a simple supper for them of rocket salad, and tomatoes from Anna Maria's *orto* and bread and cheese, she felt shy whenever she caught Luigi's gaze on her.

When he kissed her goodnight on the doorstep, it felt suddenly right to be enfolded in his arms and his kiss stirred something in her which surprised and delighted. Luigi had always been there in her life. Always. And the missing part of her had been waiting all this time, and she'd never even realised.

Two days later, Luigi came to the door. He hovered on the threshold and they were awkward with each other. Devora felt unusually shy as he stood there.

'Are you free tonight, Devora? I mean, would you have supper with me. Just you,' he blurted, his words tumbling out as Alfredo appeared at her side.

'Just me?' she stuttered, annoyed that her cheeks felt hot.

'Of course she's free,' Alfredo piped up, a grin on his face. 'And before you start fretting about what I'm going to eat, Devora, *don't*... I'm good at slicing bread and cheese.'

A nervous laugh, followed by, 'That would be wonderful, Gigi. What time?'

'I'll come for you at seven. Don't dress up.'

'I haven't got anything else to wear than this anyway,' Devora replied, pulling at her skirt.

'Perfect,' Luigi replied, looking his usual relaxed self.

. . .

He handed her a bunch of daisies when he turned up at five to seven. On his back, he carried a knapsack.

Devora's only concession to her evening look was a patterned silk shawl of her mother's, found at the bottom of her parents' trunk. It had a small moth hole in one corner, but it brightened up her everyday outfit.

'Be good!' Alfredo had called as they made their way down the alley and it was on the tip of Devora's tongue to tell him not to be so cheeky.

Luigi reached for her hand as they climbed towards the Fortezza and she liked the fit, the feel of his fingers knitting through hers. It felt strange but it felt good too, their steps keeping pace together as they climbed. She was a little breathless when they reached the top and she was even more breathless when, as they leant against the still-warm stones of the fortress wall, admiring the view over their city, lights once again shining from the houses, he reached to kiss her.

She pressed closer and their kisses deepened.

He was the first to stop and pull away. 'I think we should eat,' he said, setting down his rucksack. 'I didn't want to be with anybody else in a stuffy restaurant tonight.'

She watched him produce a cloth, a bottle of wine, and two packages wrapped in paper, one containing warm *cresce* and the other half a roasted chicken, wishing she was still in his arms, rather than him fussing over their supper.

They sat, leaning against the wall, tearing off bits of meat and the fried flatbreads. Luigi poured wine into two pottery beakers and they toasted each other.

'Thank you for this, Gigi. Thank you for... everything.'

'Thank you for you, Biondina,' he said, leaning in to wipe a crumb from the corner of her mouth and following it with a lingering kiss.

The rest of the supper was forgotten. They had the place to

themselves and when Luigi pulled Devora down to the grass, their passion increased.

She rolled off him, lying on her side, and guided his hand to her breasts, closing her eyes as he began to unbutton her blouse and then trace his lips gently over her nipples.

But then he stopped.

She opened her eyes to see him sitting against the wall, his arms crossed.

'Gigi. I don't mind. I really don't.'

'I don't want our first time to be like this: a quick fumble on the grass like a couple of teenagers. I want it to be special.'

She came to nestle next to him, fastening her buttons as she spoke. 'You are such a gentleman. I really don't think I'm lady enough for you.' She turned her face up to his. 'I really wanted you to make love to me.'

He smiled. 'Will you—'

She didn't let him finish. 'Yes, Gigi. Of course I'll marry you. Let's not waste any more time.'

He laughed as she pulled his head down to kiss him long and deep.

'I have no ring yet, but we'll choose one together,' he murmured when they came up for air.

She paused. 'I'd like to have one made... from Mütti's jewellery. Would you mind, Gigi?'

'Of course I don't mind. I love you, Biondina. I love you so much,' he said, rubbing gently on her ring finger. And this time, when he took her in his arms again, he didn't hold back.

They married three months later in the little abbey of Castel Cavallino, faded frescoes and jars of daisies picked from the meadows fitting adornments to a simple service conducted by don Cecchetti. Alfredo was their witness and had written prayers of celebration, a combination of Catholic and Jewish sentiments. Ida travelled from the north with Nechama and her postman, Primo, to celebrate. In the hostelry in the village afterwards, Luigi's freedom fighter friends sang as they shared wine and *cappelletti* pasta, roast chicken and a honey cake, baked by one of Devora's neighbours.

They had no money for a honeymoon but Luigi's parents lent them their country house near Castel Cavallino. Late that night after Luigi had picked grains of rice from Devora's hair, thrown over them on the steps outside the church, he drew back the curtains in the bedroom to reveal a full moon silvering the hills. They kissed, their sighs one with the breeze sifting through the trees, moving slowly at first, until they abandoned themselves to each other. It was Luigi who shed tears, thanking her over and over, telling Devora that he'd never dreamt he could be so happy and it was Devora who kissed his tears away and apologised for lost time, telling him they had a whole life together and she must make it up to him.

'On this first of many more,' she whispered, turning to face him, '*facciamo una notte bianca*. Let's stay awake for the whole night. We don't need to sleep,' she said, kneeling up to kiss him on the mouth and moving slowly down the rest of his body.

EPILOGUE

20 AUGUST 1988

DEVORA

Unhunch those shoulders and unclench that jaw. Words Devora had used on so many of her patients as they'd sat opposite her in the clinic but it was one thing to say, and another to do as she walked towards the central bar with Enrico.

She'd been dreading this day but Luigi had encouraged her to keep their fifty-year reunion date.

'It will give you closure,' he'd said, using the terminology she used herself in her treatments.

'What if it doesn't?'

'Go with it, *tesoro*. I'll be at your side.'

But he wasn't at her side now, and she needed him to hurry up and join her. The car park was busy and he'd told her to make her own way up to the piazza to meet Enrico in case he thought they weren't coming. Was he being artful? Contriving a showdown? But Luigi wasn't like that.

'You're looking as beautiful as ever,' Enrico said. 'No way do you look sixty-nine.'

She pulled a wry grin. 'Ever the charmer, Enrico. I'm sixty-eight actually. One year makes a big difference at our stage.'

He pulled out a chair for her in the shade of an umbrella. His silver-steel hair was longer now, falling fashionably to touch his collarless shirt, the top button open to reveal a bronzed chest and gold medallion with a lucky-thirteen charm. But his complexion was blotchy. He wasn't the Rico of fifty years ago. *None of us are*, she chided herself. *Of course we've changed.*

'Gigi won't be long,' she said, hoping this was true, worried what she might blurt out without his calming presence. 'He's finding a parking space in the market square. Urbino's packed with tourists.'

'So you don't live in the city any longer?'

'We moved to Castel Cavallino soon after Alfredo met Monica. Apart from giving them privacy, it meant I could get away from my patients who'd regularly bump into me in Urbino with their problems. In the country I switch off from psychiatry. It's the same for Gigi. He's mayor now, you know.'

'I *didn't* know.'

Luigi emerged from the portico across the way, panting a little. 'I swear those steps from the market square increase in number each time I climb them,' he said, extending his hand to Enrico. 'Long time, no see!'

'Too long, I'd say.' Enrico looked at Devora and she turned away.

Luigi mopped his face with a handkerchief. 'I need a drink before I melt.'

Swifts soared high above the buildings, catching insects, and Luigi pulled out a pair of pocket binoculars to peer at them. 'Won't be long until they gather to migrate,' he said. 'I do love to hear them as they scream and swirl around the towers. And it will mean this infernal weather will start to cool down, thank God. But enough of my obsession... let's talk about what you've been up to, Rico.'

Enrico attracted the attention of the waiter by clicking his fingers and the action grated on Devora. But she reminded herself it was his way. *I click my fingers and they come running*, she'd heard him say more than once in the past.

'I'm having a large glass of Morro d'Alba. You two?'

'Iced tea for us. But shouldn't we wait for Sabrina?' Devora said. She hadn't seen her school friend in years and she had questions for her too.

Enrico shook his head. 'She's not coming.'

'Is she unwell?'

Enrico fiddled with the menu. The waiter was hovering and he gave the order.

'I'm sure you know,' he continued, 'the tom-toms in Urbino being what they are – that we married ten years after the war.'

They nodded. 'Word did get round, yes.'

Devora wondered how Sabrina had eventually snared Enrico. She'd always had the hots for him.

'And am I right in thinking you live on the coast?' Luigi asked.

'Indeed. Cattolica. Sabrina wanted to distance herself from her mother. We have a son. Totally unexpected as Sabrina was told she'd never conceive. Giacomo is thirteen now. Born when Sabrina was gone fifty. Bit of a miracle, but... he needs constant care. She... decided it was best not to come today. With his wheelchair and everything... Urbino is so steep.'

The 'and everything' spoke volumes to Devora. Despite the passage of time and Luigi telling her it was water under the bridge, she still dwelled on Enrico's and Sabrina's behaviour during the war. Sabrina had shunned their friendship and changed sympathies like a weathervane.

There'd been an informant after their mission. She'd been plainly told that by her torturer. The nightmares still stole upon her in times of stress. Yes, Enrico had provided them with a truck and averted a disaster. But had he or Sabrina been responsible for her arrest, too? Despite racking her brains, she could think of nobody else. Luigi had insisted on this meeting in an effort to put an end to her questions, but if either of them had been responsible for her arrest, she didn't know if she had it in her to forgive.

Forgiveness was hard, even though she always advised her patients to let go of their pasts. She doubted her own pain would ever disappear. Even her decision not to bring children into the world had been formed because they would never know their maternal grandparents. She'd known some Holocaust victims cover their loss by creating fresh families but you could never replace a lost one. Alfredo was happily married and had provided them with four wonderful nephews and Luigi and Devora frequently holidayed with them at Alfredo's villa on the island of Elba. Her nephews were like sons.

Enrico was still talking and she dragged her attention back.

'I was a widower when Sabrina and I got together. You probably didn't know.'

'I'm sorry,' Devora said, not knowing what else to say.

'You both knew her actually.'

'Your first wife?' Devora asked.

'Shira,' he said, knocking back his wine.

Devora gasped and looked at Luigi.

'That woman was the love of my life,' Enrico continued. 'I can say that out loud because Sabrina's not here.'

This information floored both of them.

'Shira? From Villa Oliveto?' Devora said, her expression puzzled. 'So you must have seen her after that day... when you came to visit the camp... I remember you disappearing with her to the fortress... I don't understand.'

'I loved her. I was actually the one who arranged to have her transferred to Villa Oliveto. I'd met her a long time before that occasion. We'd lived together when I was fighting in Tobruk. I arranged for papers showing she was a registered British citizen.

All forged, of course, but it meant she could be shipped to Italy as a prisoner rather than to Giado camp in Libya. A notoriously awful place. I'd sussed out your Oliveto camp from letters you'd sent me and also from that visit you remembered, Devora.'

'Letters I believed you'd never received. You certainly never replied. I do remember Shira confiding in me that she'd been in love with a British *tenente*... and that she hated him for abandoning her.'

'That was me all along. We invented a false name.'

'So, she lied to me,' Devora said. 'It's a long time ago but I felt I knew her.'

'We all lie in war. To save our skins.'

Devora narrowed her eyes. Enrico was a liar, but hadn't she herself told lies each time she'd disguised herself and used false identity papers when she was in hiding? Survival involved deviousness. But treachery of one's friends was another matter altogether. Was he a traitor too? Doubt niggled at her like a maggot in a wound.

'So, what happened to you? We never saw you again, after our mission to rescue the Jews from the hospital. I was arrested soon afterwards,' Devora continued, unable to still her tongue, Luigi watching her carefully. 'And I was told somebody had informed on us.'

'*Caspita!* Good God! I didn't know about that,' he replied, shock in his voice.

Luigi was frowning as he listened. Then, Enrico, glass poised mid-air, stopped. '*Dio!* You can't possibly think I had anything to do with that.'

'You disappeared, Enrico... like you always did,' Devora said. She felt strangely calm as she confronted him. 'We didn't know what to think.'

'It was not me. I swear on my son's life.'

'Where did you go?' she continued, wondering what fabrication he would conjure.

'We left Italy. Bribed a cargo ship's captain to get us back to Libya. And we lived there, far from my parents, who would never have approved of our marriage. For ten years I worked for a petroleum company and we were happy.' He paused, lifting his glass to his mouth again, draining it in one. And Devora recognised only too well the sadness in his eyes. Taking a deep breath, he resumed his account.

'It's a beautiful country. You should visit some time. I shall never return. Too many reminders of my beautiful Shira, you see. She died of typhus fever. Undetected.'

Moments later he was Enrico again, his tone jocular. 'Now, if *you'd* been there, Devora *bella*, you could have saved her. But it was too late by the time I took her to hospital.'

He called for another glass of wine, his words running into each other, yo-yoing between emotions. 'I cannot believe you think I betrayed you. You're my friends.'

When his glass was replenished, he took a long swig before setting it down hard on the table and banging his head with his palm. '*Per Dio*. Olinto... it must have been him, the slimy *bastardo*. It *must* have been. He loaned me the truck. At first he asked for money... *figlio d'un cane*. Son of a dog. Wait until I confront him...' He called again for the waiter.

Devora had no idea who this Olinto character was and she still didn't know if she could trust Enrico's explanation. He was a pitiful sight, his eyes glazed, fingers trembling as he tried to light a cigarette.

Luigi went to his aid, taking the matches to strike and Enrico leant in, cupping his hands round the flame and inhaling on his cigarette. Devora stared at the hands. Luigi's hands were the hands of a good man but Enrico's? Were they the hands of a traitor?

'I've missed you both, *amici miei*. My wholesome friends who kept me on the straight and narrow while you could.' He toasted them. 'Are you sure you won't join me in another round?' Enrico leant forwards conspiratorially. 'Put me out of my misery, you two lovely, perfect people. Tell me what mischief you've been up to? Nobody in this life can be lily-white forever. *In vino veritas*, as they say.'

His voice raised; customers at near tables stared at the mayor and his wife, keeping company with a drunkard.

'Is everything all right, signor *sindaco*?' the proprietor asked, approaching the table.

'*Sì. Sì.* We're leaving. Can I have the bill?' Luigi stood, looking over Enrico's head at Devora. 'Come home with us, Enrico, and see where we live now.'

'As long as you have good wine to share. *Volentieri*.'

Walking on either side of Enrico, both supporting him, they faltered across the piazza and down the alleys of the ghetto area. They passed the simple house where Devora had lived for a while with Luigi and Alfredo. It was now a holiday rental and Devora nodded at the blonde Dutchwoman sunning herself in a deckchair in the patio area where decades ago Anna Maria had planted vegetables.

During the eight-kilometre drive to the tiny hamlet of Castel Cavallino, Enrico nodded off and Devora and Luigi talked softly in the front of the car.

'You are so much kinder than I am, Gigi. I don't think I can bear his company much longer.'

'But you wanted to find out what happened. And we can't leave him to travel back in this state.'

She sighed, wondering if Enrico had told the whole truth. There were so many things in the past not hers to know: what really happened to her family being the major unknown. Perhaps it was for the best. She looked through the car window at the parched countryside without taking it in, her mind so tired of questions. Luigi, dear Luigi, took one hand off the steering wheel for a moment to squeeze hers and she turned to smile at him.

'I'm sorry,' Enrico said, waking up as Luigi parked the car in the shade. 'Did I embarrass you back in Urbino? Sabrina tells me I've turned into a bore with my love of wine.'

'Eat something with us, Rico. Line your stomach,' Luigi said.

'*Grazie, ma no.* Call me a taxi and I'll get back to Cattolica.'

'I insist. I'll take you to the bus station after.'

While Devora was busy in the kitchen, Enrico nursed a glass of water.

'I know I'm an alcoholic,' Enrico said. 'I should lay off it.'

'Maybe cut down?' Luigi said.

'I shouldn't touch it at all. I can never stop at one glass.'

He drank half the water, grimacing. 'Disgusting stuff!' Then he looked at Luigi. 'Hang on to her, Gigi. She's a special woman. I had my chances. I blew them.'

'I shall never let her go. Don't you worry about that, Rico.'

The two men were quiet for a moment and then Enrico said, 'I'm not a traitor. You have to believe me.'

While Luigi took Enrico back to catch his coach, Devora sat for a while on the bench set against the low wall of the mediaeval hamlet, enjoying the view, gazing at the abbey perched on the top of a hill in the distance. It was where she and Luigi had married. The parched fields of sun-pink corn stubble fell away to the horizon, the sight for her like a well-worn comfort blanket. She loved her home in Castel Cavallino. The lime trees near her bench rustled like silk petticoats in the breeze that always started gentle at this time of the afternoon.

She thought back to the carefree days before war had shattered their lives. If she'd had a magic wand back then, she would have used it to banish despots and ensured nobody died prematurely in such barbaric ways. The magic wand would have kept her family safe.

But magic existed only in children's fairy tales. And if she had felt very much like a child when the war started, she had very quickly grown up.

When Luigi returned, she was still wrapped in thought.

He bent to kiss the top of her head. 'I'm bushed,' he said. 'Let's have a siesta. It's too hot to do anything much else today.'

She lay on top of the covers beside him, listening to his steady breathing. Usually, staring up at the ceiling fan, watching its slow, steady circling, lulled her to sleep. But seeing Enrico again had been sobering.

She turned on her side to watch Luigi sleeping. He was not beautiful to look at, like Enrico had been once upon a time, but he was beautiful inside. And very modest. Two years earlier, on the fortieth anniversary of the Republic, he, along with other *partigiani* and members of the public, had been presented with military medals in recognition of their courage in the fight for freedom. He kept very quiet about it and stored it in a box at the back of his shirt drawer.

Life with him was good. He made her feel special. He had always been there for her: helping nurse Alfredo back to health, standing in as big brother, father-figure and wise counsellor in his darkest moments. Luigi was possessed of so many simple, sweet kindnesses. He knew her idiosyncracies: the way she preferred to eat ice cream with a teaspoon. She loved how he cut fresh peaches for her in the summer and brought them to her served in a glass of good red wine in one of her mother's remaining crystal goblets; she loved it when he massaged her shoulders in the way only he knew how to relax her after a day listening to troubled patients. She loved the way he read passages aloud from her battered copy of *Vita Nuova* when she couldn't sleep. He made her feel cherished all the time, even when she was tired and grumpy. She hoped she made him feel special too.

Luigi woke to find her still staring at him. She reached for his hand and kissed his palm.

'Do you think we'll ever meet up again?' Devora asked. 'I can't see it happening myself. And Sabrina hurt me too much. I'm glad she didn't come today. Enrico might be wrong about that Olinto fellow, whoever he was... Do you think Sabrina might have been my informer and that's why she didn't come today?'

He pushed back a strand of her hair. 'Who knows? But I believe what Enrico told us and I think you need to trust him. I'm not going to say let bygones be bygones, but you need to let this bitterness go, Biondina.'

'Well, you *have* said it.' She sighed. 'You know how I feel, Gigi. If I were to forgive what was done to my family, then it would be like denying what they went through. I'll let God forgive – *if* He even exists. *I* can't. The perpetrators would have to ask *me* for forgiveness. But can you imagine that happening? I can't. The Nazis were pure evil. No, I need to hold on to the pain. It's a part of me. If I let go of it, then I let go of Mütti, Vati and little Arturo. Not to mention all the other victims.'

She brushed away the tears. The annoying tears that had a will of their own. It was a long time since she'd wept. Being with Enrico had opened her wounds.

Luigi gathered her into his arms. 'I'm not saying you have to forget. But if you keep on reliving these past events, you'll never be able to rebuild.'

'I know all this, Gigi. I constantly tell my patients these things. It's hard.' She looked at him, her eyes swimming with more unshed tears. 'But you and I... we've built something really good together, don't you think?'

He kissed the end of her nose. '*Certo, amore mio.* Of course, my love. And I wouldn't have it any other way.'

Her missing family would never leave her heart. Time was a balm that had soothed her pain somewhat and she had learned strategies over the years to switch off from her torment. Caring for Alfredo, watching him bloom into a confident, loving husband and father had helped.

But most of all, it was Luigi who lifted her. She settled into his arms and let herself be loved.

A LETTER FROM ANGELA

Thank you so much for reading *The Girl Who Escaped.* I invested a lot in creating this story and I hope you enjoyed reading it. It has been a work of love for me and there have been times during my research when I was moved to tears at the suffering I uncovered. However, I hope you feel that there is a positive side to the story in the way the human spirit can conquer evil.

If you did enjoy it, and want to keep up to date with all my latest releases, just sign up at the following link. Your email address will never be shared and you can unsubscribe at any time.

www.bookouture.com/angela-petch

I love to hear from readers and when I read that my words have moved you, it makes all the little struggles worthwhile. It isn't always easy to do justice to a story like *The Girl Who Escaped*, knowing that so many people suffered in such barbaric ways during World War Two. We should never forget what ordinary people went through. So, I would love to hear what you thought about *The Girl Who Escaped.* Did it make you cry? Did you learn something about the plight of Jews in Italy and the courage of their saviours? Did you fall in love with Luigi, as I did? What did you think of Devora? At the start of the story, I tried to convey the innocence of a young girl. Did she transform into a feisty, brave young woman for you? Did you know anything about Urbino before you read the book? It's the most beautiful, compact city, rich in art and architecture. After reading my book, would you love to visit one day? Or have you already visited the region of Le Marche, but did not realise how the city coped during World War Two? If you enjoyed the story, I would absolutely love it if you could leave a short review. Getting feedback from readers is amazing and it also helps to persuade other readers to pick up one of my books for the first time.

My first four historical novels are set in Tuscany but I am beginning to move further afield. My last book, *The Postcard from Italy*, is set mainly in the fascinating region of Puglia. There will be more locations in Italy in my future books for you to explore.

Thank you for reading and I hope to hear from you. I always try to respond.

With very best wishes – *cordiali saluti*,

Angela Petch

www.angelapetchsblogsite.wordpress.com

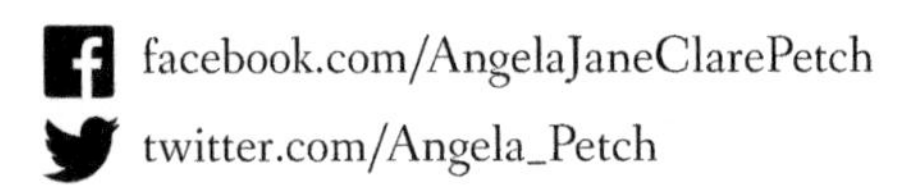

AUTHOR'S NOTE

RESEARCH

Whilst writing this book, I felt a weight of responsibility to get everything right. In a way – and I hope this doesn't sound pretentious – I wrote it as a kind of homage. A homage to Italians, to their courage and extraordinary compassion. I think the fact so many Jews' lives were saved in Italy, as compared to elsewhere in occupied Europe during World War Two, should be more widely broadcast.

The statistics speak for themselves:

> At the end of September 1943, in occupied Italy, there were 38,994 Jews (33,452 Italian Jews and 5,542 foreign Jews). Approximately 80% of Jews in Italy survived. In the rest of occupied Europe, approximately 80% perished.

Rescuers and helpers were from all classes: men, women, clergy, civilians, police, doctors, lawyers, drivers, farmers, the famous, housewives, university professors. Put simply, people who had a moral conscience.

When I visited the Jewish museum in Ferrara, there was no mention of those statistics. 'You should be so proud of your nation and what you did during the war to save so many lives,' I told the manageress. She looked slightly baffled. It was as if she didn't understand the fuss I was making: it was normal, wasn't it, to help victims? Whilst researching many personal accounts of Jews who were rescued in Italy, I kept coming across the phrase, '*Siete Cristiani come noi*' – You are Christians like us. But the word 'Christian' in this sense has nothing to do with religion. It is how Italians say, 'You are human beings like us.' I'd read this attitude before when studying accounts of Italian peasants helping escaped prisoners-of-war trying to make their way back to the allies. 'If my son were in the same position, I hope he would be helped like I am helping you,' and 'They are sons of somebody,' were comments recorded over and over again.

This generosity of spirit was huge especially after Italy moved over to join the allies in 1943. Now, the plight of escaped prisoners and Jews worsened. Another little-known fact, which I have tried to describe in Villa Oliveto – a real place that I visited near Arezzo – was about the conditions in the majority of camps for detained Jews in Italy. Internment camps were set up predominantly in southern and central Italy. There was a stark difference between these and the death camps elsewhere in Europe, and Jewish people in Italy were generally treated with dignity and respect. I am indebted to Elizabeth Bettina's amazing book of true accounts: *It Happened in Italy: Untold Stories of How the People of Italy Defied the Horrors of the Holocaust.* It is crammed with detailed personal memories of internment camps where guards made toys for the children, weddings were celebrated, concerts were enjoyed, children went to school. Life, despite total lack of freedom, sometimes seemed like 'a picnic', some internees said, although I should stress that some camps were better than others and conditions deteriorated as more internees arrived.

Another important, extremely informative book I consulted was *Salvarsi* by Liliana Picciotto: a comprehensive volume of studies and anecdotes about Jews in Italy who escaped from the Shoah during 1943 to 1945. It took the author nine years to compile and shows 'the other side of the coin', as the introduction says. Before this book, nobody had carried out a proper study of those Jews saved, by whom and how. It is a humbling testament to the human spirit. A reminder again that evil can be conquered.

In no way do I want to draw attention away from the approximately 20% of Italian Jews who tragically perished in such camps as Dachau and Auschwitz. There were four Italian camps where Jews were sent, before being transported to extermination camps outside Italy, (in Italian they were termed '*anticamere*', antechambers): Fossoli (Modena), Grosseto, Bolzano and Borgo San Dalmazzo. Only one extermination camp existed in Italy: Trieste, built by the Nazis after occupying Friuli Venezia. La Risiera di San Sabba is now a monument. Of course there were traitors amongst the Italian population too, but returning to the point about numbers of Jews saved, I wanted to write to show that goodness exists amidst evil.

PERSONAL CONNECTIONS

My husband's Italian grandfather, Luigi Micheli, is the inspiration behind Luigi Michelozzi. He was a partisan, although for his job at the Town Hall in Urbino he had to be enrolled as a member of the fascist party. In name only, because he was encouraged by his fellow partisans to do so, being more use to the cause if he pretended to be 'on the inside'. He was a socialist, ardently anti-fascist, and in his role of registrar he courageously forged identity details of Jews in the city, so that when the German occupiers came to consult the census in his office, no

Jews were found. If this had been discovered, the penalty would have been death.

He was a meticulous man, keeping records of everything including all the letters his young daughter wrote from England as the new bride of an English army captain. I used some details in my first novel, *The Tuscan Secret*. After he died, my husband came upon his papers. Hidden in a pile of folders was a medal, received from the Italian state in recognition of Luigi's outstanding courage as a *partigiano combattente* (active partisan) during the war. He was a principled man and I remember heated discussions around the dinner table. His brother's politics were the opposite of his and eventually his mother – who ruled the household with her schoolteacher's rod – banned all political discussion at mealtimes, fearing fights would break out. I am so grateful to our historian friend from Urbino, Professor Ermanno Torrico, who spoke at length to me about the occupation of Urbino and Luigi's participation in the city's liberation. He has included his story in one of his own books. As with so many of my parents' generation who endured the war, Luigi did not talk about what he had gone through. We did not realise the extent of his involvement while he was alive. It is important to record these memories and learn from them and that is why I include true stories in my novels.

THANK YOU

The numbers of Jews in Urbino are depleted and the synagogue is rarely used nowadays for worship. But it is still possible to visit the synagogue, typically hidden away behind a façade that does not advertise itself as a place of Jewish worship. My thanks to Signora Maria Luisa Moscati, who opened the building for my husband and me and answered my many questions. A writer herself, she invited us to her house round the corner and we sat in her beautiful library to talk at ease. Her home had been occupied first by the Germans and then by the British after they liberated the city in August 1944. I apologised when she told me British officers had burned some of the family's books in her magnificent fireplace as fuel in the harsh winter. I set Devora's cleaning job in this impressive *palazzo*.

Castelcavallino is a real village. I married in its rural mediaeval church where I located the secret meetings held by fictitious don Cecchetti and his fledgling band of *partigiani*. When I visited our special place again last summer, an elderly inhabitant wandered out of his house and was pleased to talk. 'We don't get many visitors around here,' he said. 'You've livened up my day.' When I explained I was researching the Second World War, he hurried inside and returned with a biscuit tin full of photographs and letters. He was nine years old when a group of German Todt construction engineers were billeted in the village and he showed me a small black and white image of one who visited frequently. 'He liked my family. He was homesick,' he told us. 'One day he showed me how to use his machine gun. Imagine! A nine-year-old with a dangerous toy. I aimed it at the trees and I couldn't believe how the leaves were torn to strips.' After his stories, out came a bottle of home-made vinsanto and we promised to visit again. And we will. His description of the soldier made its way into this book in the person of Kurt. *Grazie*, Tonino, for sharing so much with us.

RELIGION

I always have in my head that history is for everybody when I write my books. It's hard to keep a balance and not overload the fiction with facts and I hope that I have done justice to Devora's development from a flawed teenager to a determined, independent young woman. In the writing, as I was brought up Roman Catholic, I was constantly fearful of making mistakes about Judaism and I read extensively. Any mistakes or misrepresentations are my own. Although not about an Italian Jew, I was extremely moved by the true account of Lily Ebert, a Hungarian survivor of Auschwitz. Immediately after the Covid pandemic she said to her great-grandson, Dov Forman, 'Let's do something.' With his help she wrote her war testimony. *Lily's Promise* is an honest, harrowing yet ultimately uplifting message of tolerance against all the odds. Similarly, Primo Levi, another Auschwitz survivor, and his account *If This is A Man* written immediately after the war, was a great source. Extremely moving, truly upsetting and unbearable at times, but it should be read by everybody to show to what depths man's cruelty can sink and how the human spirit can pull through.

The Catholic Church comes into criticism for its role during World War Two and especially Pope Pius XII for his silence on the fate of millions of Jews killed during the Holocaust. Controversy still exists. He had been a Vatican diplomat in Germany before becoming Pope and some argue that this was why he was cautious and did not do enough to intervene. The counter argument is that by appearing to be neutral and diplomatic, the Catholic Church presented a cover for what was really going on: that the Pope strongly condoned provision of sanctuary to hundreds of thousands of Jews. There are countless accounts of Jews hidden in convents and churches, of parish priests actively involved in saving their lives and organising groups of freedom fighters. Cardinal Ildefonso Schuster of Milan, born in Italy but the son of a German immigrant tailor, publicly denounced fascism from the pulpit and enabled funds for rescues. The Cardinal of Florence, Elia Dalla Costa, was another church figure who aided and organised rescue efforts. The underground Assisi network run by the Catholic Church to protect Jews during the German occupation offered harbour in convents and monasteries. Don Cecchetti in this book, don Andrea and the nuns of the convent of Santa Caterina are a small representation of these efforts.

WHY?

Whilst preparing to write this book, I came across a passage in a history book and, returning to my point about the humanity of wonderful Italians, it spoke reams to me.

> From a letter to the German Embassy in Rome sent from Foreign Minister Joachim von Ribbentrop.
>
> *January 13, 1943*
>
> There are considerable differences between the official Italian and German position on how to handle the Jewish question. Whereas we have recognised Jewry as a disease that threatens to corrupt the body politic and hinder the reconstruction of Europe, the Italian government tends to think of Jews as individuals and reserves preferential treatment for individual Jews or certain groups of Jews. The Italian government also protects Jews abroad if they hold Italian citizenship, especially if they are influential in the economy.

All I can say is, thank heavens for the Italian people and their 'preferential treatment'.

ACKNOWLEDGEMENTS

My thanks to Deborah Rodriguez, friend and retired midwife, who looked over a couple of my medical scenes and 'pushed' me to give birth to the descriptions (awful pun, sorry). Thanks also to all my writing friends, whether I meet them online or face to face. I hope you know who you are. If I listed you individually, I'd be fearful of leaving somebody out. I love our generous, supportive writing community.

As mentioned earlier, particular thanks go to two experts in their fields on the history of Urbino: Signora Maria Luisa Moscati Benigni, who graciously spent time with me in the synagogue, and Professor Ermanno Torrico, firm friend and university tutor, always prompt with answers to my many questions. Their help has been invaluable.

I want to specially thank Ellen Gleeson, my editor at Bookouture. She knows how much I have struggled to get this book right. I hope she doesn't feel like a punchbag each time I wrestle with her structural changes and edits. She is the one who trains me to grow fitter and without her input my books would be all the poorer. Similarly, thank you to the whole of team Bookouture for the hard work you do in promoting our books, acquiring translation rights, coming up with stunning covers and generally being a surrogate writing family.

To my patient husband, Maurice, who championed my idea for putting his beloved Nonno Gigi onto my pages and who uncovered information from his documents: I promise we shall have more hours together and thank you for letting me get on with my writing.

And last but definitely not least, thanks and praise be to readers who send me such wonderful emails and post comments and reviews. You are in my head when I write and you inspire me to keep going. *Grazie mille.* A thousand thanks.

Printed in Great Britain
by Amazon